THE DEAD DOG DAY

A Cora Baxter Mystery

THE DEAD DOG DAY

A Cora Baxter Mystery

Jackie Kabler

Published by Accent Press Ltd 2015

ISBN 9781783752270

For my sister Deborah, 1970-2010.
I miss you.

ACKNOWLEDGMENTS

There are so many people who contributed, knowingly or not, to the writing of this novel. These are just some of them.

The late, great GMTV legend Billy Pond, who told me the dead dog story. He swore it was true. I was never quite sure, but it was always one of my favourites.

My friends Judith, Sophie, Dione, and Gillian, who inspired the characters of Rosie, Nicole, Wendy, and Sam. Simon, Jason, and Chris, my longest-serving crew in my GMTV years, who may recognise little bits of themselves in Nathan, Rodney, and Scott. There's also a smidgeon of some of my other favourite crew members Ted, Pete, and Mick in those characters. I miss you all and I couldn't have done it without any of you!

My darling husband JJ, who always believes in me even when I doubt myself.

My mum who, when I was seven, was told by one of my teachers that I would 'go far in English', and who says she always knew I would.

My beloved Cheltenham – Cora's home town as well as mine.

And of course my agent, Robin Wade, and everyone at Accent Press. You all made a little girl's dream come true and a big girl very happy.

1

Monday 18th December

'THE DOG IS DEAD? ARE YOU *INSANE*, CHRISTINA? HOW THE BLOODY HELL CAN THE DOG BE DEAD?'

The furious voice of Jeanette Kendrick rang across the newsroom, and everybody froze. It was 4 a.m. and the usual pre-programme hum, which had been building nicely, faded to a whisper, and then to silence. Cora Baxter, who was on Monday morning newsreader duties, suddenly stopped scrolling through the running order, her heart pounding. She had been on the receiving end of a Kendrick rant once or twice before, and it was pretty hellish.

She swivelled in her chair. Down at the far end of the long room, just visible behind the piles of DVDs and newspapers stacked on every desk, the breakfast TV programme editor was standing outside her glass-walled corner office, hands on Armani-clad hips. In front of her Christina Evans, a young trainee producer, was visibly shaking.

'I'm really sorry, Jeanette, but … well, I just rang the hotel to confirm the 6 a.m. car pick up, and … and … the guest said he'd just woken up and found the dog dead next to him, in the hotel room … he's in a terrible state, I mean … what can I do?'

'BUT IT CAN'T BE DEAD!' Jeanette was roaring now, her piercing blue eyes burning into poor Christina. 'IT'S THE BLOODY 8.10, GODDAMN IT!'

Cora gulped and turned back to the running order on her screen. Jeanette's reaction was way over the top, but everybody knew that, at this hour of the morning, losing the item planned for 8.10 was not good. It was the most watched slot of the programme, following as it did the eight o'clock news, and it was always saved for the biggest talking point of the day.

'WELL, WHAT ARE YOU GOING TO DO ABOUT IT?'

Jeanette was showing no signs of calming down. She took a step towards Christina and stamped her foot. She was shod as always in beautiful Jimmy Choos, silver-grey today to match the tailored Armani suit. Christina cowered backwards.

'Well ... erm ... erm ... well ...' She was stammering now, and sounded close to tears.

Cora quickly scanned the 8.10 link on the running order. The story was about a Newfoundland which had won an international 'hero dog' award after rescuing dozens of people from a passenger boat disaster in France the previous year. The dog, plus owner, was supposed to be on the *Morning Live* sofa to help launch a 'Britain's Bravest Pet' competition. The contest was sponsored by the show, and viewers would be voting for their favourite animal. No wonder Jeanette was so mad – phone-in competitions made big money for the breakfast programme, and this could scupper the whole thing.

Down the newsroom, Christina had started to sniffle.

'I'm sorry, Jeanette, I don't think there's anything we *can* do,' she said, and let out a little sob.

Jeanette glared at her, but the tears had done the trick. She took a deep breath and ran her hands through her elfin-cropped, dark hair.

'OK, Christina, I'll tell you what *you're* going to do, shall I?'

She'd stopped shouting, but the newsroom still held its breath, waiting to hear the magical solution she was about to produce.

'What *you* are going to do, Christina, is ring the man back, give him our deepest condolences for the death of his dog, and then ask him to bring it in anyway. We'll pretend it's asleep.'

She turned on her four-inch heels and marched back into her office. Wide-eyed with horror, Christina stared after her. Everyone else in the newsroom gaped at each other, aghast. She couldn't be serious – could she?

Christina was rooted to the spot. 'But ... Jeanette ... *I can't* ... I just can't! He was in tears ... he'll never agree to it ... really, do you *really* want me to tell him to bring it in? I mean ... it's *dead*!'

'Do it, or find me another 8.10,' said Jeanette dismissively, and slammed the door. A moment later she snapped down the blinds on the glass wall facing the newsroom – her usual signal that the conversation was over.

Christina, still open-mouthed with shock, scurried off. Drama over, the newsroom hum started up again, although it was somewhat subdued. Everyone knew that when Jeanette blew once, it could happen again at any moment, and nobody wanted to be next in the firing line. Cora, who was still feeling fragile from a fairly traumatic weekend, suddenly had an overwhelming urge to laugh hysterically. Muttering something about tea under her breath, she leapt from her seat and ran out of the newsroom, nearly barrelling into somebody coming the other way in the corridor outside. She reached the grubby little kitchen down the hall at the same time as her friend, and today's senior programme producer, Samantha Tindall, who'd been hot on her heels.

'Sam!' gasped Cora. 'Did you hear that?'

Sam nodded, shaking with suppressed laughter. She grabbed Cora's arm and dragged her into the windowless box of a kitchen, slamming the door behind them. They collapsed on the grimy lino, howling.

'"Tell him to bring it in anyway, we'll pretend it's asleep!" Have you ever heard anything like it?' There were tears running down Cora's cheeks.

Sam was wiping her eyes. 'Oh my goodness, that's the funniest thing I've heard in weeks. Bring it in anyway! Bleedin' thing will have rigor mortis by now – can you imagine it, stiff as a board on the studio floor ...' She buckled again, choking with laughter.

Cora clutched her stomach. 'Stop it, stop it, I can't bear it! Picture Alice on the sofa, having to coo over the poor exhausted sleeping dog ... imagine her face! And the lights – it would

3

probably start to smell and everything ...'

Sam wrinkled her pert little nose, imitating newsreader Alice Lomas – who was covering the main presenter's job on the sofa today, hence Cora's call to replace her at the news desk – and they shrieked again, clinging to each other.

They were just starting to pull themselves together when the door burst open and Wendy Heggerty skipped in, red Irish curls bouncing.

'No need to ask what you two have been talking about!' said the graphic designer. 'Wow, Jeanette has lost it this time, hasn't she? Scary bitch boss from hell ... I saw poor old devoted Clancy drop her off this morning. At this hour! Seriously, I don't know *how* she puts up with her.'

Clancy Carter was Jeanette's long-term love. Both big players in the television world, Jeanette's star had somewhat eclipsed her civil partner's in recent years – Clancy was head of Chrysalis Productions, a production company responsible for some of the rather less successful TV reality shows. And, while Jeanette's reputation was terrifying, Clancy was known as a bit of a sweetie. Few could understand how they'd ever got together.

Still tittering, Cora and Sam heaved themselves off the floor, and Cora bent down to give Wendy a hug.

'Hello, dwarfy. Great to see you.' Cora was on the road as a roving reporter for much of the time, so it was always a treat to be called in to cover news reading duties. It meant she could have a long overdue catch up with her friends, who nowadays were all too often just voices on the end of a phone, discussing time slots or graphics ideas for her live reports.

'You too, you big giraffe.' Wendy's pale blue eyes grinned up at Cora. Just five foot two, Wendy was buxom and curvaceous, all wild hair and heaving boobs. Today she'd encased them in a tight green jumper.

'You look fab, Wendy.' Cora grinned at her friend.

'She always does.' Sam was crouching in front of the microwave, attempting to use its door as a mirror as she tried to wipe the rivulets of mascara off her cheeks. 'I don't know how

4

you do it, Wend – I always look like a dog on nightshifts.'

She straightened up, pushing her wavy caramel bob back out of her eyes, and started to smirk again. 'I wonder where poor Christina got to?'

'Ooh, I'm dying to find out what happened – but you'll have to update me later. I'm just here for a cuppa – got a load of maps to do for the news yet,' said Wendy, reaching for a polystyrene cup. 'But I'll see you both later, OK? And we need to rip that ex-man of yours to shreds too, Cora.'

She stuck a tea cartridge into the machine, and the boiling water streamed into the cup underneath. She grabbed it, splashed in some milk, and headed for the door, just as a pale-looking Christina wandered in.

'Alright, Christina?' Wendy grimaced at Cora and Sam as she left, wildly making a 'call me' sign with her free hand. Christina didn't seem to hear her. She shoved a coffee cartridge clumsily into the slot, and stood staring into space as the hot liquid gushed out.

'Er – Christina – *are* you OK? What did the guest say?' said Sam, tentatively. 'Did you – erm – call him back, about the dog? Christina?'

Christina twitched slightly, as if suddenly registering that there were other people in the room.

'Oh, hi, Sam … Cora. No, thank God, Gerry from showbiz saved me. Went in and told Jeanette if we had a dead dog in, it was bound to get in the papers and we'd get a right mauling. He's called in a favour and got that new barmaid off *Coronation Street* to come in to fill the slot at short notice – you know the one, she's about to have an affair with David Platt?'

Sam and Cora nodded.

Christina rubbed her eyes. 'Jeanette's not happy, but what can you do? We're going to launch the pet competition tomorrow instead – there's a cat that woke its owner up after a gas leak or something that should be able to come in. I'm going to be cacking myself tonight – Jeanette will fire me if anything else goes wrong. I've only been here for three months, I'll never be able to get another job if I'm sacked …'

Her voice tailed off and a fat tear rolled down her cheek. Cora felt a sudden massive wave of sympathy, and slipped her arm round the younger girl's shoulders.

'Don't cry, Christina. You won't be sacked, it wasn't *your* fault! I remember what these nightshifts are like – they're hell, and being so tired just makes everything seem worse. It'll be OK, you'll see – Jeanette will have forgotten all about it by tomorrow.'

Christina wiped her eyes and managed a little smile. 'Thanks. But she won't, you know that. I hate that woman. I really, really hate her. Anyway, I'd better go … I have loads of stuff to do before we go on air. See you later.'

Shoulders hunched, she picked up her coffee with a shaky hand and slipped out of the room. Cora and Sam looked at each other and smiled ruefully.

'I have to agree with Christina. Jeanette will get her comeuppance one of these days, mark my words. Karma and all that,' said Sam.

Cora nodded, and headed for the door. 'Just another night at the Fun Factory, eh? Right, I'm going back – coming?'

'I'll be right behind you when I've made my tea, my little news bunny. Want to chat you through the six o'clock bulletin. Dead dog or no dead dog, the show must go on.'

The person who would be the real star of today's show looked down at slightly shaking hands and took a long, deep breath.

Sod the dead dog. There was only one dumb animal who deserved to be dead today.

And that was Jeanette Kendrick.

How lucky, then, that she soon would be.

2

*Morning! Rodders in orange trousers 2day like gangly satsuma.
Want us 2 hunt down n kill bastard boyf? L8R. N x*

Cora grinned as she caught up on her text messages. Settling
into her chair in the cosy make-up room, she reached over and
pulled the blinds so the early morning window cleaners couldn't
sneak a peek later on. Then she took a bite of the bacon roll
she'd snaffled from the green room, wiped her fingers on a
nearby towel, and tapped a slightly less than honest reply into
her BlackBerry.

*Don't worry Nathan, over him already! Nice and cosy in
here ... ha! Love C xxx*

She took another mouthful, watching the three make-up artists
buzzing around laying out their brushes and tubes, and wiped
ketchup off her chin. It was freezing outside and Nathan Nesbit
and Rodney Woodhall, her usual camera and sound crew when
she was on roving reporter duty, were up in Nottingham with
one of the other reporters this morning, on a prison
overcrowding story. As a white gown was whipped around her,
Cora smiled, her difficult past few days forgotten for a while.
Much as she enjoyed being a reporter it was, she thought, very
nice to be indoors for a change.

'Cora, darling, it's been ages! What are you wearing today?'

The cheerful Scottish burr of Sherry, her make-up girl, broke
into her thoughts.

'Got some gorgeous new colours this morning, you can be
my wee guinea pig!'

'Lime suede jacket.'

Cora peered at the fantastic line-up of bottles, powders, and eyeshadow palettes in front of her.

'Wow, Sherry, I wish I had you on the road with me. You've got stuff here I've never even seen in the shops. I love that one.' She pointed to a soft brown shadow with iridescent green flecks.

'Well that will go perfectly, especially with your green eyes.'

Sherry set to work, pulling Cora's straight shoulder-length brown bob back into a hairband and running a critical eye over her skin as she began applying powder and concealer. Cora watched her in the mirror, grimacing inwardly. These early mornings, most of which were spent outside in all weathers, were taking their toll. Half-listening to the early news on the TV in the corner of the room, she shut her eyes and relaxed as the make-up artist's experienced fingers patted and smoothed. She adored this ritual, the soothing minutes before she entered the pressure cooker of the live studio. The magic of the make-up room never ceased to amaze her, taking in as it did weary, baggy-eyed people and, without fail, spitting them out again a short time later looking like polished professionals.

The peace was shattered suddenly as the door was flung open.

'Oh, hell! How long are you going to be, Sherry? I need you to dry my hair and *everything* this morning!'

Cora opened her eyes at the familiar, whiny voice. Alice Lomas was standing in the doorway, a petulant expression on her beautiful face. Her long, poker-straight blonde hair was damp, making dark stains on the tight navy T-shirt that clung to her voluptuous chest.

'Well, good morning to you too, Alice,' Sherry said primly. 'Come back in fifteen minutes, I'll have Cora out by then.'

Alice pouted and walked off, swinging her hair. She'd totally ignored Cora, as usual. Thirty-two, but claiming to be just twenty-nine, Alice had already been a national newsreader for six years, making her one of the youngest news anchors in the country when she'd started. With no university degree, and distinctly average A level results to her name, she had still somehow managed to land a job as a weathergirl and occasional features reporter on a regional news programme after leaving school. But exactly why Jeanette had taken her on to present national news had long been a puzzle to the *Morning Live* staff, who had finally concluded that the editor, along with men across the UK, must simply have fallen for her stunning looks. It was a view reinforced by the fact that, despite having limited journalistic experience, she'd recently started filling in on the sofa when Jane, the main presenter, was away. The Lomas ego, always big, was becoming massive, and Cora couldn't stand her.

'Cow. Nice of her to say hello!' she said, shutting her eyes again as Sherry started to apply her eye shadow. 'Ben and Danny aren't doing anyone at the moment – why can't she just have one of them do her?'

'Och, she's alright really. You just have to know how to handle her,' Sherry replied soothingly. 'She's just used to me, that's all, I do her nearly every day. It's all insecurity, you know – you're a way more experienced journalist and she feels threatened when you come in to read the news – probably scared Jeanette's gonna put you on the sofa instead of her.'

'Seriously? Do you think so? Gosh, there's no chance of that. I mean, I'd love it – being on the road is so utterly exhausting, and being in the studio is SO much easier – shorter hours, no driving, more money, it's a no-brainer really. But Jeanette would never replace a babe like that with me! I mean, look at me, Sherry. I look like a right old dog first thing in the morning. No wonder Justin dumped me.'

Sherry squeezed her shoulder. 'I heard earlier – sorry about that, Cora. But you'll find someone else, gorgeous girl like you. Now shut up so I can do your lips.'

Cora adjusted her earpiece as the PA in the gallery began the countdown to the opening titles. She felt the usual little surge of adrenaline as she straightened the scripts on the news desk in front of her. Grant, the weatherman, poised by his map, winked at her, fiddling with the orange tie that matched his slightly overdone fake tan. On the big yellow sofa to his right, Alice, looking stunning in a taupe Donna Karan trouser suit, simpered at her co-presenter Jeremy and then turned smartly to Camera One as the music died and the red light came on.

'Good morning, it's six o'clock on Monday the eighteenth of December, and you're watching *Morning Live*. A great show lined up for you this morning …'

'Coming to you in fifteen, Cora.' The director's voice rumbled in her ear.

'… all that coming up shortly, but first let's go over to the news desk for the rest of the day's stories, and we've got Cora on the desk this morning, how lovely! In from the cold, Cora?' Alice smiled amiably across the studio.

Two-faced cow! Cora thought. She smiled sweetly back. 'Yes, good morning, Alice, it's very nice to be here!'

She turned to the camera in front of her, and the autocue rolled. 'And good morning to you too! Our top story this morning …'

The show whizzed by. Floor managers, flustered beings whispering urgently into headsets, whipped the usual mixed bunch of guests in and out of the studio, among them Christopher Biggins promoting his Christmas panto, and the Defence Secretary talking about festive gifts for troops on missions overseas.

Cora had a bulletin to read every quarter of an hour, and by the time she'd finished the 7.30 news she was feeling decidedly shiny. Making sure she wasn't in shot, she slipped quietly from behind the news desk, pushed open the heavy studio door and headed for make-up.

'Hey, Cora.'

'Scott! Hi, babes – forgot you were here today. The old disciplinary, eh? How did it go?'

The burly six-footer grimaced, and Cora reached up and pecked him on a slightly sweaty cheek. Scott Edson was her usual satellite engineer, number four in the on-the-road quartet

10

she spent most of her time with. He'd been called to London today too, for an early morning telling-off from Jeanette for falling asleep on the job.

'Not too good. On a written warning,' Scott muttered in his broad Bolton accent.

'Oh hun, I'm sorry. Don't worry, you know what Jeanette –'

Cora stopped abruptly as Scott brushed roughly past her and headed off up the corridor.

'It doesn't matter. See you on the road,' he said over his shoulder, and disappeared round the corner.

Puzzled and a little hurt, Cora stared after him for a moment, then wandered into the make-up room. Scott wasn't normally so off-hand, although he hadn't been himself recently. No wonder he was grumpy though – who ever heard of a 7 a.m. disciplinary hearing for goodness' sake? But that was Jeanette's style – she was at her desk from three, so everyone else simply had to fit around her schedule. The editor was on exceptionally fine form this morning though. How many other people was she going to upset?

As if on cue, Christina hurried into the room. If anything, she looked worse than she had earlier. Still red-eyed, she now had a slightly manic expression on her face and beads of sweat on her forehead.

'Tissues!' she said frantically. 'Tissues! I need tissues for dressing room three!'

Sherry opened a drawer, pulled out a packet and thrust it into Christina's shaking hands.

'There you go sweetie. Anything else you need?'

'No … no … that's fine. Thanks,' Christina stuttered. She stumbled back out into the corridor and vanished.

Sherry shook her head and caught Cora's eye in the mirror.

'Now, that looks to me like a girl on the edge.'

'I know.' Cora plonked herself into the chair for her touch up. 'Poor Christina. I'm not sure she's going to last the course, to be honest. Not tough enough, bless her.'

She closed her eyes as Sherry got busy with the powder puff, suddenly feeling exhausted.

'Not even eight o'clock and we've already had tears, tantrums, and a dead dog,' she thought. 'Good old *Morning Live*!'

And, freshly powdered and glossed, she headed back to the studio.

Usually, as the clock ticked towards the *Morning Live* closing titles, Jeanette Kendrick would be fiercely scribbling on her pad, ready to savage a few producers at the post-programme debrief.

There was still an hour to go, but in the newsroom several were already nervously gulping coffee and swapping anxious glances, steeling themselves for the completely unjustified mauling they would all shortly receive over the dead dog debacle.

They would have been greatly relieved to know that right now, a deceased canine was the last thing on the editor's mind. Jeanette was rarely fazed by anyone or anything, but as she listened to the quiet words being directed at her, fear twisted her stomach.

'I didn't know … I had no idea … I'm so sorry. So terribly, terribly sorry. Please, if …' she stuttered.

For once, though, the boss's words were being completely ignored. And minutes later, it wasn't just the unfortunate dog that had passed away on that chilly December morning.

Jeanette Kendrick was quite, quite dead.

3

@srharrison65 @CoraBaxterMLive I like to draw picshurs of allien animals. I am drawing u an allien hors and will post it 2day. Luv Kevin. PS. I luv u.

Cora laughed out loud. Alien animals indeed. She thoroughly enjoyed getting Twitter messages from *Morning Live* viewers, but there were some real crazies out there, bless them. She shoved her BlackBerry back into her coat pocket then jumped as a large, yellow shape loomed out of the darkness to her right.

'These feet are ridiculous,' said the man in the chicken suit. 'I'm surprised hens don't fall over more often, really I am.'

Cora tried to look sympathetic. It was just before 6 a.m. on a freezing Friday, and she was standing in almost total darkness on a roundabout in the middle of a Devon A-road, surrounded by chickens – and people dressed as chickens.

'And then there was light,' muttered Nathan, and Cora winced as two hefty spotlights popped into life, illuminating the scene. The hens that had been pecking quietly around her feet jumped in fright and scattered, and the man in the yellow costume tugged his over-sized beak further down over his eyes and groaned, his breath hanging in the air like ghostly candy floss.

'Bloody bright, those lights, aren't they? How long till we're on, Cora? There's a few not here yet – need to go bang on some doors.'

'Don't worry, we've got about twenty minutes yet, but I

want to do a run-through as soon as I can, so the faster you can get everyone out here, the better!'

The man nodded his big furry head, dropped the homemade protest placard he was holding, and stomped off awkwardly into the darkness, his chicken feet crunching across the frozen grass of the roundabout.

In her pocket, Cora's BlackBerry beeped again and, not for the first time, she marvelled at the ridiculousness of her job. After nearly three years on the show she had certainly covered her share of quirky stories, but some days were definitely more surreal than others. In today's bizarre, pre-dawn scene on the icy edge of Exmoor, Cora and her team would be broadcasting live with a group of protesters, who were trying to save the feral chickens that had roosted on a local roundabout for over a century but had now been deemed a traffic hazard by the local council.

'Everything OK, Cora?' Nathan pushed his dark, floppy hair out of his eyes, zipped his Arctic-weight, navy fleece even further up under his chin, and started his daily fumble with the camera tripod.

'Yep.' Cora stamped her feet. She was freezing, despite the thermal socks, long johns and long-sleeved vest she'd struggled into as usual in her hotel room earlier. There was no place for sexy undies in the wardrobe of morning TV reporters at this time of year, sadly. The male viewers who regularly wrote to Cora and her female colleagues extolling their virtues and asking for photos of them in their underwear would be sorely disappointed; Cora had often been tempted to send out photos of herself in her old faithful Marks & Spencer grey thermals, just for a giggle.

'First hit 6.20, and then another one later, time TBC – you know what "Fun Fridays" are like!'

'Fun Friday? More like Freeze the Crew's Balls Off Friday,' said a gloomy voice, as Rodney appeared, his mixer slung around his neck and his hands full of sound equipment.

'Got your earpiece, Cora? Oh yeah, I see it.' Rodney adjusted his headphones. 'Give us a voice level, eh?'

'OK – I've been in a different town every single night since Sunday, I'm exhausted, and here I am, freezing cold at stupid o'clock on a roundabout in the middle of nowhere,' said Cora. 'That OK, Rodders?'

'Fine,' replied the soundman, pushing his little round glasses higher on his nose and adjusting a couple of knobs on his mixer.

Cora smiled at him, trying to ignore his trousers. Much as she loved Rodney, he did have spectacularly bad dress sense. Today he was wearing the most lurid yellow and green camouflage-patterned combats she had ever seen, their hideousness 'enhanced' by bright red loops and tabs, making him look from a distance as though a mad knifeman had slashed him several times across the legs.

'Well, if you're happy, Rodney, I'm happy.' Nathan appeared at Rodney's elbow and slapped him on the back. 'We just seem to be missing a cable …'

'I'm here, I'm here, don't panic.'

Scott appeared out of the darkness unrolling the long satellite cable behind him.

Nathan stopped blowing on his cold hands and winked at Cora and Rodney.

'So, Scott – what are your plans for the weekend then? Doing any gardening?' he said, trying hard to conceal a smirk.

'No, I sodding am not. It's bloody December. Bugger off!' But Scott was grinning as he dumped the end of the cable on the ground next to Nathan's tripod and marched off back to the warmth of the satellite truck.

Cora, Nathan, and Rodney looked at each other and sniggered, Cora feeling a little relieved. Scott had been grumpier than usual lately, so it was nice that he'd taken the joke so well today. They'd been riling him about gardening for months, ever since the summer when he'd been redoing the garden of his new family semi and decided he wanted to trail some pink clematis across the back wall. Unfortunately, he'd instead managed to ask an elderly garden centre assistant if she could provide him with some chlamydia.

Cora snorted again, and then suddenly pulled herself

together as another disembodied voice boomed in her earpiece.

'Morning, Cora – you're obviously having fun – everything OK there? We're going to be with you in just over twenty minutes.'

Cora recognised the slightly stressed Scottish tones of her friend. 'Oh, it's you, Sam. Morning! Yes, we've been Scott-baiting again – you know, the clematis story? But everything's under control – all chickens present and correct. Talk to you in a bit!'

'Thanks, Cora. And if you could stand by for possible extra hits through the morning that would be great – items dropping like flies today, Jeanette's going bonkers,' Sam replied, and disappeared.

Cora looked at her watch and gestured to Nathan and Rodney, who had also been listening to the exchange on their headsets.

'Er – chickens, can you all gather round please? Nearly time to go on, so let's just make sure we all know what we're doing!'

'Scott, you are a star,' said Cora gratefully as the engineer handed her a steaming mug of Earl Grey.

The first broadcast of the morning successfully out of the way, and the giant chickens temporarily back in their houses, the crew were thawing out in the satellite van.

Nathan stuffed a Jaffa Cake into his mouth and then sighed heavily, delicately spraying Rodney's glasses with crumbs.

He swallowed. 'Ugh. A weekend of Christmas shopping to look forward to – can you believe it's only ten days away! I've done nothing!'

'Mmmm, shopping for me too,' said Scott, 'Elaine's spotted this clock she fancies. Edwardian. Inlaid mahogany, white enamel dial. Nice actually.'

Rodney surreptitiously picked up the sleeve of Nathan's discarded fleece and began to wipe his glasses.

'I don't get your antique fetish, Scott, really I don't. Although I'd rather go antiquing with you than do what I've got to do later – bloody got to help bloody Jodie with the sound at her bloody nativity. BOR-ING!' he said, gloomily.

'Oh, Rodders, it will be fun!' Cora tried to sound enthusiastic. Rodney's girlfriend ran a nursery, and the soundman was often roped in to help give the kids' shows a professional edge.

'Yeah, right. You come then,' retorted Rodney.

Scott and Nathan tittered, and Cora smiled and shrugged. It wasn't that she actually disliked children – she adored several of her friends' offspring. It was just that when biological clocks were being handed out she, it seemed, was given a double dose of ambition instead. Child-free and happy, that was Cora, and she had always chosen boyfriends who felt the same way.

'Well, Justin and I don't have plans really – we're staying at home, just the two of us. I want to snuggle up and not see *anybody* all weekend. It's been *mad* recently. What wouldn't I give for a nice easy studio job?'

'One of these days I'll go to London and shoot that snobby Alice Lomas cow and then you can have her job at the news desk.'

Scott raised two fingers, pretending he was aiming a gun.

'It's a doggy dog world, this TV game, after all …'

Nathan and Cora looked at each other and grinned.

'Er – it's a dog *eat* dog world, not *doggy* dog,' Cora said.

'Is it?' Scott sounded surprised. 'Oh, well. You know what I mean.'

'I do, and thank you. But I don't think murder is the answer, sadly. Especially as you're being hauled in front of Jeanette on Monday morning as it is.'

Scott's face darkened. 'Thanks, Cora. I've been trying to forget about that. Old bitch. It's my second disciplinary too, shitting myself actually.'

Cora reached over and stroked his arm. 'Sorry, sweetie, I shouldn't have mentioned it. It'll be fine, you'll see, she's not that bad, honestly …'

Her voice tailed off, as the three men looked at her sceptically.

'She's exactly that bad,' Nathan said flatly. 'None of us can

17

stand the woman, Cora, no point in pretending otherwise. But chin up, Scott mate, it won't help to get in a state about it.'

'MCR IN LONDON CALLING THE CREW IN DEVON! CAN YOU HEAR ME, DEVON?'

A voice suddenly boomed through the speakers next to Scott's chair, causing Rodney and Cora to jump so violently they both spilled their tea.

'Bloody hell, now what?' Scott flicked the switch that allowed him to speak directly to the master control room in London.

'Yes, MCR, we can hear you – problem?' he said into the microphone.

'WE NEED YOU BACK UP AT 0710 – THE PRIME MINISTER WAS MEANT TO BE ON THE SOFA BUT HE'S GOT HELD UP SO WE'RE DOING THE CHICKENS AGAIN INSTEAD.' The technical director's voice echoed round the truck.

'Oh, darn it!' Cora was frantically wiping tea off her jeans. 'That gives me ten minutes to round up those blooming chicken people – they're all in their houses! Tell them it'll be tight, Scott, but we'll do it.'

She leapt out of the truck, pulling on her coat as she ran. Nathan and Rodney followed at a more leisurely pace. Ten whole minutes to get ready – no problem!

The watery sun was starting to melt the frost on the roundabout as Cora finally heard the show's closing credits and gratefully removed her earpiece. The boys whooped and began to pack their equipment neatly away in their cars, looking forward to their usual big cooked breakfast at the nearest café.

'I'm going to be a party pooper today,' Cora said. 'I want to get home.'

She slid into her car. 'And I probably won't see you next week – I'm covering in London, remember? Don't miss me too much!'

'OK – have a good one.' Nathan leaned into the car to give her a goodbye kiss on the cheek.

'See ya!' Cora honked her horn and waved at Scott and Rodney as she eased off the grass verge and on to the road. The boys stopped winding the cable back on to the drum in the back of the truck and blew massive kisses, Rodney leaping in the air like a garish, multi-coloured salmon on a fishing line.

For what would be one of the last times today, Cora grinned inanely. Post-live hysteria, they called it. Everyone always felt a little giddy at this time of the morning, especially on a Friday. She turned Radio One up loud, and glanced at the clock as she pulled away. 9.10 a.m. If she managed to stay awake and do it all in one go, she should be home by midday.

'Hooray!' She put her foot down, happily accelerating towards what was going to be a very bad day indeed.

In contrast, a rather satisfying day lay ahead for the person who would very soon end the life of Jeanette Kendrick. The plans, which had taken a long time to formulate, were all in place. Just the weekend to get through, and then the day would be here. The soon-to-be killer, casually tossing a roll of duct tape from hand to hand, wondered with a small smirk if Jeanette Kendrick liked Mondays. If so, she wouldn't be quite so keen on her next one.

4

In a luxurious apartment in central London, Benjamin Boland flicked his gargantuan plasma screen off and sank back into the stack of fine Egyptian cotton-covered pillows that adorned his queen-sized bed.

He'd been watching *Morning Live* a lot recently. It wasn't a bad little show actually, he thought. *He* wouldn't work on it of course – and he had been asked to, not so long ago. He'd turned Jeanette Kendrick down flat though. No way was *he* going to get out of bed at the crack of dawn, not while he was still getting primetime stuff to present – but still, it did make quite entertaining viewing. Some hot women too.

Relishing his lie-in, the TV star gazed out of the huge floor to ceiling window opposite. He loved this place, which was on the fifteenth floor of a new, ultra-modern high-rise on the South Bank, just down the road from TV Centre. Without stirring from his bed (newly acquired from the Versace home range), he could see the Thames snaking by below, the weak December sun glinting on its curves. Towering over the riverbank, the London Eye, the great Ferris wheel which gave sightseers an unparalleled view of the capital, was already slowly turning, its transparent pods dotted with the first tourists of the morning.

He ran his hands through his dark, curly hair, which was even more unruly then usual at this time of day, and turned to pull the duvet off the bed completely, looking with anticipation at the sleeping figure of the skinny blonde in red, 'Mrs Santa' style lingerie sprawled next to him. She had bored him almost to tears with her conversation last night but then, most of them did nowadays. He vowed there and then to stop dating models. Well, maybe just over Christmas. Then, no more. Still … asleep, this one looked seriously sexy. Her long, wavy hair extensions draped softly over huge, quite obviously surgically enhanced breasts, the curls almost reaching the taut tanned stomach and firm little bottom below. Benjamin leaned over, slipped his fingers inside her bra cup, and gently tweaked her large, pink nipple. The blonde moaned softly and half opened her eyes, her dark lashes flaky with last night's mascara.

'Well, good morning, big boy,' she said huskily. 'You up already?' She reached out a scarlet-tipped finger and ran it gently up his leg.

Oh yes, thought Benjamin. I am very definitely up already …

A hundred and twenty miles away in the Gloucestershire flat he shared with Cora Baxter, Justin Dendy was packing. Feeling slightly nauseous, he moved slowly around the neat lounge, trying to ignore the glittering Christmas tree he had helped his excited girlfriend decorate last weekend. Picking up a CD here, a book there, he carried on until he had collected the last of his belongings. Returning to the bedroom, he tossed them into a large sports bag, zipped it closed and carried it out to the small pile of suitcases and boxes already stacked outside the front door.

With a final glance around the bright apartment he'd called home for the past ten months, Justin shut the door and locked it behind him.

He called the lift, lugged all his gear into it, and hit the button for the ground floor.

Five minutes later, the boot and back seat of his Volvo straining with luggage, he shut the driver's door, sat back in his seat and pulled his mobile from his jeans pocket. He couldn't put it off any longer. It was time to ring Cora.

5

Monday 18th December

M is for Monday – M is for murder! OMG Cora – what the hell? N x

Cora shook her head as she read Nathan's text. What the hell indeed, she thought.

It was all a little hard to process. She'd been feeling dreadful enough today after spending most of her weekend in tears, thanks to Justin. And now Jeanette was dead. Not just dead either, if the rumours racing round the newsroom were to be believed, but *murdered*. She'd never been a popular woman – well, if we're being honest here, she was probably the most unpopular person I know, Cora thought. But still – murder?

She snuggled deeper under the crisp white duvet on her hotel room bed and shut her eyes. It was only 6 p.m., but she was desperately tired, and she had to be back in work at 3.30 tomorrow morning. It had been quite a day. Quite a few days, in fact. Yes, today had been awful. But – Friday. Friday had quite possibly been one of the worst days of her life.

She'd made it quite a long way after Justin's phone call – all the way along the A39 in fact, fists clenching the steering wheel so tightly they ached, eyes fixed unblinking on the road ahead, her stomach contracting.

It wasn't until she'd reached the motorway that the crying had started, and she'd had more than one curious look from overtaking drivers as she crawled along in the slow lane sobbing, mascara streaking down her cheeks, the tears blurring her vision until she decided the only sane thing to do was just to stop. Pulling up in the furthest corner of the busy Sedgemoor services car park, away from prying eyes, she had howled until her throat hurt. Justin had dumped her. He had, in fact, already moved out. It was all over.

'I just didn't see it. I didn't see it coming! Why didn't I see it?' Cora had cried out loud, banging both hands on the dashboard.

She'd sniffed again and pulled another fresh tissue from the pack in her glove compartment. OK, so they hadn't seen much of each other recently, and she wasn't a particularly easy person to be involved with, she knew that – her work always came first for her, and she was always so tired ...

But she and Justin had been together for two years, ever since they had fallen lustfully into each other's arms at a mutual friend's wedding in Oxford. She had been instantly smitten by this tall, clever, creative man with his hard rugby player's body, and he had fallen equally quickly for her, the pretty brunette he had been watching on morning TV for months. They had lived together for nearly a year, for goodness' sake! They were going to have that big party after Christmas to celebrate! Fresh tears had come to Cora's eyes and she'd wiped them away viciously.

They had seemed so right for each other. Justin worked almost as hard as she did, commuting daily to a big Birmingham design studio and, like her, wanted to get to the top of his profession, maybe retire early, travel, have a couple of properties abroad. No children, that had always been the plan. It was one of the things she had been so awed by when they first met – the fact that, unlike every one of her previous boyfriends, who all, when pushed, admitted a desire to procreate somewhere down the line, this one genuinely seemed to want the life she did. Just the two of them, in love, happy together, needing nobody else. And now he had landed this on her.

'It's partly that I just never see you, but it's also the kids thing, Cora,' he had said, as she sat in stunned silence listening to his farewell speech. 'I want them. I know I said I didn't, but I do. I just haven't admitted it to myself until now. I'm going to be forty in a couple of years, and I want kids. I want kids, and a wife who's at home with them. I know it sounds old-fashioned, but I think deep down that's what I've always really wanted.

'The big plans, the making our fortune, the homes in the sun, it all sounded great, and for a while I thought, yes, that's the life for me. But it isn't, Cora. Well, I do want some of it, but I want a wife and kids there doing it with me. And I know that's not what *you* want, so there's no point. I'm so sorry, Cora, I know it's Christmas and everything but I thought, you know, a new year and all that, a clean break …'

And that was it.

'Two years down the toilet,' Cora said to herself. 'And to be dumped by *phone!*'

She huddled deeper into her duvet, feeling utterly miserable. Lost in thought, she jumped as her mobile began to ring on the bedside table.

'Hello?'

'Cora – evening, darling. You OK? Hell of a day, eh?'

'Sam! You're not back in the office already? Did you get ANY sleep? So – fill me in! What's the latest?'

Justin temporarily forgotten, Cora propped herself up on her pillows, eager for news. The police had allowed her, and all the crew members who'd been down on the studio level at the time of Jeanette's death, to leave the building by mid-morning, and she had heard very little about the on-going investigation since.

'Well – as you know, she was found outside, more or less below her office window, and that's why at first everyone just presumed she'd jumped. I mean – seven storeys up – if you want to kill yourself, it's pretty much guaranteed, right?'

'Yes – but then the police said there were signs of a struggle, inside her office, didn't they? They think somebody threw her out, pushed her. I know all this. What else?'

'Well … oh hang on, Cora – what?'

Sam's voice tailed off as she turned to talk to someone in the newsroom. Cora rolled her eyes and impatiently rearranged her duvet, then grinned as she listened to the distant conversation.

'A pig? Why would I want a pig on the sofa on Wednesday?' Sam was saying.

'Well, it's that self-sufficiency story – you know, that "New Year, New Start" thing we're doing after Christmas? We're previewing it on Wednesday and the woman from the self-sufficiency organisation says she can bring a pig in.' It was a young male voice that Cora didn't recognise.

'Well – how big is the pig? We can't have a monstrous great pig crapping all over the studio!' Sam sounded exasperated. 'Tell her if it's a cute little piglet, she can bring it in. Otherwise, no pig. Right – Cora – sorry sweetie, what were we talking about?'

'*Sam*! Come on – we were talking about Jeanette!' Cora sat bolt upright in bed, eyes bright. She instantly felt guilty about how excited she felt about getting the latest gossip on the case. She'd been deeply shocked by Jeanette's murder – of course she had – and saddened too, which had come as something of a surprise to her, as she'd wished bad things on her detested boss too many times to count over the past couple of years. But she couldn't help it – she'd always loved working on crime stories. There was nothing quite like a good murder, even if this time it was a little close to home.

'Oh, yes – well, according to rumour, the security guard who found her claims she wasn't quite dead. I mean – she was still alive for a few moments when he reached her. Pretty astounding, considering how far she fell, I would have thought she'd be mush as soon as she hit the ground, but you know Jeanette, tough as old boots. And there was that case last year, of that guy in New York who survived a fall of twenty storeys or something mad like that, remember? Anyway, I digress – this is the intriguing bit. She said something.'

Cora gasped. 'What? What did she say? Oh, for goodness' sake, Sam!'

Sam paused again. 'Well – it's a bit spooky really, considering what happened with Christina and the dead dog thing. It was "Chris". She said Chris.'

6

Jeanette Kendrick's killer glanced at the clock: 4.30 a.m. Nearly twenty-four hours had passed. It had gone rather well. So. A little break now, let the dust settle. And then on to the next. The murderer looked in the mirror, and smiled.

'OK, look, I know this is weird. Super weird. But, you know, the show must go on and all that …'

Sam paused, looking from face to weary face. Cora gave her friend an encouraging smile. At this hour the newsroom was normally buzzing. Not so today. Nobody had liked Jeanette, but without her, nothing felt right. Her empty office, police tape still hanging forlornly across the doorway, was like a brooding presence at the end of the big room.

We miss her, Cora thought. Who'd have believed it?

Sam cleared her throat and continued her little pre-show pep talk.

'So – as I'm now in temporary charge, please, I need your support.'

There was a flash of pride in her eyes, and Cora smiled again. She knew how much this promotion, even if temporary, meant to Sam, who lived, slept, and breathed the breakfast show.

'The decision's been made upstairs that we carry on as normal …'

Sam was interrupted by a loud sniff as Alice Lomas entered the newsroom, her face tear-streaked and eyes puffy.

'Er, morning, Alice. You OK?'

Alice glanced at Jeanette's office and a huge sob wracked her skinny body. Clutching a large Fendi handbag to her chest, she scuttled past, head down, and disappeared through the door to the stairs to the studio level.

Sam raised her eyes heavenwards and continued where she'd left off.

'As I was saying, the decision's been made that we carry on as normal. Viewing figures have never been higher and they'll probably go up, if anything, after what happened yesterday, you know how ghoulish people can be, so – well, have a good show. And thank you.'

Sam stood still for several seconds, her eyes fixed on Jeanette's office, and Cora again saw that look of pride in her eyes, but this time mixed with something else. Grief? It was an expression Cora had never seen on her friend's face before, and she watched her, mesmerised, noticing too a slight shake in Sam's hand as she put the coffee cup she'd been holding back on her desk. Then she sat down, and the spell was broken. There was silence for a moment, and then the office hum gradually resumed, if a little more sombre in tone than usual.

Cora sighed. Poor Sam. She was clearly uncharacteristically nervous, knowing she had a tough job ahead of her now. And what was going on with Alice? What a drama queen. Probably scared she'll be exposed as a complete airhead now Jeanette's not there to watch her back, Cora thought.

She drained her mug of Earl Grey and turned back to her news scripts. *Police have launched a murder investigation after* Morning Live *editor Jeanette Kendrick was found dead yesterday morning outside TV Centre. Officers are talking to staff in an effort to establish* :...

'Never thought you'd be reading that in one of your bulletins, eh, Cora?'

Cora jumped. 'Oh, morning, Wend. No, flipping heck. I still can't really believe it, you know? I just keep staring at her office. It's so – bizarre. I mean, I know the newsroom is frantic in the mornings, and any number of people always popped in and out to see Jeanette all the time, but – how?'

Wendy heaved a pile of newspapers, all with lurid headlines about Jeanette's murder, off the chair next to Cora and plonked herself down.

'Dunno. I really don't. She had the blinds down of course – remember, she pulled them down after the Christina thing? So once somebody was in there, I suppose none of us out here would be able to see what was going on anyway. But to go in, somehow throw her out the window, and then calmly walk out again as if nothing had happened … and for nobody to notice a thing? I can't get my head round it.'

'It's bonkers.' Cora saved her script and hit print. 'I can't stop thinking about it. It's this "Chris" thing that's the weirdest – any ideas? I mean, it can't be Christina, can it?'

Wendy rubbed her hands together in glee. 'Intriguing, isn't it! Of course, we're not even supposed to know about it – not the sort of thing the police are going to make public.'

'I know. But Bob on security's so damn indiscreet. I bet the whole building knows by now. Impossible to keep a secret in this place.'

'Indeed! Well of course, we hear "Chris" and we all think "Christina", don't we? Maybe not, apparently. I mean – *I* don't think for a minute she's got killer potential, but after Dead Dog-gate quite a few people mentioned her to the police – sort of had to, you know?'

Cora nodded.

'But as she's in work this morning, and not locked up … not that she'd be strong enough to push a cat out of a window, would she? She's tiny!'

Cora nodded. 'Or brave enough. She hated Jeanette, but she was scared of her too.'

Wendy brushed an errant curl out of her eyes. 'Exactly. Anyway, she spent ages with the cops yesterday, but sounds like she's in the clear. She was down in Reception sorting out a delivery while Jeanette was flying out of the building – CCTV footage from down there will prove it, or so she says.'

Cora stared into space, chin on her hand. 'So, if it's not Christina – who else? Who else is known as Chris?'

Wendy shrugged. 'No idea. Don't know anyone else called Chris. Or Christina, or Christopher. Anyway, got to go. Weather graphics calling. See you later.'

'See ya.' Cora sighed, logged out, and headed for make-up.

'How many are we expecting?'

Detective Chief Inspector Adam Bradberry frowned as he surveyed the conference room. He'd asked all the *Morning Live* staff to assemble here after the programme, but he wasn't entirely sure the room he'd been allocated was large enough.

The young detective constable who was fiddling with a TV in the corner looked up.

'Around sixty, I think, boss.'

'Right. Well, most of them will have to stand. Got that working yet?'

'Almost.'

Adam nodded. Good. He sat down and flicked through his notes again. This was a funny one, and no mistake. Virtually everyone in the damn newsroom had to be considered a suspect, but there were definitely a few persons of more significant interest, and the sooner he started eliminating people, the sooner he'd get it sewn up. He ran his fingers through his cropped blond hair. He was definitely feeling the pressure this morning. A high-profile killing like this ... he sat up straight as somebody knocked gently on the door.

'Come in!'

The door opened and, looking both wary and weary, the programme's production staff filed in.

In the newsroom, Sam had just finished briefing Cora.

'We won't do updates every day – just when there's some significant news. But I want you to do it Cora. You're back on the road after this week anyway, and you're good at crime. You always get the tone right, unlike some of the others. So if you fancy making friends with the senior investigating officer after our little film show this morning, feel free – it can only help.'

They slipped into the conference room. The email they'd all

had earlier just said there was some CCTV the police wanted staff to look at so they could eliminate a suspect from their enquiries, and everyone was speculating in excited whispers. What were they about to see? The low murmur in the room faded as a tall, fair man in a brown jacket raised his hand.

'Ladies and gents – thanks for coming, I know how busy you all are and what a difficult time this is, so this won't take long.' He paused and smiled. 'By the way, I'm DCI Adam Bradberry, senior investigating officer. You're probably going to see me around quite a lot in the days to come – sorry about that!'

Sam pressed her mouth to Cora's ear. 'He's *hot*!' she hissed.

'Shhh!' Cora elbowed her friend in the ribs. Sam was right though. He really was quite attractive. Actually, if she was being perfectly honest, he was rather gorgeous. Not that she was remotely interested in men at the moment, of course.

The policeman was still talking, '… so, if you could all just take a look at this. This man was seen loitering outside the building for quite some considerable time yesterday morning, and for no obvious reason. There may be a perfectly innocent explanation of course, but we need to be sure. We'll be releasing it to the news channels later today, but if anyone here knows who he is it would save us a lot of time.'

He pressed a button on the remote control in his hand and the big screen flickered into life. It was a shot of the front of TV Centre. The police officer pointed to a figure in a hooded coat leaning against the front wall, a metre or so away from the big revolving main door.

'That's him, there. We have several hours of footage of him – he first shows up around 4 a.m., which is unusual in itself if he's not staff. Comes and goes a bit, then vanishes for good after eight, and we're really not sure what he's doing there. A few times he looks like he's about to come into the building, then seems to change his mind. Then he disappears for a bit – see here? – goes round the corner out of CCTV range, then he comes back. We can't rule out the possibility he might have entered the building through another entrance at some point, and he's not in his position at the front there at the time your boss was murdered, so we need to find him so we can eliminate him – or not. As I said, probably completely innocent, but we need to make sure. I know you can't see his face in this footage, because of the hood on his coat. And I say "his", but actually, I suppose it could be a woman. Anybody recognise him – or her?'

Cora stared at the screen. All around her, her colleagues were shaking their heads, faces blank. But there was something … something familiar about the individual on the screen. The coat. The way the figure moved. Then, as the images continued, a hand came up and the person on the CCTV pictures rubbed his or her nose. Cora's stomach rolled. She knew that gesture. And yes, she knew that coat too. No, she thought. Please, no. But suddenly, there wasn't any doubt in her mind. Yes, it was most definitely a man. A man she knew very well indeed. A man who'd recently hurt her very badly.

The person the police were trying to identify was Justin.

7

Friday 22nd December

'Soho, please – the A-Bar.'

Cora slammed the door of the black cab behind her and settled back in her seat as the driver pulled away from the kerb. Normally on a Friday night after a week in the studio she would have checked out of her London hotel and rushed straight back to Gloucestershire and Justin, but tonight there was nothing to go home for. She fished in the little chocolate leather Ted Baker bag on her lap for her lip gloss and smoothed on a final layer, lurching slightly as the cab left the hotel forecourt and joined the evening traffic.

It was eight o'clock, and snowing lightly. Cora's breath steamed up the cold window and she huddled a little deeper into her faux fur jacket. Outside, tightly wrapped people laden with festive shopping bags scurried along the rapidly whitening pavements. The taxi slowed and stopped at a red light on Regent Street, and Cora watched as two excited children in matching blue and white striped hats and scarves hauled their mother towards the massive windows of Hamleys toy store. They stopped, the mother hooking an arm round each child and pulling them close. The display *was* wonderful, thought Cora. A magical Christmas woodland scene, it was filled with movement and colour and light that spilled out onto the darkened street, warming the chill air. Animated fairies looped across a starry sky, sprinkling gold dust onto rabbits and bears gambolling below. On a frosty hillock, mechanical elves jerkily wrapped presents in shiny purple paper. Above them all, a silver moon studded with crystals glittered and shimmered. For a moment, Cora felt the stomach-fluttering thrill she remembered from her childhood but, almost immediately, reality hit and she took a deep breath. It was three days until Christmas, and she was on her own again.

She rested her head against the icy glass of the side window and shut her eyes as the lights changed suddenly and the taxi jolted and moved away. She couldn't get Justin out of her head. Despite the CCTV footage running repeatedly on all the TV news programmes for days now, nobody else seemed to have realised it was him and nobody had come forward. But it WAS him, she knew it was. His face was unrecognisable in the video, but the coat had been the first clue – it was the one she'd given him for his birthday just a few weeks earlier. She hadn't seen him wear it before, but she knew she was right. And then that gesture, when he rubbed his nose ... so painfully familiar. There was absolutely no doubt. She'd spoken briefly to the police officer, DCI Bradberry, after the meeting, as instructed by Sam – introduced herself, told him she'd be covering the story for the programme – but she hadn't said a word about what she'd just seen, not to the police, not even to Sam or Wendy. If it *was* Justin, there had to be an explanation. It was just that, at the moment, she couldn't think of one.

It had gone round and round in her head for days – what on earth could he have been doing there? Had he come to see her, to say he'd changed his mind about leaving her? But if so, why hadn't he come in? Why hadn't he just called her? And she couldn't get hold of him to ask him. She'd tried and tried, but his mobile was permanently off, and she had no idea where he'd gone when he'd moved out of their flat. She'd spoken to all his friends, even called his parents, and they had no idea where he was either. Nor, it seemed, had any of them recognised the hooded figure on the CCTV footage, or at least they hadn't mentioned it to her; probably, Cora surmised, because nobody except her would have known he had a coat like that. It seemed he hadn't even told anyone he and Cora had split up. He'd simply disappeared. But she couldn't tell the police. She just couldn't. He might have hurt her, but Justin wasn't a killer – was he?

"Ere you go, luv. A-Bar, right?"

The driver's Cockney tones interrupted her musings, and she clambered out of the cab, paid him quickly and ran across the snowy street to the bar. The black-clad bouncer nodded her in, and as she pushed the door open a tidal wave of heat and noise hit her. A Lady Gaga track was booming, and her mood lifted as she weaved through the hordes of drinkers, slipping off her jacket as she made her way to the corner where, she hoped, Sam and Wendy would be waiting for her at their usual table. This was their favourite bar, with a nice crowd normally – not too young but still quite trendy, mostly media and marketing types, too cool to bother with the odd TV presenter who wandered in. The theory was immediately disproved by a middle-aged woman in a plunging scarlet satin dress and flashing bauble earrings who suddenly grabbed Cora's arm, making her jump.

'Wow! You're that woman off the telly, aren't you? I watch you every morning! Tell me, is that Jeremy as skinny in the flesh?'

Cora smiled weakly. Everyone always wanted to ask about Jane and Jeremy. Jeremy was actually extraordinarily skinny and was the only person she knew who looked even *smaller* on screen than he was in real life, but it would have been disloyal to say so. She muttered something about TV cameras being misleading and politely disentangled herself from the woman, who patted her drunkenly on the bottom and wished her a happy Christmas.

Cora carried on pushing through the crowd. She was attempting to side step a puce-faced man unsteadily pouring champagne from a magnum when she heard a familiar shriek.

'Cooorrrrraaa! Over heeeeeere!'

Peering over the heads of the rowdy mob, she could see Wendy, standing on the orange suede banquette that ran along the back wall. She was waving ecstatically, a large glass of red wine in one hand, breasts spilling out of a tight black corset.

Cora mouthed 'Hi' and waved back, and Wendy jumped down from the bench and disappeared. By the time Cora reached the table twenty seconds later, Sam was sloshing white wine into a glass and pushing it towards her, grinning. Cora squeezed onto the end of the long seat and took a grateful gulp of the cold Sauvignon. The Merlot bottle on the table was almost empty – it looked like they'd been there a while.

'About time, Baxter!' Wendy poured the last of the red wine into her own glass, at the same time winking lasciviously at a spotty young man in an ill-fitting suit who was standing nearby, staring at her chest as if transfixed. He flushed bright red and turned away abruptly, looking mortified, and Wendy snorted. She'd backcombed her corkscrew curls and, with her pink cheeks and glorious cleavage, she looked like a Titian goddess.

'Yeah, we thought you weren't coming!' Sam squeezed her hand. She looked gorgeous too, Cora thought – she'd straightened her soft brown bob into a sleek curtain, and a simple white shift dress skimmed her slim body. Cora suddenly wished she had made more effort with her own outfit – she just hadn't been in the mood tonight. She gave herself a quick once-over – soft gold metallic shirt, the top few buttons open to show a flash of cleavage. Then tight 7 jeans and her favourite fabulous Gucci knee-high boots, her only jewellery the diamond cuff bracelet she'd bought herself when she'd landed her *Morning Live* job. She looked OK, she supposed – slightly underdressed next to Sam and Wendy, but it wasn't as if she was on the pull or anything.

She sighed, and then jumped as Sam poked her in the ribs.

'Oi, you, stop looking mopey. We are out to have fun, fun, fun!'

Cora poked her back.

'OK, OK.' She took another sip and scanned the room. The bar was heaving, the usual Friday night crowd even more rambunctious than usual with Christmas just around the corner. Further down the orange banquette a plump girl and a man wearing slightly crooked reindeer antlers on his head were snogging fervently. Nearby, a group of office workers, ties loosened and apparently already completely sozzled, howled in appreciation, and without ungluing his lips the antler-wearing man flicked them a V-sign. The girl, oblivious, hitched a podgy leg around his waist, and the watching men leered and cheered. Despite the unpleasantness of the scene, Cora felt a sudden twist of pain. She'd never kiss Justin again. She immediately pushed the thought from her mind. Whatever he was up to, and wherever he was, he had chosen to be there instead of with her, and there was nothing she could do about it. She turned back to the table, suddenly aware she was being spoken to.

'So I take it everyone knows now? About you and Justin?' Wendy was saying.

Cora hesitated, wondering if she should now mention her fears about the CCTV footage, then changed her mind. 'Yep. Told my mum and dad last night too. They were quite nice about it actually. Mum was really shocked – she liked Justin, you know? And for once she didn't even go on about the kids thing too much – she knows better by now.'

She gulped down another mouthful. 'Now, enough – no more horrible ex-boyfriend talk this evening, OK? It's Christmas and I want a nice cheerful night out.'

'Fine by us.' Sam picked a cashew nut from the bowl on the table in front of her and nibbled it delicately. 'Can't believe it's Christmas – what a mad year, eh? Seriously, I think the stories we cover are getting more and more bonkers! I mean, look at all the stuff you've done this year Cora – remember the naked ramblers?' She shook her head and washed down the nut with another gulp of wine.

Cora laughed. She'd spent a week in the summer trailing a couple that had decided to walk from Land's End to John O'Groats with no clothes on. Remarkably, they hadn't been arrested till day three, when they'd gone into a supermarket naked to stock up on supplies. They'd actually been really nice people, and once Cora and Nathan had got used to the strangeness of watching the bloke's sizeable willy bouncing along beside them as they filmed, it had been quite a fun time.

'Yeah, we've had some strange ones recently. I just wish the hours weren't so long, you know? It's definitely got worse. I drove all the way to Manchester last week to do that arson story, and when I got there Jeanette suddenly decided arson was too miserable for December and I had to turn round and drive to Cornwall instead to interview that bloke who was giving away all his belongings to raise money for the local hospice. Nearly nine hours in my car – I couldn't feel my bum by bedtime.'

Sam and Wendy laughed and leaned over to clink glasses. Cora smiled fondly at them. It was good to be out. Her hours had been ridiculous recently. Justin had often gone on about it, and what a bitch Jeanette was to make her work so hard. Cora's stomach lurched and she took another swig of wine. Surely he wouldn't have killed her because of that ... No. Stop it. How would he even have got into the newsroom without anyone noticing? He didn't even know what floor it was on. Did he? Oh, for goodness' sake. She shook her head violently, trying to get the thoughts out of her head.

Wendy scowled at her. 'Cora, you look like a cow shaking off flies when you do that. And I know what you're doing – stop thinking about him. More alcohol, that's what you need!'

She stood up, waving the empty red wine bottle.

'Another one of each?' She wandered off in the direction of the bar, not waiting for an answer. As usual, every man she passed did a double take, gaping at her stupendous cleavage. Wendy wiggled her hips and pouted as she squeezed through the crowd. Happily ensconced in a relationship with Dan, a video editor at the studio, whom she fully intended to marry and have a brood with, she had no real interest in other men, but she certainly enjoyed a good flirt when she was in the mood.

Cora and Sam watched her and chuckled. 'She's a right one. Wish I got that much male attention.' Sam sighed.

'Oh shut up, you do alright, farmer girl.' Cora playfully punched her friend on the arm. Sam had of late become a serial dater, determined to find her Mr Right. She was working her way through the books of a 'young farmers' dating agency, hoping to find someone to slot in with the latest of her constantly changing big plans for her future, which currently involved climbing as high as she could in the TV industry before she was forty, then packing it in and moving to the country with pigs, donkeys, and a houseful of kids. Cora didn't fancy that herself in the slightest, but she very much looked forward to visiting – although she knew from past experience that Sam's future plans would probably involve something entirely different by this time next month.

She smiled at her friend and drained her glass. It was Christmas, and it was time to start having fun.

8

Less than a mile away, in the central London police station from which DCI Adam Bradberry was co-ordinating the hunt for Jeanette Kendrick's killer, there was very little in the way of festive cheer. A tatty artificial tree, scarcely three feet tall and with several branches missing, drooped miserably in the corner near the photocopier, a solitary cracked silver bauble and two battered elf ornaments nestling in its faded foliage. One elf, which only had one leg, had its face turned to the wall as if mortified by the whole sorry spectacle. On the table beside the coffee machine, a big round tin of Roses chocolates sat with its lid askew, surrounded by bright yellow and purple sweet wrappings. Adam swiped the offending packaging into the bin right next to the table with a sigh, then walked back to his desk, slumping into his chair and fixing his eyes once more on the still picture on his computer screen.

It had been five days since Jeanette's body had been found – five days during which Adam and his team had accomplished, in his weary eyes, absolutely nothing. They had questioned every single person in the newsroom, appealed for witnesses and information on every news channel and radio show, and in every paper, and had gleaned nothing. He knew from past experience that if he didn't get a lead soon, the papers would stop being supportive and turn on him, but he was running out of ideas. It seemed impossible that a woman could have been thrown out of a window so close to a busy office, and for nobody to see or hear a single thing, and yet this, it seemed, was exactly what had happened.

Deeply frustrated after another day of dead ends, Adam had finally told his team to go to the pub for an hour and then come back refreshed in the morning. Discouraged and weary, they'd needed no second bidding, pulling on coats and gloves and gratefully heading for the door, although he'd been touched that several had called out to him to join them as they'd passed his desk. He'd told them he'd be along shortly, wanting to spend a few minutes reading through his notes on the case yet again. Adam Bradberry wasn't really the anxious kind, but he was definitely anxious today. He knew very well that a murder like this, without doubt the most high-profile of his career to date, could make or break him. Catch this killer quickly, and his climb up the ladder would be expedited. He was ambitious, and all ambitious cops longed for a case like this – a well-known victim, plenty of media coverage – but it would benefit his career only if he could crack it quickly, and efficiently. Fail, and his failure would be in the spotlight just as much as, or maybe more than, a successful outcome.

Adam gazed at the hooded figure outside Television Centre, frozen in the still taken from the CCTV footage of the front of the building – the footage that had been running non-stop on the various TV news programmes, eliciting nothing of any use whatsoever.

'Who are you, and what are you up to?' he said out loud. 'And why, on day five of the investigation, are you still the only half-decent lead I have?'

He paused for a moment, as if expecting the figure to respond, then shook his head and turned his computer off. Then, feeling more than a little despondent, he grabbed his coat and headed for the pub.

In the street just yards from the A-Bar, his broad shoulders lightly dusted with snowflakes, Benjamin Boland was signing autographs for a group of open-mouthed girls. His two friends, Carlos and Edward, stood nearby, hands thrust deep in pockets, looking resigned. It was always like this when you went out with Benj. The girls jostled for position around him as one of them nervously pointed a camera phone, hands shaking with cold and the thrill of it all. Benjamin smiled seductively, and the girls, eyes wide with excitement, nestled closer. Picture taken, they thanked him profusely and scampered off, shrieking and pulling out mobiles to text their friends. Benjamin Boland! They couldn't believe it! And he was so *nice*!

Benjamin strode across to where Carlos and Edward were now huddled under a jeweller's shop canopy.

'Morons,' he said, brushing snow from his heavy black Prada coat. 'Right, where are we going? Shall we just pop into the A-Bar till this weather stops?'

The others nodded their agreement and the three walked smartly down the street. The shaven-headed bouncer, who was slouching against the door trying to keep warm, straightened up abruptly when he saw Benjamin, and even opened the heavy door for them. By the time they had pushed their way to the bar, a buzz had already started, as here and there the slightly more sober members of the throng began to recognise the TV star. Benjamin didn't mind. They might stare and whisper, but mostly he didn't get bothered in here.

He nodded at the barman, who immediately rushed over, wiping his hands on his white waistcoat. Benjamin glanced at Carlos and Edward, and sighed. Edward was gently picking a snowflake off Carlos's long dark eyelashes. Benjamin liked going out with his gay friends – no competition – but sometimes they were a bit tedious. He nudged Edward.

'Champagne?'

'Naturellement!' Edward put on a fake French accent.

Benjamin turned back to the barman.

'Dom Pérignon please,' he said, and pulled his black American Express card from his wallet. 'We'll start a tab.'

The barman nodded and rushed off to find the champagne. Benjamin leaned on the bar and gazed slowly around the room, looking for talent. A busty redhead carrying two bottles of wine squeezed past him, and he watched as she wiggled her way to a corner table. His eyes widened suddenly as he realised who else was sitting there. Wasn't that – what was her name again? From *Morning Live*. That reporter, the cute one. Kara. No, Cora. She looked even hotter in the flesh. She was always covered up on

TV, but even at this distance he could see that her shirt was slightly open, revealing a nice cleavage and a hint of lacy bra. And boots – long leather boots. Nice. He turned back to the bar as the champagne arrived, and smiled at Carlos and Edward as he poured the amber bubbles into the crystal glasses. A couple of glasses of this, and he'd make his move.

'Honestly, I thought I was going to be *sick*, I was laughing so much!'

They were back on the dead dog story again. Cora was bent double over the table, clutching her stomach, while Sam, who always cried when she laughed, dabbed her mascara-streaked cheeks with a tissue, then used it to wipe the table as Wendy snorted into her wine glass, sending a spray of red wine onto the polished wood.

As usual, the talk was still mainly about work, tonight mainly a string of increasingly drunken anecdotes from Cora, who was feeling slightly hysterical and had decided this year had *definitely* been the most bizarre of her life.

'Insane stories all year, and then Jeanette gets bumped off. We'd never have predicted *that* this time last year, would we?'

Sam and Wendy shook their heads. They were both starting to look a little dazed.

'Hey – another possibility for that Chris thing – heard a few people talking about it in the office today.' Sam put her glass down on the table a little too heavily.

'Go on!' said Cora, then tutted as she slopped a little wine onto her jeans. 'Now what?'

'Well – Jeanette used to call Clancy Chris, or Chrissy, sometimes apparently. From the name of her company, Chrysalis Productions? It had become a bit of a nickname.'

Wendy and Cora looked at her, then at each other.

'No way,' Wendy pronounced. 'Clancy adored Jeanette. Dropped her off at work early doors every day and everything ...'

'Exactly.' Sam picked up her glass again. 'So she was there, at the studio, in the early hours. Could have hung around, come back later, shoved her out the window. Easy.'

Cora frowned and took another glug of wine. It was starting to slip down worryingly easily.

'I doubt it. Anyway, the cops are talking to her, aren't they? Talking to everyone. We'll soon hear if she's a suspect. I'd be amazed though. Now – can we please change the subject? Murder is NOT very festive.'

She swayed slightly in her seat, and then squinted as a familiar face on the other side of the room caught her eye.

'Hey, hang on, look who it is – there, by the bar – isn't that Benjamin Boland?'

Sam and Wendy jumped to attention. All three were spectacularly unimpressed by 'celebrity', having met enough so-called stars at *Morning Live* to realise that most of them were deeply uninteresting. But a decent sighting was a decent sighting, and Benjamin Boland was the man of the moment. His primetime extreme travel show, *Go!,* had been getting huge ratings for months.

Wendy wagged a finger and took another slurp of wine. 'Oh yeah, I saw him earlier when I was at the bar, forgot to mention it. He's verrrrrry tall. He's so bloody macho on screen I thought he might be a shortarse trying to compensate, but he's not. Verrrrrrry tall.'

'Everyone's tall next to you, Wend,' Cora giggled.

'Hey, Cora, you could do worse than him, you know.' Sam, who was the most sober of the three, poked her in the arm. 'Go and chat him up, I dare you!'

'No!'

'Oh, go on!' Sam craned her neck. 'Phwooaarr. He might be a macho idiot, but he's undeniably attractive. *Gorrrrrr*geous in fact. If he was a farmer, I might even be tempted. Go on, Cora, be a devil.'

Cora drained her glass. 'No way! Anyway, he only goes out with Kelly Brook types. I'd have every lingerie model in the country trying to scratch my eyes out. However ...'

She eyed the latest empty bottle speculatively. 'There's no harm in a little flirt. And we do need a refill ... I could just casually stand next to him while I order it, and see what happens …'

They all grinned at each other, and simultaneously turned to peer at the bar. Benjamin was leaning casually on it, a flute of champagne held elegantly in one hand as he chatted animatedly to two handsome Mediterranean-looking men in matching black polo necks. His dark curls brushed the collar of a tight fitting white shirt, casually untucked over a pair of expensive looking black trousers. Shiny leather loafers that shoe-addict Cora instantly recognised as Versace completed the oh-so-casual-but-incredibly-sexy look.

Her mind was made up. 'I'm doing it.'

'Woo-hoo!' Sam and Wendy clinked their empty glasses. Cora got up, smoothed her shirt, winked at the girls and headed, a tad unsteadily, to the bar.

Carlos and Edward, who both worked behind the scenes on *Go!*, were in the middle of a funny if rather shocking story about the sexual proclivities of an in-the-closet children's TV presenter. Benjamin was having a good time, but after several glasses of champagne, the urge for some female company was growing. He was very proud of himself having, in line with his brand new 'no models' policy, already turned away three busty girls with no brains who had invited him to come back to theirs for a 'private party'. It was a pleasant surprise, therefore, to suddenly find Cora Baxter ordering drinks at his elbow.

Benjamin gave her a surreptitious once-over. Yep, even better close up, he decided. She was patently a little the worse for wear, but that would just smooth his path. And he knew from watching her on TV that she was bright, and funny … and yes, seriously cute – glossy brown hair, sexy cleavage under that shirt, great arse in those tight jeans. And those boots! He'd get her to keep those on later …

He tilted his head and Carlos and Edward got the message immediately and moved discreetly away. Benjamin arranged his features into their most alluring expression, waited till the barman went off to get Cora's order, and touched her gently on the arm.

'Hey, beautiful. It would give me great pleasure to buy you a drink – will you let me?'

She turned pale green eyes on him. 'Well that's very kind of you, but no thanks. I don't accept drinks from strange men.' She turned back to the bar, but she was smiling.

'OK ...' thought Benjamin. He tapped her on the shoulder again.

'Let me introduce myself, then. Benjamin Boland. I'm only a little strange. And I know who you are. I wake up with you on a regular basis, Cora.' He held out a hand and beamed disarmingly. Cora hesitated for a moment, then took his hand and grinned back.

'OK, I know who you are too. But you still can't buy me a drink.' She rocked slightly on her heels and clutched the bar. 'Actually – I think I may have had enough already!' She giggled and wobbled again.

'Whoops!' Never one to miss an opportunity, Benjamin slipped his arm around her waist. She looked at him for a moment, and then leaned in, her breast soft against his chest. Her face tilted towards his, and their eyes met for a long second. Benjamin suddenly felt more turned on than he had in a long time. His voice was husky, close to her ear. 'In that case, let's forget the drink. What say you come back to mine and make babies instead?'

Cora flinched, as if he'd just spat in her face. She moved sharply away, and something flashed in her eyes. '*Make babies*! You know what? I'd rather ... I'd rather clean toilets for the rest of my life in a ... in a home for people with incurable diarrhoea!'

Benjamin looked at her, shocked and puzzled for a second, and then laughed out loud. Cora laughed too, and the sudden awkwardness vanished as quickly as it had appeared.

'Sorry,' she said. 'I'm just a bit drunk. No offence. I should get back to my friends.' She grabbed her wine from the bar and turned away.

'Oh – well, OK. Nice to meet you ...' But she was gone, already swallowed by the riotous rabble. Benjamin stared after her. He wasn't used to being turned down, but fine. He was pretty sure he hadn't been mistaken about the chemistry between them. If she wanted to play it cool, then that just added to the fun. He knew where to find her, after all.

He turned back to the bar.

'Ooooh! That didn't go very well, did it?'

Edward handed him a fresh glass of champagne with a smirk. Next to him, Carlos was prancing, making an 'L for Loser' sign on his forehead. Benjamin ignored them. He smiled to himself. He wasn't quite sure what had gone wrong this time, but the chase was on. He wouldn't be a loser for long.

9

Saturday 23rd December

It was nearly lunchtime the next day by the time a rather weary and hung over Cora had finally dragged herself out of London and reached the outskirts of Cheltenham. Her spirits lifted a little, as they always did, as she drove into her hometown. It was just so – nice. Tall Regency buildings, tree-lined streets, clusters of quaint antique shops here and hip boutiques there, the town always somehow had the effect of melting away her stress and making her smile. Even today in December, people were enjoying the winter sunshine, sipping lattes under the outdoor heaters at Mattino's, Cora's favourite little café.

She turned into her driveway and manoeuvred round the side of the building to her parking space, the wheels of the BMW crunching on the white gravel. She and Justin had moved into the five-storey building in the smartest part of Cheltenham last February. They had decided it was too soon to buy a place together so had rented their two-bedroomed flat, and as Cora hauled her suitcase out of the boot and locked the car, it suddenly struck her that from now on, she'd be paying the rent alone. She could afford it – her salary was reasonable, although telly certainly didn't pay as much as some people thought – but she'd have to economise a bit. She'd been a little too numb last weekend, the weekend of the big break-up, to think of practicalities like that. She grimaced as she struggled up the steps to the handsome red front door with its neat row of doorbells. *Baxter/Dendy*, the top one said. She paused and ran her finger sadly over the letters. Another practicality. She'd have to change that later.

Stopping only briefly to stroke the silky head of Oliver, her neighbours' sleek black cat who was sitting regally on the doorstep, she took the lift to the fifth floor, a hard little knot forming in her stomach. Was there a chance – a tiny chance – that he might have changed his mind, be waiting for her inside? Taking a deep breath, she turned her key in the lock and pushed the door open. Silence. She shut the door and, dumping her suitcase in the hallway, headed for the living room. Idiot. Of course he was gone. *Really* gone.

The room seemed bleached of colour, faded somehow. The plump sofas, bright modern artworks, gleaming dining table were all still in place, but to Cora's dejected eyes they had lost their lustre, as though someone had come in while she had been away and sucked out all the soul. The DVD rack in the corner was half empty, as was the white Ikea bookshelf, which ran the entire length of the back wall. She cast her eyes around the spacious room, looking again at the gaps. Gone were his iPad and iPod, which normally sat on the big cherrywood table. And the wall clock, the funky Alessi one his brother had sent him for his birthday.

Cora glanced out through the patio doors that opened out on to the roof terrace. The aluminium table and chairs were still there, but there was something missing – why hadn't she noticed that last weekend? The barbecue, he'd taken the barbecue. Fine. Cora didn't really do cooking anyway.

Her head pounding and legs feeling decidedly wobbly, she made her way unsteadily across the room and sank down onto one of the vast brown suede sofas with their hot pink cushions. She picked one up and hugged it to her tightly. Justin had hated having pink cushions – there was no danger he'd take these with him!

Cora sat back and stared at the mantelpiece opposite, where her favourite photo still sat. Somebody had taken it at that wedding in Oxford the day they first met. Cora, cheeks flushed with excitement and wine, in a red and white silk dress, smiling at the camera. And Justin, in a sexy dark suit and bright tie, arm loosely wrapped around her waist, grinning too, gazing at Cora.

And now, he was gone. And, even worse, he was a potential suspect in a murder case. Cora shook her head, still staring at the picture. It was all just bizarre. If only she could talk to him, ask him what was going on. But how? Emails were bouncing back, and texts and phone calls didn't seem to be getting through. Had he changed his phone number?

She turned to look at the Christmas tree by the window, lavishly decorated with pink and silver baubles to match the room, and suddenly felt desperately in need of a drink. She dropped the cushion, stood up wearily and went down the hall to the tiny galley kitchen. She opened the fridge and pulled out a bottle of Sauvignon Blanc, shoving it in the silver cooler that always sat on the granite worktop. Grabbing a glass from the shelf, she made her way back into the lounge, and poured herself an enormous drink.

As she took her first mouthful, tears sprang to her eyes. Her friends. She needed her friends. Cora lifted the phone from its cradle on the coffee table in front of her and dialled Rosie's work number.

'Good afternoon, Rosie's! Rosie speaking.'

Her friend's cheerful voice sang in her ear, and Cora let out a huge sob.

'Rosie? Rosie, it's Cora …'

'To Cora. I luv u. This is the picshur of an allien hors I promissd you. I drawed it for u. Luv frm Kevin. PS. I luv u.'

Ah, the return of the alien-drawing tweeter, thought Cora. This time he'd used snail-mail, and the note was written in green ink – always a worrying sign. More perturbing was Kevin's return address – HMP Nottingham. She hadn't had a prison one for a while. Wonder what he was in for? Murdering the English language, probably. Despite the brutal pounding in her head, Cora smirked at her own wit.

She rubbed her throbbing temples, glared at her wine and decided a hot chocolate would be a much more sensible choice. She staggered into the kitchen and made herself one, squirting a load of cream on the top for good measure as her mind wandered back to last night. What on earth had possessed her? Benjamin Boland must think she was a complete idiot. *Incurable diarrhoea*? She blushed red at the very thought, then decided there was really nothing she could do about it and wandered back into the living room, taking a slug of her chocolate as she went.

Lowering herself gingerly back onto her chair, she put the weird drawing onto her 'no-need-to-answer-but-keep-in-case-ever-need-to-show-police' pile. She put the cup down and wiped a blob of whipped cream from her nose. Ouch. Even her nose hurt! Never mind a *picture* of an alien horse – she felt like alien horses were thundering around racing each other inside her head. Accompanied by alien elephants. And some of those giant chickens from Devon too, probably. Ugh, hangovers. She rarely drank enough to get one any more, but today's was a humdinger.

She whimpered and pushed aside the pile of post she'd been attempting to sort through, picked up from her studio pigeonhole during her week in London. It was the usual stuff. Around fifty per cent was just sweet letters asking for signed pictures – notes from nice, normal viewers who simply wanted to say how much they enjoyed watching her. The other half was the stuff her friends loved to read with a glass of wine – either the alien horse type from, presumably, mad people, or the filth type from perverts.

Cora picked up her mug and rose carefully from her seat at the dining table. Trying hard not to jar her pulsating skull, she walked slowly over to the patio doors and leaned her forehead against the cool glass. She looked at her reflection in the window. She couldn't see her face clearly, but she knew she looked dreadful. Her eyes were still pink and puffy from her lunchtime bout of crying, her hair matted, old make-up from last night streaky on her cheeks.

She really needed to pull herself together. It was just being back here, with all the memories … and that damn CCTV thing. Where the hell was Justin, and what was he playing at? She sighed, balanced the mug carefully and pushed the doors open.

It was one of those gloriously bracing, fresh December afternoons, the last rays of sun sparkling and dancing on the shiny metal of the terrace table. Yellow winter pansies glowed in the four oversized grey pots dotted around the decked floor. Pulling her cardigan tightly around her, Cora sat and gazed at the quiet street below.

Rosie and Nicole, her best friends in Cheltenham, would be here soon. Cora smiled, looking forward to seeing them, and started giving herself a stern talking to. OK, so she was single again. But she had a lovely home, wonderful friends, a job hundreds of journalists would kill for – what was there to be sad about? There must be men out there who didn't want kids, men who wanted the sort of life she wanted – mustn't there? And had she actually really, really loved Justin? They'd said it to each other a lot, but had it just been one of those things you say, when you're cosy and comfortable with someone? Certainly the early months of their relationship had been incredible, passionate, exciting – but recently it hadn't been like that. She'd just accepted it, she supposed, as how things were in every relationship after a while. But maybe it had been more than that. Maybe they were never meant to be. Well, they were pretty obviously not meant to be, actually, seeing as she was sitting here on her own.

She sighed and picked up her BlackBerry. A quick look at Twitter and she'd go and sort herself out. She whizzed through all the news feeds she followed, catching up on the day's events, then clicked on to her messages. There were the usual few from viewers, but one in particular made her pause.

@a-friend *@CoraBaxterMLive Cora – please follow me. I need to DM you urgently. Please. It's important.*

She clicked on the tweeter's profile. A private account. No photo and just one tweet, the one to her. No followers.

'Hmmm. Why do you want to direct message me, stranger? Probably a weirdo, but what the heck,' she said out loud, and sent a follow request. 'Let's see what's so important, Mr or

Miss *@a-friend*!'

She shivered and stood up. Time to go in. She needed painkillers and a hot shower, in that order.

10

'OK, what the *hell* is that?'

Nicole was standing by Cora's dining table, holding the picture of the alien horse between finger and thumb, her nose wrinkled as though someone had just thrust a rotten kipper under it.

'What?' Cora, hair still damp from her shower, appeared in the doorway, straining under the weight of an enormous tray laden with teapot, mugs, and a mountain of cream cakes. She dumped it onto the table with relief. 'Oh, that. An alien horse, apparently.'

Rosie, who was sprawling on the sofa, sat up and peered over the back.

'Gosh, Cora, you do attract some nutters,' she said.

'Tell me about it.' As she dumped the tray on the table, Cora's BlackBerry beeped. She took a quick look. Her follow request to the mysterious *@a-friend* had been accepted. Good. Now let's see what you've got to say for yourself, she thought, as she picked up a chocolate éclair and took a rapturous bite.

'Mmmm! I should get dumped more often; this is delicious, thank you!' she mumbled, spraying pastry over Nicole's sleeve.

Nicole dropped the drawing back onto the pile and frowned at Cora, brushing the crumbs from her black jumper neatly onto the table.

'Pig,' she said, reaching across to select a custard slice from the plate. Rosie leapt off the sofa and joined them, and the three friends sat in companionable silence around the big table, chomping contentedly.

Cora finished her first éclair, chose a second, and took a big gulp of tea. She looked gratefully at her two friends. They'd

55

brought wine as well as cakes, but after last night she thought it might be wise to hold off on the booze for a while.

Rosie finished her cheesecake and wiped her mouth. 'Yum. I might have to have a chocolate muffin now – the baby wants one, don't you, my love?'

She patted the minute bump under her grey jumper dress and smiled. Rosie was four months pregnant with her third child, but you could barely tell. Tiny, her short red hair dusted with blonde highlights and with perfect alabaster skin, Rosie always made Cora feel like a great galumphing hippo. She ran her own florist's, and her friends always thought she looked a bit like a flower – a perfect little rose, with a sweet personality to match.

'Go for it. You've hardly put on any weight yet anyway, cow,' Cora said affectionately, pushing the plate in Rosie's direction. She and Rosie had been mates since they'd met at secondary school aged twelve, and in all these years Cora had never seen her friend get even vaguely fat, despite her pregnancies.

Nicole nodded vehemently, mouth still full of custard.

'I don't know how you do it,' she said, swallowing. 'I was like a heifer with Elliot from about day two!'

Rosie smiled serenely, carefully extracting a chunk of chocolate from the top of her muffin. 'Good genes,' she said. 'But you lose it quicker, Nicole. You were back in your size eights ten minutes after Elliot – it took me months to deflate.'

She glanced at Cora, obviously suddenly realising the turn the conversation was taking.

'Oh – sorry. Look, no more baby talk, OK? Do you want to talk about Justin, Cora, or something entirely different? Like the murder? Gosh – how exciting that must be, your boss being murdered practically in front of everyone!'

Cora ran her forefinger around her plate to wipe up the last smears of cream. She wondered for a minute if she should mention the CCTV footage, and then changed her mind again. No, not yet.

'I'm a bit murdered out today, to be honest. And as for Justin – well, I still can't believe he did it by phone. But I suppose I'm sort of counting my blessings. My job's going well, and I've got you lot, and the guys at work ... I mean, I kind of wish it wasn't Christmas, but I'll be OK, I really will. It just wasn't meant to be, you know. The kid thing and all.'

She stopped, suddenly feeling sad again. Nicole pushed the cake plate to one side and took her hand.

'Exactly,' she said gently. 'But Cora – don't get cross – you are sure, aren't you? I mean, really, really sure? Because Justin used to say he didn't want kids, but he obviously ... I don't know ... had a void or something that he suddenly realised needed to be filled. Are you sure that isn't going to happen to you, somewhere down the line? I mean, if you're starting to lose relationships over it. I just don't want you to end up old and lonely, and regretting it.'

Cora tried to snatch her hand away but Nicole held it fast. Across the table, Rosie was starting to look worried.

'Please, not this again! I don't have a void, Nicole, you should know that by now! There are loads of men out there who don't want children, I just need to find one, that's all. And since when does having kids guarantee you won't be lonely? That's just a stupid thing to say. I have loads of friends – and I'd rather find my own than give birth to them.'

'OK, OK, I'm sorry, you're right.' Nicole dropped Cora's hand and stood up, pulling an elastic hair band from her wrist. She caught her long, dark hair up into a ponytail and looped the band deftly around it, pulling it back from her face. In her customary black, today wearing tight jeans and a long silky jumper which clung to her leggy form, she looked like an elegant spider as she stretched her arms out to loosen the tension in her back, and sat back down again.

'Oh, it's fine. I know you're only saying it 'cos you care.'

Cora exhaled heavily. She loved her friends, but why could they not accept this one aspect of her personality? Why were they so insistent that she was wrong? It drove her crazy, but she was so used to it by now that she never stayed cross with them for long. She leaned back in her chair.

'Last cake, anyone?' she said.

Rosie, who hated rows, stopped nervously fiddling with a silver bauble she'd picked off the Christmas tree and looked relieved. She stretched over and selected the cream slice, pointing to her belly remorsefully.

'Baby's still hungry … come on, let's put the telly on or something.'

The three of them got up and moved to the sofas. Cora and Rosie sank onto one, Rosie cradling her cake, while Nicole kicked off her spiky black boots and arranged her long legs under her on the other.

'Sorry,' she said again.

Cora, who was flicking disconsolately through the channels, threw a cushion at her.

'Shut up, it's fine,' she said. 'Honestly.'

Nicole stuffed the cushion behind her back and grinned. 'Thanks, I'll keep that. Had to deliver a bugger of a calf this week – nearly did my back in.'

'Oh, don't start, please, unless you want me to vomit.' Cora shuddered and carried on channel-hopping.

A vet who normally specialised in small animals, Nicole occasionally got called out to nearby farms in emergencies. Cora and Rosie had met her at a party six years ago, and although the three of them had been inseparable ever since, some of Nicole's stories were a little hard to stomach.

'Yuk,' Rosie agreed. 'I can't imagine sticking my hand up a cow's bum. I don't know how you do it, Nic.'

'Well, I can't imagine pottering around with flowers all day. I mean – poncy *flowers*,' Nicole retorted. 'And as for you, Cora, what did I see you doing earlier in the week – oh yes, standing in the dark at some ungodly hour, in Liverpool of all grotty places, pretending to be *reeeeeally* excited and impressed by some completely insane people who had about a zillion Christmas lights all over their house and garden. I mean, honestly. You do have a crap job.'

Cora and Rosie looked at each and started to giggle. Nicole was funny when she went off on one.

'I know. I hate Christmas lives. But you weren't saying that

58

when I interviewed George Clooney, were you?' Cora threw another cushion across the room.

Nicole caught it with one hand and added it to the pile behind her.

'OK, I'll give you that one ... oh, stop flicking, look! It's that travel thingy, with that Boland bloke, whatever his name is – now, he's almost as yummy as Gorgeous George, don't you think?'

Cora's heart sank as they all stared at the screen. Benjamin Boland was striding across a desert somewhere, his dark hair damp with sweat but still managing to curl sexily around the nape of his neck. His white shirt, open at the chest, clung to his tanned, hairless torso.

Oblivious to the blush spreading across Cora's cheeks, Rosie stroked her bump dreamily. 'Oh yes. Now that, Cora, is a man who doesn't want to be tied down with kids, I bet. A real adventurer, roaming the world – crikey, look at those thighs! I bet he is *fantastic* in bed.'

'Cora – Cora, what on earth is wrong with you? Why have you gone all red and sweaty?' Nicole was leaning forward on the sofa, sharp eyes taking in her friend's fiery complexion.

'Cora?' Rosie sat up too, looking perturbed.

Cora sighed and stood up. 'Anyone for a glass of wine? And then, I have a rather funny story to tell you ...'

11

'Baby, you look seriously hot! Come watch with me!'

The tiny Japanese girl curled up on a huge purple leather beanbag beckoned to Benjamin with a manicured finger. Her shiny black bob swung as she turned back to the TV. On screen, Benjamin was now hacking his way through a rainforest, the muscles in his forearms bulging as he swung the axe. The shot cut to a python slithering through the undergrowth, and the girl let out a little scream, and then giggled.

Benjamin, who was standing by the window of his South Bank apartment, gazing down at the river through his shiny new telescope, suddenly felt irritated. He'd done it again, hadn't he? Last night when he and the boys had moved on to a club. This one wasn't a model – he'd at least managed to stick to that part of his pre-Christmas resolution. She was a – receptionist? In a gym? Something like that. And she was stunning, there was no doubt about that. But she was still stupid. And he was bored. Bored rigid in fact. Fed up of these beautiful but vacuous females, most of whom only wanted to hang out with him because he was on TV. But what could he do about it? In the world in which he moved, these were the only women he met most of the time.

Ignoring the girl, he went to his bedroom and shut the door. He slumped onto the red velvet chaise longue by the window and put his head in his hands. He'd just have to stop dating altogether, it was the only solution. He would not go out with another woman until he found a real one – an equal, somebody he could actually talk to, for heaven's sake. Surely that wasn't too much to ask? He thought again about Cora, and the way she'd rejected him so amusingly in the A-Bar, and wondered how he could wangle another meeting. Somebody like her, that was what he needed.

Benjamin stood up and crossed the room to his enormous walk-in wardrobe. Pushing past the rows and rows of designer suits and shirts, he reached in to the back of one of the shelves and hauled out a small cardboard box. Digging under old cards and personal documents, he found what he was looking for. It was a picture, yellowing around the edges and slightly torn. He returned to the chaise and stared at the photo, gently running his finger across the faded faces. A woman, in her early thirties, with dark, curly hair. A man, maybe a little older, with smiling eyes and a shiny grey suit. And between them, a little boy, six or seven years old, with the same dark curls as the woman. He had an arm looped around each of their necks, and a shy grin, big eyes looking straight into the camera.

'That's what I want,' Benjamin thought. 'I want what they had. I'm thirty-five years old. It's time.'

His contemplation was interrupted as the bedroom door opened, and he jumped and stuffed the photo under the cushion of the chaise. The Japanese girl popped her head in.

'Hey, baby, what you doing in here on your own? I'm lonely.'

'I was just coming to talk to you, actually, er, Chloe. You see, the thing is, I really …'

He paused as Chloe stepped into the room, totally naked. Benjamin felt his willpower drain away as he watched her perfect little body with its smooth honey skin sauntering across to the big bed. She hopped up and draped herself seductively on the white duvet, one knee cocked, eyelashes fluttering coyly.

Benjamin got up slowly. OK, one more night. One more night and that would be it. Tomorrow, he'd dump her, and find a real girlfriend. Buoyed by the thought, he whooped, ripped his clothes off, and went to join her.

It might have been Saturday, and almost Christmas, but it certainly wasn't a day off for DCI Adam Bradberry and his team. Slugging down a mouthful of tepid coffee, Adam stood up and stared again at the incident board covered in notes and scene of crime photos at the far end of the room. Reinvigorated by their pub visit and early night yesterday, the murder investigation team had attacked today with new vigour, but Adam couldn't help feeling there was something he was missing here, something they were all missing.

'OK – let's go through this again,' he pronounced. Fifteen heads, some still on telephones, turned to look at him. Everyone else was out of the office, trying desperately to get some sort of angle on what had happened before the Christmas festivities started. They all knew it wouldn't be much of a Christmas otherwise.

'I just need to get it all clear in my mind. Gary, can you recap what we know at this stage?'

Detective Constable Gary Gilbert, young and slightly scruffy-looking in a check shirt, put down his pen and shuffled up to the whiteboard.

'Right.' He cleared his throat. 'Well, what we definitely know is that at approximately eight a.m. on Monday the eighteenth of December, that's the Monday just gone, forty-two-year-old TV editor Jeanette Kendrick was found dying on the ground outside TV Centre. She was lying almost directly under her office window, which was open. Seven storeys up, that room is, and her injuries were consistent with a fall from that sort of height. In fact ...'

He paused for a moment, studying the scrawl on the board. 'In fact she probably fell just before eight o'clock – say, 7.58, 7.59 – because the security guard who found her was very adamant that he always leaves on his eight o'clock rounds bang on time, and he would have taken a minute or so to check the front of the building and then make his way round the side to where she was. Probably got to her about, say, 8.01 or 8.02. Post-mortem showed she probably landed on her feet first, sounds weird to me but apparently it's not uncommon, then bounced and landed on her head ...'

He flicked through a sheaf of papers. 'Injuries – well extensive, as you'd expect. Multiple injuries to internal organs, multiple skeletal fractures, head injuries, spinal cord transected. Died of respiratory failure within a minute or two, but was amazingly able to mutter a couple of words, which may or may not end up being of some help to us. Coroner was amazed she could speak at all, vast majority of people would be dead as soon as they hit the ground, although he did say he'd heard of some incredible survival stories too, all down to how you fall and how you land I think. Anyway, he reckons she certainly wouldn't have lived more than two or three minutes with those injuries, and she was just about alive when the guard found her.'

Adam nodded slowly. 'So – just before eight o'clock, she's pushed out of her office window by a person or persons unknown. Definitely pushed, not suicide – tell us why, again?'

'Yes, definitely. There were signs of a struggle inside the office near the window – a vase knocked off, other bits and pieces. I mean, I suppose she could have knocked stuff over if she was jumping out, but there was other evidence of foul play too. It says here, look – small linear contusions on both arms. Grab marks, basically. Bruising. She'd tried to fight somebody off. And bruises also across the front of her thighs, probably from her legs being bashed on the windowsill. If she'd jumped by herself, those bruises wouldn't be there. Also, there was a sticky substance on her face, consistent with her mouth being taped over at some point before she died. No sign of the tape though. Bit weird – maybe the killer wanted to shut her up for a bit but then ripped it off again before shoving her out? Anyway, somebody helped her out of the window, no doubt about it.'

'And the security guard saw nothing amiss on his rounds, did he? But the victim managed to speak those couple of words to him before she died. "Chris. Chris." Any luck with finding anyone else of that name? Friends, family, workmates?' Adam looked around the room.

There was a general negative murmur.

'Forensics then. Very little, but we have some fibres on her body that definitely didn't come from her own clothing. Black, wool. Like you'd get from a black jumper, or gloves. Some caught in her fingernails, as if she was trying to cling on to someone to save herself, poor woman. But a black top, or jumper – hardly unusual in Britain in winter, eh?'

Gary looked glum. 'Exactly. And could easily be stuffed in a bag afterwards too, so it's not going to help us much trying to track down everyone who was wearing black that day. Which incidentally, was about seventy per cent of the people in the building. What is it about media types and black? Anyway, nothing else, forensic-wise, apart from the tape residue which appears to come from a standard roll of duct tape, available anywhere. No sweat, saliva, fingerprints, nothing. Bloody annoying.'

Adam sighed. 'A forensically aware killer then, maybe. Or somebody who just got lucky. OK. So. CCTV. No CCTV in Kendrick's office or in the newsroom itself. Good shots from the front of the building of people coming in early for work, but no solid reason to suspect any of them at the moment. We still haven't identified that lurker have we?'

Again, a murmured 'no' from the group.

'Also CCTV from the rear entrance and the east side of the building. Again, nothing much of interest, except the trickle of people coming in and out as you'd expect. But for some reason, the bloody CCTV cameras covering the west side, where Kendrick's office is, were conveniently not working. Coincidence or design?'

'Bleeding coincidence,' said Gary. 'Fairly sure of that, anyway. Apparently it had been playing up for a while, according to security. Sod's Law. There aren't any main entrance doors on that side though, just fire doors and delivery areas. But it means we have no shots of her actually coming down. And no shots of anyone who might have entered or left the building via any of the doors on that side. The CCTV footage from further up and down the street has been checked too and there's no sign of anything suspicious. A few people wandering along the road in the minutes after it happened, but just looks like people heading to work. And of course, we have no reason to think the killer left the building. Could have just gone back to his duties once he'd shoved her out. Got to be a cool customer, given he did the deed just feet away from a roomful of people.'

He cleared his throat and flicked through his notes again.

'House to house enquiries – well, mainly office to office in that area – turned up sod all as well. Most of the offices with a line of sight to the TV building were still empty at 8 a.m., bit of a slow-down in the run-up to Christmas, and the few staff we did find who *were* already in didn't see anything. Well, they wouldn't would they, unless they were staring out the window at the right time? And, of course, even though it was eight o'clock, it's still almost dark at that time in December. It was just a few days before the twenty-first, the shortest day of the year. Also, the window the victim was pushed out of is positioned at the back of the building, so it wouldn't have been easy to spot her coming out even if anyone *did* happen to glance that way at the right time. And the river runs behind the building, but there's a big wall, so no chance of anyone viewing anything from that side at all.'

Adam perched on the corner of the nearest desk, scratched his blond head and sighed.

Gary continued. 'Of course, we *do* have CCTV from the reception area and the three lifts inside the studio building. But there aren't any in the emergency stairwells, so it's feasible that if somebody with murder in mind did come in from outside, they could have used the stairs to get up to the seventh floor. We're going through all the CCTV frame by frame, but it's a big job – huge, busy building, hundreds of people arriving for work between about 3 a.m. and the time of the murder. They start early in TV land, it seems. And as we have no idea who or what we're looking for, I'm not sure how valuable it's going to be, unless we spot anyone obviously acting weird. All we have is loads of probably perfectly innocent people wandering about – impossible to know which one is a killer.'

Adam nodded. The DC was right. Simply looking at people entering, leaving and walking around the building wasn't going to get them very far unless they could find somebody who actually had a reason for wanting Jeanette Kendrick dead, and prove they were in the newsroom that morning.

Gary was pointing to a photo of Jeanette's office.

'Now, normally those high office windows are sealed – you know, for Health and Safety? But this woman – well, from all accounts, what she wanted, she got. And she was a bit of a fresh air freak, so she'd had them unsealed so she could open them whenever she wanted.'

'A decision that cost her her life.' Adam shook his head. 'And that, I presume, was common knowledge, certainly among the staff?'

Gary nodded. 'Yes, that's coming through in all the interviews we've done so far. They all knew about it. Anyway – other potential witnesses. There were some window cleaners working that day but they didn't start until about 8.30 – it was still dark until quite late of course, being December, as I said earlier. Sunrise was – let me see – 8.04 a.m. that day. So they're no good – I've checked, none of them got there before about 8.20. And there doesn't seem to have been anyone else around. No deliveries till later on, apart from newspapers which came in much earlier, around 2 a.m. The sides of the building aren't well lit anyway, and on a freezing cold morning, when it was still so dark ... seems like nobody else saw her coming down.'

Adam frowned. 'Right, let's move inside. The office is right at the far back corner of the newsroom.' He stopped to study the photographs pinned to the board.

'Two external walls, both with windows as it's a corner office, and two internal glass walls, but the blinds were down. So as long as somebody was able to slip in and out without anyone noticing – which is quite possible in that place, I've spent enough time there this week to know it's crazy in there while the programme's on air – then it's an easy job. Even if she'd screamed, there's so much noise going on I doubt anyone would have heard it.'

Gary agreed. 'Nobody heard a thing. There are TVs and radios on everywhere, and a lot of people work in headphones. If she did scream or shout, it went unnoticed. And it seems her mouth had been taped up at some point, remember.'

Adam stood up and moved closer to the board.

'Suspects so far then. We still need to rule out Mr or Mrs Lurker from outside the building – definitely weird behaviour there. I can't understand how it's taking so long to get an ID.'

Detective Constable Karen Lloyd, a small, dark-haired woman in a white shirt, raised her hand. 'I'm working on that – it's mainly because it's impossible to make out the face, so we're trying to at least find out where the coat might be from. Not proving easy though. It's not clear enough. And no joy at all from all the telly airings.'

'Thanks, Karen. Then there's this young producer, Christina, who had a massive row with the deceased a few hours before. The "Chris" thing clearly works, but sadly I'm fairly sure we can rule her out at this stage – she's on CCTV at 7.59 down in the reception area, which would only have given her a minute at most to commit the crime and get down there. From seven floors up that's a tall order. And I just don't see her doing it. By all accounts, there was no love lost between her and her boss, but …'

Gary interrupted. 'And she's tiny. I'd be amazed if she'd had the strength, you know?'

Karen spoke again. 'Yes, but you never know – anger can make people do terrible things – it's like they get superhuman powers from somewhere. Remember that young girl in Ealing last year? Took out her twenty-stone boyfriend.'

A few of the other officers nodded.

'OK, fair enough. But the timing is still wrong. I'm not convinced. I'm ruling her out for now. Who else?'

'Well – almost everyone really!' Gary laughed. 'The woman wasn't exactly popular. We're looking into her background – she seems to have pissed off pretty much everyone she worked with, but we need to find out if there's anyone out there she's pissed off enough to want to top her. No reports of any recent big arguments or anything, though, and she hadn't had any threats from anyone, or certainly none that we can find at this stage.'

He consulted his notes. 'We're obviously looking at her partner too, as in civil partner. Clancy Carter, another media hotshot, but by all accounts not doing so well as her lover. We're looking at a jealousy angle there maybe? Although by all accounts they were pretty happy. You never know though. And the "Chris" thing sort of works again.'

He pointed to a picture of Clancy on the whiteboard. 'It's a bit tenuous, but Kendrick called her "Chrissy" sometimes. Some sort of nickname.'

'And we know she dropped Kendrick off earlier that morning,' said Adam. 'She says she dropped her outside, and that stands up on CCTV, but did she come back later? Slip in through one of those side doors somehow? Or bundle up in a hat and scarf and sneak back in through Reception?'

Gary nodded. 'Maybe. It's a much easier job in summer, isn't it, when we can see their faces! We should get through all that CCTV by the end of the weekend. It'll be a bit clearer then. Although we've obviously spoken to Carter – she claims she was back home and had gone back to bed at 8 a.m., though there's nobody to verify that.'

Adam rubbed his nose. 'So that's where we are. A woman everyone hated, killed right under the noses of about sixty people. With the exception of the few who were actually on air at the time, or down on the studio level, any one of the others *could* have done it – and nobody saw or heard a thing. Either that, or everyone's taken a vow of silence. No decent suspects, no leads. Great. Just great. Happy bloody Christmas, guys.'

And feeling more despairing than he had in a long time, he slouched off to the coffee machine. It was going to be a long night.

Meanwhile, the person who had caused Jeanette's demise was feeling anything but despondent. Almost a week, and nothing. Nobody had a clue. Sipping from a cold glass of white wine, the killer gazed out of the window into the darkness of the early evening and smiled. So, a nice Christmas, and then time to formulate a plan. Number two might not be quite so easy.

12

Cora was on her hands and knees, scrubbing a filthy bathroom floor. Suddenly the door burst open and a wild-eyed man in a grubby grey nightshirt staggered in, whimpering and clutching his stomach. Ignoring her, he hitched up his gown and flung himself onto the toilet with a groan. Cora looked up, aghast.

'What – what are you doing? I'm cleaning in here – you can't …'

'Have to … have to … no choice … incurable diarrhoea … totally incurable …' gasped the man, and a loud splatter resounded from the toilet bowl.

Cora recoiled and banged into her bucket, sloshing stinking water over her knees. Then she jumped as behind her, she heard a familiar chuckle. A shirtless Benjamin Boland was leaning on the doorframe, looking down at her, tanned, muscular arms folded across his smooth, bare chest, laughing and laughing …

TRRRINNNGGG! TRRRINNNGGG!

Cora snapped into consciousness and bashed the alarm clock, which was flashing '9.00' at her. She was panting slightly, and even in the darkness of her bedroom she could feel that she was blushing. How mortifying! She was even dreaming about it now. Shaking her head to wipe out the vision of Benjamin Boland's smug face, she snapped the light on and clambered out of bed, suddenly aware that it was Christmas Eve and she wasn't exactly organised.

After a quick shower and hurried breakfast, she shrugged on her sheepskin coat and a pair of brown leather gloves and headed out. It was another bright, crisp day and Cora's spirits lifted as she took her favourite shortcut across the park to Cheltenham town centre. A Jack Russell in a green plaid coat yapped frantically as he scampered across the grass after a ball, and in the play area a little boy in a yellow Puffa jacket, face barely visible under the huge hood, screamed with excitement as he flew higher and higher on the swings.

As she reached the pavement on the far side of the park, a doll's house bedecked with fairy lights caught Cora's eye in the window of the old-fashioned toyshop on the corner and, despite herself, she got that old familiar rush of pleasure. She loved Christmas, and she would be damned if she was going to let Justin, Jeanette, or Benjamin bloody Boland spoil it for her. The bell jangled overhead as she pushed the door open, and the warm fug enveloped her like a comfort blanket. After fifteen happy minutes of browsing she emerged clutching a bagful of goodies – a gorgeous little, hand-made wooden train set for her godson Elliot (Nicole had quite enough revolting coloured plastic in her house – Cora refused to add to it) and, for Rosie's two, an exquisitely dressed, baby doll for five-year-old Ava, and a drawing set for the already artistic little Alexander. She paused by the door to cross the three names off her list and, across the street, the Salvation Army brass band suddenly struck up, the opening bars of 'We Wish You a Merry Christmas' floating across the heads of the harried shoppers like a soothing breeze.

'Where do they go, the rest of the year?' Cora wondered idly, smiling at the scrubbed faces under the navy hats. As she headed down the Promenade, she found herself humming along. Her hastily rearranged Christmas with Rosie and Nicole was going to be lovely. And, now that she didn't have to fork out for the expensive new games console Justin had been angling for, she could afford to splash out a bit more on her *real* friends.

She stopped outside WHSmith on the High Street and scrutinised her list again. It wasn't too bad actually. She'd already exchanged bottles of perfume and champagne with Wendy and Sam in London, and family presents had been posted off a few weeks ago – Cora's parents were spending

72

Christmas abroad and she and her sisters had agreed they'd all do their own thing this year. Nathan's present was alive and on its way – two ridiculous-sounding but very sweet Ginger Nut Ranger chickens for the growing menagerie at his Gloucestershire cottage, to be delivered after New Year. He'd be thrilled, thought Cora happily. He and his boyfriend Gareth were becoming a right pair of domestic goddesses. For antiques freak Scott she'd found a World War One compass in a little curio shop in Yorkshire a few weeks ago when they were on a story, although he'd been so miserable recently she wasn't entirely sure he'd appreciate anything she chose for him this year. And for Rodney, a pair of green and white checked golf trousers. Rodney didn't play golf, but she knew he'd adore them. Both presents had been delivered days ago, with strict warnings not to open them till tomorrow. The children she'd just done, so that left Nicole, Rosie, and their husbands. Easy.

As she folded the list back into her jeans pocket, a familiar face caught her eye in the shop window behind her, and her cheeks suddenly burned again. Benjamin Boland's face smouldered at her from the cover of this week's *OK!* magazine. Urgh. Could she *never* get away from that man? Standing on a ski slope, dressed completely in black, he looked devastatingly gorgeous, and despite her mortification Cora suddenly felt a tiny flicker of desire. That moment when he'd slipped his arm around her, the way their eyes had met …

'Oh shut up, you complete cretin!' she said out loud, to the surprise of an elderly man who was standing quietly in the shop doorway lighting his pipe. He glared at her.

'Oh – I'm so sorry – I was talking to myself, not to you …' The man continued to glare and, flustered, Cora backed away from the shop, straight into somebody coming the other way.

'Oh gosh, I'm so sorry …

The woman she'd crashed into tutted and stalked off.

Crikey, this wasn't going very well, was it? Oh well, on with the shopping, if you can manage that, you blithering clumsy moron, she muttered to herself, as she made her way through the revolving door into the welcoming warmth of the big

73

department store. And shaking her head, she pulled out her list again, and headed to the handbag department.

'Just a note to say I love your hair. I was wondering, if I may, whether when you go to the hairdressers you ever keep any of the old, cut hair? I am building up a small collection of organic matter from television personalities and would love to add some of your hair to it ...'

Did they ever stop? Slumped on her sofa, exhausted and surrounded by carrier bags, Cora was astounded as she read the latest email that had pinged on to her BlackBerry.

'I mean, someone who collects *organic matter* from TV presenters? What sort of nut job does that?' she thought. It wasn't unusual for presenters to *receive* 'organic matter' from viewers – and the less said about that the better – but she'd never heard of it happening in reverse. She dreaded to think what else he – and it was always a 'he' – had in his collection.

She sighed. It was already nearly dark outside, and through the window she could see Christmas tree lights twinkling and flashing in the apartments opposite. She looked at her watch and heaved herself up again to fetch the champagne she'd put in the fridge before her shopping trip. It was something her mum and dad had always done, a Christmas Eve tradition that she'd planned to share with Justin this year – wrapping presents while sipping champagne and watching a good old festive movie. Now, she was determined to carry on the tradition by herself, and *The Sound of Music* was about to start. She flicked the TV on just in time to catch the opening scene, and as the familiar music swelled and the helicopter camera zoomed in to Julie Andrews twirling on the mountain top, Cora sipped the cold bubbles and felt almost happy for the first time in days.

Setting her glass down on the coffee table, she spread out her wrapping paper, bows, tags and sticky tape and dipped into the nearest carrier. A leather D&G hobo bag, black of course, for Nicole. Cora stroked it. Gorgeous. She tipped out the rest of the bags. A skinny black scarf with a hint of metallic shimmer, also for Nicole. For Rosie, a soft, baby blue cashmere cardigan, delicately beaded, plus some expensive and delicious-smelling body lotion for her bump. Nicole's husband, Will, who taught science at a local secondary school and was always missing his favourite TV programmes because he had so much marking to do, was getting a box set of the latest cult sci-fi series, and she'd found a book on contemporary American furniture for Rosie's hubby Alistair, a furniture designer who was always on the look-out for new ideas.

She put the presents aside for wrapping and delved into another bag. Yum. Goodies to take to Rosie's, where she and Nicole and her family were all spending Christmas – bought, rather than made, naturally. Cora really couldn't cook, and after the time she'd suggested she bring a plate of toast to an 'everyone bring a dish' dinner party, arguing that everyone likes toast, she'd been banned from ever 'cooking' for her friends again. Hence her purchase of a three-pound pungent Brie, some divine-looking handmade chocolates, an apple and gingerbread loaf, some raspberry and cappuccino cupcakes from Mattino's, and of course a case of champagne, already chilling in the fridge. Gathering the food, she staggered into the kitchen, popped the Brie in the fridge, and plonked the rest on the worktop, ready to take in the morning.

As she sank down onto the sofa again, her Twitter direct message alert beeped. She clicked on to the page and her stomach turned over. The message was from her mystery tweeter, @a-friend.

@a-friend @CoraBaxterMLive Cora, it's me, Justin. I'm sorry. I'm so sorry. I screwed up big time.

What? This @a-friend character was Justin? Was it really? And what did he mean, he'd screwed up? Her hands shaking, Cora stared at the screen. Then she frantically typed a reply, fingers slipping on the tiny keys in her haste.

@CoraBaxterMLive @a-friend What do you mean? What did you do? Where are you? Why were you at TV Centre? You were

on CCTV! Call me!

Breathing heavily, she waited. Seconds later, the reply flashed up.

@a-friend *@CoraBaxterMLive I'm sorry. Needed to get away. I'll be in touch soon, I promise.*

What the hell? What was going on? And why on earth wasn't he just calling her or emailing her? She paused, then started typing again.

@CoraBaxterMLive *@a-friend Justin – why all the secrecy? And the police are looking for you. You have to come back.*

She waited. Then:

@a-friend *@CoraBaxterMLive I know. But I didn't do anything. Please trust me. I'll talk to them soon. I'm SO sorry. Bye for now.*

Frustrated and angry now, Cora banged out another message.

@CoraBaxterMLive *@a-friend Justin – I NEED to talk to you. Call me, call your family, anybody. Please.*

Ten minutes later, there was still no reply. If *@a-friend* was really Justin, he'd logged out. Confused and annoyed, Cora pushed her phone out of sight and tried to make sense of what had just happened. At least she knew he was alive and, presumably, well. But why had he gone away? Where was he? Did she believe him when he said he hadn't done anything? Honestly – yes. But it still didn't explain why he hadn't come forward to the police, when he was obviously aware of the CCTV footage. But what could she do? She wasn't prepared to tell the police about this, not until she'd had a chance to talk to him properly. It might be a decision she'd live to regret, but it

76

was the only one she felt she could make, for now at least. She sighed heavily and grabbed her champagne.

'Right. It's Christmas. Forget Justin, forget weird murders. I am *not* dwelling on this now.'

She drained her glass, refilled it, turned the TV up, and started wrapping.

13

Christmas Day, 9 a.m. Trying not to think about what her Christmas morning *should* have been like, Cora grabbed a suitcase and started packing up the presents piled in the corner of her bedroom. She added clothes, toiletries, and her hair straighteners and then sat back on her heels, looking fondly at the little pile of gifts on the bed. Nathan had arrived on her doorstep last night with a bag from himself, Rodney and Scott – and the boys had excelled themselves. Cora stretched over and picked up the beautiful Calvin Klein boots, black and white snakeskin with kitten heels, that they'd clubbed together for. She kicked off her shoes and tried them on again. Perfect. As well as the boots, the boys had each given her a useful little stocking filler – from Nathan, a big flask for those early morning in-car cuppas, a gift nicely complemented by Scott's, a box of weird and wonderful teas from around the world. Rodney, who had a torch fetish and a huge collection of them stacked neatly in the boot of his car, had presented her with a bright pink Maglite, which would be useful when they were in the middle of nowhere on dark winter mornings. She knew they were being extra sweet to her this year, and she was touched.

Fortunately, the boys had all rung her first thing this morning, equally thrilled with what she'd chosen for them. Nathan had been ecstatic about the prospect of two new chickens for his garden, and said he'd be spending Boxing Day fixing up his old coop in preparation for their arrival, while Scott had been so impressed with the old compass that for a moment Cora thought he might actually be a little tearful.

Rodney, meanwhile, had vowed to wear the golf trousers for all of his Christmas celebrations, giving Cora a sudden pang of guilt when she thought of his long-suffering girlfriend Jodie. Overall, though, a most satisfactory gift exchange. Cora stuffed the snakeskin boots into the top of her case, zipped it up, and headed for the kitchen to pack up the food.

By the time she lifted the brass knocker on Rosie's battered, blue front door she was actually feeling quite perky for the first time in days, and determined not to let last night's Twitter encounter with Justin ruin her day. She'd already decided not to tell her friends he'd been in touch. She'd worry about the whole sorry mess after Christmas, she vowed.

'CORA'S HERE!'

Cora laughed as she heard her friend's shriek. Moments later, Rosie wrenched the door open, Nicole thundering down the hall behind her, closely followed by Ava, Alexander, and Elliot. At the same time Alistair appeared at the top of the stairs, a broad smile on his handsome face, and Will popped his head out of the sitting room door, clutching a book and grinning.

'Gosh, what a welcome!' Cora giggled.

'Come in, come in! It's CHRISTMAS!' Rosie pulled her into the hall and slammed the door.

'OK, OK! Hello, all of you. Now, is it too early for a Christmas drink? I have champagne, naturally.' Cora thrust her food bags at Nicole, kissed her and Rosie, and then climbed a few stairs to greet Alistair, who even on Christmas day looked as if he'd just come out of his workshop. She pecked him on the cheek, trying to avoid his dusty old navy jumper, but he pulled her into a hug and laughed.

'It's only sawdust – you're not getting out of giving me a hug that easily, Miss Glamour Puss!'

Cora gave in and hugged him back.

'Oh alright, you messy pup. Now go and get cleaned up – what are you doing working on Christmas Day, anyway?'

She slapped him on his big bottom, and he tittered like a schoolboy and raced back upstairs. Cora wiped sawdust off her black jacket and turned back to the hall. Will, tall, gangly and studious-looking as always with his little, black-framed glasses and floppy, brown hair, emerged fully from the sitting room and enveloped her in a bear hug.

'Glad you're here, babe. It's going to be great, all of us together for Christmas.'

'Yes, it is, isn't it? Thanks Will. And where are my favourite babies then?'

Ava, Alexander, and Elliot were still standing there, staring at her, and she crouched down so they could inspect her properly.

Elliot reached up a chubby hand and touched her hair.

'Christmas. Santa came,' he said, beaming.

'Ooh, lucky boy! Did you get nice presents?'

Elliot considered for a moment, then nodded solemnly. 'Very nice presents.'

'Very nice presents,' echoed Alexander.

Cora wrapped an arm around each two-year-old and pulled them close. 'I'm very pleased for you both, my darlings. You must have been very good boys.'

Ava tapped her on the arm. 'I saw you on the telly wiv a talking pig, Auntie Cora. It was funny! You look pretty, Auntie Cora,' she said shyly, and Cora let go of the boys and held out her arms to the little girl.

'Thank you, angel. Not as pretty as you though – what a lovely dress! Are you a Christmas fairy?'

'Yes! And now you're here we can open all our other pressies soon – hooray!'

Ava giggled and wiggled and Cora kissed her red mane and let her go. All three ran off down the hall, Ava waving her wand, the net skirts of the glittery blue dress she was wearing bouncing. Her little brother, stocky and blond like his dad, toddled after her, tiny jeans slipping down over his nappy, closely followed by Elliot, dark curls bobbing as he followed his friends into their playroom.

'We're in the kitchen!' Rosie's distant voice sang out.

'Be there in a mo – just going to unload the presents.'

Cora wheeled her case into the sitting room and stopped, awed. Rosie and Alistair had been doing up their six-bedroom Regency house, just a few streets away from Cora's flat, for the past three years – a slow process, which had gathered pace in recent months as Rosie's florist shop and Alistair's furniture design business had finally started to make real money. The large sitting room at the front of the house had been the most recently transformed, with almond white walls, dark red sofas scattered with cream and taupe cushions and a shiny walnut floor but, while Cora had seen it before, it hadn't looked quite this stunning. An eight-foot Norway Spruce wafted a soft fragrance across the room, its branches heavy with red, beaded baubles and sparkling, glass butterflies. Holly branches, artfully entwined with ivy and tiny, maroon and white fairy lights, trailed over the fireplace. On the table in the corner, candles flickered on a bed of snowy pine branches. Bowls of nuts and oranges sat on various shelves, surrounded by delicately scented tea lights. The whole room glowed, and Cora thought she had never seen anything more cosy and welcoming.

'Rosie, you've surpassed yourself!' she yelled.

'Thank yooooou!' Rosie's voice echoed from the kitchen.

Cora unzipped her case to tip out her gifts and added them to the tottering pile already under the tree. Then she returned the case to the hall and followed her nose, throwing her jacket onto the groaning coat rack as she passed. She stopped again as she reached the kitchen door. The vast steamy room at the back of the house was filled with an aroma so rich and festive it could have been no other time of year. The old pine worktops were crammed with food – fragrant mince pies fresh from the oven sat on a cooling rack next to an enormous fruity Christmas pudding, while bottles of red and white wine and port jostled for position with an entire fresh salmon, a pot of cranberry sauce, and a bowl of creamy brandy butter. On the wooden table in the centre of the room, a colossal, and as yet uncooked turkey, oozing stuffing, sat nakedly beside a pile of shortbread and a big white Christmas cake with a wonky Santa sledging across its snowy icing.

'Oh – my – goodness!' Cora suddenly felt ravenous. 'I hope we are *all* going to forget being sensible for the next few days – this is some spread, Rosie.'

She picked up a slice of shortbread and took a bite, then licked the sugary crumbs from her fingers. Rosie, who was unpacking Cora's offerings, oohed and aahed as she added them to the feast.

'Ooooh! I adore these cupcakes! We might have to demolish these right now ...'

Nicole, corkscrew in hand, peered over her shoulder.

'Yum! Pass me those glasses, Cora?'

Cora picked five champagne flutes from the stack at the end of the table, and Nicole filled them. The boys appeared just as they were clinking, and they all stood in a circle and smiled at each other.

'Well – Happy Christmas, everyone!' Rosie, cheeks pink and eyes bright, took a guilty sip and patted the little bump under her green velvet dress. The others glugged happily, Alistair slightly less dusty than earlier in a clean Aran sweater, Nicole slinky as usual in a long, black skirt and crocheted tunic, Will casual, blue shirt untucked over jeans, his arm around his wife's waist.

'Happy Christmas!' they chorused, and Cora felt tears prick her eyes as she looked at her friends, the two couples, so happy and secure. She turned away quickly, on the pretext of refilling the glasses. It would be a happy Christmas, it really would. And maybe next year, she'd have a partner to share it with too. Preferably one who wasn't wanted for murder.

Later, the girls lolled on the sofas in the candlelit sitting room, full and contented. Will and Alistair were next door in the playroom, arguing over the table football with bottles of beer. The kids, exhausted and happy, had been put to bed, the three of them cuddling up together in Ava's room – 'the only five-year-old I know who has a double bed!' Cora had exclaimed, as she'd kissed their weary little faces goodnight with a teeny sense of relief. They were definitely all lovely children, but she'd rather had enough for one day.

Now Rosie sprawled on one sofa, eyes closed, looking worn out but happy. Nicole and Cora sat at opposite ends of the other, Nicole sipping red wine, Cora still on champagne.

'I still can't believe you turned down Benjamin Boland.' Nicole carefully put her glass down on the wooden floor, stretched luxuriously and lay back on her cushions. 'You could be off spending Christmas in some glamorous hideaway with him if you'd played your cards right. Incurable diarrhoea!' She poked Cora with her long toes.

Cora grimaced. 'Don't remind me! I'd rather be here with you guys for Christmas though, honestly! But, yeah, ugh … I really did blow it, didn't I? I'm hopeless.' She shook her head at the memory.

'You are. You're a total numpty.'

'Yes, I'm a numpty. I'm a numpty from Numpty Land. In fact, if there was a Queen of the Numpties, I'd be it.'

Nicole snorted, and Cora started to giggle. They were both a bit drunk. Rosie, who wasn't, joined in with the sniggering anyway.

'You are funny, Cora. You're bound to bump into him again, though – I mean, you know where he hangs out now, don't you? And you're always up and down to London for work, aren't you, so you might be able to salvage it.'

Cora sighed. 'Maybe. I doubt he'll come near me again though. And I'm going to be so busy, especially until Jeanette's killer is found.' She covered her face with a cushion and groaned.

'You're a disaster. And don't you get lip gloss on my cream cushion, Queen of the Numpties!'

'Sorry.' Cora put the cushion down again, and they lapsed into a companionable silence, which was suddenly ruined by a triumphant roar from the playroom next door, followed by a 'Na na na-na-na!' in Alistair's deep voice. Rosie sat up and banged on the wall and the noise subsided.

'Those boys! Big kids – they'll wake the children!'

She collapsed again. 'I'm exhausted. Shall we go to bed? It's nearly midnight, look. And we have another day of drinking and debauchery tomorrow.'

'Good idea.'

Cora and Nicole heaved themselves off the sofa and all three of them waved goodnight to the boys from the door of the playroom and tiptoed up the stairs.

They all stopped outside Ava's bedroom and peeped in. The children were snuggled together like kittens, Alexander lying sideways, his soft, blond head on Ava's chest, Elliot's stout little arm draped across Alexander's legs. Nicole and Rosie had a brief, whispered debate about whether to rearrange their sleeping offspring, but decided against it. If they woke them now, they'd never get them down again. Back on the landing they all hugged.

'See you on Boxing Day!'

Cora shut the door of her room, and sat on the edge of the bed as she slowly wiped off her makeup, her heart twisting a little. Today had almost been like a little break from reality – the reality she knew she would have to face again tomorrow, the reality of a murdered boss and a missing ex-boyfriend and weird Twitter messages. She'd surreptitiously checked her phone about fifty times today, but there had been nothing from Justin. A 'happy Christmas' would have been nice, she thought wryly. Although an explanation of exactly what the hell he'd been doing when he became a potential suspect in a murder case would have been even better.

She shook her head to dispel the thought and gazed around her. This room hadn't been done up yet, but she liked it. The faded wallpaper, wide blue and white stripes, at least matched the worn blue carpet. Rosie had put a fresh navy duvet on the bed and filled the white painted fireplace with candles, flickering now like drowsy eyelashes. Cora pulled on her pyjamas, ran a comb through her hair and went to blow the candles out.

She paused by the window on her way back to bed, pulling aside the slightly tatty white curtains. The street outside was silent and empty, a light drizzle softening the yellow light from the street lamps. Suddenly a fox appeared, snuffling around the gatepost opposite, its sharp nose worrying the nooks and crannies, looking for dinner. A car drove past, and in its headlights the fox's eyes flashed emerald green. It slunk into the shadows and was gone.

Urban foxes. There was something fascinating about them, Cora thought, those clever, wild creatures scavenging in town centres when everyone was asleep, surviving and thriving so far outside their natural environment. She climbed into bed, recoiling as her feet hit hot rubber. Rosie thought of everything! She pulled the hot water bottle up and hugged it against her chest as she sank into the soft, old mattress. Out on the landing, she heard creaks and whispers as Will and Alistair came up to join their wives, and then all was silent.

Before sleep slowly overcame her, Cora's thoughts drifted yet again back to Justin. Damn, she missed him. And yes, there was undoubtedly something very odd going on. But she was as certain as she could be of one thing – her ex-boyfriend was not a killer. Behaving suspiciously, yes. Very. But capable of murder?

'No. Definitely not,' she murmured into the darkness. But who then? Who on earth killed Jeanette? Who could have wandered through the newsroom, unremarked upon, made their way into the editor's office without challenge, and then left again? Cora's final thought as her heavy eyelids finally closed was a chilling one. Could the murderer really, possibly, be somebody she knew?

14

'BRRRRRR! BRRRRRR! BRRRRRR!'

On her bedside table, Cora's mobile was ringing like a thing possessed. Dragging herself out of a deep sleep, she glanced at her alarm clock before she pressed the call button: 1.30 a.m., and she'd only gone to bed at 11.

Here we go, she thought.

'Hello. News desk, I presume?'

'Morning, Cora. Happy Wednesday – sorry to start you so early.' Sam sounded apologetic.

Cora groaned, sinking back onto her pillow in the inky darkness and pulling the duvet over her head to make the most of her last few seconds in bed. 'Where am I going then? I'm obviously in for a long drive if you're calling this early.'

'We need you to go and find snow, I'm afraid. Reports coming in of quite a bit starting to fall in Derbyshire, possibly around Buxton? We're not sure really though. See what you can get. The crew are going to meet you at Frankley services and you can go in convoy from there. We're hoping for lives from six. Sorry babe. Oh – and we'll get you to do an update on Jeanette later too – I'll fill you in when you're properly awake. Thanks. Speak later.'

Cora sighed. 'I'm on my way. Later.'

She put the phone down and shut her eyes for a moment in her warm cocoon, still trying to put off getting out of bed. Her job was a pain in the bum sometimes. While the producers in the newsroom in London were able to get *some* guidance from the Met Office and the programme's weather forecaster, it was

87

pretty hard for anyone to *guarantee* there would be snow in a particular location while the show was on air. So the only way to make sure a reporter was standing there in snow was for that reporter to get out there and find it. Cora exhaled loudly and grumpily, poked a hand from under the duvet and flicked the light on. Living alone had its advantages – Justin would have been huffing and sighing by now. Blinking, she rolled out of bed and, already shivering, headed for the bathroom.

A few hours later she was huddled in her car, heater blasting, as she poured the first cup of tea of the day from the new flask Nathan had given her for Christmas. He and Rodney, parked up behind her on the grass verge of a twisty road in the middle of the Peak District, were having a quick pre-live snooze, but a little pool of yellow light emanated from the truck, and inside she could see Scott on the phone, sorting out satellite clearance. It was dark as a dungeon outside, but at least there was a fine dusting of snow, and it was still falling gently. By six, there should be enough to make a decent live. There had flipping better be, after that icy drive through the night. Cora sipped her tea and watched the flakes landing softly on her windscreen like tiny white feathers. It was ridiculous, she thought, how excited the programme got about snow. In fact, about any bad weather at all. Still, at least they'd managed to find a live location pretty easily this time – it was even more stressful when six o'clock was approaching and they were still tearing around, trying to find somewhere, anywhere, to broadcast from.

She opened the door a crack and tipped the dregs of the tea out, shivering as the icy air rushed into the car. Then she shoved the cup back into her glove compartment and looked at the clock on her dashboard. Ten past five. She opened the door of the car, stepped out gingerly, walked carefully round to the boot of her car and started rooting. Her Emu boots, definitely needed those today. She pushed aside a waterproof coat and trousers and some long, green waders and finally found her red fleece and a matching pair of thermal gloves. Shrugging the fleece on with some difficulty – she was already wearing a long-sleeved thermal vest and a thick polo neck – she zipped it to the neck, slammed the boot closed again and headed warily to the truck, pausing on the way to knock on Nathan and Rodney's car windows. They gave her sleepy thumbs up signs, both grimacing at the prospect of the morning ahead.

In the van, Scott was raising the satellite dish.

'Everything OK?' Cora slammed the sliding door behind her.

'Fine, fine. So – good Christmas? Justin a dim and distant nasty memory?'

Cora settled into the passenger seat and started pulling off her trainers to replace them with the boots.

'Yes, he damn well is. I am officially forgetting he ever existed,' Cora lied.

And then, more truthfully: 'And yeah, really good Christmas, thanks. I just hung out with the girls really – Christmas at Rosie's. You have a good one?'

'Not really, no.'

'Oh no! I'm sorry, Scott – why? What happened?'

Scott didn't reply. Frowning, he pressed a few buttons. 'Bastard thing. Keeps getting stuck. I'm at my wick's end with this dish.'

'Wit's,' said Cora automatically.

'OK, wit's end then. Hang on – think it's locking up now – yes! We're in business.'

He turned back to Cora. 'So … Christmas …' He paused.

'Well … to be honest …' He paused again.

'Oh, nothing really. It was just a quiet one, that's all. Me and Elaine and the girls, and the parents popped in. I got a fantastic pressie from Mum and Dad though – a Victorian toilet mirror, satinwood frame, little hinged velvet trinket tray, the works. Looks brilliant in the downstairs loo. Well impressed.'

He smiled, but Cora could tell something wasn't quite right. Was he having marriage problems or something? It would explain his recent moodiness. She was about to press him further when the door slid open and Nathan and Rodney leapt in, already bundled up in their outdoor gear.

'Find friggin' snow! Well, we've found some, I suppose. It's not exactly blizzard conditions though, is it? I mean, it is December – hardly unusual to have a little bit of snow. Bloody stupid.'

Nathan stamped a few flakes off his boots, and they melted immediately, leaving a minute puddle on the truck floor.

Cora stood up, and pulled her coat on over the fleece.

'I know, I know! You know what it's like, though – I had half a feeling when I went to bed last night that we'd be called out. Come on, let's get out there and try and make it look half decent. I've spoken to Sam – she said as long as it keeps snowing they'll come to us every half an hour.'

'Arse!'

Nathan slapped Scott good-humouredly across his shaved head with a glove. Scott shoved him back. Rodney, who was wearing his new green and white golf trousers with a purple Gore-Tex jacket, pinched Nathan's bum hard, and Nathan turned and whacked him. Cora shook her head and climbed out of the truck. Honestly, sometimes it was like working with five-year-olds.

'So – Christina's definitely in the clear? Gosh, that's a relief.'

A few minutes before the eight o'clock news, Cora was getting an update on Jeanette's case from Sam.

'Yes – she might have been angry and upset on Dead Dog Day, but she didn't kill anyone. Apparently the cops worked out the timeline properly over Christmas and they don't think it could have been her. I think they're still looking at Clancy though, from what I've heard on the grapevine. Well, they always look close to home first, don't they? And she has no alibi, you see – she says she was back home in bed by the time Jeanette was killed, but there was nobody else in the house. They're trying to get proof of that somehow. Seem to think she could have sneaked back in to the newsroom later, sometime after she dropped Jeanette off. Although I certainly didn't see her. Anyway – we obviously can't mention any of that, it's come from Clancy, not the cops! What they DO want to do is one final appeal on that CCTV footage. The weird guy – or woman, whatever – outside the building still hasn't been identified, so they want to give it one more go. Clutching at straws I reckon, but hey …'

Cora gulped slightly and tried to disguise it as a cough.

'You alright love? Anyway – just recap the murder, link into the CCTV pics and then wrap. A minute will be fine. OK?'

Cora cleared her throat. 'Sure, no problem. Yes, yes that's perfect. Talk to you later.'

She ended the call and sank back in her seat. That bloody CCTV. The more it was out there, the more likely it was that *somebody* would recognise Justin, and her ex-boyfriend would officially be prime suspect in a murder. What on earth was she going to do? If only she could talk to him properly before anyone else did, find out what he was doing there. There'd still been nothing else from him on Twitter since their unsatisfactory exchange on Christmas Eve. She clenched her fists in frustration. Where *was* he? Unless he really *did* have something to hide? Cora sighed. Hands shaking a little, she reapplied her lip gloss, took a deep breath and got out of her car.

'Thanks so much for letting me know, it's very good of you. I really appreciate it, Jean. Well … goodbye then.'

'Bye, Cora, love.'

Cora pressed the end call button and stared numbly out of her car window at the traffic whizzing past the lay-by she'd hastily pulled into when Justin's mother had called, with what she'd said was 'great news' about her missing son.

Justin, it seemed, was in Spain. It appeared he'd taken Cora's advice to phone somebody, and had called his parents on Christmas Day, telling them he'd taken a sabbatical from work, needed a break to 'get his head together' after splitting with Cora, and would be back soon. He was fine, just wanted a bit of space to decide what he really wanted to do with his life, and nobody was to worry. He'd got himself a Spanish mobile number, but for now he apparently had decided he'd prefer not to give it to anyone, promising to call his parents regularly instead.

This news apparently came as a huge relief to his mum and dad, who'd finally decided they'd better tell his now ex-girlfriend to put her mind at ease too. Somehow though, Cora wasn't feeling particularly reassured. Spain? Wasn't that one of the places Ronnie Biggs ran to after the Great Train Robbery? Wasn't leaving the country an even bigger sign that Justin had been up to no good in the CCTV footage? And should she now, at this point, put loyalty aside and tell somebody her suspicions? If not the police, then at least one of her friends? In despair, Cora sank her head onto the steering wheel, accidentally beeping the horn in the process and making herself jump. She was kidding herself. There was no way she would tell anyone, she knew that. It was so late now, for a start – the police might even arrest *her* for covering it up for so long, accuse her of attempting to pervert the course of justice or something. And she knew, deep down, that Justin wasn't a killer. There would be an explanation, and one day soon she would speak to Justin and he would tell her what it was. And in the meantime, the real killer would be caught. He, or she, simply had to be.

'So forget the CCTV. Nobody's come forward. Nobody will. Forget it,' she said out loud. She flicked on her indicator, moved smoothly out into the traffic, and headed for home.

15

'Alice has been acting like a crazy person, seriously.'

Sam and Cora were huddled in the corner of the newsroom, cradling coffee cups and having a quick catch-up before Cora hit the road again. She'd been called to London in the early hours to stand in for Sue the political reporter, who'd gone sick, and had popped in to the newsroom on her way home to wish Sam and Wendy an early Happy New Year.

'Honestly, talk about over the top,' Sam continued. 'She won't stop crying and she's been foul with everyone. I mean, she's always foul. But *really* foul. It's a nightmare.'

Cora screwed up her nose. 'I don't get it really. I know Jeanette gave her a job she wasn't really cut out for, and was incredibly supportive of her for whatever reason. But they never struck me as *personally* close, particularly. It's odd, isn't it?'

'It is. I think she's just attention seeking. The papers splashed a picture of her leaving the building looking all weepy and tragic last week and you know what she's like – loves the publicity …' Her voice tailed off as Alice wandered past, looking miserable.

'Oh, hi, Alice!'

Alice glanced at Sam, said nothing, and carried on walking.

'Cow. See what I mean? I give up with her, I really do. Sodding Alice Lomas. Lo-Intelligence more like.'

'Or Lo-Cut-Top.' Sam and Cora both tittered childishly at the silly joke, then Cora glugged the last of her drink and stood up.

'Right, I'm out of here. Home for a sleep. Please try not to call me again till tomorrow? Love you. Happy New Year.'

Sam gave her a hug. 'Love you too, babe. Have a good one. Drive carefully.'

As she emerged from the lift into Reception, Cora stopped as a familiar face approached.

'Ah – DCI Bradberry. Cora Baxter, remember? I'm covering Jeanette's murder.'

The police officer smiled. 'Cora, of course. Nice to see you. Hey – you were at Westminster this morning, weren't you? I've been at my desk since six – got into the habit of watching the programme seeing as I'm working on the murder of its editor.'

Cora nodded and shifted her heavy handbag to her other shoulder. 'Yes, I get around. And always happy to have another viewer.'

'So – do you have a specialist subject then? Or how does it work?'

Adam looked quizzically at Cora and she thought once again how attractive he was, then gave herself a mental shake. She was off men, remember?

'No, no – we have a political reporter, who went sick today so I stood in, and a doctor who does the health stories, but the rest of us have to be experts in a different field every day, really. I read all the papers online, check Twitter all the time, and watch the news non-stop – it becomes a bit of an addiction, but it's the only way to keep on top of everything.'

'Interesting. I guess you never get bored, then? And crime – do you do much crime?'

'A fair bit, yes. It's one of my favourite areas, to be honest. I find it fascinating. So – what about Jeanette? Anything new for me?'

'Don't think so – hang on.' He started flicking through the notepad in his hand, frowning. Cora couldn't help staring a little. He really was extremely fit. Muscular, but not too beefy. That sexy cropped blond hair. Dark green eyes, unusual shade …

Adam looked up suddenly from his notes and caught her looking at him. Cora felt herself flushing.

He smiled. 'To be honest – nothing for you really. We're floundering a bit on this one. But we hope to have finished going through all the CCTV we've got in the next twenty-four hours, so maybe then? Give me a call.'

He reached into the inside pocket of his jacket and pulled out a card.

'Here – my mobile number. I know what it's like getting through to the press office – can take for ever. Call me direct and if I know anything we can release to the press, I'll give it to you first. Only fair – she was your boss, after all.'

Their fingers touched as he handed her the business card and a jolt went through Cora, leaving her stomach fluttering. Crikey. That didn't happen to her very often. She'd only just split with Justin, she shouldn't be reacting like this to other men. But if she felt like that when he touched her hand, what would it feel like if those fingers were to touch her in other places?

Flustered, she fumbled in her big bag and pulled out one of her own cards.

'And here's mine. Just in case, you know, there's some big breaking news.'

Adam tucked the card into his pocket. 'Thanks. Right – have to run. My little boy's arriving tomorrow for the weekend and we have a LOT to get through at work before then.'

For a reason she couldn't quite put her finger on, Cora's heart sank a little.

'Oh – you have a little boy? That's … er … nice.'

'It is. He lives with his mum in Swindon, but I get him alternate weekends – here he is, look. Proud dad, sorry – always showing him off.'

He held out his mobile phone and showed Cora the screensaver. A serious-faced little boy, hair a few shades darker than his dad's but – the green eyes. Unmistakable.

'He – he's lovely. Very sweet.' She smiled, but inside she was feeling uncomfortably perturbed.

'I think so. Well, nice to see you again, Cora. Hopefully there'll be some developments to report soon. I'll be in touch.'

'Thanks, er … Adam. Bye now.'

She wandered out into the street and clambered into her car, suddenly feeling rather low. It was hopeless. Not that she was looking at the moment, obviously, but it was looking highly likely that she'd be single for ever, let's face it. She rarely met *anyone* she fancied, and there'd miraculously been two in the few days since she split up with Justin, yet she'd managed to act like a bowel movement-obsessed crazy woman in front of one, and the second was a doting daddy who'd run a mile once he found out she wasn't exactly stepmother material.

Oh well. There were always chocolate and banana muffins. A stop at Mattino's on the way home was definitely needed today. She turned the key in the ignition and pointed the car towards Cheltenham.

16

Today's hotel, somewhere in Cambridgeshire, wasn't a particularly pleasant one, and Cora shuddered as she pushed aside the slightly mouldy shower curtain encrusted with soap residue. Sadly, despite her request to Sam, the news desk had called to divert her as she headed for Cheltenham yesterday, meaning yet another night away from home.

To their credit, the *Morning Live* travel desk did their best to book the crews into decent hotels most of the time, understanding that when you spent most of your working life away from home, it wasn't really acceptable to be accommodated in dumps. But sometimes there just wasn't anywhere nice available, especially in the more remote areas. In fact, there had only been one room free in this hotel – Rodney and Nathan had been put in what sounded like an even worse place a couple of miles away. Scott never stayed in hotels – his contract meant his working day started at midnight, so he simply drove the truck through the night to wherever he needed to be and then drove home again to sleep.

Forty-five minutes later Cora was scrubbed and polished and ready for work. Mindful of the other guests, she slipped out of her room, closed the door quietly behind her and tiptoed down the long, dimly lit corridor with its garish red and brown swirly carpet. At the reception desk, the night porter was sitting with his feet up, flicking disconsolately through yesterday's copy of the *Mirror* and picking his nose. At the sight of Cora he sat up abruptly, with a look of great surprise on his face.

'Morning!' she said brightly.

The porter looked at his watch.

'Er – morning, madam.'

He eyed her up and down, frowning slightly. Cora sighed inwardly. It was happening again – he thought she was a hooker. The problem with hotel night porters was that they never recognised her, because they never watched breakfast TV as they were always working when it was on air. Therefore, when a woman left their hotel in the early hours of the morning, glammed up with heels, perfume, and lipstick, they all automatically presumed she was on the game. When she had time or was in the mood, Cora sometimes stopped and explained *why* she was apparently sneaking out at 4.30 a.m., but she really couldn't be bothered today.

'I'm just going out for a few hours – I'll be back for breakfast later,' she announced, as she marched smartly through Reception.

The porter looked at her even more suspiciously.

'Well – alright then,' he said slowly.

'*Madam*,' he added sarcastically.

He stared after her as she walked to the door and Cora, feeling his eyes boring into her back, suddenly wished she had a condom in her pocket so she could 'accidentally' drop it in front of him. That would give him added spice for the story he'd no doubt be telling in the pub later. The problem was that by the time she did make it back for breakfast, he'd be off duty, so he'd never discover what she really did for a living. There were hotel porters all over Britain who thought she was a prostitute. Marvellous, wasn't it? Cora smiled to herself as she fumbled for her car keys. People thought her job was so glamorous – if only! At least there was no ice on the car windows this morning. No scraping required – a good start to the day for *Madam* Cora.

She tapped the address into her sat nav and zoomed off into the darkness. She was only about fifteen minutes' drive away from today's location, and her BMW quietly ate up the miles as she navigated the empty roads. The through-the-night DJ twittered away on Radio One, and Cora reached one hand into the door pocket for a sweet and popped a chocolate caramel into her mouth. She felt bored already. Today's story was one of those tedious tales of a small child who had dialled 999 and saved his mother's life after she'd collapsed with some illness or other, and Cora couldn't summon up much enthusiasm for it.

After a few years, the job had become a bit 'groundhog day' – the same stories cropped up over and over again. She'd done versions of this one at least twice before. Still, at least it was indoors – another bonus on a wintry morning. She'd actually got her legs out today for a change, choosing a slim charcoal pencil skirt teamed with black patent heels and a tight-fitting grey sweater.

Cora slowed down as she saw the satellite truck parked under a lamppost up ahead and pulled up neatly behind it. She waved at Scott, who was standing in the middle of the road, rubbing his woolly-hatted head and frowning over his compass as he worked out the best way to position the dish, and he waved back. There was no sign of Nathan and Rodney yet, so she locked her car and made her way up the path of number 12, the only house in the street with lights blazing. It was always weird knocking at somebody's door at 5 a.m., and Cora was constantly amazed that so many people agreed to have a TV crew in their home at such a stupid hour. That though, as Jeanette had never tired of pointing out, was the power of *Morning Live*. It was a big show, and people wanted to be a part of it, no matter how early they had to get up.

The woman who opened the door was wearing a maroon velour tracksuit and no make-up. She looked exhausted, but she was smiling and excitedly ushered Cora inside. The living room was small and faded, but cosy and immaculate. A large flat screen TV dominated the space, and a huge gilt-framed photo of a little red-haired boy in a navy school uniform hung over the fireplace.

'I can't believe it, Cora Baxter in my living room!' the woman enthused.

Cora beamed back. 'Well, it's very nice to meet you. And this must be little Ronan.'

The ginger-headed boy from the photo, now wearing Thomas the Tank Engine pyjamas, was poking his head around the living room door, grinning shyly.

'Ronan, Ronan, come and meet the lady. This is Cora, off the telly. You recognise Cora, don't you?'

The little boy inched his way into the room and clutched his mother's tracksuit bottoms. Cora crouched down to say hello.

'So, you're the little star who rang 999? What a clever boy! You're going to be on television now too, isn't that exciting?'

The child stared at her with big, blue eyes and said nothing. Oh dear, Cora thought. Live TV and a child who won't speak. Great. She smiled and stood up. Thank goodness they had the tape of the 999 call to play.

The woman started bustling around the already tidy room, manically straightening cushions.

'Cup of tea, Cora? I'm going to tidy up and get us both dressed and then I'll put the kettle on. Or maybe I should put the kettle on now, what do you think? We're not on until after six, are we – gosh, I'm so nervous, I've never done anything like this before ...'

She stopped and clasped her hands to her mouth.

'You'll be fine, honestly,' Cora said soothingly. 'We'll have a rehearsal before we go on, don't worry. But it's just like you and me having a chat, it's easy. Don't panic!'

The woman took a deep breath. 'OK, I won't. Thank you. I'll go and sort out that tea – make yourself at home.' She gestured towards the worn red sofa.

'I will in a minute, thanks – just going to check on my crew, they seem to be running late.'

Cora reluctantly made her way back out into the chill air and breathed it in deeply. Her head had started to swim with tiredness. Thank goodness it was Friday. But it was nearly 5.15 – where were the boys? Worried now, she pulled out her phone and speed dialled Nathan. He answered after two rings, sounding out of breath.

'Sorry, sorry, we'll be there in ten minutes. Shit-hole hotel, no night porter, door locked, had to climb out window ... you know, the usual … see you in a mo …'

The line went dead. Relieved, Cora went back inside. This happened all the time too. Small hotels often didn't have night porters, and even though she and the boys were always careful to point out when they checked in that they would need to leave in the early hours, harassed receptionists sometimes forgot and locked the doors. When that happened, your only option was to find a window to climb out of and hope you wouldn't set the burglar alarm off. It happened surprisingly regularly, and the travel desk always had a go at the hotel later, asking them what would have happened if there had been a fire and guests had needed to get out urgently. The hotel managers were always terribly embarrassed and apologetic – the boys would probably get a free breakfast later – but it didn't really help. Getting to location on time was nerve-wracking enough without having to climb out of windows to get to your car.

The boys arrived a few minutes later, Rodney panting slightly as he lugged his gear into the living room where Cora sat running through her notes.

'That was close,' she said, relieved.

'Damn hotels. Caught my trousers on a nail on the windowsill too – look! Jodie's going to kill me, she got me these for Christmas!'

He turned and Cora stifled a giggle. There was a long rip in the reasonably normal-looking, dark green canvas jeans the soundman was wearing, revealing a far from normal pair of luminous yellow boxer shorts with a ghastly green mushroom and pepper print.

Nathan appeared in the doorway.

'Oh for heaven's sake, Rodney, where do you even *buy* underwear like that?' he exploded. 'I mean, is there some special secret shop somewhere, specialising in weird soundman clothes? Would you *look* at those pants! They look like a tea towel gone mental!'

Rodney looked offended. 'These are my favourite pants, *actually,* Nathan. I don't comment on *your* underwear, do I?'

'That's because I wear *normal* underwear that doesn't merit a comment. Jeez, if I came home in those Gareth would die laughing! Seriously …'

They were interrupted by the woman clanking in from the kitchen with a tea tray.

'Oh – morning, gentlemen! Ronan, the camera crew are here too now! How exciting!'

The ginger child poked his head in again and stared. He had yet to utter a word.

The woman was still fluttering.

'I made tea *and* coffee,' she announced proudly. 'Toast on the way!'

She scuttled out, her maroon velour bottom wobbling, and Cora held up her hands as Nathan opened his mouth again.

'OK, enough, Nath. Rodney, if you tie that fleece around your waist, the pants will be forgotten, right? Let's just drink our tea and get this show on the road.'

'OK, OK.' Nathan submitted.

'Alright. Three lumps in mine.'

'Yeah, yeah, I know.'

Cora poured tea and, peace restored, the organised chaos that always preceded a broadcast got underway as the boys set up lights, connected up cables and generally turned the front room of a suburban semi into a mini TV studio. Cora, cup in hand, picked her way carefully through the equipment and lifted the net curtain at the window. Outside, the dish was locked in place. Good. At least Scott hadn't had any drama this morning. Reporter being mistaken for a hooker, crew locked in hotel … and this had been a relatively *quiet* morning. She smiled into the darkness and shook her head. If only the viewers knew what went on before a live broadcast. They just wouldn't believe it.

Later, as they packed up, Nathan pulled Cora aside.

'There's something weird going on with Scott.'

Cora nodded. 'I've been a bit worried about him, to be honest. He's been so grumpy, and distracted. And I don't think he had a great Christmas. I thought maybe him and Elaine were going through a rough patch or something? Do you know

102

what's happening?'

'I don't think it's Elaine. I don't know what it is for certain. But – see what you make of this. I called in last night on the way here to drop off that jacket I borrowed from him. And you know what the house is normally like – so packed with antiques you can barely get in the door?'

Cora smiled. 'Sure do. I've never seen so many old bits of furniture and knick-knacks in one place. They could open a shop.'

Nathan shook his head. 'Not any more. They're all gone. Apart from the compass you gave him for Christmas, and some little mirror in the downstairs loo, there's not one antique in the house. Not much of anything, in fact. Half the furniture is gone, and Elaine looked mortified. Tried to keep me on the doorstep, except I was desperate for a wee so she had to let me in. Muttered something about a change of style, trying minimalism, but I didn't buy it.'

Cora looked shocked. 'But – why? He's obsessed with antiques, they both are. Why would they get rid of them all? Unless …'

Nathan nodded slowly. 'Money? That's what I thought. I think our Scott has money troubles. *Big* money troubles. The question is – why?'

If Scott's ears weren't burning, they should have been, because at that very moment he was also being avidly discussed by a police murder investigation team.

'Look, see here.' Gary paused the CCTV footage and everyone huddled closer around the TV monitor. He pressed play.

'He gets into the lift, on the newsroom floor, and there's somebody else in there. Then two floors down, the other person gets out. And as soon as the doors close – look. He starts punching the wall. Once, twice, three, four times. What's all that about then?'

Adam Bradberry was watching closely. 'He's very angry, that's pretty obvious. And we're sure about who he is?'

Gary nodded. 'Yes, it's Scott Edson. An engineer who works mainly on outside broadcasts. Kendrick had called him in that day for a disciplinary hearing. Seven in the morning, odd timing but just her style from what I've heard. Fell asleep on the job and missed a broadcast apparently – and a second offence. One more strike and he'd have been out.'

Adam stroked his chin thoughtfully. 'So, no love lost for Ms Kendrick then. And not looking very happy here, is he? What time was this?'

Gary checked the timecode on the monitor. '7.40. He comes out of the lift and leaves the building. So yes, he was gone about twenty minutes before Kendrick was killed. Unless …'

'Unless he came back in through one of those side doors, and took that temper out on Ms Kendrick instead of on the lift. I like your thinking, Gary. Let's have a chat with Mr Edson. Good work.'

'Thanks sir. We'll head over there then. Nice to get this wrapped up before New Year, wouldn't it?'

It certainly would, thought Adam. It would be very nice indeed.

17

Tuesday 2ⁿᵈ January

'Hmmm – shall I bring the thong, or not?'

Benjamin Boland stepped back from the Louis Vuitton suitcase he was packing and held up a scrap of black fabric with a large front pouch and a miniscule back. He turned it this way and that, pondering for a moment, then decided against. He was off to Finland after all. Probably better to bring some slightly larger pants – keep the crown jewels warm …

He put the thong neatly back in his colour co-ordinated underwear drawer and selected several pairs of tight white Dolce & Gabbana boxer briefs instead. Folding them precisely, he added them to the case and then started to choose socks. He should have packed yesterday really, but he'd been so hung over after New Year's Eve. And then, just as he was starting to feel better, he'd been tempted out for a meal at Nobu with some of the boys, and then on to a lap-dancing club, so by the time he'd got in he was a little the worse for wear all over again. The car wouldn't be here to collect him till nine though, so he still had over an hour.

He was quite looking forward to this trip – he'd had a quiet Christmas, for him, and he was feeling in need of an adrenaline fix. It was just a five day shoot, but it should be fun – a husky safari through one of the few real wildernesses left in Europe, the forests and frozen lakes of western Lapland. The temperatures could drop as low as minus twenty-five, and the crew would be staying in wood cabins at night with no running water, toilets or electricity, but he could cope with that for a few days. In fact, he couldn't wait. It would be a bit of a challenge, and he needed one. He hadn't been feeling very happy recently – lonely sometimes, if he was honest, despite his exciting job and big circle of acquaintances – and he didn't like it. Maybe a serious blast of cold air would sort him out.

He wandered into the depths of his walk-in wardrobe to find his thermal long johns and gloves. As he emerged, he glimpsed a familiar face on the TV that was burbling away quietly across the room, and to his surprise his stomach did a small but unmistakeable back flip. He reached for the remote and turned the volume up. On the vast screen, Cora Baxter was chatting animatedly to a plump woman in a chavvy-looking kitchen. Benjamin sat down slowly on the bed. Hell, she was looking good. Stunning in fact. Her swishy bob swung around her chin as she turned back to the camera, her green eyes sparkling, a tight red top emphasising her curves. She handed back to the studio and was gone, and the weatherman popped up instead, white teeth flashing in his luminous face.

Instantly bored, Benjamin turned away from the screen, and then chuckled softly to himself as he remembered their brief meeting. She'd been flustered and acted a little strangely, but there had definitely been something there. He snapped his suitcase shut, stood up and pointed at himself in the mirror.

'You, Boland,' he said firmly. 'You are going to go to Lapland, and then you're going to come back and go on a date with Cora Baxter. Deal?'

The face in the mirror grinned back at him. 'Deal!' it said.

18

'So no, I didn't bloody kill Jeanette. In case you're wondering.'

Scott banged his mug down and glared at his colleagues.

'Scott! Of course we weren't wondering. Don't be ridiculous,' Cora said soothingly.

'Honestly, mate, as if!' Nathan reached out and squeezed Scott's shoulder, while Rodney shook his head and smiled sympathetically.

'Well – thanks. That means a lot,' said Scott, sounding somewhat mollified. 'I wish the cops had as much faith in me though. They've told me they'll want to speak to me again, you know, after 'further enquiries'. Elaine's in bits. Me, questioned for murder, just because I thumped a lift! I only did it because that woman pissed me off so much.'

The others looked at each other and grimaced. Poor Scott. They'd all been horrified over New Year to hear that their friend had been questioned about Jeanette's murder, and desperate to hear the details. Finally back on the road together today, they'd had the blow-by-blow account, and while none of them thought Scott was remotely capable of murder, it seemed his little show of temper as he left the *Morning Live* studios had raised police suspicions.

'So, what further enquiries are they making? Did they tell you?' asked Cora, and took another bite of her sausage sandwich. They'd all stopped at a little roadside café for breakfast after the morning's lives, and as usual she was starving.

'Dunno,' said Scott sullenly. 'Told them I drove straight off and never came back to the building, which I didn't. They have my reg details, so I s'pose they'll look at traffic camera footage or something. I dunno. I'm just pissed off with the whole thing. I'm going. See you tomorrow, unless I'm in bloody jail or something.'

He pushed his egg-smeared plate away angrily and stood up, chair scraping loudly on the grubby tiles, then slouched out of the café without another word, letting the door slam behind him.

'Phew-wee.' Nathan leaned back in his red plastic chair and ran his fingers through his hair.

'You don't think … do you?' Rodney pushed his glasses higher onto his nose, anxiety wrinkling his forehead.

'No. No! Of course not. But something's going on.' Cora rubbed her temples. She could feel a stress headache brewing.

'I mean, this business at his house, with all the antiques disappearing? Which none of us have had the guts to ask him about yet, have we?'

The boys shook their heads.

'And he has been incredibly grumpy and acting quite strangely recently. And, let's face it, he was definitely edging closer to getting the sack – Jeanette was getting really fed up with him. So yes, something's very wrong with our Scott. But murder? No. No way.'

'Agreed,' said Nathan. 'But let's hope the cops decide he's innocent sooner rather than later. He's already on the edge, and I dread to think what will happen if he tips over it.'

'Oh, he's putting his socks in his pudding now! Elliot! Stop it, that's not very nice, is it?'

Elliot giggled and Zoë, his nanny, shook her head good-naturedly and pushed his high chair back from the table, out of reach of his bowl of fruit and yoghurt. She grabbed his wiggling feet, peeled off his now soggy little green socks, and waved them at Cora, who was flicking through a newspaper across the table.

'Cora, would you mind keeping an eye on him for just a minute? Nicole's still in the shower and I'll have to go and rinse these out – the yoghurt will start to stink if I leave them in the washing basket.'

Cora, who'd popped round to see Nicole for a rare mid-week visit, reached out and tickled Elliot's toes, and he kicked his feet and shrieked with delight.

'Course I'll keep an eye on him – little monkey. I wouldn't worry about it though – you know what a state Nicole's clothes get in at work. That washing basket could probably walk off on its own, a bit of yoghurt's nothing!'

'I know, but I'll do it anyway. Back in a mo!' She tousled Elliot's dark curls and he gazed after her as she headed for the utility room. Young and pretty in a freshly scrubbed, no make-up kind of way, Zoë had been Elliot's nanny since he was six weeks old. He adored her, to the extent that Cora – and sometimes even Nicole – got quite jealous, but Zoë was such a sweet, down to earth girl and Nicole and Will relied on her so much that they willingly put up with sharing the little boy's affections.

Cora got up, grabbed a wet wipe from the pack on the table and brandished it at Elliot.

'Right, mucky mush, give me that face!'

The toddler grimaced as she scrubbed at the tomato sauce, fish finger crumbs, and yoghurt smeared across his cheeks, then beamed and held up his arms for a cuddle. Cora unstrapped him from his chair and hauled him out, kissing his damp pink nose.

'Gorgeous boy.'

She held him close, and his chubby little arms wrapped tightly round her neck. Cora waltzed around the kitchen with him, humming softly, and he snuggled in, his head heavy on her shoulder. She loved Elliot so much, but sometimes she preferred to cuddle him when nobody else was around, just to avoid the inevitable 'oh, you're so good with him, I can't believe you're not having your own' comments. To Cora though, enjoying a cuddle with a cute kid was a million miles away from actually wanting to give birth to one. It drove her mad that even her close friends still gave each other knowing looks when they saw her with a small child – almost as mad as when people said, pityingly, 'and who's going to look after *you* when you're old?'. As Cora delighted in pointing out, nursing homes were full of old people who never had visits from their children, because they'd fallen out or emigrated or just couldn't be bothered. In Cora's view, it was much safer to work hard, save your money and provide for yourself in your old age – and what a selfish reason to have children, just so you could have a more comfortable retirement ...

'Right, young man, it's nearly seven o'clock and I make that bath time!'

Zoë bustled back into the room and Cora, startled out of her reverie, reluctantly relinquished her charge.

'Thanks, Cora, you're a star. Nicole said she'll be down in a minute, and to help yourself to the wine in the fridge. I'm going to bathe Elliot and put him to bed before I go home, so you two can catch up. See you soon – say goodnight to Auntie Cora, Elliot!'

Cora planted a kiss on the little boy's head. 'Night night, darling.'

'N'night,' squeaked Elliot, and flapped both hands at her in his cute toddler wave.

Cora waved back until he'd disappeared down the hall, poured herself a small glass of wine in case her work phone rang later and sank down at the table again. Wearily, she glanced at her BlackBerry. No messages. She'd tried contacting @a-friend, aka Justin, several times since their Christmas Eve encounter but he'd never replied, leaving Cora deeply uneasy. It was impossible to shake the constant feeling of anxiety she'd had ever since the day of Jeanette's murder – the horrible knowledge that the killer was very probably somebody she knew, that it was highly unlikely that some random stranger had managed to slip in and out of the newsroom unnoticed. Justin's silence was making everything worse, her mind swinging wildly from complete faith in the innocence of a man she knew so well, to extreme doubt. She was still pushing the doubts viciously from her head, but she wasn't sure how long she'd be able to keep that up. It was becoming exhausting.

She sighed heavily and tried to think more positively. It

would be nice to have a few hours of quality time with Nicole. Will had already headed off to the local pub for a snooker night with the lads, so it would be just the two of them, something that didn't happen very often.

Nicole and Will lived in a beautifully restored Grade II listed cottage two miles outside Cheltenham. Dating back to 1830, it had all the character you would expect – an inglenook fireplace, beams, flagstone floors – but Nicole had managed to combine its country charm with contemporary décor, so for a building with such small windows and low ceilings it had a surprisingly bright and modern feel about it.

As in every good cottage, the kitchen was the heart of the home, and they rarely sat anywhere else on their girls' nights in. It was a big messy room, every surface always liberally scattered with toy bricks, cars and children's books, but with its massive oak table and grey leather sofa, the squishiest Cora had ever sat on, it was the perfect place to sprawl, especially in winter when the heat thrown out by the shiny cream Aga meant you rarely needed to wear anything much warmer than a T-shirt.

Cora, already heating up, slipped off her cardigan and sipped her wine sleepily. She was just getting stuck into an article on the latest suspected terrorist arrests in Birmingham when Nicole wandered in, knotting the belt of her black velvet dressing gown, looking fresh-faced and rosy after her shower.

'That's better! I was reeking – had a dog with chronic diarrhoea today and I didn't get out of the way fast enough!' She tittered. 'Oh, sorry – we're not supposed to mention diarrhoea, are we?'

'Ha bloody ha.'

Nicole tipped a bag of crisps into a bowl, sloshed some wine into a glass and slumped onto the sofa. 'And then ...'

She paused to take a slurp.

'I got home to find Elliot wandering around naked because he'd just climbed into the loo and Zoë had had to strip him off, and while she was shoving his clothes in the wash he did a great big poo right in the middle of the dining room floor, which I walked straight into!'

Cora groaned. Nicole ignored her. 'So I had dog diarrhoea all over my jeans and baby poo on my shoes and …

'Tra la la la LA LA LA …' Cora stuck her fingers in her ears and sang loudly and tunelessly.

Nicole laughed. 'OK, OK, I'll stop! Come on, tell me your news, then. I don't seem to have any that doesn't include bodily functions.'

'Thank goodness for that.' Cora pushed her chair back and came to join Nicole on the sofa. 'Well – not a lot going on really. Things are really odd, with the murder enquiry, and all this Scott stuff. Although he seemed in a better mood today, thank goodness.'

Nicole selected a crisp from the bowl in between them and pondered.

'A date, that's what you need, young lady. Cheer you up, stop you mooning over Justin. Nothing serious, just a bit of fun. Come on – what about the hot cop? Sounds like there's chemistry there, from what you've said?'

Cora held up her hands. 'No, stop right there – not even in the running. He has a child he sees at weekends. Way too much baggage. So no point in even going there, sadly.' She pouted and got up to refill their glasses.

Nicole held hers out. 'It's what you're going to find more and more though, Cora, you know that don't you? At our age, all the single men either have baggage, or they're single for a reason, cos they're peculiar! It's highly unlikely you're going to find many men in their late thirties or early forties who are attractive, intelligent, and normal, *and* still single. I know you don't want your own kids, but you might have to compromise and put up with one being around now and again. Is that such a big deal? I mean, you actually quite like some kids, don't you?'

Cora sat down again. 'I do, yes. But I think it is a big deal, Nicole. I fully intend to join the long list of women in history who lived life happily and successfully while being totally child-free.'

Nicole wrinkled up her nose. 'OK – name five, then!'

Cora rubbed her hands together. 'Easy! Jane Austen. Coco Chanel. Oprah Winfrey. Er ... Barbara Windsor. Amelia Earhart. See – all successful, all talented, all normal, all *with no kids*!'

Nicole laughed and poked Cora in the ribs. 'Only you could have a list like that to hand. Alright, point taken, nutter.'

Cora smiled with satisfaction as Nicole flicked the TV on to the Comedy Channel. Then she took another sip of wine, and settled back on the cushions to watch *Frasier*.

19

Monday 8th January

'Brrr. I'm going to wait in the car – I'm freezing!'

It was nearly 6 a.m. and, run-through done and still with twenty minutes to go before the first hit of the morning, a shivering Cora turned and nearly walked straight into a gently swaying man who had wandered up behind her. He smelt strongly of stale beer.

'What ya doing?' he slurred, pleasantly. 'Ish thish televishion?'

Cora giggled and Nathan, who was now adjusting the lens of his very large television camera, stared at the drunk.

'No, mate, it's radio.'

The drunk gaped at the TV camera.

'Oh, that'sh a pity,' he said, disappointed. 'I thought it wash telly. Alwaysh wanted to be on telly. Never mind.'

He turned and drifted unsteadily off into the darkness. Cora raised her eyebrows at Nathan, who shook his head.

'Somewhere, this morning …' he began.

'… a village is missing its idiot.' Cora finished the sentence and they both laughed.

Meeting people who were still coming home from the night before was an occupational hazard when you worked this early in the morning. If you ever attempted to stop and ask directions on your way to a location, nine times out of ten the only person around would be inebriated. She usually let Nathan handle the wandering drunks – he treated them with utter disdain but impeccable politeness, which always made her chortle.

'Right, I'll be back in a few minutes. Stay warm.'

Nathan, who was wrapped up like an Eskimo, grunted. Pulling her scarf up over her nose, Cora trudged off to her car. Another Monday, another week. Wonder what this one would bring?

Monday. Three weeks to the day. Jeanette's killer took another sip of coffee and gazed at the dull dawn. A new plan was needed. There was still one more to go, and extra care would be needed this time. Getting away with it once had, it seemed, been relatively easy. Twice might be trickier. So. First, more coffee. Then, later today, when things were less busy, time to plan a murder. What a satisfying way to spend a Monday.

On the doorstep of the elegant home where the late Jeanette Kendrick had lived, DCI Adam Bradberry said a brief goodbye to her tearful partner Clancy Carter and marched down the white-painted steps, Gary hot on his heels. In the car, they both sat in silence for a moment, frustrated at what appeared to be yet another dead end. The police automatic number plate recognition system, known as ANPR, had indeed shown that Clancy had driven straight back to the couple's home after dropping Jeanette at TV centre at 3 a.m.

'And OK, so there was no sign of her car coming back again between then and 8 a.m. But I still thought she *could* have done it. Got a taxi or something back later, or borrowed a car, or even got the Tube or a bus,' Gary mused sadly.

'Another theory scuppered by a delivery guy,' sighed Adam. After further questioning, the distraught Clancy had suddenly remembered that a delivery van from John Lewis had arrived on the morning of the murder. An hour ago the driver had been traced and confirmed he'd spoken to Clancy at her front door at 8.40, when he came to deliver a chair to her neighbours and they weren't in.

'Yep. Unless she was in a helicopter or something, no way she could have killed Kendrick and been back at home at that time, not in rush-hour traffic. Another one bites the dust, eh?'

'Looks like it. Any joy with the Chris thing?'

'Nope. It's a bugger. No idea what she was trying to say. But I'm starting to think maybe we shouldn't put too much emphasis on that, you know boss. Security guard could have misheard – we've only got his say-so that that's what she said.'

'Maybe. And she did have pretty severe head injuries. Could have just been talking rubbish. OK, you're right, let's not put too much emphasis on that for now. So what about Scott Edson's vehicle? He where he says he was too?'

'Still working on that one. Sorry, boss. Too much to do, not enough staff. You know how it is.'

'I do. But we need to get a result on this one fast. Three weeks and nothing. It doesn't look good, Gary.'

Gary nodded morosely and started the engine. As they headed slowly back to the station in the morning traffic, Adam reached into his pocket for his phone and a piece of cardboard fluttered out. He grabbed it. Cora Baxter's business card. He looked thoughtfully at it, feeling a little regretful that he didn't have any news on the case to share with her at the moment. She was a very attractive girl, and he had a small inkling the feeling might be returned – he was sure she'd been staring a little the other day. He didn't know if she was attached or not, but if not maybe when all this was over he'd ask her for a drink or something. It had been a long time since he'd had a date. He slid the card carefully into his wallet, then located his phone and carried on with his day.

'Right – how do I get hold of her?'

Benjamin Boland surveyed his slightly wind-burned nose in the mirror and frowned. His trip to Finland had been excellent, but he wasn't entirely happy with what it had done to his skin. A serious facial would be needed.

Carlos shrugged. 'Email, I guess? Seeing as you didn't manage to get her number. You know, that night you failed to chat her up.'

Benjamin glared at him. 'Oh shut up. OK, email. How do I find her email address then?'

Carlos tapped his smartphone. 'They're all the same over

there at TV Centre. First name dot surname at MorningLive –
all one word – dot co dot uk.'

Benjamin was scribbling the address down.

'Bet she says no again.' Carlos smirked and then ducked as
Benjamin threw a hairbrush at him.

'Bet she doesn't. Nobody *ever* says no to me twice.' But
Benjamin wasn't as confident as he sounded. Please say yes, he
begged silently. Please.

He flipped open his laptop and began composing an email to
Cora Baxter.

20

Tuesday 9th January

'I need a can of beans, a tin of drinking chocolate, a packet of digestive biscuits, and a Noodle Pot. And I'm in a huge hurry – so, quick as you can, please.'

Cora looked at her watch, feeling increasingly stressed. She'd still heard nothing from Justin and the whole thing was making her feel ill. Plus, it was 3 a.m., she had a two and a half hour drive ahead of her and she was trying to buy props for this morning's broadcast from a garage shop assistant who seemed to be somewhat less active than a sloth.

'Can of beans. What were the other things again?' he said slowly, squinty eyes peering at her from a blubbery face.

'Drinking chocolate, digestives, Noodle Pot,' Cora snapped, finding it hard to conceal her irritation. She hated the security measures that meant you couldn't actually go into most urban garage shops during the night, but had to ask the staff to get your shopping for you and pass it through a hatch. Especially when she was tired and grumpy.

'Drinking chocolate, digestives, Noodle Pot,' repeated the cashier, and lumbered off again.

Cora sighed and tapped out a quick text to Nathan to tell him she'd probably be a little late on location this morning. They were broadcasting from a restaurant kitchen in Liverpool, along with a nutritionist who'd be talking about 'high salt food'. Apparently half a tin of beans had as much salt as five bags of crisps, and the other items on her list were equally surprisingly salty.

The assistant was back. 'Got your biscuits and your drinking chocolate. Wot flavour Noodle Pot?'

'I don't care. Anything,' said Cora, who'd never eaten a Noodle Pot in her life.

'But there's loads to choose from,' the boy said, frowning. He started counting on his fat and not entirely clean fingers. 'There's beef and red pepper, chilli chicken, tikka masala, sweet and sour ...'

'I DON'T CARE.'

Cora spoke rather more loudly than she'd intended, then paused as the cashier pouted sulkily. 'I'm sorry – it's just that I really am in a hurry. I honestly don't care what flavour, I'm not going to eat it. Just get the nearest one. Thanks.' She smiled, mentally urging the boy to get a bloody move on.

He looked at her wide-eyed, seemingly bemused that somebody was urgently buying food at three in the morning but was not going to eat it, then shrugged and shuffled off to the grocery shelf again, coming back moments later with the packet.

Gratefully Cora paid, ran back to her car, threw the bag onto the passenger seat, and hit the road. Once she was on the motorway and doing a steady eighty miles an hour northbound, she was able to breathe again. This sort of stress really wasn't good for you.

She flicked the radio on and relaxed a bit, smiling a little as the eighties music show brought back school-day memories. Positive thoughts, that's what she needed. Otherwise she was going to go mad, which wouldn't help anybody. Positive thoughts. Paint on a smile. She forced her lips into a wider grin, which suddenly became a natural beam as she remembered what she would be doing on the coming Friday night. Because, amazingly, on Friday night she, Cora Baxter, would be going on a date. And only with Benjamin bloody Boland!

The email she'd received from him yesterday had actually been very sweet, once she'd got over the shock. No mention of diarrhoea. Simply a nice message, saying he'd been thinking about her since they'd met in the bar, and that he would really like to see her again, and if by any chance she was free on

Friday night he would be honoured if she'd let him take her out for dinner.

'Honoured? *Honoured*?' Nicole had snorted down the phone when an excited Cora had rung to fill her in.

'What's happened to him – has he acquired a time machine and gone back to the 1950s on that travel show of his or something? Who says *honoured* nowadays?'

But she was genuinely pleased for Cora, as were Rosie, Wendy, and Sam who'd all received similar phone calls in quick succession. Cora – their friend, Cora – was going out with Benjamin Boland, *the* hottest man on television.

'I cannot WAIT till Saturday to hear all the gossip. Seriously, Cora – do NOT get too drunk,' Sam had warned her. 'You need to be able to remember *every minute* of that date.'

Now, as she drove in the dark on the M5, Cora started planning what to wear on Friday, a little flutter of excitement building inside her. It had been so long since she'd had a date with somebody new.

'Just don't make a prat of yourself with him again,' she said to herself sternly.

And, Justin and mysterious murders temporarily forgotten, she turned the music up and sang along loudly and happily all the way to Liverpool.

21

Fridays were pretty much the same as any other day of the week for a police murder investigation team. Especially for a police murder investigation team which was rapidly running out of suspects, and ideas. But as lunchtime came, and the rustle of sandwich bags and crunching of crisps temporarily replaced the tense buzz in the incident room, things suddenly stepped up a gear.

'Look at this, boss.'

Adam looked up from his bacon and egg, all-day breakfast roll and wiped a smear of brown sauce from his top lip. He swallowed.

'What is it, Karen?'

'OK – so Scott Edson, the angry engineer who'd been in to see Jeanette Kendrick for a 7 a.m. disciplinary, went down in the lift and left the building around 7.40, right?'

'Right.' Adam took another nibble of his roll.

'And when we brought him in, he told us he drove straight home. So he should have headed out west, this way – look – along the Victoria Embankment, and then onto the A4 and M4.' Her index finger with its bitten nail traced the route on a map on the wall.

'OK. So – problem?'

'Yes, problem. Well, problem for him anyway. We've tracked his van, and he certainly didn't go straight home. For a start, we have CCTV footage showing the vehicle at a Shell garage *here*' – she pointed again – 'at 8.20. That's about forty minutes after he left TV Centre. He should have been miles away by that time.'

Adam stared at the map. The garage Karen was indicating was on Southwark Bridge Road. Not only was that, at a guess, less than five minutes' drive from TV Centre, but it was in completely the wrong direction for Edson's drive home.

'So he lied. He didn't go straight home.'

'Looks like it. TV Centre to that garage is about a four-minute drive if the roads are quiet. Even if it took, say, ten or fifteen minutes maximum to get there in rush hour traffic, that still leaves a lot of time unaccounted for. So what was he doing between 7.40 when he left, and 8.20 when he's still only a few minutes' drive away? And most importantly, did he come back into the building during that time and chuck somebody out of a window?'

Adam nodded slowly. 'Let's talk to him again. Lean on him a bit. Actually, lean on him a *lot*. And find out exactly where he went after he pulled out of the TV Centre car park. Good work, Karen.'

Adam took a long slug of coffee, screwed his brown paper sandwich wrapper in a ball, and aimed it at the bin opposite his desk. Bull's-eye.

For breakfast TV staff, Friday was always the best day of the week. As soon as the *Morning Live* closing credits rolled at 9.30, the weekend officially began, with no more work until Sunday afternoon when the dreaded call from the newsroom would come, telling the show's crews and reporters where in the country they were needed to be for Monday's programme.

For Cora, this particular Friday was an extra good one. After her morning broadcasts in Reading she'd driven to London and checked into her usual hotel. Now she opened her wardrobe door and surveyed the six outfits she'd brought with her.

'So, Benjamin – which one is it to be?' she said out loud. Pulling each garment out in turn, she held them in front of her and studied herself critically in the mirror. Not the orange dress – why had she brought that? Too clingy, although she looked great in it on a thin day. But, no. She didn't want to look as though she was trying to emulate one of her date's usual model types.

The black shift? Possibly. Simple, classy. But a bit too plain, maybe, for a Friday night out in London? She threw the two dresses on a chair and grabbed a black pencil skirt with a full-length zip down the back, and a sleeveless print shirt. With her black killer heels, definitely a sexy look. But – maybe too 'secretary'?

'Aaagh, I just don't know!' Cora groaned, wishing one of her girlfriends was around. She sat on the bed and looked at the black dress. Justin had always loved her in that.

Justin. She thought about him for a minute, her continuing anxiety about the situation suddenly turning into a flash of irritation. He'd said in that last message that he'd be in touch – why on earth was he taking so long, and ignoring her repeated messages? She was still determined to somehow get an explanation for his weird behaviour outside TV Centre, and for his disappearing act, no matter how long it took. But there were limits to her patience, and she was definitely reaching them. She was about to go on a date with someone else, and she needed closure with Justin. So if messages begging him to contact her weren't working, what else could she do? An idea struck her and, impulsively, she picked up her phone and tapped out a Twitter direct message.

@CoraBaxterMLive @a-friend Justin – get in touch. I haven't said anything to the police about you in the CCTV. But I might. IF YOU DON'T CALL ME.

Would that do it? It wasn't exactly a threat, but it might spur him into action. Satisfied, she put the phone down and reached for the wardrobe again. The final three outfits were a pretty, purple, one-shouldered dress, with one full-length sleeve – another possibility, thought Cora – a white knitted maxi-dress (quickly dismissed for being too 'Snow Queen'), and a grey silk shift with a low-cut back.

Cora picked up the black, purple and grey dresses for a second time, laid them all out on the bed and gazed at them for a full minute. Then, still undecided, she sighed and went to run a deep, bubbly bath. A minute later, she returned to the bedroom, opened the mini-bar and grabbed a quarter-bottle of champagne. She looked at the dresses once more and made a snap decision.

'I choose – you,' she said dramatically, pointing at the grey shift. Then she and her champagne headed off for a delicious soak.

An hour and a half later, she brushed on a final coat of mascara and checked her reflection in the full-length mirror on the back of the hotel room door. The soft grey silk skimmed her curves, the scooped back showing off her lightly bronzed skin (courtesy of a subtle spray tan expertly applied by Rosie two nights earlier). Her favourite, diamond cuff bracelet, grey skyscraper-high Vivienne Westwood heels, and a studded clutch bag completed the look. Satisfied, but feeling more than a little nervous despite the champagne, Cora grabbed her coat and headed off for her date with Benjamin Boland.

22

'A *traffic* exhibition? Seriously? You're winding me up!'

Benjamin laughed, perfect teeth flashing, and Cora grinned back at him.

'Seriously. There's loads of them. Road traffic technology. I had to do a live broadcast from the NEC with traffic cones and make them sound interesting, I kid you not. I get all the glamorous jobs, you know.'

Benjamin shook his head in amazement and held out his glass. 'Well, cheers to you then, Miss Baxter. You're even more brilliant than I thought you were!'

They clinked glasses, and Benjamin gestured to a passing waiter for another bottle of champagne. Cora leaned back in her seat, relaxed and more cheerful than she'd felt in ages. Who would have thought it? Her date was actually incredibly good company – charming, funny, and intelligent, and a lot less arrogant than his TV persona suggested. Obviously a little vain, but she was starting to suspect he wasn't quite as outrageously confident as he seemed. He was quite sweet actually. Delighted that she'd agreed to go out with him, Cora sipped her drink happily as Benjamin told her about the antics of his crew on a recent filming trip to Lapland. Justin – Justin who?

They'd been swapping television tales for nearly two hours now, ensconced in a cosy booth with purple velvet sofas in the VIP area of a trendy hotel. It was actually the after-party of the latest Guy Ritchie film premiere, although they hadn't gone to the film itself. Instead, Benjamin had taken her for a delicious meal at Claridges, before suggesting they pop in at the party on the way home.

Cora had been amused and slightly horrified when they were papped on the red carpet on the way in – photographers didn't normally bother her when she was alone, but as Benjamin Boland's date she was suddenly, it seemed, fair game. Thankful she was wearing a nice dress, she'd pulled her stomach in and posed like a pro, Benjamin's arm protectively round her shoulder.

Once inside, he'd whizzed her round the room at breakneck speed, exchanging hearty handshakes and air kisses with supermodels, soap stars, and Premiership footballers, before whisking her into the VIP area. And there they'd sat, sipping Dom Pérignon and nibbling on arty finger food, oblivious to the wall-to-wall celebrities around them.

To his credit, Benjamin had waited until the date had been at least two hours old before he'd mentioned diarrhoea. Eyes sparkling mischievously, he'd leaned across the restaurant table and hissed: 'So – any joy with that cleaning job then?'

Cora had stared at him, bemused.

'Pardon? What cleaning job?'

'You know – the one in the home. For the people with that awful incurable condition. The one you said you'd rather do than sleep with me.'

He'd grinned widely as Cora blushed beetroot red.

'OK, OK, I suppose I owe you an explanation,' she'd muttered, mortified. And quickly, without going into too much gory detail, she'd explained about Justin and the baby thing.

'It was just bad timing – and an unfortunate turn of phrase, you know, when you asked me to go and make babies. I didn't mean I don't want to sleep with you. Er, not that I'm suggesting I do, of course,' she stuttered, blushing furiously again.

'Of course not,' he'd replied, raising an amused eyebrow.

Then to Cora's immense relief, he'd taken pity on her, stopped teasing, squeezed her hand and changed the subject.

Now, her embarrassment forgotten, she tried not to think about how incredibly attractive he was as they chatted, knees gently touching under the table in a way that kept making her stomach do little somersaults.

'So – how did you get the *Morning Live* job in the first place? You said you started in regional news, right?'

Cora nodded. 'Yep. Newspapers first, then local TV news. Then I saw a job ad for an overnight producer on the national breakfast show and got a six-month contract. I never really wanted to be a producer, but it seemed like a good way in. The night shifts were awful though – I hated them.'

Benjamin nodded sympathetically and topped up their glasses. Cora watched him, trying to ignore the young *EastEnders* star and her pop singer boyfriend frantically making out in the next booth. She dragged her attention back to the conversation as the girl vanished under the table. Good grief!

'Anyway …' she continued. 'When a reporter job came up I applied and because Jeanette already knew me and – amazingly – sort of trusted me, she gave me the job. And here I am!'

'You're here – but she isn't, eh? Weird, that murder thing, wasn't it?' Benjamin said. 'Police got any ideas yet?'

Cora shook her head. 'If they have, they're not telling us. I'm supposed to be doing regular updates for the programme, but there's been practically nothing to report so far. She wasn't exactly popular though – did you ever meet her?'

'Several times.' Benjamin grinned. 'She was definitely a ballbreaker. I could see straight away why she had such a bad reputation in the industry – no interpersonal skills at all, really quite unpleasant. She tried to get me involved in *Morning Live* a while back, did you know that? Wanted me to do holiday cover for Jeremy what's-his-name, said it would attract a younger female audience. Couldn't pay me enough though. I don't do getting up early, and I don't do sitting on sofas. That show would bore the pants off me. No offence.'

His eyes twinkled and Cora punched him gently on the arm. Wow, muscles, she thought, and then turned as there was a sudden commotion at the entrance to the VIP area. Tara Kilcoyne, the British acting sensation who'd just landed her first role in a Hollywood blockbuster, flounced in, her killer figure barely covered in a tiny sequinned minidress. She was flanked by three hugely tall men in black suits and, despite it being night time, indoors and dimly lit, dark sunglasses.

Strutting towards the bar, she spotted Benjamin, pouted and waved a skinny hand bearing an enormous emerald ring, then wiggled past.

'You know her, then?' Cora looked down at her own modest dress, feeling a little inadequate.

'Oh, not really. We had a snog once at some do. It was ages ago, before she hit the big time. She's gorgeous, but thick as a ... thick thing. Anyway – what were we talking about?'

'Er ... career paths, I think! So what about you? How did you get to be TV's action hero?'

Benjamin shrugged modestly and gave her a quick summary of his journey from personal fitness trainer to TV star.

'Right place, right time. Used to train this TV producer, and when she heard about this new travel show that wanted an unknown she suggested I audition. And the rest is history.'

Cora was right though. Benjamin Boland was, at thirty-five, becoming a bit of a British TV legend. Host for the past five years of the BBC's flagship adventure travel show, *Go!*, he revelled in the exhilarating and often perilous activities the show demanded of him. The prime-time programme had been launched as an antidote to the tired old travel show format in which presenters did nothing more exciting than wander along beaches and sip cocktails in glamorous locations. *Go!* was entirely different, with its team of presenters, led by Benjamin, travelling to some of the most remote destinations in the world. Five years on, he was rarely out of the papers or off the 'Sexiest Man on TV' lists. Plus, with his fat fee – which he'd managed to re-negotiate *again* this year despite all the budget cuts in TV nowadays – as well as all the cash from guest appearances and celebrity magazine deals, he was making a small fortune. He was at the top of his game, and he was loving it.

'It's peculiar though, isn't it, this fame thing,' Cora was saying.

'I mean, I only get recognised a bit, but you must get it non-stop.'

Benjamin nodded. 'I do. But I don't mind. It has lots of advantages. Good restaurant tables, party invitations,

130

money … I'm not complaining.'

Cora swallowed a tiny parmesan biscuit with a quail's egg on top. Despite the large meal she'd had earlier, she was definitely starting to feel a little inebriated. She picked up another biscuit, hoping the nibbles would soak up the booze. Next door, the *EastEnders* actress finally emerged from underneath the table grinning tipsily, wiping her mouth, hair in disarray and lipstick smeared. Her boyfriend, one hand doing up his trousers, high-fived her with the other, and the two of them burst into raucous laughter.

Cora dragged her eyes back to Benjamin and carried on talking. 'For me, the worst is when people who don't know me ask what I do for a living. And then, when I say I'm on telly, they say "Well, I've never seen you!" in a really accusing sort of way, as if I'm making it up. So I say, "Well, do you watch *Morning Live?*" and they say "no", so I say, "well if you don't actually watch the show that I work on, of course you haven't seen me". It all gets very … er … tedious …'

Her voice tailed off as she suddenly realised Benjamin was looking very amused. 'Sorry – I tend to go on a bit when I drink champagne,' she giggled.

Benjamin shook his head and laughed with her. 'No, it's great just to have a normal conversation with somebody for a change. The women I usually date, well – they just want to know what sort of car I drive and who I can introduce them to. You're a breath of fresh air, honestly.'

Cora flushed. 'I suppose when you're in the same business, it's different. You're not so easily impressed, because you know it's just a job really.'

'And a tough job,' Benjamin said. 'I've lost count of the number of times I've let my friends down, I'm always having to cancel plans at the last minute because of work – that's the downside I guess.'

'You and me both!' Cora drained her glass. 'But at least if you're both in the industry, you understand. Justin wasn't, and he ended up hating my job. Anyway, enough about him …'

'Indeed.' Benjamin leaned forward, picked up Cora's hand

and stroked it gently, and she responded by moving closer, her eyes soft.

'So, Cora Baxter. Fancy going somewhere a little quieter? Get to know each other properly? And no baby-making, I promise.'

Cora paused, visions of Justin racing through her head. Then she took a deep breath and made up her mind.

'I think that sounds like a very good idea, Mr Boland,' she whispered.

And without another word, they slipped out of the party, hailed a taxi and headed for the South Bank.

23

Trying to move as little as possible, Benjamin reached a hand from under the duvet, groped on his bedside table for a slim black remote control, and pressed a button. Almost silently, the white blinds on the huge window opposite started to open, the weak mid-morning sunshine brightening the big room.

He pressed stop and dropped the remote on the floor, as Cora moaned softly next to him. He leaned over and kissed her softly on the forehead.

'Sorry, sleepy-head. I was trying not to wake you. Coffee?'

Cora blinked and rubbed her eyes, grimacing as she realised she hadn't done a very good job of taking off her make-up last night, despite Benjamin's extremely well stocked bathroom cabinet.

'Never touch the stuff. Got any Earl Grey tea?' Her voice was hoarse and she cleared her throat and tried again. 'Earl Grey, black, no sugar. If possible?'

'Think I've got some somewhere. Back in a jiffy. Don't go anywhere.'

'I won't.' Cora watched sleepily as Benjamin slipped out from under the heavy, white duvet and padded across the thick carpet, stark naked. Wow. Incredible body. Great thighs. And, er, other things. She felt herself blushing yet again as she remembered the events of last night, and pulled the duvet over her head in sudden embarrassment. Gosh. She'd slept with Benjamin Boland. What on earth had come over her?

She squeezed her eyes tightly shut, trying to work out how she was feeling. Physically, definitely a bit hung over. Dry mouth, slightly pounding head. Could be worse, though.

133

Amazing, considering how much champagne she'd put away last night. But how was she feeling, well, emotionally? She pondered for a moment. Well, she definitely liked him, quite a lot actually. He was so different from his telly image, and he'd treated her so well last night, been such a gentleman. But she *never* normally slept with anyone on the first date. Rebound sex, that's what it had been. Good sex though. Bloody incredible sex, actually …

'One Earl Grey tea, black. Here you go.'

Cora emerged from the duvet, still feeling a little hot and bothered, and sat up cautiously, suddenly aware that she was naked in a very bright room with an equally naked man.

'Er, thanks. Very kind,' she murmured, and reached out for the smoked glass mug with one hand, the other clutching the duvet to her chest.

'Pleasure,' Benjamin said, smiling at her, his large penis bobbing slightly. Cora gulped down a mouthful of tea. He really was extraordinarily body-confident.

She averted her eyes slightly, trying to concentrate on her drink, as he slipped back into bed and edged closer to her. Then she nearly choked as a finger started to stroke its way up her thigh in seductive circles.

'Erm – I think I'd better put this tea down. Don't want to spill it on your nice bedding,' she spluttered.

'Good idea, Ms Baxter. Excellent in fact,' whispered Benjamin.

Cora leaned over and carefully placed the mug on her bedside table. 'What *am* I doing?' she thought. For a moment she paused, unsure. But the circling finger was too much.

'Oh sod it!' And all shyness forgotten, she pushed the duvet off and flung herself on top of the grinning, gorgeous man beside her.

Adam looked at the clock. 11 a.m. already. He pushed a few piles of paper around his desk in a half-hearted attempt to tidy it, then gave up and slumped back in his chair, feeling gloomy.

He'd questioned Scott Edson himself earlier today,

determined to get to the truth about why his van had been in the wrong place at the wrong time on the day of Jeanette Kendrick's murder. The man had been cagey and defensive, finally saying he'd popped in to see a friend on the way home and didn't think it was important enough to mention it before. He'd refused to give the friend's name, saying he didn't want him or her involved, and without any real evidence, there wasn't much more Adam could do. He simply didn't believe that was all there was to it, but with his team still working on tracing the van's movements, he had no proof Scott had returned to TV Centre. Not yet, anyway.

'We'll be talking to you again. Don't leave the country,' he'd snapped, as the surly engineer marched out of the interview room.

Now Adam groaned and rubbed his eyes. Sodding murders. Who'd be a cop, eh?

On the South Bank, Cora waved again to Benjamin as her cab pulled away from his apartment block and then sank back in her seat, simultaneously thrilled and exhausted.

She started to dial Sam's number then stopped herself. Maybe not in a taxi. Too many deliciously naughty details to share – the taxi driver had already given her an interested look when he'd recognised the TV star who'd waved her off. No, no phone calls yet. She'd go back to her hotel, get out of last night's clothes and pick up her car, then zoom home to Cheltenham first.

The cab stopped at a red light and a heavily pregnant woman in a straining black coat shuffled across the road, pushing a screaming toddler in a buggy. Cora's mind wandered back to last night, when Benjamin had pointed out a pregnant footballer's wife at the party and then apologised for bringing up kids again.

'Oh don't worry, honestly. I know you probably think I'm weird not to want them,' she'd said hesitantly. 'I just never have. You know when you're young and people ask you how many children you'd like to have? Even when I was about

135

twelve, I was always surprised that everyone just assumed you'd have them – I always said none! And everyone always told me I'd change my mind, but I never have. And never will.'

To her great relief, Benjamin had simply nodded and agreed with her. 'Don't blame you. They're not for everyone. And certainly no room for them in MY life – too busy having fun!'

Cora sighed a happy sigh, gazing out of the window at the Saturday crowds as the taxi slowly weaved its way through the London traffic. She suddenly realised she hadn't thought of Justin for hours. He hadn't replied to her message from last night either, but suddenly she didn't care. Good. It was about time she forgot all about him and got on with her life. If Justin *was* involved in Jeanette's murder, let the police sort it out. She was going to be a little bit too busy to care. Benjamin Boland, she decided, might well be very good for her indeed.

24

'Rodney – can you just test the boom for me?' Scott's voice came through the soundman's earpiece.

'Sure. OK – talking into the dog now. Talking into the dog, talking into the dog …'

The man who was standing nearby dressed in a big game hunter's outfit stared at Rodney, and started looking around in a confused manner. Rodney gestured to the grey, fluffy microphone cover on the end of his boom pole.

'No, mate, this is what we call a dog, don't worry!'

Cora laughed. 'Technical terminology,' she explained, and the man smiled, still looking a little puzzled, then wandered off to take a call as his phone rang.

Cora shivered. She was wearing a khaki suit too, completely inappropriate for the freezing weather.

'Brrr. I'm going to sit in the truck, I'm so cold,' she said. 'I swear Sam is turning into Jeanette – can't believe she made me wear this!'

Rodney, snug in a shockingly ugly, pea green ski jacket, grinned. 'Yep, she's making the most of being the boss, isn't she? Suits you though. Go on, I'll mind the kit. But send Scott out here with a couple of cuppas for me and matey boy, will ya?'

Cora nodded and skipped off to the satellite truck, silently cursing the locals who'd claimed they'd seen a crocodile swimming in a Gloucestershire river over New Year and drawn it to the attention of the breakfast show. As a result, Cora had spent her Sunday trying to track down a crocodile expert and trawling fancy dress shops to find them both costumes for this morning's broadcast.

She hopped into the truck, where Scott and Nathan were involved in a heated discussion about the merits of one X-box football game over another, and slid into the passenger seat, leaning forward and waving her stiff fingers in front of the heating vents in an effort to defrost them.

Her phone beeped and she slid it out of her pocket awkwardly. A text.

Morning, gorgeous. Looking sexy in your croc hunter suit on my telly. I'm still in bed – wish you were here. B x

Cora's heart skipped a beat. Lustful text messages had been flying back and forth between her and Benjamin since she'd left him on Saturday, and she was thoroughly enjoying herself.

She giggled as she tapped out a reply.

Scott and Nathan stopped talking and watched her.

'Oooh, who's a smitten kitten then? No prizes for guessing who's got you acting like a schoolgirl,' cooed Nathan.

'Shut up,' Cora said, then raised her eyes heavenward as Scott reached for his copy of the *Mirror* newspaper and waved page five at her for the sixth time that morning.

'Scott, put that away and bring Rodney and the guest some drinks, will you? Please?'

'Oh alright.' He threw the paper at her and she caught it, smoothing it out to look again at the photo that had brought her so much teasing. It was a paparazzi shot from Friday night, Benjamin looking tall and handsome, her leaning into him, both of them looking very happy under the cheesy headline, which read 'COR-A! WHAT A COUPLE!'

'No chance of keeping anything quiet when you go out with someone like him, is there?' Scott said over his shoulder as he spooned coffee into two mugs.

'I s'pose not. I don't mind really though. It could be quite good fun,' Cora mused.

She tore the page out carefully and slipped it into her pocket. Whatever happened with Benjamin, it would be a nice keepsake. She glanced through the rest of the paper, pausing halfway through to read a tiny, three-paragraph article about

Jeanette's murder. It said little, only that police still had no idea who killed her, were continuing to question a number of people and were appealing for more help from the public. From being front-page news for the first few days, the story was slipping further and further down the news agenda. Cora knew that if there was nothing new to report soon, the papers would finally lose interest altogether.

Scott glanced at the page as he headed for the door, clutching two steaming drinks.

'Mention me, does it?' he said sarcastically.

'No, of course not. Look – don't worry, Scott. The police will soon stop pestering you, I'm sure. We all know you didn't do it!'

'They've got channel vision when it comes to me. They think I did it, and that's that. Whatever,' Scott muttered, and marched off, coffee slopping onto the grass.

'Tunnel. Tunnel vision,' Cora whispered, as Nathan followed Scott outside, grimacing at her as he went.

She watched them go and sighed. Scott was not a happy man, but there wasn't much she could do to help if he wouldn't talk to any of them. He'd told them earlier that he'd been questioned by the police again over the weekend, but had refused to say why, getting so irritated when they tried to get more details out of him that they'd simply given up. He was definitely hiding something – but what?

Cora's phone beeped again, and she instantly stopped worrying and looked at it eagerly, expecting another message from Benjamin.

'Oh.' It wasn't a text, but a tweet. Disappointed, she clicked on it anyway, expecting a silly comment from a viewer about her choice of outfit. Then, a little shiver ran up her spine as she read the short message.

@a-friend @CoraBaxterMLive Cora, I got your msg. But a warning for you. Be very careful. Watch your back.

What? Maddened, she quickly typed a reply.

@CoraBaxterMLive @a-friend What do you mean, be careful? Is that a threat? What the hell is going on, Justin?

She waited. Nothing. Angrily, she tossed her phone into her handbag, her good mood ruined. OK, she had sort of threatened him, she reasoned, by saying she might go to the police. So maybe he was playing the same game. Fine. If he was going to be childish, let him.

'Two minutes, Cora.' A voice buzzed in her earpiece. Bracing herself against the cold, she reluctantly stepped out of the warm truck and stomped off across the grass to join her crew.

25

'There's only one thing for it. We're going to have to cut the whole side of the car off. Sit back as far as you can mate, and don't move.'

The fireman stood back, decision made, and his colleagues nodded. Nearby an ashen-faced taxi driver looked on in horror as a huge electric cutting tool started whirring. Inside the silver Mercedes, the anguished face of an enormously fat man in a multi-coloured shirt stared out at the assembled group, pink with humiliation.

Huddled together on the pavement outside TV Centre, Cora and a gaggle of researchers and producers watched, agog.

'So – tell me again – WHAT happened?' Cora hissed.

'Well ... he's the guest for the 8.40 alternative health slot – some sort of naturopathy expert. You know, all the sort of natural treatments – homeopathy and so on?' Angela, a young researcher, turned her brown eyes on Cora expectantly.

'Yes, yes, I know.'

'So. He lives in Reading, so we send a car. He did tell us on the phone last night that he was quite – well – large, and specifically asked for a big car, so we booked the Merc. Anyway, the driver says he got in OK, just about – he had to give him a bit of a shove, apparently, but he fitted through the door fine.' She paused as the screech from the electric saw reached ear-splitting levels.

'Gosh. I hope they've given him earplugs. Anyway – they drive from Reading to London, and pull up here, and well, he can't get out. The driver tried pulling him, and then called the newsroom and a few of us came down and opened the other

141

door and tried pushing him. But he literally couldn't fit through the door. It's like he swelled up on the journey or something.'

Cora spluttered. 'Oh come on! That's impossible, surely.'

Angela shook her head. 'Well, either that or the door's shrunk. That's why the fire brigade have to cut the whole side off. They tried just taking the door off but he still couldn't get out. Now they're taking away that bar thing between the back and front doors as well. Car's going to be massacred. Poor driver – looks like he's about to pass out ...'

Cora glanced at the man, who did indeed look extremely pale, and then turned away quickly to conceal her giggles.

'Crikey. Only on *Morning Live*, eh!' she snorted.

She looked at her watch. 'Damn, it's half eight. I need to get going – I'm going upstairs to grab my stuff, presume I can tell Sam she'll need another 8.40?'

'She already knows, don't worry. Don't think this poor man will be in any fit state to talk healing when he gets out of there ...'

Still giggling, Cora made her way back up to the newsroom. She'd had to come down to London in the early hours yet again to do a quick turn on the sofa talking about the latest unemployment figures, and as usual she was exhausted. It was, however, weariness tempered with some excitement, because last night Benjamin had called to say he HAD to see her again and would join her this evening, no matter where in the country she happened to be.

'Ooooh.' Cora hugged herself as the lift travelled up to the seventh floor. She was still amazed by how much she liked him, as well as being incredibly flattered that he seemed so keen on her.

Already fantasising about tonight, she wandered dreamily into the newsroom and went to gather her bag, coat and phone from Christina's desk where she'd dumped them earlier.

The young producer was in a huddle with two of the runners and jumped when Cora appeared at her side.

'Oh, Cora, thank goodness. I thought you were Alice for a minute.'

'Ooh, why, are you talking about her? What's the gossip then?'

'Oh, nothing really. She's just been such a *cow* recently. Honestly, since Jeanette died I reckon Alice is trying to take over as Queen Bitch. She's so rude to all of us, even ruder than she used to be. She's unbearable, seriously, Cora.'

'Gosh, I'm sorry to hear that. Ignore her. She's just an attention-seeker. I've got to go – see you soon, keep smiling!'

'Bye, Cora. Get some sleep, you look knackered.' Christina paused and pointed to the copy of yesterday's *Mirror* on her desk.

'Oh – and Benjamin Boland! Nice one, Cora. Very nice!'

The three girls giggled and Cora grinned soppily. There was no getting away from it, her new relationship was public property. Too happy to care, she bounced out of the room and headed for home.

Down at the other end of the newsroom Adam Bradberry, who'd popped in for another chat with TV Centre's security officers, had also spotted the *Mirror* picture.

'I thought she'd have more taste, really,' he thought, then put the paper down, wondering why he felt slightly disconcerted. He had a few minutes to kill before Bob, the security guard who'd found Jeanette's body, was due on duty, so he wandered into the late editor's still-empty office and stood at the window, gazing down at the ground below.

'What happened here?' he murmured. 'What the hell happened, and why is it taking me so long to figure it out?'

It was a solid motive that was really eluding the investigation team. Although Jeanette, it seemed, had been universally disliked professionally, there seemed to be nobody in her life with a strong enough reason to want to kill her. Her father had died some years ago, she got on well with her mother, and she even had a decent circle of friends outside work, who all said she was very different socially to how she was perceived in the TV industry. A bit of a sweetie, a couple of them had even said.

'She was just a tough boss who wasn't that popular with her colleagues,' Adam thought, as he looked again at the spot where her sprawled body had lain. 'Nothing very unusual in that. Who hated her enough to want to get rid of her?'

He turned as he heard a loud sniff behind him. Alice Lomas was standing in the doorway, a tear running down her perfectly powdered cheek.

'Hello. You OK?'

'Fine. Just … yes, I'm fine. Just – Jeanette, you know. Sorry.'

She turned sharply and scurried away, shapely bottom straining against her tight blue wool dress. Adam watched her for a minute, then checked himself and looked at his watch. Time to do some work.

26

For once Cora was awake before her alarm. A sleeping Benjamin's arm thrown across her, her long legs entwined in his muscular ones, she smiled into the darkness of her Wolverhampton hotel room as she watched the clock tick towards 4 a.m.

'I feel happy,' she whispered to nobody. 'Really, really happy!'

True to his word, Benjamin had driven up from London last night after she'd phoned to tell him she was being sent to the Midlands. The assignment had been pretty grim – tasked with filming a story about the teenage yobs terrorising a housing estate, Cora, Nathan, and Rodney had at one stage had to take refuge in their locked car as the youths rampaged around them.

How blissful then, to return to the hotel just after 9 p.m. to find Benjamin already there, a room service trolley with chilled white wine, Irish soda bread, and smoked salmon parked in the bedroom, and the bathtub filling up with hot, scented water.

They'd fallen on each other like ravenous tigers, the food forgotten. Two hours later, they'd surfaced and sipped Sauvignon Blanc as they snuggled together on the big bed, telling each other their life stories. Now, as Cora reached out to shut off the alarm seconds before it started buzzing, she calculated she'd probably only had about two hours' sleep.

'And I don't care,' she said softly, and bent to drop a light kiss on Benjamin's tanned shoulder.

He stirred, opened one eye and smiled sleepily. 'Morning, gorgeous. You leaving me already?' His early morning voice was husky.

'Sorry. But I'll be off air at 8.30 and back here by 9, if you care to wait for me?'

Benjamin reached up and pulled her face down towards his. 'Just try and stop me,' he murmured.

It was closer to nine o'clock that evening when the day suddenly improved for Jeanette Kendrick's murder investigation team.

'Boss – can you come over for a minute? I think we've finally bloody got him!'

Adam looked up. Gary, slightly pink around the earlobes, waved at him from across the room. Karen, nervously biting her lip, hovered next to the monitor they'd been using to trawl through CCTV footage from the streets near TV Centre.

'Really? Ouch, dammit.' Adam nearly tripped over an overflowing wastepaper bin in his hurry to cross the room. 'You'll make my day if you have. Come on – put me out of my misery.'

'OK. So, to recap, Edson left the television building at approximately 7.40 a.m., should have been heading out west to go home but then we spotted his van at that garage on Southwark Bridge Road at 8.20, right?' Gary's words tumbled into each other in his haste to tell the story.

'Yes, yes. And when I questioned him he just said he'd gone to see a friend before going home and hadn't thought to mention it. So?'

Karen put a calming hand on Gary's shoulder and hit play on the control pad.

'Look, boss – here.' She pointed at the grainy image. 'We tracked his van, spotted it at various points on the ANPR cameras but nowhere really relevant. Until we found this. That's his van. It's not very clear, because it's almost out of range of the CCTV camera on the corner of that street, but we've enhanced the number plate so we're certain.' She hit pause and looked round at Adam.

'OK, I believe you – and the time on the screen is 0750. So, what, about ten minutes after he left TV Centre? So where is he – what street is that?'

Karen took a deep breath. 'It's Ditchley Street. It's small and there's nothing much there, but boss – it's two minutes' walk from TV Centre. And look.' She hit play again.

On the screen, a figure emerged from the van, paused for a minute as if looking around, and then walked quickly away.

'He's got a bag, look – over his shoulder. And he's walked off in the direction of TV Centre.'

Adam leaned forward, his heart beginning to pound slightly.

Gary took over again. 'And if we fast forward about twenty minutes – look. It's 0810, and he's back. Hops in to the van, still with that bag, and drives off. Probably to that garage we saw him at, the timing is right.'

'Sooo – he leaves TV Centre in a foul temper. Parks up the van in this little – Ditchley Street did you say? Grabs a bag with – what? Gloves? Some sort of disguise? Walks the two minutes back to TV Centre, gets back up to the seventh floor via the stairs, wanders into Kendrick's office without anyone noticing – they all know he was around that morning for his disciplinary so nobody would bat an eyelid – kills her, walks out again, and back to the van. All in twenty minutes. Then heads to that petrol garage, it's probably the nearest one if he was low on fuel, and then off he goes. It's doable, isn't it?'

'We're going to go out and check the timings now – park up and do the walk ourselves, up into the office and back again, just in case we're wrong. But yes, I think it's doable. He did it, boss, I'm sure he did.'

'OK. Good work, guys. Brilliant work. Do the checks tonight, and if you're sure as you can be, we'll nab him first thing in the morning.'

Gary and Karen grinned at each other. Adam smiled at them, then wandered thoughtfully back to his desk. It sounded right, it looked right. But did it feel right? He wanted it to, but he wasn't entirely sure. And at the moment, he couldn't put his finger on why.

27

Thursday 18th January

If the residents of a certain Midlands street were trying to have a lie-in on this Thursday morning, they were out of luck. The howls of laughter coming from the satellite truck parked halfway along it were currently so loud it was amazing nobody had called the local council's noise abatement team.

'A hooker? Wow, Scott, your luck's changed hasn't it?'

Nathan, grinning widely, thumped Scott on the back as Rodney wiped tears of delight from under his little glasses. Cora joined in, delighted that everyone was in as good a mood as she was this morning. Since Benjamin Boland came into her life things had definitely looked up.

Scott pushed Nathan away good-humouredly. 'Yes, a friggin' prossie! There I am, minding my own business, sitting in the truck having a cuppa and she knocks on the window. And when I said no thanks, she got all offended! Demanded to know what I was doing sitting here at 4 a.m. if I didn't want business! I mean, how was I to know it was smack in the middle of a sodding red light district – thanks for the warning, Cora!'

'I didn't know either! They're not labelled on the map, you know!'

The boys laughed again.

They were on location in Birmingham this morning, broadcasting from a newsagent's that had been the victim of an armed robbery last weekend. Remarkably, seventy-eight-year-old proprietor Asha Gupta had managed to beat the would-be robber off with a broom handle. Snug in the truck between hits, and sipping the delicious hot chocolate Mrs Gupta had just brought out to them on a tray, Cora gazed contentedly out of the slightly steamy window as the boys carried on teasing Scott. It was so good to hear him laughing – maybe whatever had been bothering him had been sorted out at last and they could get back to normal. He certainly seemed happier today.

Outside, the early morning traffic was starting to build, moving slowly past the once elegant redbrick Victorian terraces, the paint around their bay windows now cracked and dirty, the brickwork stained. The prostitutes had gone now, home to sleep off the night, and instead bleary-eyed people were emerging from their homes, walking briskly towards bus stops, dragging recalcitrant children with trailing schoolbags, reclaiming their streets and starting their morning.

'Nothing in the papers about old bitch-face's murder at all the past few days,' Rodney mumbled through a mouthful of Jaffa Cake. He flicked through the last few pages of *The Sun*, threw it onto the pile in the corner and picked up the *Mail*.

'Not surprised. I knew that would happen. I've been nagging Adam Bradberry for news every day and he's had nothing for me,' Cora sighed. 'Looks like they've hit a dead end, eh?'

She turned to look at Scott just in time to see a flash of irritation cross his face. 'Sorry, Scott, I know you've had just about enough of Jeanette. Let's change the subject, OK?'

'S'alright, don't worry,' Scott muttered. He grabbed a pen from the pot on the side and reached for *The Times*. 'I'm going to do the crossword – see if I can finish it by the time you lot come off air.'

Cora, Rodney and Nathan exchanged surreptitious glances. Touchy, touchy, thought Cora. Hmmm. Maybe he's not feeling better after all. She took another sip of her drink and leaned back wearily in her seat, eyes returning to the street outside. At the door of her shop just across the road Mrs Gupta, her beautiful, peacock blue silk sari worn rather incongruously with a tatty, thick, navy cardigan, was chatting excitedly to three younger women, snippets of the conversation floating through the chilly air.

'We saw you – on the telly! You're famous!'

'Ah now ... have to do it again in half an hour. Lovely they

150

are though, the crew. Treating me really nice … come in, come in, it's cold!'

The group disappeared through the shop door just as a police car pulled up outside. Cora watched idly as two officers got out, straightening their jackets. Then she sat up, suddenly aware of something.

'Hey, look, Nath. That's a Met Police car. Bit out of its patch, isn't it?'

'Oh yeah!' Nathan leaned across her to peer out of the window. 'Wonder what … hang on. They're coming over … '

Cora put her mug down carefully on the dashboard. They all looked at each other, three of them puzzled, Scott suddenly pale.

'Scott – what is it? Are you OK?'

He didn't answer, and Cora felt a little lurch of fear. BANG! BANG! She jumped at the loud knock on the satellite truck's sliding door. Rodney slid it open.

'Scott Edson?' The taller of the two policemen barked his question at Rodney, who instinctively took a step back.

'No – I'm Scott Edson.' The engineer's voice was uncharacteristically quiet.

The other officer stepped into the truck, pulled out some handcuffs and in one swift movement snapped them on to Scott's wrist.

'In that case – Scott Edson, I'm arresting you on suspicion of the murder of Jeanette Kendrick. You do not have to say anything, but it may harm your defence if you do not mention when questioned something which you later rely on in court. Anything you do say may be given in evidence.'

Cora gasped as Scott, white-faced and silent, half-walked and was half-dragged from the truck. Rodney was rooted to the spot, eyes huge behind his glasses. Only Nathan seemed able to speak.

'But – officers – seriously? You're arresting him for *murder*? Is this some sort of joke? And we're in the middle of a live broadcast. What are we supposed to do now?'

'Sorry, sir. But we're in the middle of a murder enquiry. I

think that rather takes precedence, don't you?' the taller policeman said tersely over his shoulder. He started to cross the road, his colleague gripping Scott firmly.

'Hang on – please, just one minute,' Scott begged, his voice hoarse.

The officers paused. Scott turned to look at his friends, his eyes anguished.

'Guys – I'm so sorry about this. I need to talk to you … tell you something …'

'Come on, that's enough. Save your telling for the station.' The policemen led Scott briskly across the road, the taller one holding up his hand to stop the traffic, and bundled him into the back of their car. A minute later, it sped off down the road and was gone.

Feeling weak with shock, Cora sank back onto her seat. Rodney was still standing stock still, wide-eyed. Nathan ran his hands frantically through his hair.

'What the hell? Seriously – they can't be serious – can they?'

'I hope not, Nathan. I mean, he didn't do it, I don't believe he did for a minute. But – they've kept coming back to him, haven't they? There must be a reason, it can't just be because he punched a lift. And he was so angry that day, Nathan. I'm scared …'

Cora's voice tailed off.

'There's no way. No way. Not Scott.' Rodney somehow found his voice.

'And – what do we do now, Cora? We're on again in fifteen minutes.'

Cora pulled herself together and sat up. 'Well, that's not going to happen, is it, without Scott? I'll ring the desk and tell them what's happened, they'll just have to drop the last hit. Nathan – can you ring the programme organiser? They'll have to send another engineer to pick up the truck. And Rodney – go and see Mrs Gupta, apologise – you know the score.'

The boys nodded and stepped sombrely out of the truck, Nathan grabbing his phone as he went.

152

Cora picked hers up too and hit the speed dial for the news desk, suddenly realising her hands were shaking slightly.

'Sam? Sam, it's Cora. You're never going to guess what's just happened ...'

Two minutes later, she and a shocked Sam agreed the next step was to speak to the police and see if they could get any more information. If charges were imminent, this was going to be a huge story.

'It can't be real though, Sam. They won't charge Scott – not with murder. I know him, he's a gentle giant. He wouldn't hurt anyone.'

Sam sighed down the phone. 'Cora, I admire your loyalty and I can only imagine how hard this must be for you, you guys have been friends for years. But the simple hard truth is he's been arrested on suspicion of murder. Of the murder of *our boss*. And it doesn't matter who he is, we have to treat this like we would any other arrest on a high profile murder case. Talk to the cops, get all the details and we'll run it as a news flash. I'm sorry Cora, I have no choice.'

'I know. OK, I'll call you straight back.'

With a heavy heart, Cora dialled Adam's number. She didn't feel much better after she'd spoken to him.

'Well?' Nathan was standing at the open door of the truck, watching her. 'What are the cops saying?'

'Nothing really. He was really abrupt. Just confirmed Scott was to be questioned later today on suspicion of murder, and he'd tell the press as soon as there was anything more to say. This is just bloody awful, Nathan. I feel sick.'

'Come here.' Nathan stretched out his arms and Cora stepped out of the truck and into his comforting embrace.

'It'll be OK. Our Scott didn't do anything, I'm sure of it. It's a pigment of their imagination, as he'd say.'

Cora couldn't even raise a smile.

'There's something going on with him, we know that. But not this. It can't be, I refuse to believe it.' Nathan pulled Cora closer.

'Me too. But I'm frightened, Nath. I don't like this.' Her

words were muffled by her cameraman's thick fleece as she buried her face in his shoulder.

Nathan stroked her hair. 'Nor do I, babe. Nor do I.'

28

'Sweet dreams tonight Cora – dirty ones hopefully! Filthy, in fact. But not diarrhoea filthy – the good sort of filth!'

Nicole cackled as she wrapped her big, black scarf tightly round her neck, then leaned forward to kiss Cora on the cheek before stepping out into the icy evening.

'Oh, Nicole, you're so one-track minded!' Rosie giggled and gave Cora a hug, then followed Nicole outside. They linked arms and turned to wave as they crunched down the drive. Cora waved back and blew her friends a kiss, watching until they turned left onto the road and vanished. She was about to shut the door when something caught her eye – a shadow by the hedge at the end of the driveway. It moved briefly, then disappeared. Was somebody there?

Cora stared into the darkness for a moment, but the light from the streetlamps didn't penetrate far enough inside the gateway for her to see clearly. Then a movement by her right foot made her jump violently.

'Oliver! You nearly gave me a heart attack!'

The black cat peered haughtily up at her and walked disdainfully into the hall, swinging his tail.

Cora glared after him.

'Was that you, lurking down there by the gate?' she hissed. The cat, now bounding up the stairs towards his first floor home, ignored her.

'It WAS you, wasn't it?' Oliver's bottom disappeared round the bend in the stairs. Flipping heck, she was talking to cats' bottoms now. What next? She slapped herself on the cheek and closed the door firmly. But still feeling slightly uneasy, she bounded up the stairs to her apartment two at a time and double-locked her door.

Telling herself not to be paranoid, she quickly tidied away the debris of a late afternoon tea with the girls, poured herself a small glass of red wine and snuggled up on the sofa, pulling a fake fur throw over her knees. It was only six o'clock, she was as yet unassigned for tomorrow morning's programme and had been told that was unlikely to change, and *Midsomer Murders* would be on soon. A recipe for a perfect Sunday evening, if only she could quell the anxiety that kept bubbling up inside her.

She sipped her wine and lay back on the cushions, reflecting on the past few days as she waited for the programme to start. Friday had been weird – with a temporary satellite engineer taking Scott's place on the truck, Cora and the boys had been live outside the police station where their friend was being questioned. Having to tell the nation that a member of *Morning Live* staff had been arrested on suspicion of murder was one of the hardest things Cora had ever had to do.

'At least I didn't have to give his name – small mercies,' she thought, and took another deep gulp of Shiraz. Despite several calls to Adam and the police press office over the weekend, she'd gleaned nothing except that officers had been granted extra time in which to question Scott. But that time was running out. She did a quick calculation. He'd been arrested on Thursday morning – the 96-hour rule meant they'd have to either charge or release him by first thing tomorrow morning.

'Please, please let him be coming home,' she sighed, heaving herself off the sofa to top up her glass. Then she snuggled down again, pushing Scott out of her mind and smiling soppily. The rest of her weekend had been rather good. Pretty fantastic in fact.

Benjamin Boland. My boyfriend. Crikey. Who'd have thought it?

Her boyfriend was currently on a plane to Dubai. Placing his champagne glass carefully on the little table next to him, he

156

stretched luxuriously in his First Class seat and shut his eyes, mind drifting back to Friday night.

Cora had been distraught when she'd rung him on Thursday, tearfully telling the story about how her friend had been arrested. He'd tried his best to comfort her over the phone, and insisted that as soon as she finished work on Friday she come straight to his place so he could cheer her up properly. When she arrived not long after ten, pink-cheeked and damp and still a little emotional after a morning broadcasting from outside the police station, he had been surprised at the depth of feeling she stirred in him. Wrapping her in his arms, he'd vowed to get her smiling again by Sunday morning. Luckily, it didn't take that long, as they'd instantly fallen into bed and were both smiling rather broadly when they surfaced again at midday.

After tea and toast with Stilton and strawberry jam – an unusual combination that it turned out they both adored – they'd dragged themselves out of the apartment for a walk in Hyde Park. It had turned into a perfect winter afternoon, sunny and cold, and as they'd strolled hand in hand among the joggers, cyclists and nannies and parents with prams, Benjamin kept glancing sideways at his new girlfriend, fascinated by the way her eyes flashed an even brighter green in the winter sunlight. She'd grinned up at him and slipped her arm round his waist.

'What are you looking at, Mr Boland? In your, I have to say, rather strange hat.'

Cora giggled and reached up to pull the red and white striped monstrosity further down over his eyes.

'Oi!' Benjamin laughed and straightened it again. 'It's my disguise – nobody's ever bothered me when I wear this in public. I'm such a style king normally, no one would expect me to go out in this!'

'Dead right.' Cora yanked the hat down again and wriggled out of his grip, shrieking as he gave chase. She skidded to a halt at the bank of the Serpentine, snorting as Benjamin, still half-blinded by his hat, almost fell over a duck. He sank down onto a wooden bench and hauled her onto his knee, panting.

'Aargh. Out of breath just chasing you, you little minx. I'm supposed to be desert hiking in Dubai on Monday – you're wearing me out!'

Cora leaned in for a kiss and then squeezed his biceps through the thick wool of his jacket.

'Oh, I think you're pretty fit, I wouldn't worry too much!'

She slipped her arms around his neck and for a moment they sat in silence. Benjamin rubbed his nose against the soft skin of her neck, inhaling her musky scent. He hadn't felt like this for so long. He hadn't even looked at another woman for – what? – ten days now. Or maybe it was nine, since their first date? Anyway, he hadn't even thought of going out girl-hunting since he'd spent that first evening with Cora. And for him, that was a record. A first, in fact. And at the moment, he was quite happy with that. More than happy. Content, that was the word. Content just to spend his time with this one woman. It was a feeling he was not very familiar with, and he was very much hoping it would last.

'Right, Cora Baxter. It's freezing, and I need warming up. Time for tea?'

'Mmmm, yes!'

'Race you to the café then!'

They'd spent the rest of the day and night in a loved-up haze, eating, drinking, and laughing, when they weren't wrapped in each other's arms.

Now, with a few days of working abroad ahead of him, Benjamin drained his glass, waved away the steward who rushed over clutching a new bottle of Moët and pulled down his eye-mask. He'd ring her as soon as he landed, he vowed, and fell into a deep, contented sleep.

29

Monday 22rd January

'The member of Morning Live *staff arrested on suspicion of the murder of programme boss, Jeanette Kendrick, has this morning been released on bail pending further investigations, police have confirmed ...'*

Hugely relieved, Cora sank back onto her pillows as she watched Alice Lomas read the seven o'clock bulletin, her voice unusually tremulous as she mentioned Jeanette's name.

'Drama queen,' thought Cora. 'Surprised she hasn't burst into tears live on air, just for the attention.'

Nestling back into her warm bed, and luxuriating for another long moment in the joy of being unassigned on a Monday morning and actually watching the show from home for a change, Cora smiled to herself about Scott's release, then thought for a minute and started to worry again.

What was the wording Alice had used? 'Released on bail pending further investigations'? OK, so Scott was free. But that wasn't the same as being released without charge – all that meant was the police didn't have enough evidence to charge him. There was every chance he could be taken into custody again.

'Dammit, Scott, why won't you tell us what's going on?' Cora shouted to the empty room, and thumped her pillow.

She suddenly decided she couldn't wait a second longer. Grabbing her phone from the bedside table, narrowly avoiding knocking her water glass to the floor in the process, she punched in Scott's number and waited.

He answered within two rings.

'Cora! Hi. Yes, I'm out. It's been awful. You OK?'

159

'Shit, Scott, we've been worried sick! Scott, look …'

She paused, unsure what to say, and then ploughed on.

'Er, look, we've all been wondering what's going on. Not whether you were involved with Jeanette's murder, don't think that, we all know you couldn't have been.'

She started talking even faster, not giving him a chance to interrupt.

'But it's just … well, you've been acting so strangely recently. And being so evasive. And we know the police saw you thumping that lift because you were cross with Jeanette, but there has to be more to it, Scott. They wouldn't have zoomed in on you like this otherwise. You said when you were being arrested that you had something to tell us? We just want to help, but we can't if you won't tell us what's going on …'

Her voice tailed off. At the other end, Scott sighed heavily.

'Cora, I can only imagine what you've all been thinking. Look – I'm sorry I've been grumpy with everyone. I've just been really tired recently, you know, the hours getting to me. And then the disciplinaries and all that. It's just been doing my head in, that's all.'

He coughed and carried on. 'And about the cops, and what I wanted to tell you … well all it is, is that I wasn't entirely honest with them the first time they spoke to me. I said I went straight home that day, because what I actually did was call in to see a … er, a friend for a few minutes, and I didn't want to get the friend involved. And they found out – saw the van parked up on CCTV – and got suspicious, and thought I might have parked up to go back and shove old bitch-face out the window. But I didn't, honest.'

He paused.

'So – do they believe you now, the police?'

'Think so. Got the friend to agree to back me up after all so there's not much they can do. Think they still want me as prime suspect though, but there's no evidence. Mainly because I didn't do it, Cora.'

'Well, that's great.' She hesitated. 'And … is everything else OK? You know, at home and everything?'

'Fine. Everything's fine. And talking of home, I need to get back there. Elaine's going ballistic. I only got out of the cop shop an hour ago so I've been shovelling down bacon sarnies and coffee at Heston services. Cop shop food is shit. I should be back on the road tomorrow – see you then, OK?'

'OK, Scott. I'm so glad you're out. See you tomorrow. Drive carefully.'

'I will. Later, hun.'

Cora pressed the red button to end the call and stared at the ceiling, her mind working overtime. Scott's explanation seemed reasonable enough, but it didn't explain why he appeared to have sold half his possessions. And who was this 'friend'? Why would he not have mentioned him – or her – to the police on day one? Was he having an affair? None of it really made sense.

She exhaled heavily and clambered unwillingly out of bed. Her phone was bound to ring shortly with her story for the day, and she suddenly felt the need to soak away her worries in a long, hot bath. As she wriggled into her soft velour robe, her phone beeped. She glanced at the text and suddenly cheered up. Good morning, Benjamin!

'Er … Yorkshire? In an hour's time? I'm in Gloucestershire, Mark. Unless Concorde is back in service, and taking off from my driveway, the answer is no, I can't make the press conference.'

Cora raised her eyes heavenwards. Sometimes she despaired. Did the duty news editors ever actually look at a map? Although at least this one had a bit of an excuse, being an Australian freelancer.

'OK, no worries. We'll skip the presser. Back to plan A. Call me later when you're sorted.'

'Fine. Talk to you later.'

Cora grabbed her always-packed overnight bag, locked her front door and headed for Yorkshire. She'd only been on the road five minutes when the phone rang. She hit the button on her hands-free kit and Samantha Tindall's lilt filled the car.

'Hey, darlin', enjoy your lie-in today? It's been a while, eh?'

Cora hit the brakes as she spotted a speed camera a hundred yards ahead.

'Certainly has, thank you! And good news about Scott too. So how are things there?'

'Yeah, fine! Ellie on autocue staggered in still smashed at 4 a.m. and we had to send her home, but otherwise it was a reasonably sane morning. Hey, you were lucky though – the night team nearly called you at 2 a.m. to send you to Manchester on a story they found in the first editions – fat woman who lost twenty stone so she could donate a kidney to her best friend's dog. Hang on – that can't be right. Must have been niece or something …'

Cora laughed. 'Phew! Glad that didn't happen then. I *hate* diet stories – as Rodney so charmingly says, I'd rather sit on a bed of hot coals, plucking my pubic hairs out one by one!'

'Good old Rodney. Anyway – just checking you got the message about the flags. For the snails?'

'Yes, I got the message. That's my evening sorted then. Can't wait …'

'Sorry, love. Have fun, catch you later!'

'Bye, Sam.'

Later, in her snug hotel room, Cora laid out glue, scissors and paper on the desk and set to work, half-watching *Coronation Street* as she trawled through a pile of celebrity magazines to find the right faces. In the morning she'd be broadcasting live from a snail farm where they'd be filming a live snail race, and Cora's ludicrous task this evening was to make little flags to stick on the back of the snails, each bearing the face of a TV presenter or reality star.

'It's one of Clancy Carter's shows, actually,' she explained to a bemused Nathan who'd just checked in and popped by to say hello before he went to bed. '*Celebrity Cycle Challenge* – have you seen it?'

Nathan raised a quizzical eyebrow.

'OK, silly question, me neither. It's about a group of celebs cycling around the coast of Britain. It ends this week and we're supposed to be trying to predict the winner – whichever snail wins the race, that's the celeb who'll win the show … '

She tutted as she squeezed the glue tube a little too energetically, squirting a sticky mess onto the desk. Ignoring Nathan's smirk, she wiped it up with a tissue and then carefully stuck a picture of Davina McCall onto a tiny, flag-shaped piece of paper.

'There! Last one done!'

'That's mental. I would have thought we could stop promoting Clancy's shows now Jeanette's gone.'

'Yeah, I know. Think we'd already agreed to it though, so Sam's honouring the deal. Anyway, it's an indoor job at least. And the snail farm's promised to cook us breakfast, so count your blessings!'

'Fair enough. Long as they're not cooking the snails. Anyway – spoke to Scott earlier. He told me what he told you, and I agree, it's not really a proper explanation. I'm worried Cora. He's our mate, and I want to trust him, but it doesn't add up.'

Cora pushed her flags into a neat pile and nodded. 'I know. It's beyond me, Nath. Maybe Rodney can get something out of him, they've always been particularly close?'

'Yeah, maybe. I'll have a word. Anyway, sleep well. See you in Reception, 4.30 a.m.?'

'Night, Nathan.'

The cameraman closed the door quietly behind him. Cora yawned and flopped onto the bed. She'd just watch the end of Corrie then have a deliciously early night.

The person who had murdered Jeanette Kendrick was making neat notes on a red, leather-bound memo pad. The second victim, of course, had already been decided. Decided a long time ago. It was just the timing and the method that had to be selected. It would need to happen soon though. Once it was done, life would be great. No point in delaying too long. The police were clueless anyway. Get it done. And then back to nice, happy, normality. The killer shut the notebook with a satisfied smile.

30

'Sam – big train crash in the Alps!'

Christina tapped at her keyboard, frantically trying to get more information before the journalists around her started screaming for details. 'Right – it's in a big holiday resort area, so lots of skiers probably on it … '

'Brits?' barked Sam.

'Just looking … yes, it says dozens of British tourists thought to be on board …'

'Oh good. Are they dead?'

Cora, who'd been called to London yet again in the early hours and was standing behind Sam's chair waiting to have a quick chitchat, punched her friend on the shoulder.

'Sam, I swear you've been possessed by the ghost of Jeanette Kendrick! You get more like her every day.'

'Well hopefully I'll live a bit longer than she did – that's the plan anyway,' muttered Sam.

Cora smiled. Sam really was grabbing this opportunity with both hands. At just twenty-nine, she was a few years younger than Cora, but had risen through the ranks of producers at an astonishing rate, her sharp mind and unerring nose for a good story making her stand out from her contemporaries. She'd even been awarded a place on *Broadcast* magazine's annual 'hotshots' list a few months back, much to the delight of all her friends.

As Cora watched admiringly, Sam grabbed her phone and quickly assigned the programme's Europe correspondent to the story, then slammed it down and turned round with a grin.

'OK, my lovely, I can take fifteen minutes now. Canteen?'

'Sounds like a plan. You're loving it, Sam, aren't you? This job I mean. It's so nice to see.'

Sam nodded, her eyes bright.

'I really am. It sounds terrible, Cora, but whoever killed Jeanette did me a huge favour. I'd never have been given this chance if she hadn't died so suddenly.'

She turned to stare at the glass-walled office in the corner, and Cora saw something flash in her eyes. For a moment she sat there motionless, as if deep in thought, then dragged her gaze back to Cora.

'OK, let's go. Clock's ticking.' Sam stood up, grabbing her mobile from the desk and shoving it into her jacket pocket.

They headed for the café on the third floor, banging on the door of the graphics suite as they passed and picking up Wendy, who eagerly agreed that 9 a.m. was definitely not too early for a Danish pastry. Choosing a cosy blue sofa by the window, they quickly caught up with the latest gossip.

'So you and Mr Boland – hot couple or *what*?' Wendy shoved a large piece of Danish into her mouth and chewed ravenously.

'It IS going rather well, I must admit.' Cora beamed and broke off another chunk of double choc muffin, delicately removing a large chocolate chip and swallowing it.

Sam followed suit with her own muffin. 'I'd say! What are you doing this weekend then – he's back from Dubai tonight, isn't he?'

Cora nodded. 'He's invited me to his again. I'm zooming home now for an early night and driving back up tomorrow afternoon. Not sure what we'll do, but I can't imagine we'll get much sleep …'

She raised her eyebrows lasciviously as the others chortled.

'Anyway Sam, enough about me – how's your latest farmer boy? Got down and dirty in the hay yet?'

'Not yet! Give me a chance, it's only our second date this weekend. I'm far too busy being the boss at the moment. Although he is *very* nice …'

Her voice tailed off. Cora followed her gaze. While they'd been chatting, Alice Lomas had settled herself at a table right behind them. She smiled icily as Sam gave her a half-hearted wave, and took a tiny sip from her glass of sparkling water.

'Hello.'

'Er – hi, Alice,' Cora replied.

'So, Cora – saw you and Benjamin in the paper. I was quite surprised you were dating to be honest – I mean, he's just SO good looking.'

Cora, unsure what to say, said nothing.

Alice took another sip, dabbed the corner of her lip-glossed mouth with a napkin, and stood up.

'I guess he gets sick of all those gorgeous models throwing themselves at him. He probably wanted to try, well – a different type, for a change,' she said bitchily, and tossed her blonde mane.

The three friends stared at her, speechless, as she turned and stalked out of the cafeteria, hips swinging.

'Seriously, what is her problem? That girl is *vile*,' spat Sam.

'She is, but she has a point,' mused Cora. 'He *is* incredibly good-looking, and he *does* normally go out with those dolly, modelly types. But what she doesn't realise, what I think a lot of people don't realise, is that he really isn't as shallow as he seems. He honestly is a really nice guy under all that macho exterior, and I genuinely do think he likes me. I know he does, in fact.'

'Well, good, we're delighted for you. Alice can take a running jump into the Thames as far as I'm concerned, stupid bimbo.' Wendy crossly wiped crumbs off her tartan miniskirt onto the carpet.

'She doesn't bother me,' said Cora. She sat back and gazed out of the big window at the river, and the morning joggers pounding along its bank. 'Really. She can think what she likes. I know the truth, and I'm very happy at the moment. He's certainly helped me get over Justin in record-quick time, that's for sure.'

She hesitated, for the five hundredth time wondering if her

decision not to tell anyone at all about what was going on with Justin was the right one. But she knew her friends – they'd only tell her what she knew already, which was that she should have gone to the police on day one, and angry though she now was with her ex, she knew she wasn't prepared to do that. Not yet anyway. Things were complicated enough with the investigation focussing so closely on Scott, and she honestly didn't think she could bear it if the spotlight was on yet somebody else she was close to.

'Well, hooray for Benjamin Boland!' cheered Sam, and they all clinked mugs. Cora drained hers and plonked it on the table with a sigh.

'Right, I'm off. Home to get some beauty sleep. Catch you both next week sometime – have a fab weekend.'

'Bye, you. Have fun.'

Cora wiggled her eyebrows again. 'Oh, don't worry. I intend to.'

Upstairs, DC Adam Bradberry was standing yet again in Jeanette's office. He turned away from the window with its distant view of the London Eye and sat in the late programme editor's big leather chair, looking intently around him at the room he already knew by heart: the silver-framed picture of Clancy Carter on top of the filing cabinet, dozens of DVD show reels sent in by TV wannabes stacked on top of the bookshelf, the antique print on the wall next to the window and, on the desk, a paperweight in the shape of a Gucci handbag, holding down a neat pile of letters and scribbled notes.

The key to finding out what had happened to Jeanette Kendrick was right here, inside these four walls, or certainly inside this newsroom, he was sure of it. He knew he'd find it sooner or later, despite the fact that everything in here had been gone through in the tiniest detail before being returned to exactly how it was on the day of the murder. That seemed important to Adam for some reason – he was sure that if he visited here enough times, and just looked at the room, eventually it would give up its secret.

It was just that, at the moment, he seemed to have come up

against a brick wall. The team had drawn a blank in trying to trace the strange lurking figure in the CCTV footage, and there was no evidence he or she had entered the building anyway. The young producer, Christina, who had seemed such a promising lead on day one, had been ruled out for now, as had Jeanette's partner Clancy. He was wary of dismissing any suspect *completely*, certainly at this stage of the investigation – that was a rookie mistake, and a clever criminal could always find a way that may not be instantly obvious to the police. But he was as sure as he could be right now that neither of those two women were responsible for the murder. And then he'd been so optimistic that Scott Edson might have been the answer, but once the engineer presented them with an alibi …

Adam sighed and picked up the *Daily Mail* he'd tossed on the desk when he'd arrived. There'd been intense speculation in the papers earlier in the week about exactly which member of Jeanette's staff had been arrested on suspicion of her murder, but the *Morning Live* management team had made sure only a handful of staff had known it was Scott, and none of them had said a word. A few days on, the tabloids had lost interest again, apart from a couple of editorials questioning why on earth the police were taking so long to solve what should be a simple case. Adam tried not to take them to heart – he'd learned very early in his police career that news didn't stay news for long.

He flicked disconsolately through the newspaper. He wasn't ruling Scott Edson out entirely either, not yet, but he was devoid of ideas, and the horrible feeling was dawning on him that this enquiry was now at a dead end. Deeply discouraged, he closed the paper again and stared out into the newsroom, smiling briefly as his eyes met those of the producer, Sam Tindall, who had just entered the newsroom and sat down at her desk. It was she, he knew, who had now taken over the deceased woman's duties, and who he had several times during recent visits spotted gazing – rather covetously, in his opinion – at the ex-editor's office. He had asked staff not to use the room for now, and he remembered the disappointment that had crossed her face when she had reluctantly agreed. She was clearly fiercely ambitious, and as he watched her, now speaking animatedly on the phone, he wondered briefly if she might be ambitious enough to kill. There'd been nothing about her so far to raise any real suspicion, but still ...

His gaze continued to wander across the rows of busy producers and journalists until it came to rest on Alice Lomas, who was sitting at a desk halfway down the room, idly stirring something in a mug while staring blankly into space. Her long, blonde hair was tied back in a loose ponytail and she was wearing a pale pink jumper which clung to her curves. As Adam watched, she turned her big blue eyes towards Jeanette's office and visibly winced. Then, quite suddenly, she leapt from her chair, sending it careering back into a recycling bin which wobbled violently and fell over. Seemingly oblivious, the newsreader rushed from the room, and as she passed the late programme editor's office Adam could see tears streaming down her cheeks. There was a brief lull in the usual newsroom buzz and a few heads turned to watch her curiously, but nobody moved, and seconds later all was as it had been before.

Hmmm. Adam reached into his inside jacket pocket, pulled out a notebook and flipped through it until he found the relevant notes. Alice Lomas, unlike the other presenters and studio crew, hadn't actually been down on the studio level at the time Jeanette died, but she hadn't been considered as a potential suspect because various people had vaguely remembered her rushing about out in the newsroom at around the time of the murder. Now Adam wondered if maybe they'd been too hasty in ruling her out. On the few occasions he'd seen her, her behaviour hadn't exactly been normal.

He studied the neat list of Alice's movements on what he now knew programme staff had dubbed 'The Dead Dog Day'. She'd left the studio at 7.55, as soon as the programme had cut to a commercial break, and returned approximately 13 minutes later, in time to do her 'hello' from the sofa as soon as the 8.00 news was over. There was a list of three people who had spoken to her in various parts of the newsroom during that period but, Adam noted with interest now, none of them had been able to be precise about the time. So, could she have slipped into Jeanette's office just before 8 a.m., done the deed and then calmly re-entered the newsroom to chat to various colleagues to give herself an alibi? It was possible, Adam mused. She wasn't a big woman, but she was extremely fit – a fitness freak, by all accounts, terrified of putting on an ounce of fat. But could she have thrown an equally fit woman of similar size out of a window? Was that why she was so upset now? Or was she, as he'd heard many of her workmates comment, just a drama queen? Not entirely convinced either way, Adam shrugged and put his notebook back in his pocket, then stood up and headed back to the police station.

31

Benjamin Boland was lying on his big, white bed, flicking through the hundreds of channels on his immense plasma and thinking about Cora. She would be here in an hour and he was genuinely getting rather excited, which was extremely unusual. It was usually the girls who got excited about seeing *him*, not the other way round. He really wasn't sure what had got into him lately.

Flinging the remote aside, he lay back on a mountain of snowy, duck-down pillows and let his mind drift. Could he actually, seriously, be getting to the point where he might feel like – he hardly dared say the words – *settling down*? He'd always presumed he'd be at least fifty, and not in his mere mid-thirties, when that thought reared its head. And he'd only been seeing Cora for a couple of weeks. But there was something about her …

Benjamin leapt acrobatically off the bed, went to the wardrobe and retrieved his precious little cardboard box. He sat on the end of the mattress and carefully removed the old photograph, gently smoothing its creases.

'Hello, Mum,' he whispered. 'Hey, Dad. I wish you could meet her. You'd really like her, I think.'

He stared at his six-year-old self, so happy and innocent. Six years old. Just months before his world was shattered. He hadn't told Cora yet about the plane crash that had claimed the lives of both his parents and devastated his childhood, had told very few people in fact, despite the rage and despair he still felt when he let himself think about it. For a long time his anger had frequently been out of control, his younger self flying into frenzies that used to terrify those around him. Now he had managed to get mostly on top of it, was a calmer person. It was in the past, and that was where he liked it to stay. He had no time for people who blamed their tragic or tough upbringing for their present day woes. But if he was serious about Cora ...

'I might tell her, Mum. Because I think she's special, like you were.'

He gazed at his mother, floating away into memories. He'd loved her so much. He missed her, even now. Missed both of them. He felt the old fury rising up inside him for a moment. Would his life have been different, if they hadn't died? He'd have been just as successful career-wise, of that he had no doubt. But emotionally? Would he have been such a ... womaniser, lothario, sex addict even – all those names the papers called him – if he'd had a more stable upbringing? Why was he like this? Was he searching for something? And had he, possibly, now found it in Cora Baxter?

On the big TV, Big Ben suddenly struck to mark the start of the six o'clock news. Benjamin jumped and, suddenly feeling like a soppy fool, quickly pushed the old photograph back into the box and returned it to its hiding place.

Idiot, he told himself. Pull yourself together. She'll be here in a minute. And spirits suddenly soaring, he raced to the bathroom to get ready for her.

Later that night, as they shared delicious, soft shell crab at a discreet corner table in Hakkasan, Cora was also feeling remarkably close to this man she'd known for only two weeks. There'd been no further contact from Justin, but her anger had dissipated now and she'd barely given him a thought in recent days, her mind filled with Benjamin. He'd been so thrilled to see her earlier, and after a passionate reunion that made her cheeks flush even now as she nibbled her seafood, Benjamin had dug out an old cardboard box and told her about his past. As they'd cuddled up together under his enormous duvet, Cora had been in tears at the thought of the scared little boy this wonderful man had once been.

Now, she smiled at him and reached across to wipe away the sauce that was dribbling down his chin.

'Sorry,' he mumbled, mouth still full of food. 'I'm a slob.'

'No, you're not, you just like eating – that's one of the reasons why I love you!' Cora beamed, then suddenly realised what she'd said.

'I mean – er, I love that you love food, like I do, not that I, er …' she stuttered.

Benjamin swallowed and smirked.

'You just said you loved me, Cora. Can't back out of it now.'

'But I didn't mean … it was just …'

'Haha! Got ya!'

He leaned back in his chair, grinning. Cora threw her napkin at him.

'Stop being so smug. It was a slip of the tongue!'

Benjamin leaned forward again and reached for her hand.

'No it wasn't. At least I hope it wasn't. Because I feel the same, Cora.' His eyes were suddenly serious as he gazed into hers. 'Yes, it's only been a couple of weeks, but when you know, you know. At least, I think you do. I'm not sure I've ever really been in love before. I've certainly never felt like this …'

His voice tailed off and he dropped his lips to her hand and kissed it. Cora's heart melted.

'Oh Benjamin. You're so sweet. And yes, it's so soon, and I've only just split up with Justin, but – I don't know. This feels like something special to me. We just seem to fit, don't we?'

Benjamin nodded. 'We do. I love it. I love you, Cora Baxter.'

'And I love you,' she said simply.

He smiled and squeezed her hand gently. Cora gazed at him for a moment, then cleared her throat.

'It's just that – I mean, obviously it's WAY too early to be talking about kids – but you do understand, if we've got to this stage already … you do understand that I'm not interested in having them? Ever? Because I'm scared, Benjamin – I can't even think of starting to get serious in another relationship if the man is secretly hoping I'll change my mind, like Justin was.'

He shook his head. 'I told you before, I'm not bothered about kids. It's not an issue, Cora.'

'OK. But if you change your mind – just tell me, Benjamin. Straight away. Don't pretend, don't lie to me. Never lie to me, please? Because, essentially, that was what Justin did, you know? He accepted a childless future, when I told him very early on that that was what it would be if he stayed with me – and that acceptance was a lie.'

'I won't lie to you. What's the point? Why did he?'

'I don't know. I guess he was just driven by lust, at the beginning, and thought it would all be OK, that we were enough for each other.'

She paused as a waiter appeared at her elbow and briskly cleared away their starter plates. Benjamin was still watching her intently.

'But then there was all the other stuff – lazy lie-ins, spontaneous nights out, last-minute weekends away,' she continued, when they were alone again. 'We both always said how great it was that we could do all that without having to worry about anyone else, we both said how having a child just wasn't for us. That's why it was such a shock, that he changed his mind like that.'

Benjamin nodded. 'Did you ever – even for a minute – think that you'd made a mistake? When he left?'

'Only for a moment. That day, when he rang to tell me it was over, and why, I was almost tempted to say OK, I'd have a baby if he'd stay. But I couldn't bring myself to do it. I couldn't do it, and I won't. Love means compromise, yes, but the absolute certainty that I don't want children is too much an integral part of me to ever compromise on. Do you understand that – really?'

She looked beseechingly at him.

'Yes, I do. And I'd never ask you to compromise like that. I promise.'

She nodded, suddenly fighting back tears.

'To be fair, Justin didn't either. I suppose he knew me too

well. If he wanted a baby, the only solution was to leave me, and even in amongst all the grief I felt when he left, I was grateful to him for that. That probably sounds weird, but I was.'

'No, I can understand that,' Benjamin said softly.

'Thank you. Sorry, this has got a bit heavy, hasn't it?' She used her free hand to wipe away a tear that had escaped and looked at him affectionately. 'But thank you for listening. I feel better now!'

He nodded and looked tenderly at her for another few seconds, then squeezed her hand again.

'Dim sum?' he asked.

Cora snorted. 'Ah, I see the romantic moment didn't last long while there was still food on the table!'

'Hey – we need energy for the romantic moments we'll be having when I get you home!' Benjamin winked in an exaggerated fashion, and speared a prawn dumpling with a chopstick.

Cora laughed and tucked in. He was right – and the food was just too divine to ignore.

An hour later, stuffed and happy, they ambled out into the frosty Mayfair street.

'Ooh – freezing! Hang on a mo.' Cora stopped under a streetlight to wrap her cashmere scarf more tightly round her ears.

'It's Baltic, isn't it?' Benjamin scanned the street for a cab, then tutted.

'Nothing. Let's nip round the corner to Berkeley Square – there's always loads there.'

He slipped his arm around her shoulders and they headed down the road, to Cora's great amusement Benjamin beginning to merrily extoll the virtues of the food they'd just eaten as if she hadn't been there.

'It was scrumptious, seriously. The jasmine tea smoked chicken was to die for ...'

He chatted on, but Cora was suddenly distracted. Her sharp ears had picked up the soft footsteps of somebody close behind them. A mugger? Or just paparazzi? She turned quickly, and sure enough a shadowy form a few metres back stopped abruptly and melted into a shop doorway.

'What's up?' asked Benjamin, his restaurant review brought to a premature halt.

'Nothing. Just a pap, I think. Don't worry, he's slipped into a doorway. Oh look – a cab, quick!'

They sprinted to the corner, Benjamin waving frantically, and the cab screeched to a halt at the kerbside. Settling into the blissful warmth, Cora snuggled up to her boyfriend and grinned as his fingers began to discreetly stroke their way up her thigh and under the hem of her short skirt. But the figure behind them had left her feeling uneasy. Was it really a pap, out to get a quick snap of Benjamin Boland? If so, why hadn't he just done it as they'd left the restaurant like they usually did? Why follow them, and then hide? Weird.

She suddenly remembered the vague feeling she'd had last weekend that somebody had been lurking outside her gate in Cheltenham as she'd said goodbye to Rosie and Nicole. Was somebody following her? And then there'd been an incident a few days ago when, for a scary five minutes, she'd been convinced that somebody had been in the flat while she'd been out. The drawer where she kept all her keys, spare batteries and takeaway menus was half open, and Cora *never* left drawers ajar – it was a particular bugbear of hers. As nothing else in the apartment had been disturbed and there'd been no sign of a break-in, though, she'd eventually decided she must have been in even more of a hurry than normal when she was rushing out that morning, and dismissed her fears. But now, again, somebody lurking in the dark, waiting for her ...

'Oh don't be ridiculous,' she told herself. 'All this Dead Dog Day murder mystery stuff is making you paranoid. Why would anyone want to follow *you*?'

And putting any such thoughts firmly out of her mind, she leaned closer to Benjamin and planted her lips on his deliciously soft mouth, flicking her tongue between his teeth. He responded eagerly, his hand moving higher on her thigh and then stopping just outside the line of her knickers, his index finger gently circling until she thought she might actually pass out from anticipation.

'Er – driver? Any chance you could go a little faster?' she croaked. The driver glanced over his shoulder, raised his eyebrows and put his foot down.

Benjamin snickered. 'Good grief, Cora Baxter. You'll be getting me a reputation!'

'Tonight, Mr Boland, I really couldn't care less,' she proclaimed. 'I couldn't be happier.'

'Me too,' he said softly. And he reached for her lips again, and kissed her until the cab driver coughed loudly to announce their arrival on the South Bank.

32

@ilovelegs2 @CoraBaxterMLive Morning Cora. Please can you tell me if you have stockings on under that sexy green rubber? Thanks.

Cora sighed and shoved her phone back into the pocket of her waterproof jacket. How on earth could men find waders sexy? She checked her watch and splashed her way back through the knee-high water that was flowing down the street in the centre of Worcester, narrowly avoiding a swan outside Boots. After three days of horrendous rain, the River Severn had once again burst its banks, turning the towns and cities it passed through into watery nightmares for their residents, and giving the ducks and swans interesting new routes to investigate.

She turned into a steep side street and stomped up the hill, the floodwater gradually getting lower and lower until she reached the dry ground at the top where Scott had parked the truck. Relieved to be out of the water, which really didn't smell very nice, she stamped her frozen feet and leaned against the wall to take her waders off, wrinkling her nose.

'Urgh – it stinks, doesn't it?'

Rodney poked his head out of the truck, then jumped out and ran over to give her a hand.

'Yes, it does. Can't imagine how horrible it must be for all those poor people with this stuff in their living rooms. No wonder it takes a year or more to get it all properly cleaned up. Vile.'

She leaned on Rodney's arm as she wriggled out of the second wader and stood in her socks on the dry ground. Rodney grabbed her rucksack which was lying nearby and pulled her Emu boots out.

'Thanks – you're a star.'

'Hey, Cora ...' Rodney dropped his voice, looking surreptitiously at the truck to check that nobody was within earshot.

'Tried to have a word with Scott, while you were on the phone – asked him about you know what. No joy, won't even go there. And he's denying any money troubles too. Still insists he's just trying out 'minimalism' at home,' he hissed.

Cora sighed, as she finally got her boots on and straightened up. 'Oh well, you tried. It's such a worry Rodney. I just have no idea what to make of it all. He's just so damn quiet, and SO moody.'

'Tell me about it ...' He stopped as Nathan appeared at the door of the truck. 'Are we done then?' he shouted. 'Was that definitely the last hit?'

'Definitely!'

'Amen to that,' replied Nathan. 'I've had quite enough of that honking water.'

'Me too. Especially after that near miss earlier ...'

They'd been halfway through the eight o'clock news hit, Cora walking down the High Street pointing out the flooded shops and submerged benches and telephone boxes to the camera, when out of the corner of her eye she'd noticed two men in fluorescent jackets gesticulating wildly at her. Steadfastly ignoring them, she'd carried on with her broadcast, but as soon as she'd been given the all-clear she marched across to where they were still standing, watching her.

'Did you not realise we were live on air? That was really distracting,' she'd said, mildly irritated.

'Well, did you not realise there were open manhole covers all the way down that street? You could have disappeared!' the taller of the two replied crossly.

Now, Nathan snorted with laughter as he recalled her face as she'd realised what could have happened.

'I wish it had – we'd be on *It'll be Alright on the Night* for

182

ever and a day!' he grinned.

'Well, at least we learned something – flooding can cause manhole covers to lift! Every day's a school day.'

'True, true. Come on, let's go and find some breakfast, I'm starving. And I am DYING for a wee.'

'Me too – it's all this water,' Cora laughed.

And cheered by the thought of toilets and breakfast, they banged on the side of the truck to alert Scott and headed off to find a cosy café.

At his flat in Shepherd's Bush, Adam Bradberry was enjoying a rare morning off. Slugging down his second strong coffee of the day, he stood by the window of his second floor living room, gazing idly at the bustling street below and wondering when Harry would wake up. His ex, Laura, had called him in a panic yesterday afternoon, asking him if he could take their five-year-old overnight because of some crisis at the hospital where she worked, and he'd happily obliged. He was getting nowhere at work anyway at the moment, the Jeanette Kendrick enquiry floundering like none he'd ever worked on before, and he needed a break. Plus, any chance to spend some extra time with his beloved son was more than welcome.

He turned away from the window and wandered over to the fireplace, smiling as he picked up his favourite photo from the mantelpiece. A wooden frame was filled with a laughing close-up of Harry, his huge green eyes sparkling. Adam's tired face softened and his own green eyes shone as he looked at his son. Apart from their hair – the child's was mousy-brown and curly – they were strikingly similar.

He put the picture down and picked up the one that stood next to it. Adam himself, tanned, in a white T-shirt and red shorts on a Spanish beach, his little son grinning on his shoulders. A smiling woman sat on the sand next to them, her long, brown hair blowing in the breeze. Adam and Laura, a nurse, had divorced a year ago, after seven years of marriage, but they were still friends. Soon after Harrison was born they had somehow started to drift apart, but the little boy was the most important thing in both their worlds and they had always managed to keep everything amicable. Adam saw Harry every second weekend, despite the long trek from London to Swindon and back, and took him away on regular holidays, and the little boy seemed to be as happy as he had always been.

He looked around the room, quietly contented with the home he'd created for himself and his son. He'd only moved in six months ago, and it had been hard work doing it up when his working hours were so long and his budget so tight, but it was slowly coming together. The front door opened into a small windowless hallway, which he'd brightened with halogen spots and two modern artworks Laura had agreed he could take from the marital home; then double doors opened onto a surprisingly big L-shaped, open-plan living area. It was a corner apartment, with windows on two sides opening on to a wide balcony that ran all the way round. Now, the winter sun streamed in, burnishing the polished oak floor. A huge, grey suede sofa with lime and turquoise cushions, a TV, a simple white dining table and chairs – the tabletop currently covered with Harry's crayons and colouring books – and some high stools around the breakfast bar area had been his main purchases so far, but it was definitely starting to feel like home.

There was still no sound from Harry, so Adam poured a third coffee and made a piece of toast, which he spread thickly with Marmite. Munching, he drifted into the master bedroom, with its views of the quiet, communal courtyard at the rear of the apartment block. A small water feature bubbled away in the centre, and metal benches were dotted around on the gravel paths, shaded by huge palms and gently rustling bamboo plants. He'd got lucky with this place, without a doubt. Swallowing his last mouthful of toast, he carefully opened the door to his son's bedroom and crept in, smiling as he saw the tousled curls emerging from the bottom of the bed and the slightly grubby little feet on the pillow. Sleeping upside down again – this was becoming a habit. He slipped into the en-suite bathroom and began to run a bath for his son – the excitement of a mid-week trip to Daddy's had left them both too exhausted last night –

and as the tub filled, leaned against the bathroom doorframe, waiting for his son to stir. On a shelf near the bed, two goldfish swam in determined circles. On the pale blue walls, stickers of sharks and dolphins mingled with boats and mermaids, and a large clock with Nemo's face ticked loudly, alerting Adam to the fact that it was nearly 9.30 and he really did need to get this day started.

'Hello, Daddy!'

Adam jumped as the sleepy voice interrupted his musings.

'Well, hello, sleepyhead! I thought you'd never wake up!'

Harry grinned, revealing a missing front tooth. 'I can hear the bath! Can I have my submarine? And my water pistol?'

Adam pulled back the duvet and swept the child into his arms. 'Submarine, yes. Water pistol, definitely not! I've already had my shower this morning, thank you very much!'

'Awwww!' moaned Harry, then chuckled hysterically as his dad threw him over his shoulder and headed for the bathroom.

Adam laughed too, the usual little bubble of elation fizzing up inside him. He loved his son so much. So what if this latest murder enquiry had struck a dead end, and so what if he had no woman in his life at the moment? Sometimes, Harry was quite simply all he needed. He dumped the giggling little boy onto the bathmat and then, suddenly changing his mind, he grabbed both the toy submarine and the water pistol from the shelf, threw them into the bath, and prepared himself to get very wet indeed.

33

'OK, OK, I'll come out – but I'm attached now, remember, so no trying to lead me astray!'

Benjamin grinned down the phone at the incredulous jeering at the other end and cut the call. His friends were still not convinced he'd changed, and sometimes he found it hard to believe it himself, but Cora Baxter had definitely done something to him. He walked to the window and stared out at the river for a moment. It was twilight, and the streetlights had come on, reflecting in the shimmering water. Far below his lofty home, Londoners and tourists scurried along the South Bank. A cluster of people who'd been standing on the pavement next to a burger van suddenly skipped into the road, and through his triple glazing Benjamin heard the distant sound of an irate car horn.

He looked at his Breitling. Five o'clock. Might be a good time to ring Cora. He hit her speed dial number and she picked up almost immediately.

'Hi! I was just thinking about you! What are you up to this chilly evening?'

'Not a lot at the moment – Hugo's just rung though, bit of a boy's night out later so I thought I might go along. You?'

'Oh, working – the usual! Up in Manchester, rubbish story … hang on – what? Now?'

He could hear an urgent voice in the background. A moment later she was back.

'Oh, Benj, so sorry, I can't talk to you now, got to go and shoot an interview before the bloke gets on a plane. Look – have a great night, I'll talk to you tomorrow, OK? Love you.'

'Love you too.' But she'd already hung up. Benjamin

sighed. She was always so busy and distracted during the week. One of the things that he loved most about Cora was that she had a career so similar to his, which meant she understood his lifestyle so well ... but it *would* be nice to see her a bit more often.

He went to the kitchen, made an espresso in the thousand-pound Gaggia machine he'd bought himself last Christmas, and drank it slowly, thinking about the boy's night out he'd gone on last week. As usual, women had approached him constantly through the evening – beautiful, sexy women, women he'd have taken home in a heartbeat in the days pre-Cora. And yes, he'd been tempted, a little – he was only human after all – but all he'd done this time was have a little flirt and a chat, before sending them on their way. And that was part of his job really, he mused – keeping the public happy was what a TV presenter was supposed to do.

'Any future dealings with other women will be purely platonic,' he announced proudly to the Gaggia, which spurted a little frothy milk at him in reply.

'I'm a one-woman man now.'

He wandered slowly around his apartment, straightening cushions and moving a vase a fraction to the left so it lined up perfectly with the 'Hot Hunk of the Year' award he'd been presented with by a showbiz magazine a few months back. It was beautiful here, and he loved it, but it suddenly felt rather empty.

'A woman's touch, that's what it needs. Somebody here when I get home, somebody to sleep with every night, wake up with every day,' he said softly. He pulled out his phone again and flicked through his photos to a shot of Cora. He'd taken it at the weekend just after she'd woken up. She was sitting up in bed, hair dishevelled, no make-up, clutching the duvet to her chest and grinning cheekily at him. She looked gorgeous. He smiled at her image for a moment then pulled himself together.

'Christ, man, get a grip!' he shouted out loud, and laughing, headed for the wardrobe to find something to wear. He was finding himself reaching a whole new level of soppiness here –

a boys' night out was probably just what he needed.

He opened the wardrobe and started flicking through his vast shirt collection, then paused as something on the closet floor caught his eye. He bent to pick it up. It was his passport. Weird, he thought. How did that get there? He travelled so much that he was absolutely religious about keeping his documents together for easy access when he needed them, automatically putting them in his box on the shelf behind the clothes rail every time he came back from a trip. He looked up at the shelf. The box was there, but it was slightly ajar, papers protruding from the opening. Benjamin frowned. He was almost certain he hadn't left it like that – he was tidy to the point of obsession. He felt a sudden little flicker of unease. Could somebody have been in here?

He walked quickly through the apartment again, scanning every room for anything else that might be out of place, but all seemed fine. Back in the bedroom, he sat down on the edge of the bed and thought for a moment. His cleaner was the only one with a key – well, apart from Cora of course, he'd given her one after their second or third date, happy for her to let herself in if he was ever delayed on a shoot. But he knew she'd never been here without his knowledge, and would certainly never go through his stuff, and the cleaner had always been under strict instructions never to open drawers or cupboards. He stared hard at the passport he was still clutching in his hand, then stood up and returned it to its box, closing the lid firmly. He was imagining it, he told himself. He'd obviously just been a bit careless when he was unpacking last time. Nothing to worry about. Being in love was obviously affecting him in more ways than one. And grinning again at the thought of his lovely new girlfriend, he finally selected a shirt and headed off for his boys' night out.

34

Friday 2nd February

'What the hell is wrong with her now?'

Cora nudged Sam and nodded across the newsroom to where Alice was huddled in a corner, dabbing her eyes with a tissue.

'Honestly, what's wrong with everybody at the moment – if it's not Scott on the road, it's Alice in here!'

'Oh – man trouble this time I think. She was seeing somebody for a while and he's dumped her. Don't blame him really, do you?'

'No – I suppose not,' said Cora, but she instantly felt a little bit guilty. She knew how dreadful it was to be dumped. She watched Alice for a moment, and felt a pang of sympathy. Then she glimpsed the clock on the wall opposite and stood up.

'Right, I'm off. Got a lovely girlie weekend planned with Nicole and Rosie, none of which I'll enjoy if I don't get home and get some sleep!'

'Benjamin away again?'

'Yep – flies off tonight for a few days canyoning in the Caribbean – Dominica, I think. I'm not even sure what canyoning is.'

'Sounds very manly, whatever it is. Lucky git, it'll be hot there at this time of year too – he hasn't got a bad job, your boyfriend, has he?'

'I know.' Cora sighed. 'Wish I had a job like that. Froze my ass off out there this morning.'

She picked up her blue cashmere scarf from where she'd dumped it on Sam's desk earlier and started winding it round her neck, then paused as Alice approached, still sniffing.

'Er – Sam? Is it OK if I leave now – I've finished everything I need to do and I'm, well, not feeling that great to be honest.'

'That's – that's fine, Alice. You go,' said Sam, sounding slightly surprised. Cora looked on, amazed. Never before in all the time she'd worked with Alice could she recall her speaking to anyone with anything even verging on politeness. Had she had a personality transplant, or was she just so upset that she'd forgotten to be nasty? Cora took a deep breath and decided to say something.

'Sorry to hear about what happened – with your boyfriend, Alice. I know what it's like, it's horrible.'

Alice looked sharply at Cora for a moment and then her eyes welled up again.

'Thanks. Thanks Cora. It is, it's horrible. Men are horrible.'

'Not all of them, Alice. Don't give them up entirely, eh?' Cora smiled and awkwardly patted the newsreader on the arm.

Alice gave her a watery smile. 'I'll think about it. See you, Cora.'

And she turned and walked away. Sam, open-mouthed, nudged Cora so violently she nearly fell over.

'What the buggering buggery happened there? She was … she was actually *civil*. Who is that, and what has she done with Alice Lomas?'

Cora shook her head, bemused. 'Bizarre. Maybe she's actually human after all, underneath all that hair and boobs and bitchiness? Shame we don't see it more often really – I actually sort of warmed to her there for a second, she looked so – so sort of vulnerable, didn't she?'

'Vulnerable my arse. The girl's a cow. Just after sympathy, I reckon. She'll be back to bitch mode by Monday, mark my words.' Sam decisively typed the last few words of the email she'd been writing and hit send.

'You're probably right. OK – that's it, I'm out of here, definitely this time. Have a fab weekend.'

Cora bent and gave her friend a swift hug, then headed for the lifts, suddenly aware her tummy was rumbling. It was nearly 10 a.m. – past lunchtime really, she thought, seeing as she'd been up since four. She pushed her way through the revolving door at the front of TV Centre and hesitated. Left to the car park or right to the café?

A minute later she was pushing open the door of Media Café, the delectable aroma of strong coffee hitting her nostrils as she weaved her way between the closely packed tables to the counter. It was busy as always, windows steamed up as dozens of telly types and tourists sought refuge from the morning chill. Cora ordered a hot chocolate and a fat, moist slice of Dorset apple cake, then cast her gaze around looking for a spare table. She spotted one tucked away in the corner and, balancing her tray carefully, headed towards it. She was about to put her tray down when she heard her name.

'Cora? I thought it was you!'

'Oh – DCI Brad … I mean Adam … hello. Sorry, I didn't see you there.'

In an alcove at the back of the room, Adam Bradberry was sitting across the table from a small boy.

'Come and join us? There's plenty of room.'

'Er – yes, OK, why not?'

Awkwardly side-stepping a large man in a dusty raincoat, Cora shuffled her way over, dumped her food on the table, and sat down next to the child.

The little boy smiled shyly at her. 'Hello. I'm Harry.'

'Hello, Harry. I'm Cora. Very nice to meet you.' She looked at Adam and smiled.

Adam beamed at his son. 'Cora's on the telly, Harry. And Daddy's been working with her a bit.'

Harry nodded solemnly then turned his attention to the enormous Danish pastry on his plate. Adam turned to Cora, who was slightly nervously sipping her drink. Why was she nervous? She had a boyfriend now, other men shouldn't have any effect on her at all. He was gorgeous though. Those eyes …

'So – busy?' He interrupted her reverie.

'Erm – yes, as always. So glad it's Friday – just needed a bit of sustenance before the long drive home. I live in Gloucestershire – lots of driving.'

'Ah, I didn't realise that. Nice part of the world though?'

'Yes, it's wonderful, I love it.' Cora broke off a small piece of cake and nibbled it. Yum. She was starving.

'So ...' She swallowed. 'Day off for you? No breakthroughs in a certain high profile murder case?'

Adam sighed and shook his head. 'Nope. One or two potential suspects still around but nothing concrete.'

He took a mouthful of black coffee. 'And to answer your other question, yes, I actually have a day off, and on a Friday too, wonders will never cease. Harry's with me for a few days, which is brilliant, isn't it, mate?'

He patted his son's hand, and the little boy grinned up at him, green eyes crinkling, his entire lower face covered with sticky pastry. He took another huge bite and turned back to the Superman comic that was spread out in front of him.

'He's very cute,' Cora said genuinely. She might not want children of her own, but she could still spot a good one.

'Thanks – I think so. You got any plans to have any – with, er, Benjamin?'

Cora almost choked on her cake. She gulped down a mouthful of hot chocolate and coughed.

'Gosh, well, first, it's a bit soon – we've only been seeing each other for a few weeks. And second – well, I actually don't want kids. Never have.'

Adam nodded, but looked slightly taken aback.

'I like them though,' Cora added hastily. 'Just don't want my own.' She smiled at Harry, who had stopped reading and was looking up at her intently.

'They can be little monsters at times, to be fair. Although I wouldn't be without this particular little monster.' Adam ruffled Harry's hair, and he grimaced and buried himself in his comic again.

'He does seem very good. Not every child of his age would behave this well in a café,' Cora commented.

'Yep, he's alright is my Harry.' He leaned forward suddenly on the table, and the light scent of a delicious-smelling aftershave wafted across at Cora, making her stomach lurch slightly. For goodness' sake, she thought. You have a gorgeous boyfriend. Calm down. She took another bite of cake, trying not to stare at the policeman's amazing eyes.

'So – tell me some telly tales, take my mind off work,' he said.

Cora laughed. 'OK … let me think. Well, there was a time I nearly needed police help actually. Do you remember last summer when loads of rivers and canals all over the country were covered with duckweed – that thick green slimy stuff?'

'Think so, yes. There was a bit of an epidemic, wasn't there?'

She nodded. 'Well, all the news shows were covering it, with reporters just wandering along river banks and pointing at it. But of course Jeanette being Jeanette, that wasn't good enough. She made me *get in* to the vile stuff …'

Adam spluttered into his coffee. 'Get *in* to the water? Wasn't that dangerous?'

'Well, yes, as it turns out. I had a dry suit – two sizes two big, but that's beside the point – but no health and safety considerations at all. I didn't even know how deep the water was. So, as instructed, I hop in – it was revolting – and there's only a stupid shopping trolley in the bottom of the canal, and of course me being me I get my foot caught in it, and there I am, stuck fast.'

Adam was laughing out loud now, and Harry had completely abandoned his reading and was grinning with delight.

'What happened next?' he asked excitedly.

'Yes, what happened?' Adam urged. Two pairs of amused emerald eyes were glued to her.

'Well – luckily for me, the cameraman had brought diving gear in case he needed any underwater shots. So he went down and freed me – took a good half an hour though. And all the time I'm trying to tread water in this disgusting green slime, with all the early morning joggers and dog walkers laughing at me …'

She stopped and chuckled as Adam and Harry snorted with laughter.

'You're funny, Cora,' giggled Harry.

'And you're very cute,' Cora replied honestly. He really was a sweet boy.

She turned back to Adam. 'Now I've shared a telly story, how about you sharing some police knowledge?'

She paused, wondering how far to push it, then decided to go for it. They were getting on so well that it seemed to be worth a try.

'Jeanette's murder – why have you been talking to Scott so much? Scott Edson? Can you tell me anything?'

Adam's smile faded. 'Cora, I'm really sorry but I can't. We've had our reasons, that's all I can say. Sorry.'

Cora suddenly felt a little sick and pushed the remains of her cake to one side. 'But you haven't charged him. And you said there was more than one suspect ...?'

Adam shrugged. 'I can't comment further at this stage. Sorry.'

Cora nodded and started crushing bits of cake with her teaspoon, wishing she hadn't brought the case up.

'So, to change the subject ...' Adam hesitated. 'How well do you know that blonde newsreader – Alice? Alice Lomas?'

Cora looked up, surprised.

Adam took another sip of his drink. 'Just interested,' he said casually. 'She seems like a bit of a character.'

Cora grimaced. 'That's one word for her, I suppose.'

She paused, aware that she was sounding rather nasty. 'Well, what I mean is that she's not exactly ... popular. None of us are quite sure why she's here. Jeanette gave her an amazing job that, to be honest, she's not really cut out for, but instead of being grateful for it she's kind of horrible to everyone all the time. Even more so now that Jeanette's dead. Although we think that might be because she's scared she might lose her job now, because nobody else really rates her.'

'Could be that, yes.' Adam smiled.

Cora smiled back, and for a long moment their eyes locked. Again, her stomach lurched. Oh for goodness' sake. She stood up so suddenly that Harry jumped, startled, and nearly knocked over his milk. He grabbed it with a sturdy little hand and steadied it just in time.

'Oh, sorry! I just need to go – it was a very early start and I have a busy weekend ahead, got to squeeze in an afternoon nap before tonight if I can.'

'Of course, don't worry. Well, it's been very nice. We must do this again sometime – you know, if you have time.'

Cora felt herself blushing. 'That would be great, yes.'

She dragged her eyes reluctantly away from Adam. 'And lovely to meet you, young man. You'll have to lend me that Superman comic sometime, I'm a bit of a fan too.'

Harry beamed. 'I will.'

'OK, well – bye then.'

'Bye, Cora.'

She shrugged her coat on and made her way out of the café, turning at the door to wave self-consciously. Adam raised his hand and Harry waved wildly, making her laugh again. Still grinning, she stepped out into the February gloom and was marching happily along the busy South Bank when yet again she got the sudden feeling somebody was following her. She stopped abruptly and turned, but the street was so busy with scurrying pedestrians that it was impossible to tell if anyone was paying her any particular attention.

'Oh, don't be ridiculous!' she berated herself, and forgot about it. And feeling ridiculously and unexpectedly chirpy for a Friday morning, she headed for the car park and home.

Inside the café, Adam urged Harry to hurry up and finish his pastry and stared out of the window, lost in thought. He'd felt strangely disappointed at Cora's admission that she didn't want children, though quite why that should have any relevance to him he wasn't sure. There was definitely a mutual attraction there, he was sure of that, but she had a boyfriend, and that was that. But what she'd said about Alice – interesting. He contemplated for a moment. Maybe Cora was right – the newsreader was simply scared of losing her job. It might explain her behaviour, he supposed. Being upset wasn't a crime, after all.

'Daddy? I'm finished, look.'

Harry peered up at him, large sticky crumbs all over his chin. Adam grabbed a napkin and started to scrub, his son giggling and wiggling. Right, Adam thought. It's the weekend, I'm off, no more work till Monday. And he resolutely pushed Jeanette Kendrick out of his mind and concentrated on cleaning Danish pastry off the face he loved most in all the world.

35

Saturday 3rd February

In the cosy little pub that was one of Cora's favourite Cheltenham haunts, she downed the remains of her third gin and slimline tonic and raised her eyes heavenward as Rosie and Nicole bombarded her with questions about Benjamin.

'It's about darn time we met him for ourselves, Cora,' Nicole declared, and took a large mouthful of red wine. She banged the almost empty glass down on the long wooden table decisively. 'You need to get him to come down here for a change – it's always you rushing off to London to see him. Make him do the running!'

Rosie nodded her agreement. 'It *would* be nice to meet him, Cora.'

'We *have* talked about him coming down here – it's just that there's so much more to do in London, and I'm often there on a Friday anyway so it's just been easier,' Cora argued feebly.

'Nonsense.' Nicole was having none of it. 'We're your best friends, we need to meet him. Sort it out, girl,' she said firmly, wagging her finger in Cora's face.

'Stop it! Alright, you win, I'll invite him down. Now stop wagging and start drinking!'

Nicole smiled victoriously and took another big gulp of wine. She was a drink behind the others, having been called out on some sort of veterinary emergency involving a pig and an ulcer – Rosie and Cora had quickly declined their friend's offer to fill them in on all the gory details.

Rosie sipped her orange juice and grimaced. 'Ugh. I'm so done with babies after this one. Being in a pub when you're pregnant is so utterly boring.'

Cora rubbed her arm sympathetically. 'At least you don't get the hangovers.'

'True.' Rosie sighed and then brightened up. 'Come on – make me laugh. Any mad fan to tell us about? Have you got your very own stalker yet?'

'No – thank goodness. Although ...' she paused. 'OK, you're going to think this is weird and tell me I'm imagining it, but I have had a sort of feeling a few times recently that someone was watching me. I even caught a glimpse once, when I was with Benjamin.'

Rosie and Nicole leaned towards her simultaneously, agog. 'Really? Wow. That's a bit creepy. What exactly have you seen?' asked Nicole.

Cora counted off the incidents on her fingers. 'Well, first there was a sort of – well, shadow at the gate outside the apartment. I just had a feeling somebody was out there. That last night you two were round actually, when I was waving you off.'

'I didn't see anything,' said Nicole. She looked at Rosie, who shook her head.

'OK, well maybe I imagined that one,' Cora said, feeling a little better. 'Then there was the night I went to Hakkasan with Benjamin. There was definitely someone following us down the street – I turned round and saw them slip into a doorway.'

'Paparazzi,' Rosie and Nicole said together, and they all laughed.

'Yes, that's what I thought. But why hide – they're not usually shy!'

Nicole shrugged. 'Don't know then. Bit odd, I suppose. What else?'

'Well, I sort of thought somebody had been in my flat – there was a drawer half open, and I'm sure I didn't leave it like that. Although I probably did imagine that one – there was absolutely no sign of a break-in or anything. And then yesterday, when I was leaving the Media Café – you know, when I had a drink with the police officer and his son? I just had a feeling, again, that someone was there.'

'Did you see anything that time?' Nicole was looking a little sceptical.

'Well – no.' She paused, remembering something that had struck her as a little odd as she drove out of London. 'Although, there was a navy blue car that I thought was following me for a bit on the way home. But then it turned off, so it probably wasn't.'

Cora was starting to feel a little bit silly. Last night she'd even started convincing herself that maybe Justin had returned and was following her, after his last slightly threatening message. Now, saying it all out loud to her friends, she realised she was more than likely getting herself in a state over nothing at all.

Rosie patted her hand. 'I think you're just overtired, Cora. Lack of sleep can do strange things to your brain. Trust me, I'm the mother of two small children, I know what I'm talking about. After Alexander was born I barely slept for the first month – thought there was somebody outside chucking marbles at the window one night and spent a good five minutes screaming at them to stop, until poor Alistair managed to convince me it was just a freak hailstorm.'

Nicole and Cora hooted.

'Oh, I'm sure you're right. I'll stop being stupid. Who'd want to stalk me, anyway? Delusions of grandeur, that's what it is. Right – who's for another drink?'

'Anything but orange juice,' grinned Rosie.

Nicole waved her now drained glass. 'Wine. More wine. LOTS of wine.'

Cora gave her the thumbs up sign and wriggled out from behind the table. She pushed her way gingerly through the crowd by the bar, trying to avoid being drenched by a group of rowdy but harmless twenty-something lads who seemed to be celebrating a birthday by vigorously waving their pints in the air and singing tunelessly.

'Sorry, love – go ahead,' one of them slurred politely, stepping unsteadily backwards to let her pass. She glanced up to thank him and was struck by his lovely green eyes, albeit in a face flushed with alcohol and accompanied by distinctly beery breath.

'Thanks,' she smiled, and instantly thought of Adam. His eyes. They were so striking ...

'And here I go again!' she berated herself as she leaned on the bar, trying to avoid soaking her sleeve in a puddle of lager. She waved at the barman and he gestured that he'd be with her next. As she waited, she puzzled over why Adam was creeping into her thoughts at all. She had a yummy boyfriend who was perfect for her. She loved him, she really did, despite their relationship being so young. And she truly believed that he loved her too. They had quickly developed a deep connection, something she had never expected when she'd first agreed to go out with him. It was wonderful. So why on earth was she thinking about someone she barely knew – and someone who had a child, to boot?

'Ridiculous,' she said out loud, then, 'Oh – a gin and slimline, a large glass of Shiraz, and a pineapple juice, please,' as the barman looked at her quizzically.

Two hours later, Rosie and Cora waved Nicole off in her taxi and then walked arm in arm to the corner of Rosie's road where they parted ways.

'Are you sure you're OK, walking the last bit on your own, Little Miss Pregnant?' Cora squeezed her friend's shoulder affectionately.

'Of course! You be careful too – and get some sleep, you look knackered!' Rosie stood on tiptoe and pecked Cora on the cheek.

'OK – talk to you tomorrow – it was fun!'

'Yes, it was!' Rosie turned and blew a kiss then walked slowly off, the orange beam of the streetlights giving her coppery hair a fiery glow as she ambled the few yards to her front door. Cora watched her for a moment then huddled further into her fake fur jacket and headed for home, shivering. Roll on spring! This weather was really getting rather tedious now, she thought, wishing she'd remembered her gloves.

202

Five minutes later, she gratefully turned into her driveway, fumbling in her bag for her door key, which promptly slipped through her numb fingers onto the gravel. As she crouched to pick it up, she heard a noise behind her. Turning sharply, she caught a glimpse of a white trainer disappearing into the shadows beyond the gatepost.

'Oi!' Suddenly angry, she ran to the gate. Down the street, a figure was running, dodging the few people who were braving the chilly night. Moments later, he – or she, Cora couldn't tell – vanished round the corner. Breathing heavily, as if she'd been running herself, Cora leaned against the gatepost. So she'd been right. There WAS somebody following her. But who? And why? Could it be Justin? Was it just an obsessed fan? Trembling from more than just the cold now, she stumbled towards the door and let herself in with shaking hands.

Once locked and double-locked inside her apartment, she sank onto the sofa, clutching a cushion. Adam, she thought. I'll tell Adam. He'll know what to do. And she took herself off to bed and fell into an uneasy sleep, dreaming of shadowy running figures chasing small boys with piercing green eyes.

36

Monday 5th February

'The guy's never been faithful in his life. Anyone who goes out with him needs her head examined,' hissed Alice in a stage whisper, disdainfully shutting the latest *Hello* and dropping it on the floor.

Across the make-up room, Cora gripped the arms of her chair and clamped her lips shut.

'I will NOT rise to it. Ignore her, ignore her, ignore her ...' she chanted under her breath.

It was pretty obvious who Alice was talking about – she'd been poring over the six-page Benjamin Boland spread in her magazine for the past five minutes, muttering bitchily to poor Ben her make-up artist at a level clearly designed for Cora to hear, even over the hum of hairdryers and the chatter of the show's guests as they prepared to go on air. As Sam had predicted, the newsreader had clearly bounced straight back into nasty mode already. Ben caught Cora's eye in the mirror and grimaced apologetically, and she shook her head and smiled. Looking relieved, he continued teasing Alice's thick hair into gentle curls. He yanked the comb a little roughly through a knotty strand and Alice jumped.

'Ouch!' she whined. 'Be careful, idiot! How am I supposed to concentrate with you tugging at me like that? Where's Sherry today, anyway?'

Ben said nothing. Sighing loudly, Alice picked up a red notebook and started to flick through the pages, pausing every now and again to mouth questions she'd obviously written in advance for today's big interviews.

Cora raised her eyes heavenwards and exchanged smirks with Danny, who was putting the finishing touches to her blusher.

'So Danny – any gossip? You know, other than that in the trashy mags?'

'Oh, Cora. I could tell you, I'd love to tell you, you know that, but then I really would have to kill you. A make-up artist never ...'

'Er ... Cora. You're so clever – what does quant ... em ... quantit ... hang on ... quantitative easing mean again?' interrupted Alice, smiling sweetly over her shoulder.

Astounded, Cora whipped her white cape off and stood up. Seriously – did Alice really think she was going to help her now, after the little bitch-fest she'd just listened to? What on earth was wrong with the girl?

'Thanks, Danny. That looks great, you're a star,' she said, and headed for the door.

'Cora! Did you not hear me?' Alice's voice was so piercing Cora half expected dogs to rush into the room.

'Bye Danny – Ben,' she said cheerfully, not looking at Alice.

'Oh, I see!' the newsreader thundered. 'Very funny. HILARIOUS.'

The room was suddenly quiet, all eyes on Alice and Cora.

Cora stood in the doorway, waiting.

Alice paused for a moment, and when she spoke her voice was quiet and pure ice.

'I'm warning you, Cora – ignore me at your peril. People who ignore me live to regret it.'

She stared at her rival with steely blue eyes, and unexpectedly a chill ran through Cora. Wow, she thought. She can actually be really scary when she wants to be. Transfixed, she gazed back at Alice for a long moment, then dragged her eyes away and left the room.

'And then he – or she – just ran around the corner and disappeared. And that's it – well, for now, anyway.'

206

'And at no stage have any of these people talked to you, tried to make contact in any way?' Adam tapped his pen thoughtfully against his coffee mug as he listened. Cora definitely sounded nervous, and he thought she was unlikely to be the type to *imagine* somebody was following her, but it didn't sound like she'd actually been in any danger at any point. He wasn't sure there was much he could do.

'Well – no. I mean, I've only actually *seen* the person once, that last time. The previous times it was more like … well, shadows, or movements. Or a feeling that someone was there. I know it sounds stupid.'

'No, no, not at all. Look, Cora, all I can say for now is keep your wits about you. Try not to walk around on your own, especially at night. And if at any point you're actually threatened, or feel in real danger, call 999 straight away, OK? But try not to worry. It's a stressful time, what with your boss's murder and all that's happened since. Try and relax, alright?'

'Yes, OK. Thanks, Adam.'

Cora ended the call, feeling only slightly reassured. She could tell the police officer was a little sceptical, and who would blame him? She tossed her mobile into her handbag on the passenger seat and started her engine. As she crawled along the South Bank, her mind turned for the first time in days to the whole Justin mystery. She rubbed her throbbing brow, steering with one hand. It was beyond her. The hanging around outside the building, the fleeing to Spain, the weird messages – and especially the last one.

Stuck for what seemed an age at a red light, she picked up her phone again and flicked through her Twitter feed to her direct messages. She clicked on the last one from Justin.

@a-friend @CoraBaxterMLive Cora, I got your msg. But a warning for you. Be very careful. Watch your back.

She looked at the date. The fifteenth of January. Today was the fifth of February, so she hadn't heard from him in nearly three weeks. Three weeks. She did some calculations in her head. She was pretty certain that the first time she'd thought someone was watching her was a few days after Justin's message. Could it be him? Could he be back in the country? But surely he'd get in touch, not just hang around in the dark scaring her? And what exactly was she supposed to be careful about? It made no sense.

'None of it makes *any bloody sense*!' she said loudly, banging her fist on the steering wheel, just as a harassed-looking woman in a tight, black suit and tottering heels scurried across the road in front of her car. The woman scowled at her. Cora glowered back, her decision to keep Justin's odd behaviour a secret weighing even more heavily on her mind today. Should she at least tell Benjamin? It was the only thing she hadn't shared with him, and she was starting to feel bad about that. She pondered for a moment, then yet again changed her mind. Adam was right – nobody had actually threatened to do her any harm. And even if something odd was going on with Justin, he would never hurt her, she would bet her life on that.

Sighing, she turned Radio Four on. The afternoon play was starting. Just the distraction she needed.

That night, she felt immeasurably better as she snuggled into Benjamin's arms under his snowy duvet. Reluctant to go home and be alone, she'd suggested an impromptu mid-week meet up, and he'd been only too happy to oblige. As they'd cuddled up on the sofa, watching a classic Bond film and sipping tea, she'd felt so comfortable and happy she'd wondered why on earth she'd thought she might also have feelings for Adam. Ridiculous. Benjamin was all she needed. He was perfect.

'Shattered, babe,' he murmured now, and kissed the back of her neck gently.

'Mmm, me too. Sleep, then?'

'Think so. If you don't mind.'

'Of course not. Love you. G'night …'

She closed her eyes and drifted off almost immediately. Benjamin stroked her silky arm gently and stared into the darkness. He did love her, he really did. He'd even shrugged off the advances of several stunning women on his weekend shoot in the Caribbean, much to the astonishment of his crew. He'd been completely faithful, even when there was no chance of Cora finding out what he'd been up to. He was amazed at himself. The big question was, could he keep it up? He thought about it for a while, and for the first time, a tiny seed of doubt crept into his mind. Just a tiny one, but a seed nonetheless. Was he really ready to settle down? Had he met Cora too soon, before he really, truly, was ready to get serious?

'But I don't want to lose her. Come on, Benj. Grow up,' he thought, and pushed himself up onto his elbow to gaze at Cora, now deeply asleep. He bent his head and brushed his lips against her cheek. She didn't stir. Smiling, he lay down again. Everything would be fine.

37

'Damn thing. It was so much easier when we were allowed to have the wheels,' grumbled Scott.

He stood up and dragged his chair a few inches towards the truck door so Rodney had a bit more room to sprawl on the floor. It was an ordinary office swivel chair, but without the wheels – all the trucks had been forced to remove their chair wheels recently, after an unfortunate incident when an engineer had accidentally wheeled backwards straight out of the side door onto a busy road.

'At least you won't end up as roadkill,' mumbled Rodney, his mouth full of chocolate digestive.

'Yeah, whatever.' Scott sighed and took a loud slurp of tea. He looked thoroughly fed up, as always nowadays. Cora and Nathan, who were sharing the front passenger seat, glanced surreptitiously at each other. Several weeks after he'd last been questioned by the police, they were still no closer to discovering what their friend's problem was. He simply changed the subject every time they raised it, so much so that they'd pretty much given up.

'He'll tell us in his own time. There's no point in pestering him,' Rodney had said wisely earlier that morning as they huddled together, the wind whipping their cheeks, outside a hospital where there'd been a huge norovirus outbreak. And so they'd all agreed to leave well alone. Cora had bigger things on her mind today anyway, she thought with a grin. It had taken a few weeks to find a date that suited everyone, but tonight Benjamin was finally coming to Cheltenham for the weekend.

She'd barely seen him in the past fortnight, and as she clambered reluctantly out of the warm satellite van for the last live hit of the week she felt the usual little flutter of excitement. She couldn't wait for him to meet Rosie and Nicole, couldn't wait to show him off, couldn't wait for him to get an insight into her life away from TV, to see her beloved home town.

That evening though, as she luxuriated in a deep, hot bubble bath while she waited for Benjamin to arrive, her thoughts turned briefly to Adam again. They'd been chatting on the phone regularly recently, ostensibly because Cora needed regular updates on the murder case which seemed to have totally stalled. In reality though, she probably called him a little more often than necessary, enjoying the gentle banter that had developed between them, and the policeman certainly didn't seem to mind.

'He's becoming a bit of a guilty little pleasure,' she mused, stretching out a soapy hand to carefully pick up the glass of Sauvignon Blanc she'd balanced precariously on the edge of the tub. 'I know we'd be no good together – me and a single dad, for goodness' sake! But there's just something …'

Her mind drifted back to the telephone conversation they'd had earlier today, when she'd checked in for any updates on Jeanette's case.

'Oh Cora, I wish I had something for you,' Adam had sighed. The investigation had pretty much ground to a halt, but he thought it best not to tell the reporter that. He paused. 'So – how are you, anyway? Haven't seen you in the papers recently with, er … everything still rosy on the romantic front?'

'Er – yes, all good thanks!' Cora hoped she didn't sound as surprised by the question as she felt. 'Benjamin's coming to meet my friends in Gloucestershire for the first time tonight, actually. Should be fun.'

'That's – great. Enjoy.'

'I'll try,' she'd laughed. Now she cautiously replaced her glass and sat up in the bath, pink-cheeked and squeaky clean. He was interested, she knew he was. And she liked it. She couldn't help it. He was SO damn attractive. She wiped steam

212

from the mirror with a corner of her towel and stared at herself.

'And you shouldn't be finding him attractive, should you? So pull yourself together, numpty!'

And, suitably self-admonished, she strode purposefully into the bedroom to get ready for Benjamin.

He was still about an hour's drive away, travelling at a rather more sedate pace than he would have liked as a combination of Friday night traffic and three miles of roadworks brought the M4 to a crawl. He groaned as the cars in front braked yet again, and turned up the music in his custom-designed Range Rover Evoque. As Adele and the theme from *Skyfall* boomed from the speakers, he tried to clarify how he felt about the forthcoming weekend.

'It'll be good to see her,' he thought. 'Great in fact. We've barely seen each recently. And it'll be nice to see where she lives, and meet her friends, I guess.'

He tried to ignore the tiny wave of anxiety that suddenly pulsed through him. They'd been together for a while now, it was perfectly normal to meet your partner's friends, wasn't it? Of course it was. But in the past couple of weeks, when work had largely kept them apart, the niggling doubts had crept in again. He'd been lonely before he met her, although that was something he would never have admitted to anyone, and desperate to meet somebody, somebody he could talk to as well as have sex with, to rid him of that feeling. But he needed to get over this stupid fear of being tied down, of being with just one woman. Had he done all the stuff he needed to do, before settling down? Had he really? The same question had been running around in his head too often in recent days, and he simply didn't know what the answer was.

He flicked over to TalkSport as a fleeting thought of the beautiful woman he'd chatted to briefly in a bar last night flashed into his mind, then pushed her out of his head. This weekend, he would concentrate on Cora. Gorgeous, wonderful Cora. He smiled, and on cue the traffic began to move again. Moving smoothly into the outside lane, Benjamin grinned happily to himself, put his foot down and sped westwards.

'Well, after that delightful first conversation, how could I resist?' Cora felt herself blushing as Benjamin, Rosie, and Nicole all howled with laughter. They'd been talking about diarrhoea for a good ten minutes now. It was lucky they'd chosen a quiet booth at the back of the small bar, away from prying ears. Cora would most definitely be having words with Nicole later for bringing the subject up. Honestly, would she ever be allowed to forget it? She elbowed Benjamin in the ribs.

'OK, OK, enough now, give me a break, please!'

Still laughing, he draped his arm over her shoulders and hugged her. 'Oh, sorry darling, but you have to admit that as a chat up line killer, that was probably an Oscar winner!'

'He's right, Cora!' Rosie giggled. She wrapped her arms protectively over her bump and smiled at her friend fondly.

'Yes, yes I know. But can we change the subject now, please?'

'I know – let's talk about that time you got your jeans belt caught on a sticky-out nail in that house on live telly and ripped a big hole in your bum ...' Nicole swayed slightly in her seat, waving her pint of cider in the air.

Benjamin spluttered into his wine. 'Really?'

'Yesh, really.' Nicole was definitely rather drunk.

Cora raised her eyes to the ceiling. 'Maybe I should have said, let's change the subject and talk about something other than me and what an idiot I can be?'

'Well, we could ...' Benjamin said slowly. 'But we wouldn't have nearly so much fun ... '

Nicole snorted, and even Rosie, who was stone-cold sober, started sniggering again.

Cora sighed theatrically. 'Well, I'm going to the loo. Maybe you could all pull yourselves together while I'm gone?'

'No, no, I'm coming too!' Nicole banged her glass down on the table, sloshing a healthy quantity of cider onto Benjamin's hand. He exchanged amused glances with Cora.

'And me. For only the seventeenth time tonight. Got to love pregnancy.' Rosie stood up warily, grabbing Cora's arm to steady herself.

'Right, it seems we're all going to the ladies, then. Back in a moment, Benj ... after we've talked about you, of course!'

'I'd expect no less. I'll get the drinks in,' he replied, and Cora waved her thanks as she led her friends towards the toilets.

'So – what do you think?' she said eagerly as soon as the door shut behind them. Rosie dived into a cubicle and slammed it shut, sighing with relief.

'Well, I like him,' she announced from behind the door. 'He's not nearly as showbiz and arrogant as he seems on telly. AND he's flipping lovely to look at. Nice one, Cora.'

'Nicole?' Cora turned to the mirror where Nicole was reapplying lip gloss with a slightly unsteady hand.

'Yeah, agreed. He's alright.' She staggered backwards slightly, then leaned forward, frowning as she scrutinised her handiwork.

'Only alright?' Cora reached into her handbag for an eyeliner.

'Alright is good. I thought he'd be a dick.'

'What? Did you really? You never said that before!'

The toilet flushed and Rosie emerged. 'Well, obviously she never said it. But we both thought it a bit, Cora. Just because he's such a big star, and we don't know any telly types apart from you, and you don't count ...'

'Thanks!'

'And even though we could see he was extremely good looking, and rich and all that, and we were excited that you were dating him, we didn't really think he'd be proper boyfriend material, if you know what I mean ...'

'But we shtand corrected,' Nicole interrupted. 'Well, Rosie shtands corrected. I'm sort of shwaying corrected at the moment ...' She lurched forward, grabbing at Rosie's cardigan to steady herself.

'Crikey. How many have you *had*?'

'Erm ... about twelfteen I reckon,' Nicole slurred happily.

'OK, twelfteen isn't actually a word. I think it might be time to get you in a taxi, my love.' Rosie peeled Nicole's hands off her top and turned her round firmly. She tottered to the door and held on to it. Cora laughed and went to her aid.

'And they say people in the media are big drinkers! Remember that night not long after I started at *Morning Live,* when the senior director was telling us all how he hardly drank any more, and then got up and walked straight into a wall? I'd hate to be at a vet's night out …'

Nicole planted a sloppy kiss on Cora's forehead. 'Shut up and help me walk.'

As they weaved their way back to their corner, Cora smiled happily to herself. A big test for Benjamin tonight, and he seemed to have passed it with flying colours – that called for several more drinks!

That decision seemed less of a good one when she woke at 2 a.m. with a dry mouth and the beginnings of a pounding headache. Leaving Benjamin snoring gently, she slipped out of bed in search of water and paracetamol. As she headed back to the bedroom clutching a pint glass, she paused for a moment at the lounge window, glancing quickly up and down the quiet road. Suddenly her stomach lurched. Directly opposite her building, leaning against a lamppost and quite clearly visible, stood a figure, bundled up in a Puffa jacket and with a hood pulled around its face. He (if it was a he?) was looking down at his hands, seemingly engrossed in something he was holding – a phone? As Cora stood there, frozen to the spot, the person looked up suddenly, as if aware he was being watched. She caught a glimpse of a pale face – then, like a ghost, the figure melted backwards into the shadows of the long hedge that ran across the front of the apartment block opposite. Shaking, Cora rubbed her eyes and peered into the darkness. She stood there for another full minute, but the street was empty.

BEEP. She nearly jumped out of her skin as her mobile phone sprang into life, sounding as loud as a foghorn in the still, dark room. What the hell? It was 2 a.m.!

Trembling, she located the phone on the dining table and opened her Twitter messages. It was Justin.

@a-friend @CoraBaxterMLive *Cora, I'm deadly serious. Be* *very, very careful. Trust nobody.*

Her heart pounding so fast she felt faint, Cora tapped out a reply.

@CoraBaxterMLive @a-friend Justin – please tell me what's going on? Be careful of what? I'm scared.

She waited, trying to breathe deeply. Moments later, a reply flashed up.

@a-friend @CoraBaxterMLive Just watch your back. I can't explain properly, but I will soon. I'll be in touch.

She stared at the screen, trying to work out what was going on. A man – she thought it *was* a man, now – outside her house at 2 a.m. Doing something on a phone. And then, moments later, a message from Justin telling her to be careful. Was that him then, outside? Was he back in the UK? All she'd seen was the pale outline of a face in the moonlight. It could have been him, certainly – the height looked about right. But if so, why was he lurking around, watching her, and then sending these scary warning messages? Or did he somehow know she was being stalked by someone else, and was trying to warn her? But how would he know, if he was abroad? It made no sense.

Shivering with fear and cold, she stumbled back into the bedroom and pressed her body against Benjamin's. He stirred slightly, automatically throwing his arm across her without waking. She entwined her fingers in his, her mind racing. There was no doubt now. She was clearly in some sort of danger. And she had no idea what to do about it.

38

'And Cora's at the scene for us now ... good morning, Cora!'

The sickly sweet sound of Alice Lomas's TV voice filled Cora's ear. Ugh, she thought.

'Good morning to you, Alice. Yes I'm here at ... at ... er ...'

Horror suddenly gripped her as her mind went blank. Where on earth was she? Was it Wiltshire? Or Somerset? She had absolutely no idea. None.

'Er ... well I'm somewhere, where last night farmers barricaded the dairy here behind me in protest at falling milk prices ...'

She cringed inwardly as she launched into the story, aware that Nathan was grinning widely behind the camera and Rodney's shoulders were shaking with suppressed laughter.

As she handed back to the studio, her soundman dropped his boom pole and chortled with delight. Nathan switched the camera off and stepped out from behind it, sniggering, and even Scott popped his head out of the truck with a big smile.

'Made my morning, that did, Cora!' he announced, and disappeared back inside.

'Aargh, what an *idiot* I am!' Cora slapped her hands over her face. The stress of what was going on with Justin and her stalker was definitely getting to her.

'We're in Taunton, Somerset. Just for future reference,' Nathan cackled.

'Thanks. Can't believe I did that. Alice will be loving it, can you imagine?'

'Ah, don't worry about her. Come on, let's grab a cuppa.'

Rodney slung his arm, today clad in a startling pink anorak, around her shoulders, and led her towards the truck. Nathan trailed behind them, giggling like a teenage girl.

'What with Cora's memory, and that jacket, Rodney, we look like a right group of nutters today. Where'd you get that – nick it from Katie Price's washing line?'

Despite herself, Cora smirked.

'I bought it in a rather expensive outdoor pursuits shop, actually,' said Rodney in his most dignified voice.

'But it's bright *pink*. Why would you buy a *pink* one?'

'It was on sale. And I'm secure in my sexuality, Nathan.' Rodney sat down primly on his usual space on the floor, and accepted the mug of tea Scott was holding out.

'I give up, I really do.' Nathan picked up his tea and spooned two large sugars into it.

'So Cora – what happened? Not like you, luv.' There was genuine concern in Scott's face, despite the smiles, and Cora was touched. He seemed happier today, which made a pleasant change.

'I'm just a bit tense, I think. You know, with this weird stalker business ... '

They all nodded. The boys, like all her friends, now knew about all the strange happenings, although she was more determined than ever now not to mention Justin's unsettling messages to anyone. Trust nobody, he had said. Why had he said that?

'And still nothing the cops can do?' Rodney's question interrupted her thoughts. He put his mug carefully down on the floor next to him and reached for the packet of chocolate fingers on Scott's shelf.

'No. Spoke to them again on Monday. Adam said that unless I was actually physically threatened, no crime's been committed. And I haven't been. The stalker hasn't actually done anything. I'm just scared he might, at some point.'

'Bloody peculiar. I'd just go up and ask him, next time you see him. Probably just an obsessed fan, Cora. If you asked him to stop, go away, he might listen?'

'Maybe.' Cora fished the teabag out of her Earl Grey. Maybe she should ask Benjamin to have a word, she thought. Her boyfriend had been livid when she'd filled him in about the stalker outside her house, especially as he'd dismissed her previous sightings as paps, or possibly as Cora's imagination. Now, he was vowing to 'break the guy's neck' if he popped up again. Cora doubted he actually would – Benjamin, for all his strength and size, was more of a gentle giant than a fighter, she suspected. But it was sweet that he'd been so angry.

The boys started chatting among themselves about some intermittent technical problem with the truck, and her thoughts drifted obsessively back to Justin. She was beginning to feel she would actually go mad if she didn't get to the bottom of it all very soon. She was now increasingly of the opinion that Justin somehow knew someone was following her and was trying to warn her. How he knew, she couldn't figure out. But the prospect of her stalker actually *being* Justin seemed ludicrous in the cold light of day. Why would he stalk her himself, and also send her messages warning her to watch her back? Despite everything, he was a good man. Whatever was going on, she knew he couldn't hurt anyone. She just needed to be careful, and maybe whoever it was would get bored and give up …

'TWO MINUTES, CORA!' The director's voice rumbled through the satellite van's speakers, startling her out of her reverie.

'Taunton, Somerset. Taunton, Somerset,' she muttered as she clambered out into the cold, Rodney and Nathan hot on her tail. They both laughed, and she joined in. Thank goodness for her job. Nothing like a spot of live telly to distract you from your worries!

Two hours later, with work done for the day, Cora felt a little calmer. She had to get this into perspective, she told herself firmly as she sped homewards. If somebody was watching her, fine. Let them. Plenty of people had stalkers, and few actually got hurt. She refused to let this weirdo upset her.

She pulled out to overtake a lorry, suddenly realising that she was starving. Spotting a Shell garage up ahead, she

221

indicated left and parked on the forecourt, then wandered around the shop, picking up bits and pieces to keep her going. A big bottle of water, an all-day breakfast sandwich packed with bacon, sausage, and boiled egg, an apple, and a bag of cheese and onion crisps – that should do it. She yawned as she handed a tenner to a bored-looking cashier with straw-coloured hair and dodgy blue eyeshadow.

'There you go, luv – three ten change,' said the cashier, looking up at Cora for the first time. Cora saw a flash of recognition in the woman's eye, but hastily muttered her thanks and scooted out of the shop. The woman stared after her, scratching her bleached head.

Cora unlocked her car and got in, tossing the bag of food on the seat beside her. Despite the fact that the *Morning Live* press officers did little to raise the profile of the on-screen reporters, concentrating their efforts on the studio presenters, the job still meant she got recognised nearly every day. People were mostly nice, but she was too tired to get into a conversation about her work this morning. Yawning, she eased the car back into the traffic, glancing in her rear-view mirror as another car followed her off the forecourt. It was dark blue, navy. She looked again, suddenly remembering the navy car she'd briefly thought had been following her the first day she'd had coffee with Adam and Harry. She slowed her car a little, wanting it to overtake, but the navy car slowed too, staying about three vehicle lengths behind.

Cora squinted in her mirror, trying to see the driver, but the car was too far away. She breathed deeply, trying to quash the anxiety that was once again starting to take a grip. Come on, girl. There are thousands of dark blue cars on the road. You're imagining it, she told herself, and dragged her eyes away from the mirror.

Resolutely staring at the road in front of her, she spotted a parking area up ahead and indicated left. As she pulled in, the navy car slowed a little then sailed past, disappearing out of view within seconds. Cora sighed with relief. What an idiot she was. Grinning to herself, she reached over and pulled the sandwich out of the bag. She was about to take the first bite when a text message flashed onto her phone. She reluctantly put the sandwich down again and retrieved her mobile from the passenger seat. It was from Scott, and a chill ran through Cora as she read it.

'Hey Cora, Nath, Rodders. Made a big decision – going to tell you what's been going on. I'll hotel with you tonight if we're assigned? We need to talk ...'

39

Cora shifted position in the worn, red leather armchair and held out her hands towards the fire crackling in the cast iron Victorian grate. Opposite her on a deep Chesterfield sofa, Rodney and Nathan sat in silence. Rodney, who was wearing a plaid orange and green shirt with brown suede elbow patches, stared at the ceiling, and Cora watched as Nathan glanced sideways at the hideous garment, opened his mouth and then shut it again.

'Gosh,' she thought, turning back to gaze into the flames. 'If Nathan's refraining from commenting on Rodney's clothing, things *must* be serious.'

They were the only people in the hotel lounge at this early hour. After all three had received Scott's text, they'd arranged to meet at six at the hotel booked for them for tonight's stopover in Buckinghamshire. Cora glanced at the gothic-looking black clock on the mantelpiece: 6.15, and still no sign of the engineer.

'Wonder where he is?' she said.

Rodney lowered his eyes from the ceiling. 'Maybe he's changed his mind? About telling us whatever it is he wants to tell us?'

Cora nodded slowly. 'Maybe.'

'No, I haven't changed my mind. Sorry I'm late.'

They all jumped as Scott suddenly appeared in the doorway. He shrugged off his heavy coat and dumped it on a table, then sat down cautiously in the armchair next to Cora's. All three of his friends turned to face him, and he rubbed his hands over his face for a moment, then took a deep breath.

'So, here goes. First off, I did *not* kill Jeanette. I'm not here

225

to make a confession of that sort, just so you know.'

'We never thought that, Scott,' said Cora hastily. 'But we have been really worried about you.'

'I know, I know. I'm sorry. I was just ... well, ashamed I suppose.'

'Ashamed of what? Come on, mate, there's nothing you can tell us that can change what we think of you, you know that! We're a team, aren't we?'

Nathan leaned over and patted Scott on the knee. Scott nodded gratefully.

'OK – well – here goes. Basically – my name is Scott Edson, and I'm a compulsive gambler.'

He looked around at all three of them in turn.

'OK. Go on.' Cora's voice was gentle.

'It started a couple of years back – not sure why really, it was just a bit of fun, a way to relax after a long day. Mostly online to start with, and I won just enough to make it exciting. Was able to buy some great bits and pieces for the house, even some quite rare pieces.'

He paused. The others watched him intently.

'And then, of course, as these things do, it got out of control. I started losing, and bet even more to try to win it back, and then lost bigger ... and then when the bank account ran dry, I just couldn't bring myself to tell Elaine, so I ended up going to a loan shark. Yes, I'm an idiot, you don't need to say it.'

Rodney shook his head. 'Mate, you're not an idiot. These things happen to people. Go on.'

Scott sighed heavily. 'Well, we've done enough stories about them – you can imagine the rest. Ended up having to sell pretty much everything to meet the payments. That's why the place was stripped when you came round, Nath.'

Nathan nodded.

'Elaine went mental when I eventually had to tell her what was up. She's standing by me, amazingly. I love her so much, don't know what I'd do without her and the kids ...' His voice shook, and Cora leapt from her chair and perched on the edge of his, draping a comforting arm around his shoulders. He sank his

226

face into his hands and breathed deeply.

'So, that explains some of what's been going on – but what about the police, the murder? How does that tie in, Scott?'

Scott raised his head, an anguished look on his face.

'That day, after I had the disciplinary with Jeanette, I had one last payment to make to the loan shark. Elaine had borrowed it from her parents, enough to pay it all off, clean slate. I was shit scared after seeing Jeanette – she told me I was on my last chance, one more strike and I was out, and that's why I lost it in the lift. Thought, if I lost my job, how would I ever pay the in-laws back, make it up to Elaine, you know?'

Cora hugged him, and he smiled weakly and continued.

'So I went back to where I'd parked the van, grabbed the bag with the money – all had to be in cash of course – and went off to pay the guy. I knew there was no easy parking near his flat, you know what central London's like, so I walked instead of driving, and then walked back. Course, the cops eventually saw all that on CCTV, and to them it looked like I'd parked up nearby, grabbed – I dunno, a murder weapon? A disguise? – and headed back to kill the old bitch. And I didn't want to say anything, because I was so ashamed, and I thought the loan shark guy would never back up the story anyway. So I just stayed schtum, when the cops questioned me …'

'You've cleared it all up now, though?' Rodney sounded anxious.

'Yeah, yeah. Amazingly, the bloke said OK, he'd tell the cops I was with him and what for. Said he had nothing to fear, was running a legal money lending business and so on. And he had a security camera in his office, showed the cops footage of me in there, handing over money at around eight o'clock that morning, which gives me a solid alibi. I should have just fessed up in the first place, I'm a dick. I put you all through all that worry, and Elaine …'

His voice wobbled again and his eyes filled with tears. He wiped them away angrily.

'Oh, Scott.' Cora's eyes were wet too as she hugged him again, and Nathan and Rodney rose from the sofa

227

simultaneously and patted Scott awkwardly on the back.

'Thanks so much guys. You don't know what it means ...'

'Rubbish, mate.' Nathan's voice was gruff with emotion. 'We're just glad it's all out in the open at last ... oh bugger.'

He glared at his phone which had just started to ring loudly on the coffee table.

'Nathan here. Oh. OK. Well, we're all at the hotel already ...'

Scott, Cora, and Rodney looked anxiously at each other. Now what? Another hundred-mile drive to a different location?

'OK, great. Thanks. Have a good night!' Nathan ended the call with a grin.

'Well, that's a bit of a result! Story's cancelled, but as we're all here and the hotel's paid for, they said we might as well stay here till we're assigned tomorrow!'

'Woo-hooo!' Rodney threw his scarf in the air, Cora flung herself joyfully back into her own armchair and even Scott managed a broad smile.

Nathan was already heading for the bar. 'Two white wines and a pint of cider?' he called over his shoulder.

'Cheers, mate!' Scott was looking happier than Cora had seen him in a long time. She smiled fondly at him. Thank goodness, maybe things could go back to normal now. She stretched luxuriously in her chair, long legs warmed by the fire, as Scott suddenly noticed Rodney's remarkable shirt and started ribbing him mercilessly.

Cora listened happily. Whoever had killed Jeanette, it definitely wasn't her friend Scott. And that would do, for now.

'So that's that. Another dead end. We're screwed on this one, guys. I have no idea where to look next. Any ideas? Anyone? Please?'

Adam stood up abruptly, shoving his chair noisily backwards. His frustrated gaze swept the room, taking in the glum, weary faces. Damn it. A high profile murder like this, that seemed to have happened right under the noses of dozens of people, and they couldn't solve it? HE couldn't solve it? This was not good. Not good at all. Bloody terrible in fact. The CCTV pictures from the loan shark's office had finally confirmed Scott Edson's alibi, and Adam was all out of ideas.

'What about the newsreader – Alice Lomas? Should we look at her more closely?'

Adam glanced at Donna, the officer who'd spoken up. He shook his head.

'No. We've considered her. Opportunity – possibly. Motive – none. None that we can see anyway. Feel free to investigate her a bit more if you like, but I'm not bringing her in unless you get something concrete. She's never out of the papers, and she seems to be a right little diva – we don't need the bad publicity.'

Donna nodded and sat down.

Adam sighed and looked at his notes. The only other person on his list with a question mark against her name was Samantha Tindall, the ambitious producer who was now doing Kendrick's job, but he had nothing to actually connect her to the murder either. It was hopeless. With a heavy heart, he made the announcement he'd been dreading.

'Hence, folks, we're going to have to scale down the case. Some of you will be back to the day job as from tomorrow – I'll send a memo round as to who's staying on it with me full time. Thanks for your hard work – I'll bring you back on board if we get another lead. And we'll release the body, let her family organise the funeral, they've waited long enough.'

His voice tailed off. He turned and walked to the window, his own reflection glaring back at him, and pressed his nose against the glass. Outside, cars crawled by, 'bumper to bumper' as the cheery radio traffic reporters loved to call it. London's rush hour in full swing. Adam slowly bumped his forehead against the cold pane. Who the hell had killed Jeanette Kendrick? Why couldn't he figure this out? He stopped bumping and turned to face the room again. His colleagues were back at their desks, but there was a subdued air in the big office.

Scaling down. How he hated that phrase. But this wasn't

over yet. He'd find Kendrick's killer if it was the last thing he ever did. Failure was simply not an option. And, fortified by the thought, he headed for the coffee machine.

'And then he said … he said …' Cora dissolved into helpless giggles.

Nathan snorted and picked up where she'd left off.

'He said, in his poshest voice: "What do you think of the clitoris on the back wall? Planted it myself, you know …"'

Scott and Rodney howled. Cora was already laughing so much she could barely sit upright, and slid slowly off her chair onto the carpet.

Nathan hauled her back up, still giggling. They'd been swapping funny work stories for the past hour, this latest about a rather unpopular director who'd invited some of the studio crew round for dinner and shown them round his newly designed garden.

Scott wiped his eyes. 'Well, that beats my chlamydia cock-up, that's for sure! Clitoris! Hilarious. Clematis. Why do we seem to find that so hard to remember? Clematis. Clematis …'

He got up and headed for the gents', still muttering the word under his breath. The others looked at each other contentedly. They had Scott back. *And* they had an unexpected free night, together in a hotel. Wonderful! Cora drained her wine glass and then jumped as her phone beeped.

'Uh oh. They'd better not move us now … I've had a bit too much to drink to start driving anywhere …'

Then she sighed with relief as she read the message.

'What?' Nathan frowned.

'Just Benjamin. Telling me he loves me.' Cora grinned.

'Phew.' Rodney waved his empty glass. 'One more before we hit the hay?'

She nodded. 'One last drink, and then a proper night's sleep. How blissful.'

'How blissful indeed,' sighed Rodney.

Cora stared into the fire, and for a moment Justin and the stalker flashed back into her mind. She felt the familiar lurch of

230

unease. Then, determined not to let anything spoil the evening, she turned back to the boys. They were all together, Scott was part of the gang again. All was right with the world.

232

40

One month later – Wednesday 28th March

Adam was leaning across the table, bright-eyed with anticipation. He loved Cora's ridiculous stories about her life as a roving reporter – they were the highlight of what had become a weekly coffee shop meeting, ostensibly to pass on updates on Jeanette's murder. However, as he'd had nothing at all to report for weeks, with the investigation now at a total standstill, their little get-togethers were really just getting-to-know-you sessions, during which he always tried to forget that she was actually dating someone the magazines called 'the hottest man on telly'. He could deny it to himself all he liked, but he had become rather fond of Miss Cora Baxter.

'So, your colleagues in Solihull announced a crackdown on airguns after a spate of cat-shootings – remember, about a year ago? – and we were sent off there to do a live with this poor cat that had been shot six times and survived, but was too traumatised to leave the house,' Cora was saying.

She paused to nibble her Bath bun, swallowed and continued. 'Except, of course, when me and the boys turned up at the house at 5 a.m. to set up for the live, the flipping cat wasn't there, having gone out the night before and not come home. Honestly, I felt sick! I rang Jeanette and, well, you can imagine …'

Adam grinned as Cora drew herself up to her full height in her chair and launched into her Jeanette impression.

'WHAT DO YOU MEAN, THE BLOODY CAT HAS GONE OUT? HE'S SUPPOSED TO BE TRAUMATISED! BLOODY WELL GO AND FIND HIM THEN!'

Two elderly women sitting opposite turned simultaneously and glared at Cora. She shrank back in her seat, suddenly aware that she was being rather loud.

'Er, sorry,' she said.

The ladies tutted and returned to their coffee and croissants. Adam sniggered.

'You're hilarious. What happened next?'

What had happened was that Cora, her crew and the cat's owners had spent the next forty-five minutes stumbling around the garden in the dark, shrieking the cat's name and waking up all the neighbours. Two and a half minutes after they gave up, and just as Cora, with heavy heart, was about to dial Jeanette's number again, the cat strolled nonchalantly into the kitchen, looking remarkably untraumatised. Thankfully, he was scarred enough by his airgun wounds to *look* traumatised which, after all, was all that really mattered on TV, and the story was saved.

'So all was well that ended well. But that old telly adage, never work with children and animals – so true!' Cora said vehemently, and took a large and satisfying bite out of her bun.

Adam swallowed the last of his rhubarb crumble and grinned. 'Anyway – how's your stalker situation these days? Anything new to report?'

Cora shook her head. 'Nothing for a week now. Maybe he's got bored and given up, eh? I'm not that interesting to stalk, after all – go to work, come home, that's about it.'

She had, in fact, almost convinced herself that she'd imagined the whole thing. Why would anyone follow *her*? It made no sense. It was, she'd decided, much more likely that the strange stalker was actually a fan of Benjamin's, as most of the incidents had happened when she was with him. There were some peculiar people around, and she wasn't going to waste any more precious time worrying about it. If that was how this particular fan got his kicks, let him! Justin had gone quiet, too – no more scary warning messages. And she hadn't seen the navy car again either, deliberately not looking too closely at cars behind her as she drove. The sense of imminent danger that had freaked her so much a few weeks ago had eased.

She smiled at Adam, at the same time feeling slightly guilty that she was sitting here enjoying his company so much when she hadn't seen Benjamin for over a week. Both their schedules had been insane, and there'd simply been no days when both of them were free. She missed him terribly, but she had to acknowledge somewhat reluctantly that Adam did a rather good job of distracting her from pining for her boyfriend. She looked forward immensely to their weekly briefings, and she suspected he did too. Harry had joined them once or twice too since Cora's first meeting with him, and she'd grown rather fond of the little boy as well. It was, for some reason, a fondness she hadn't shared with Benjamin. After all, she reasoned, these were just work meetings, and as she and her boyfriend tended not to discuss the finer details of work much when they were together, there seemed no need to tell him about unimportant meetings. That was fair enough, wasn't it?

Adam was pouring himself a second cup of tea from the big pot on the table.

'Me too, please,' said Cora, pushing her cup towards him. As he obliged, she suddenly became aware of a familiar voice behind her. She turned, but saw nobody. Then she heard it again.

'I feel … sick. When I think about it. And so, so guilty. I really do,' the voice said.

Alice? That was Alice Lomas. Where was she?

Adam had recognised the distinctive whiny tones too. 'Is that Alice? Oh look – there's an alcove, there at the back. Hadn't noticed it before. She must be sitting round there,' he murmured.

Cora turned round to see what he meant. Sure enough, tucked away in the rear of the cosy café was a little booth.

'What did she say … she feels guilty? Wonder what she's been up to then?' whispered Cora.

'I wonder …' Adam's eyes were glued to the alcove.

Alice was still talking, but her voice was too low for them to make out any more of the conversation, and moments later she fell silent.

235

'Was she on the phone, do you think? Or is she with somebody?' Cora asked quietly.

'Sounded like a phone call … I only heard one voice. Oh – watch out, she's on the move.'

Abruptly, the subject of their interest emerged from the booth, phone in hand, and marched smartly towards the exit. Cora steeled herself. There was bound to be a nasty quip from the presenter as she passed by. Adam raised an eyebrow. Although he'd never seen them together, he had become well aware of the animosity between the two colleagues. Somehow, he suspected Cora was able to give as well as she got.

Alice, a distracted look on her face, was almost alongside their table when she noticed them. To Cora's astonishment, the newsreader stopped dead in her tracks and instantly flushed bright red.

'Cora. And … Sergeant, er …' stammered Alice, who never seemed to be able to remember Adam's rank.

'Good afternoon, Alice.' Adam smiled politely.

Cora stared. 'Are you feeling alright, Alice?' The girl was practically luminous.

'Yes. Fine. Why on earth wouldn't I be? Just didn't expect to see you here, that's all. Anyway, goodbye.'

'Bye, then.' Cora watched, bemused, as Alice rushed out into the drizzle and disappeared round the corner.

'Well. That was strange. Why did she go so red? And what was she feeling guilty about? More tea?'

Adam shook his head slowly. 'No idea. And yes, more tea, thanks.'

But, as Cora topped up their cups, he wondered – and not for the first time – if he'd been too hasty in ruling Alice Lomas out of the murder enquiry. Jeanette's body had finally been released to her family for burial last week, and at the funeral Alice had been practically hysterical, sobbing loudly by the grave, ashen-faced and trembling. Her behaviour had been in stark contrast to that of other members of staff, who had been respectful and solemn but not visibly distraught. This was, after all, a boss who had not been terribly popular. Even Jeanette's mother and other family members, while clearly deeply distressed, had wept in a more dignified manner than the newsreader. Yes, Alice was certainly behaving a little abnormally.

Making a mental note to go back over her statement with a fine tooth comb, Adam smiled at Cora, who'd just launched into another anecdote. Maybe, one day soon, he'd actually have something interesting to tell *her*.

41

Benjamin stared at his reflection in the mirror for a moment, then turned away and flung himself truculently on the bed.

'You're an idiot, Benjamin Boland. You really need to sort yourself out,' he announced.

He loved Cora, he really did. He told her so all the time, something he'd never said and truly meant to any woman in his life up until now. But over the past few weeks it had been difficult for them to meet up due to their conflicting work schedules, and he'd screwed up. He'd done something that a man in love really should not do. He'd slept with somebody else.

And not just once. Three times. The same somebody else. There had been no need to be unfaithful, no need at all. He felt slightly sick. The thought of losing Cora genuinely horrified him. He wouldn't do it again, he vowed, as he shrugged off his clothes and crawled under the duvet. Definitely not. Absolutely, one hundred per cent, NOT.

'Wha ... whassup? Huh?'

Cora woke with a jump so violent she banged her head on the side window. Window? Hang on, why was there a window in her bed? She rubbed her eyes and glared at it. Yes, there was definitely a window there.

'Who put that there? I don't understand ...' she croaked.

'You're in the car, stupid. Stakeout, remember?' Clarity was restored by Nathan's voice at her right shoulder.

'Oh. Sorry,' she muttered. Of course. Stakeout. Somewhere in Wales. That's where she was. She massaged her stiff neck and peered out through the windscreen.

239

'Any sightings?'

Nathan shook his head. 'Tea?' he asked, waving a Thermos flask.

Cora nodded gratefully, and glanced at the clock on the dash of his car. Three ten in the morning. She pulled the collar of her Puffa jacket up around her face and stared out into the moonlit street. Complete silence, not even a car anywhere in sight. They'd been here since nine last night, parked in a dark lane almost directly opposite the gated entrance to the Cardiff mansion of Arwyn Jones. The Welsh pop sensation was, the *Morning Live* news desk had been reliably informed, currently in the throes of a passionate affair with Jessie Jarman, lead singer of girl band Sugar Kiss. Jessie had married Burberry model Stuart Stevens in a million-pound extravaganza less than a year ago and, if the rumours about her infidelity were true, this would be on the front pages for weeks.

If Cora and Nathan could get the first pictures of the illicit couple together, it would be a major coup for the breakfast show. Normally the tabloids got hold of all of these lurid tales first, so a TV show that broke the story would earn serious kudos.

'Sorry for falling asleep. It's even more tedious doing these things when there's nobody to talk to,' she said apologetically, and took a sip of her tea.

'No worries. I need a wee. Back in a mo.'

Nathan opened the car door, letting a rush of frosty air in. Spring might be almost here, but the early hours of the morning were still bitter. Cora shivered, and watched in the rear view mirror as the cameraman disappeared into the shadows behind the vehicle. It was easy for the boys, she sighed, shifting uncomfortably in her seat and ignoring the fact that she would soon need to go to the loo too. She always carried toilet paper and a plastic bag to put the used tissue in, but finding somewhere to go in the middle of the night was always a challenge.

'Oh, the glamour of telly!' she said theatrically, as Nathan clambered back in to the car. He slammed the door and turned

240

the key in the ignition.

'Tell me about it. I'll whack the heater on for a few minutes. Brass monkeys out there. Anything?'

'Negative. No lights on or anything. If they're in there together tonight, they'll be tucked up in bed if they've any sense. It'll be the day shift tomorrow who get the pictures of her leaving, mark my words. What time are we being relieved – eight a.m.?'

Nathan nodded. 'At least we get a day off tomorrow – I'm spending *all* of it in bed!' He stretched his hands above his head and cracked his knuckles.

'Urgh, stop it!' Cora punched her friend in the arm. 'Bed though … that sounds *soooo* good. I might go to London, sleep at Benjamin's for a few hours. He's around tomorrow afternoon, and we need to catch up. It's been impossible recently.'

'How are things going then? Still serious?'

Cora thought for a moment. A few weeks ago that would have been an easy question to answer. Now, she wasn't quite so sure.

'I don't know. We have an amazingly strong connection, and I do love him … we love each other, I think. But – oh, I don't know. I've been spending some time with Adam, and I really like him too. Although that could never go anywhere, because of the kid thing … but I shouldn't be having feelings for anyone else at all, if I'm in love, should I?'

Nathan looked at her quizzically.

'To be honest, I always thought that Benjamin was just a rebound thing. And they rarely last, do they? It was SO soon after Justin that you two got together.'

'It was, I know, but he made me smile again. I probably shouldn't have jumped into something so soon, no. But it just sort of happened. Oh Nathan, I don't know. I do love Benjamin, he's sweet and funny and kind. I'll just see how it goes. It's not like we're planning to get married or even live together or anything. There are no decisions to be made, we're just enjoying each other. I just wish I wasn't also enjoying Adam.'

'He is gorgeous though. Always did like a man in uniform …' Nathan sighed.

Cora laughed. 'You're such a slut. And he doesn't even wear a uniform, you twit. He's a plain clothes detective!'

Nathan tittered. 'He can detect what's going on in my clothes anytime.'

'Oh for goodness' sake!' Cora yawned. 'More tea please.'

They settled down into a companionable silence, sipping from their plastic cups, eyes glued to the driveway opposite. Only another four and a half hours to go. Then bed. How heavenly that would be.

The person who had brought Jeanette Kendrick's life to a premature close was already in bed, but sleep would not come. Mind racing, the murderer stared at the ceiling. It couldn't wait much longer. The police were clueless, but care would still be needed with the second killing. The plan was coming together perfectly, though, and it was almost ready to be put into action. The killer's heart raced. It was very nearly time. One more, then it would all be over.

42

'I've got something really interesting for you to listen to … hang on, I'll get it.'

Benjamin bounded off the sofa and started rummaging in the leather Paul Smith bag he'd flung carelessly on the floor earlier. Cora stretched lazily and watched him, admiring the tightness of his bottom as he bent over the bag. He really was the most extraordinarily fine specimen of a man. She smiled as he returned to his seat, clutching his iPhone.

'Now – remember last week you said you overheard Alice in that café, talking about feeling guilty about something?'

Cora nodded. She sat up, suddenly intrigued.

'Well, have a listen to this. Recorded it when I was on that magazine shoot yesterday – you know, the 'Sexiest Bods on the Box' one?'

'Yes – the one Alice was on too, silly cow?' Cora was even more interested now. What on earth had he recorded?

'Yep. Agreed, she's a silly cow. Got a smoking body though.'

Cora rolled her eyes.

'But not as smoking as yours, obviously,' he smiled.

'Yeah, yeah, get to the point!'

'OK, well – we were sitting around, waiting for the lights or something to be fixed up, and she gets a phone call. Wanders off to take it. I'm dying for a wee so I head into the toilets, and suddenly I can hear her, clear as day, through the wall. She's in the ladies' loo next door, but it was only a sort of temporary partition thing, so I could hear every word. And it was so peculiar, what she was saying, especially after what you told me about last week in the café. So I hit record on the phone. Here, listen.'

He pressed play. Agog, Cora leaned forward as Alice's unmistakeable voice filled the room.

'Yes, I feel really guilty. I feel awful. I can't stop thinking about it.'

Her voice was echoey and slightly distant, but Cora could hear every word. Her eyes widened. Yet again, the guilt thing. What on earth had Alice done? There was a pause, presumably as the person on the other end of the newsreader's phone responded. Then:

'But that's what's even worse. She was – well, she was nice to me. I know I can be a bitch, but I've never done anything like this before. Not something this bad. You know that, don't you?'

There was desperation in Alice's voice, and Cora clapped her hands over her mouth as a shocking suspicion entered her head. Benjamin raised his eyebrows and nodded as the recording continued.

'Look, got to go. Talk soon. Sorry to lay all this on you. Bye.'

Benjamin pressed stop. 'See what I mean? Pretty weird, huh? She's obviously done something majorly bad ...'

Cora slumped back on the cushions in disbelief. 'Bloody hell. Could she – I mean, could she be talking about something as serious as murder? Could she, Benj? Could she have killed Jeanette? Seriously?'

Benjamin shrugged. 'Can't really imagine it. Can you, honestly? But – well, I don't really know her, babe. You work with her. What do you think? Something's happened though, that's for sure.'

Cora felt slightly sick. She thought for a moment. Horrifically, it did sort of make sense.

'That bit about someone being nice to her. Jeanette *was* nice to her – about the only person she was nice to – and Alice was nice back. They seemed to get on, for some reason. But no – hang on. Why would she kill the only person who was actually

244

on her side? She wouldn't, would she? Unless they'd fallen out or something? Oh, I don't understand. And what should we do? Anything?'

Benjamin took her hand. 'I'm not sure. Tell your copper friend, see what he thinks? I'll make a copy of the recording for you. Then at least you'll have done your bit, even if it comes to nothing.'

Cora nodded. 'Yes, I'll do that. It'll just prey on my mind if I don't. Thanks, darling.'

Prey on my mind like withholding the information about Justin lurking outside the building does, she thought guiltily. But she was still sure there was a rational explanation for that, whereas this Alice thing – this felt different, somehow.

'OK, I'll run off a copy onto a memory stick now. Then – nice glass of white?'

'Definitely!' Cora perked up instantly. Nothing like a crisp Pinot Grigio to instantly improve an evening!

The next morning she was regretting the crisp Pinot slightly as she waited for Adam to appear so she could hand over the recording. She perched gingerly on the edge of a hard and not altogether clean chair in the police station reception and massaged her throbbing temples, thinking enviously of Benjamin who was off today and, no doubt, still sprawled under his fluffy duvet.

Still, it had been worth it. A soppy smile crept over her face as she recalled the events of the previous night. One bottle of wine had turned into two, the second of which had been sipped in bed between no fewer than three sessions of rather delightful sex. Benjamin had been extra loving and tender for some reason, and she'd found herself falling for him all over again. He really was so damn …

'What's got you so smug-looking this morning then?'

Adam's amused voice interrupted her reverie. Cora jumped. He seemed to have materialised out of nowhere and was standing right in front of her, grinning down at her surprised face.

245

'Oh, nothing,' she muttered, feeling slightly flustered. 'Er, look – here it is. It could be absolutely nothing, and I feel a bit bad for even doing this to her, but it's just a bit eerie, you know, after what we overheard in the café.'

She stood up and thrust the memory stick into his outstretched hand, still a little embarrassed.

'No, you've done the right thing, thanks, Cora. We'll have a listen, see what we think. Thank you.'

He paused. 'Everything good in your world, then?'

Cora, rapidly regaining her composure, smiled. 'Everything's great, thanks. Fine and dandy! So – well, keep me posted, yes?'

'Always. Well, as far as I can, anyway,' Adam smiled back. 'See you soon.'

'Bye.' Cora watched for a moment as his broad back disappeared behind the counter and out of sight, then glanced at her watch. Bugger. She was supposed to be filming in Reading at 10 a.m. and she was running extremely late. Rummaging in her bag for some headache pills as she went, she walked quickly to her car.

43

'OK, if they don't come to us RIGHT NOW I am walking away, live or no live,' hissed Rodney viciously.

Helpless with laughter, Cora wiped tears from her cheeks, while behind the camera Nathan's face was puce, his shoulders shaking with suppressed howls. In Cora's ear, she heard the director's voice:

'I don't know what the hell is wrong with you there on the South Bank, Cora, but pull yourself together. With you in twenty seconds. Think you can manage that?' he spat, sarcastically.

Not trusting herself to speak, Cora nodded furiously, trying not to look at the boys. In particular, she tried very hard to avert her eyes from Rodney, the subject of their uncontrollable giggles, but she couldn't help it. She glanced at him again and once more subsided into hysteria. Nathan managed to last another three seconds and then joined her, clutching his stomach and guffawing.

Rodney glared at them both, stinking white and green seagull droppings gently running down his forehead from his hair, where they had landed a minute before. Hands full of sound equipment and mere seconds from broadcasting live to the nation, there'd been absolutely nothing he could do to clean himself up.

'Shut up, idiots,' he hissed again. 'Get a grip, Cora. You're on any second now ...'

With a valiant effort, Cora composed her face and stared resolutely into the camera lens. Behind it, she could see Nathan with his fist in his mouth, tears rolling down his cheeks.

'Nathan, please,' she begged, biting the inside of her lip in an effort to curb a fresh wave of mirth.

'Sorry,' he squeaked, and stuffed his fist back into his mouth.

'And Cora joins us now from the South Bank. So Cora, what's happening?' Alice's perky morning voice filled her ear, and Cora took a deep breath, digging her nails painfully into her palm as out of the corner of her eye she saw the slime sliding down towards Rodney's eye. He blinked furiously.

'Well, Alice ...' With an almost super-human effort, Cora launched smoothly into her broadcast. Thank goodness it was Friday. Rodney would need a couple of days to wash that smell off.

'We questioned Alice Lomas for nearly three hours last night. Kept it discreet, didn't arrest her or anything, just asked her to come in for a chat. She was very reluctant, but once we got going she was pretty open with us, and well – there was just nothing there. No motive, claims she got on very well with the deceased and had no reason at all to want her dead. And of course, we have no forensics anyway. To be honest, she put on a fairly convincing display of innocence. She was pretty horrified and angry about that telephone recording – we didn't tell her where it had come from, by the way, although it seemed she instantly assumed it had been made by that blonde ex-model who's now a sports presenter? Agnes somebody? She was on the shoot that day too, and apparently there's no love lost ...'

'They can't stand each other. Had an actual cat-fight in a nightclub a while back,' confirmed one of the younger detectives, who spent rather a lot of her spare time reading the showbiz gossip mags.

Adam nodded. 'Anyway, Lomas flatly denied the phone call we had on tape was anything to do with murder, insisted it was just about a silly row with a friend that she's feeling guilty about. And we can't prove otherwise. If she's our killer, she's doing a damn good job of hiding it.'

Adam looked round the room, and sighed. Everyone in the now seriously depleted team looked like he felt – seriously fed up. Normally a cheerful sort, he was becoming heartily sick of feeling like this, but there was nothing he could do about it – he knew from experience that the only cure for his blues would be cracking this case. Maybe cleaning up the incident room would help clear his mind. The big table was covered with the detritus of an early breakfast meeting, takeaway coffee cups jostling for space with bacon sandwich wrappers, half-empty instant porridge pots and a couple of browning banana skins. Adam poked at his barely touched sausage bap for a minute, then stood up.

'I'm not giving up on this one. We're going to tidy this place up, and then we're going to keep digging. We're nailing this bastard if it's the last thing we do. Right?'

The response echoed around the room. 'Right!'

'She's in the toilets now, throwing up. Ugh. Don't go in there, it's revolting.'

Christina gave an exaggerated shudder, grinned at Cora and walked off, staggering slightly under the weight of an enormous, wobbly pile of scripts topped with a large wooden cactus that had been a prop on that morning's show.

Cora, who'd popped in to the studio after her broadcasts to collect her post and have a quick gossip in the make-up room, swung round in her chair and looked expectantly at Sherry.

'Throwing up? Alice? In the *morning*? Now that's very interesting, isn't it, young Sherry? Go on – spill!'

Sherry looked coy.

'And what makes you think I have anything *to* spill?'

'Sherry, you're her make-up artist. You know everything.'

Sherry smirked and busied herself with her big, black holdall, tidying away brushes and bottles into their neat compartments. Cora continued to stare at her, moving closer and closer until her nose was almost touching her friend's ear.

'Spill, spill, spill,' she chanted.

'Och for goodness' sake!' Sherry batted her away and

249

giggled. 'OK – look, you cannot breathe a *word*, alright?'

'Deal.'

'Right then. Well – yes, you've guessed it, she's preggers. Only a few weeks, she says. And before you ask, no I don't know who the father is. All I know is she hasn't told him yet, not sure how he'll react, so I'm guessing it's not very serious.'

Cora was wide-eyed. 'Wow. So – is she keeping it? Surely she won't want a baby scuppering her career? Has she even got a maternal bone in her body?'

'Ah come on, Cora, she's not that bad.'

Cora snorted. Sherry ignored her and continued. 'She's just insecure, seriously. And she's been very upset recently, what with Jeanette's death, and now being questioned by the police, even though she's obviously got nothing to do with it ...'

Cora nodded slowly, but said nothing. It seemed that Alice was in the clear for now, but she wasn't convinced. That phone call had been so very odd.

'... she didn't have much of a family life growing up, from what I gather. So I think, from the little she's said to me, that yes, she will be keeping it. Start a little family of her own, with or without the father, whoever he is. Now – shove off, I need to run the vacuum round, had to cut Kerry Katona's fringe this morning when she came in and there's hair everywhere.'

'OK. Thanks for the gossip, see you soon.'

Cora wandered slowly out of the room, mind racing. So Alice was pregnant! Which meant maternity leave, which meant Cora would surely have a very good chance of covering it, which would mean a stint in London, which would mean being closer to Benjamin, and her London friends ...

Suddenly excited, she hugged herself and skipped off to share the news with Sam and Wendy. Then she stopped. Hmmm. Sherry had said not to breathe a word. Alright, I'll be good. Keep it to myself for now. It won't be a secret for long anyway, thought Cora.

44

Saturday 7th April

Benjamin cupped his large glass of red wine between tanned hands and gazed at Cora who sat opposite him, engrossed in conversation with Wendy. She looked gorgeous tonight, he thought, taking in the glossy swing of her hair and the gentle curves of her body under the simple navy dress with an enticing gold zip that ran all the way down the front.

It was lovely to be out in the A-Bar, the place they'd first met, with her and her friends – he liked them a lot, appreciating the way they now treated him as a completely normal person and not as a celebrity. He sipped his wine as the conversation buzzed around him. Sam, who was sitting to his right, leaned across the table to hear better as Wendy imparted some scandalous gossip about a new producer in a loud whisper, and Benjamin tried to listen in for a minute and then lost interest and sat back, grinning at their animated faces.

He took another mouthful of wine, suddenly feeling desperately sad and disgusted with himself. He loved Cora, so why had he slept with someone else? He had a problem, he knew that. But he could stop it, he knew he could. He wouldn't do it again. Because he knew Cora's views on being cheated on, and they weren't pretty. If she found out what he'd done, he'd lose her, and that wasn't something he was prepared to do. So, he vowed, still watching her beautiful face across the table, that the next time he was tempted he'd remind himself of what he was risking, and that would stop him being so bloody stupid. This was it. Cora Baxter was it.

As if she could read his mind, Cora suddenly glanced his

way and squeezed his knee under the table. He reached down and stroked her hand, and she smiled happily and returned to her conversation. Benjamin tuned in again, suddenly aware they were discussing Jeanette Kendrick's murder.

'So it seems Alice isn't the killer either. Who the heck is it, then?' Sam was saying. 'Not Alice, not Christina, not Clancy, not Scott. It does freak me out a bit, you know, thinking that there must be a murderer walking amongst us and none of us have any idea who it is.'

Cora shuddered. It was something which preyed on her mind frequently too. 'From what I gather from the police though, the enquiry's virtually over. Every lead they've had has been a dead end. I don't know if they're giving up, exactly, but they're struggling. Who on earth could it be?'

'Probably the last person you'd ever think,' Benjamin said. 'Once all the predictable suspects are ruled out – partner, work colleagues – then it's quite often somebody random, which makes it really difficult. They'll probably never find out who did it now, it's been months.'

'Hmmm, maybe,' Cora sighed. 'I'd love to know though. Still don't understand how it happened right there, practically under our noses, and we still don't know who was responsible.'

'You know what, I don't even care any more,' Wendy announced, and drained her glass. 'I think it's way better at work without her. Sam's doing a brilliant job as a stand-in, and the whole atmosphere is so much nicer without the old bag in the corner office. Whoever did it did us all a favour, and I hope you stay our boss for ever, darling girl.'

Sam blushed. 'Aww, thanks! They're looking for a new editor though, I won't be in charge for much longer. It's been fun, nevertheless.' A sudden look, a combination of sadness and anger, crept into her eyes. Cora, instantly understanding, leaned across to stroke her friend's hand.

'Well, long may it last. Now – are we all finished? Because I could eat a scabby dog. Thai or Indian?' Cora reached for her coat.

'Thai. They always give me free drinks there. It's closer

252

too,' said Benjamin, standing up. 'Is that alright for all of you?'

'Free drinks? Definitely!' laughed Cora, and the others agreed vociferously. Wriggling into their jackets as they walked, they made their way out of the busy bar, dodging a group of inebriated twenty-something girls, several of whose mouths dropped open as they spotted the handsome TV presenter wending his way through the crowd.

'Phwoar!' one of them shrieked. 'Get your kit off, Boland!'

Benjamin threw her a smouldering glance, then winked at Cora. She slipped her hand into his, secretly delighted by the attention he got and secure in the knowledge that this gorgeous man was all hers. Let them leer – she was the one who'd be sleeping next to him tonight!

They reached the door and Benjamin pulled it open and stood back, putting on his most solemn face and bowing slightly to each of them as they passed through it into the mild spring night. Cora giggled, and then stopped abruptly, causing Benjamin to walk straight into her as he followed her out.

'What are you doing?' he spluttered.

Cora pointed, face suddenly tight with rage. 'Look. Across the road. It's *him. Again.*'

The other three stared, following her finger. Sure enough, half-hidden in a doorway directly opposite the bar, stood a man. He looked up suddenly from the phone he'd been tapping on, and his gaze landed on the little group across the road. Slowly, he reached up and pulled his hood closer around his face, then moved out of the doorway and started to walk briskly down the street.

'No – not this time!' Cora yelled.

'Cora – wait!' Wendy begged.

'No – I've had enough!'

There'd been a sudden break in the traffic and she was across the road in a flash. The man glanced over his shoulder, saw her approaching and started to run, but Cora was already on his tail. Breaking into a sprint, she caught up with him and, reaching out a hand, grabbed the hood of his jacket.

'Stop!' she screeched.

The man stopped walking and turned to face her, tugging his head sideways so she lost her grip. The hood slipped away from his face and Cora stared at him. He was pale, thin, with a scruffy goatee beard and dark blue eyes. She didn't recognise him at all.

'Look – I mean no harm. I'm not trying to hurt you,' he stammered, in a soft Welsh accent.

'Well – what are you doing? Why have you been lurking around, following me, spying on me, for months?' Cora was still breathing heavily.

The man just shook his head and looked over her shoulder. Benjamin, Sam, and Wendy were fast approaching, concerned looks on their faces.

'I'm just a … a paparazzo. And not a very good one. Sorry, I have to go.' And with that he turned and jogged off, disappearing round the corner just as Cora's friends arrived.

'Well? What did he say?' Sam urged.

'Just said he was a bad paparazzo, and meant no harm.' Cora gazed down the street, her breathing steadying. 'He looked harmless enough, I suppose. I guess you were right Benj, about him just being a snapper?'

Benjamin ran his fingers through his hair, a puzzled look on his face. 'I wish I was right Cora. But now I've seen him close up, I don't think I am.'

'Why not?'

'Well, there was kind of something rather crucial missing there, don't you think?'

It was Cora's turn to look puzzled. 'Huh?'

Sam looked at Benjamin and nodded slowly. She turned to Cora.

'He's right. There *was* something missing. If he really is a pap, where was his camera, Cora? He didn't have a camera.'

Cora looked wide-eyed at her friends, her stomach suddenly tightening with fear. No camera. Of course. Suddenly shivering, she reached for Benjamin. He held her close, exchanging worried glances with Sam and Wendy over her shoulder. What the hell was going on?

45

Monday 9th April

It was Monday. A new week. And Jeanette Kendrick's killer had made a decision. There was no more time to waste. This week. This week, it was time for number two. The killer nodded slowly. It wasn't going to be easy, or enjoyable, not like the first one. But it would be done. It had to be done. The killer nodded slowly. This week.

It had been a quiet news day. Too quiet, thought Cora, as she arranged the sofa cushions more to her liking and settled back to watch *Coronation Street*. A quiet day generally meant something huge was about to happen – an unexpected storm, a political scandal, a high profile murder. Mindful of that unwritten rule of the TV news business, she'd reluctantly poured a large glass of sparkling water instead of wine to accompany her prawn stir fry. And sure enough, just as the end credits of the soap started to roll, her mobile chirruped. Cora sighed and reached for it.

'Cora – sorry, babe. Two British soldiers killed on an exercise in Canada and nobody free here. Need you outside the Home Office in the morning. Booked you into a lovely hotel though.'

Sam's tone was apologetic.

Cora's heart sank but it wasn't her friend's fault. 'No worries. I'll head down straight away then, make the most of it! See you in the morning.'

'You're a doll. Bye.'

Cora rolled off the sofa and headed to the bedroom to collect her overnight bag. Two hours later she was making her way along Chelsea Embankment, in what was ludicrously heavy traffic for 10.15 at night. Rolling her eyes as yet again a bank of brake lights glowed red in front of her, she lowered her window and breathed in the cold night air, letting her gaze wander along the north bank of the Thames, the streetlights dancing on the dark water. It was raining, the windscreen wipers flicking back and forth with hypnotic regularity and making her feel even sleepier than she already was. She glanced in her rear view mirror, and felt a sudden slight chill. Two cars behind – was that a navy car again? She flicked the switch to wipe the rain off her rear window and squinted in the mirror again. Yes, definitely a navy car. But was it the same one she'd seen those times before? She wasn't sure. Oh for goodness' sake. How many navy blue cars were there in London? Thousands. *Stop it, Cora.*

She checked the road ahead again – stationary. Groaning, she reached for the piece of paper on the passenger seat, reminding herself that her hotel was next left and left again, and then scrunched it up and threw it into the plastic bag that served as an in-car bin. Still no sign of the traffic moving. Bloody London, thought Cora. I love it, but I could never live here.

She leaned back against the headrest and watched idly as a little cluster of people passed by, still in office suits and raincoats and clutching briefcases, one of the women hobbling a little in her high heels. She grabbed on to one of her male colleagues for support and laughed up at him flirtatiously as he slipped an arm around her. Cora smiled.

Then the smile faded from her lips as the group passed by, revealing a couple who'd stopped in a doorway just a few metres down the road. They seemed to be engrossed in conversation, the woman gesticulating animatedly, the man half-hidden under a large striped golf umbrella.

'Is that Alice?' Cora thought. 'Looks like her, the cow.'

She stared at the couple, remembering that Alice did indeed live somewhere in Chelsea. She was out late on a work night, wasn't she? So who was her boyfriend then? Could this be the mysterious father of Alice's so far still secret baby? True to her word, Cora hadn't breathed a word about the newsreader's pregnancy, but she was intrigued to know who the dad was.

The traffic moved forward about a metre then stopped again, but it was enough to get Cora close enough to decide that the girl was definitely Alice. She peered through the windscreen, as Alice flicked her long blonde hair back in characteristic fashion and suddenly leaned forward to kiss the tall man in the doorway. He bent down to meet her lips and as his face emerged from under the umbrella, Cora's heart almost stopped.

Was that ...? No, it couldn't be. Suddenly shaking, she leaned forward again and stared. Oh no, she thought. No, no, no. It is. It's Benjamin.

46

For a moment, Cora sat frozen, horrified eyes fixed on the oblivious Benjamin and Alice. Then an irate horn sounded behind her, and she jumped, realising the traffic had suddenly started moving again. Spotting an empty parking meter, she indicated left and manoeuvred into the space, then turned off the engine with a shaky hand. What should she do? Only yards away now, her boyfriend and her loathed work colleague were still huddled in the doorway as the rain pounded the pavement.

In a flash, Cora made up her mind. She wrenched the driver's door open and leapt out, only narrowly missing an approaching cyclist, and marched down the street. As she got closer, her grief and disbelief turned to white-hot anger.

'Well, hello, Benjamin, Alice. Anyone care to tell me what the hell is going on here?' she spat.

The two faces turned simultaneously.

'Cora! Cora, my God! Look, it's not what it looks like, OK?' Benjamin spluttered, his face flushing, eyes wide with shock. Beside him, Alice looked horror-stricken.

Cora, her anger intensifying, pushed him hard on the arm and he actually staggered backwards a little, looking dismayed.

'It's exactly what it looks like, Benjamin. We'd all been wondering in work about Alice's new mystery man – who would have thought it would be *my* boyfriend, eh? You're disgusting. All that talk of how much you loved me ...'

Her voice cracked and she stopped. She would *not* cry in front of them.

'I DO love you. I adore you. I'm so sorry, Cora, I just ...' Benjamin actually sounded as if he might cry too.

Cora shook her head, not trusting herself to speak. Benjamin covered his face with his hands, and a tiny sob escaped him. Alice, who'd been looking from one to the other, suddenly bent down and picked up her handbag, which had been resting on the doorstep. White-faced, she looked up at the stricken Benjamin once more, then turned to Cora.

'I'm … I'm sorry, Cora. I've never had any luck with men. I thought he was different, but …' she whispered in an anguished tone. Then, her eyes too filling with tears, she stepped out into the driving rain and walked rapidly away, pulling her Burberry mac more tightly around her slim frame.

Cora suddenly felt weak. Benjamin was still slouched against the door, face in his hands.

'I'm so sorry. You can't even imagine how sorry I am. I'm an idiot. I've got a problem … I think I'm a sex addict or something. I'll get help. Please, I'm so sorry,' he mumbled.

'It doesn't matter. None of it matters. It was just all a massive mistake. I should have known better than to trust somebody like you. I'm the idiot here, Benjamin. Goodbye.'

'No – wait, please!'

Cora ignored him. Running now, tears suddenly mingling with the rainwater that was streaming down her face, she was in her car and sliding back out into the slow stream of traffic before Benjamin had a chance to stop her. As she passed, sobbing wildly at the wheel, he stood on the sodden pavement, hands running frantically through his hair.

'Cora!' His tortured roar reached her despite her closed windows and the torrential rain that was battering her roof, but she drove on, somehow making her way to the hotel car park. Then, slumped in her seat, she howled. Why? Why did this always happen to her? Why could she not keep a man? What was *wrong* with her?

Another car pulled into the space next to her, and a smartly dressed man clambered out, looking curiously at Cora as he walked past and headed for the hotel reception door. Suddenly aware of how odd she must look, Cora sat up straight and pulled down the driver's mirror, still gulping. She stared at her reflection, eyes bloodshot and swollen, rivulets of mascara drawing dark streaks down her cheeks, hair still dripping.

As she fumbled in her glove box for some baby wipes, Cora wondered if Benjamin knew that Alice was pregnant. The word at work was that she hadn't told the father, wasn't it? Benjamin had been clear that he wasn't interested in having children. Maybe he'd dump Alice then, when he found out. The thought made Cora feel slightly better, but not much. How could he? How could *she*? They weren't friends, of course, but Alice had known how happy Cora was, how much in love she was.

'Did she pick him on purpose, because she knew he was mine?' she wondered aloud. Shaking her head, and feeling the tears welling up again, Cora looked at the hotel in front of her. Another night in a hotel room, another horrible early alarm call, another morning standing outside in the cold. A wave of nausea swept over her. She couldn't do it. She just couldn't. Not today, not feeling like this. She made a sudden decision. And picking up the phone, Cora did something she'd never done before, not once in her entire career. Swallowing her sobs, she rang Sam and told her she was ill.

'Been throwing up all the way here. Had to keep stopping the car, it was awful.' She stopped, hating lying but simply unable to tell the truth about what had happened, even to her friend. Not yet. It was too raw, too painful.

'I need to go home, Sam, and sleep it off. I'm so sorry.'

'No, no, don't worry your head, babe, we'll cope. It's so not like you to be sick, will you be OK on your own?' Sam sounded worried, making Cora feel even worse.

'Why not go and stay with Benj, rather than drive all the way home?' Sam continued.

Cora struggled to hold back another violent sob. 'No! No – he's, er … away filming. Don't worry Sam, I'll be alright. I'll ring you tomorrow, tell you how I am, OK?'

'Of course. Get well.'

'Bye.'

Cora had just dropped the phone onto the passenger seat when it started ringing. She glanced at the screen. Benjamin. Angrily, she hit the red button to reject the call, then took a deep breath. Even as she'd been talking to Sam, she'd been making another decision. It was all too much – Justin, the weird goings on with people and navy cars following her, and now Benjamin. She wiped a final errant tear from her cheek, turned the ignition key and headed for Heathrow.

47

Ten minutes after Cora had driven off, Benjamin was still standing on the rain-soaked street, distraught and with no idea what to do next. He slumped against the wall of the nearest building, ignoring the curious stares occasionally thrown his way by passers-by, although most were too busy battling with their wind-blown umbrellas to notice the famous TV star with the tear-streaked face and the anguished look in his eyes.

How could he have been so stupid? The look on Cora's face ... Benjamin groaned and reached for his phone. His fingers shook as he dialled her number. He needed to explain, she had to let him explain. But as the phone rang twice and then stopped abruptly, he realised with a sinking heart that it wasn't going to be that easy. She'd been angry, really angry, and terribly hurt, and he didn't blame her one tiny bit. What a complete idiot he was. He'd finally met a girl he genuinely believed he could be happy with, and he'd screwed it up. Screwed it up so very, very badly. She was never meant to see him with Alice, it was pretty much all over, for heaven's sake. If only Cora hadn't come along when she did, if only ...

Horrified by the whole situation, he stumbled down the street towards the nearest bar. He needed to think. And drink. Drink quite a lot, actually. And once he'd done that, he'd come up with a plan to sort this mess out. It would be OK. Somehow. Benjamin Boland usually got what he wanted, didn't he? Of course he did. It would be OK. He spotted a tiny bar down a side street and staggered towards it like a dying man. It would be OK. He'd figure it out. He had to.

48

Cora opened her still-swollen eyes gingerly. Ouch. Her head
hurt. And why was the room so bright? Squinting, she sat up
slowly in bed. It wasn't her bed either, the duvet cover bright
blue and slightly scratchy. She swung her legs over the side of
the mattress and sat for a moment, head in hands, as her brain
fog slowly cleared. Spain. She was in Spain. And Benjamin was
a bastard.

Cora stood up, wobbled slightly then walked carefully to the
window, kicking an empty wine bottle out of the way and
groaning as she remembered why her head was aching so much.
She pulled the thin, white curtains back, grimacing as the light
hit her tender pupils, then stood there for a minute, letting her
vision adjust and drinking in the view. The soft morning air
filled her lungs and she pushed the window open even further,
eyes drifting across surprisingly green countryside and to the
distant hills beyond.

As she headed downstairs to the kitchen in search of tea, she
muttered a fervent thank you to her parents for the always open
invitation to pop over to their Spanish villa and, she had to
admit, an even more ardent thank you to them for actually being
away on a cruise right now. Much as she loved her mother, the
questions would have been a little hard to take in her current
delicate state.

Cora's parents lived in Moraira, a small, up-market town
about halfway between Alicante and Valencia on Spain's
eastern coast. Formerly a fishing village, the town was now a
thriving tourist destination, but also popular with the wealthy
retired, particularly of the British variety. Edwin and Doreen

Baxter had started working together when they got married nearly four decades ago, first setting up a successful cleaning business and later, when Cora and her two younger sisters had gone off to work and university, opening a seaside hotel in Cornwall. A few years ago they had sold the hotel for a healthy profit and decided to retire. Now in their mid-sixties, they lived a wonderful life in the sun, taking long holidays, playing golf, and generally making up for all the leisure time they had missed over the years.

As she pottered around the immaculate kitchen with its wood burner, the big, cream tiles cool underfoot, Cora was again filled with gratitude that their long spell as hoteliers meant her parents had got into the habit of never, ever letting themselves run out of food. They might be away on a three-week trip but the tea caddy was stuffed with teabags, there was bread, meat, fish and some unidentifiable brown lumps in plastic bags in the freezer, and three bottles of white wine in the fridge (there'd been four last night, Cora thought ruefully), along with some unopened butter and pots of blueberry, raspberry, and mango jam.

Cora snapped off a couple of slices from a frozen loaf, popped it in the microwave on defrost, then shoved it into the toaster, sipping her black tea as the bread slowly browned. Then, after liberally spreading her toast with butter and jam, she pulled her mother's orange floral dressing-gown tightly around her and carried her breakfast out onto the pool terrace, sinking into a rattan chair and wishing she'd brought her sunglasses with her. As the mid-morning sun – she had, incredibly, slept until nearly eleven – gently warmed her weary body, the events of last night came slowly back to her. It seemed so long ago, and so far away, and yet it was only a matter of hours since she'd driven frantically away from her unfaithful boyfriend and her deceitful colleague.

Cora had dumped her car in the first long-stay car park she'd found at Heathrow Airport, grabbed her overnight bag and laptop and raced to the nearest ticket desk. Luck had, for once, been on her side, and she'd managed to grab a one-way ticket to

Alicante, leaving on the last flight of the night. She'd worry about the return journey later. Once she landed, it had been a simple matter to hire a car and drive the familiar fifty or so miles north to Moraira. There'd been a moment of panic when, in the dark, Cora couldn't locate the spare key her dad always left under a big rock at the side of the villa. But after a quick fumble and a lot of cursing, she was letting herself in to the quiet hallway, a huge sense of relief flooding her and for some reason causing her to burst into tears again.

She'd dumped her bag in her usual bedroom and then headed for the fridge, still sobbing. Then, clutching a bottle and grabbing a glass from the cabinet as she passed, she'd sunk into the big, soft, brown sofa in the lounge, tuned the TV to an English language channel showing an old black and white comedy film, and poured herself a large drink. And there she'd sat until she was all cried out, and actually managing a giggle or two at the on-screen antics. She'd brought the remains of her wine to bed, sipping it as she snuggled under the duvet and the first light of dawn began penetrating the dark room, and had eventually fallen into a deep, dreamless sleep.

Now she watched idly as a tiny lizard skittered across the flags of the patio, stopping to sun itself at the edge of the small swimming pool that was her dad's pride and joy. Cora glanced at the wall thermometer hanging next to the table. It was nearly twenty degrees already. Suddenly feeling unexpectedly cheerful at the prospect of a day sunning herself, she downed the rest of her tea and headed back inside in search of a shower and some sun cream. She knew she had to make some phone calls, and decisions, but all that could wait. She'd get dressed, drive down to the local supermarket for some provisions, then sit by the pool and make a plan.

By two o'clock she was settled in a sun lounger, dressed in a lurid pink strapless dress she'd found in her mother's wardrobe, laptop and phone fully charged on the little drinks table at her side. She hesitated for a moment, then decided first things first. Her friends would be worried if they thought she was ill and not answering her home phone, so she'd have to come clean.

Taking a deep breath, she picked up her mobile and called Sam. Five minutes later, she ended the call, greatly relieved. Despite being lied to last night, her friend had been incredibly forgiving about her bunking off work, satisfyingly outraged about Benjamin and Alice, and deeply understanding about Cora's need for a few days off.

'Seriously, love, don't worry. I'll put in a sick leave form for you for the rest of the week. That should be enough, shouldn't it?' Sam had said, sounding only slightly anxious.

'That's perfect, thank you so much. I'll get my head together here for a few days and then book a flight back for the weekend. And Sam – you won't say anything to Alice, will you? Not yet? I want to handle this myself, and I haven't decided what to do yet. I need to think.'

'Well, if that's what you want.' Sam's tone was dubious. 'It's going to be hard for me to treat her normally though, knowing what I know. What a total bitch!'

Cora sighed. 'I know. I'm not letting her get away with it, Sam. But I need to think carefully. Do I ring Benjamin and tell him she's pregnant? Because I very much doubt that he knows that – from what Sherry said at work, Alice hadn't told the father yet. That's assuming he *is* the father of course. Who knows who else the little slut was sleeping with? Or maybe I'll just confront her in the newsroom, in front of everyone. Or … I don't know. It's over between me and Benjamin, that's for sure. I should have known better than to trust someone with his reputation …'

She'd paused then, tears threatening to spill once more, and quickly ended the call, Sam urging her to chill out and come back refreshed and promising to tell nobody but Wendy what was really going on.

Cora shut her eyes for a few minutes, savouring the heat, then made quick calls to Rosie and Nicole to fill them in too. Their horrified exclamations and vows of love, support and plenty of cake when she returned left Cora feeling more cheerful. Then she tapped out a quick email to her parents, deciding that was the best way to reach them on a cruise, and told them she'd decided to take a last-minute mini break at the villa but that everything was fine and not to worry. She had a sneaking suspicion they would have asked some of their neighbours to keep an eye on the place in their absence, and didn't want to cause a panic when lights were seen going on and off inside later.

Finally, a few brief texts to the boys, simply saying she'd split up with Benjamin and had taken a few days' leave in Spain. They all responded within minutes, making her laugh with declarations that she was too good for him anyway and to have a great rest/drink lots of sangria/pick up a nice Spanish hunk (or, in Nathan's case, to bring him back a nice Spanish hunk).

Duty calls all done, Cora looked at her watch. Just after three. She picked up an old crime thriller she'd found on a bookshelf in the lounge and settled back, ignoring her phone when it rang. It would only be Benjamin again, for around the sixth time today. Let him suffer, she thought coldly. I've had enough of men messing me around. For a fleeting moment, Adam came into her thoughts, but she instantly berated herself. For goodness' sake, *no more men*!

She'd concentrate on her career from now on, especially if Alice was pregnant and her job was likely to be up for grabs ... maybe she and Benjamin had done Cora a favour after all ... and maybe ...

Her thoughts became a confusing jumble as sleep overtook her, the novel sliding out of her hand and slipping to the ground as her heavy eyes shut. It was nearly five when she awoke with a jump, neck stiff and cheeks pink from the sun. She lay still for a moment, as a sudden feeling of overwhelming loneliness swept over her. Why did this keep happening to her? She'd talked to Benjamin about coming out here for a weekend, and he'd seemed so keen on the idea, promised to make her paella, get her drunk on cava and have his evil way with her ...

There was no point in thinking about that now. Cora sighed, sat up and started to gather her belongings. She was about to head back inside when out of the corner of her eye she saw something move on other side of the pool. Startled, she shaded her eyes and stared at the cluster of palms and phormiums along the back wall. Was there something there? Or – somebody? Her breath quickened.

'Is … is someone there? Hello?' Her voice was tremulous. There was silence. No noise, no movement, just a few innocent looking plants. She was an idiot, letting her imagination run away with her, that was all. Probably just another one of those little lizards. She felt herself growing calmer again. She'd go inside, have a nice cool shower, whip up some pasta and watch an old movie. It would be lovely. With one last glance across the turquoise water, she skipped into the villa.

49

In London, Benjamin Boland's mood was anything but sunny. He too had woken with the most shocking hangover, and it had taken him a full ten minutes to work out how he'd actually got home. The memories slowly trickled back into his aching brain as he moved cautiously round his designer kitchen, every clink of a cup and tap of a teaspoon hurting his throbbing head. Eventually he sank onto the sofa, strong coffee in slightly shaking hand. Swallowing two paracetamol, he shut his eyes and remembered. Remembered the grotty little bar he'd spent the evening in, knocking back first beer and then brandy. Ugh. He didn't even like brandy. And then remembered why he'd drunk so much, the horrible scene on the Embankment as Cora had appeared from nowhere and his world had fallen apart. And all his own fault. He knew that, he wasn't going to pretend otherwise. A hot flash of anger pulsed through him. He had brought all this on himself, and now he needed to fix it.

He'd stayed in the apartment all day, staring miserably out at the driving April rain and trying Cora's number every couple of hours. Each time, she refused to answer. He hadn't seen her on the TV this morning, which probably meant she was off filming somewhere. And he had no idea where, so there was no point in getting in the car and trying to find her. By four o'clock, Benjamin was close to despair. He slumped in a chair, head in hands, and then nearly jumped through the adjacent window in shock as his phone finally rang. He grabbed it, elated, and then dropped it again. Alice. He couldn't talk to her, not now.

And so the long, grey day continued, Cora rejecting Benjamin's calls and Benjamin ignoring Alice's. As the sun started to set outside his huge windows though, the plan he'd been formulating all day finally came together. He would see Alice, one more time, and finish it properly. He had to work tomorrow, but Thursday. Thursday evening would be good. And then he'd go and find Cora.

50

Cora yawned loudly and reached out a hand to flick the bedside light off. Stuffed full of crab and prawn pasta, and suddenly too weary to concentrate on a film, she'd done a quick tour of the house checking that doors and windows were locked and then headed upstairs. She glanced at the clock. Only nine o'clock. She was so rock and roll, honestly. She managed a smile as she snuggled down under the duvet. An early night would do her good. Tomorrow she'd go and pootle around the shops in Moraira, treat herself to a new handbag or a piece of jewellery, maybe have tea and a pastry in one of the sunny coffee shops. Then she'd look into flights home. She wasn't quite sure yet how she was going to deal with Alice, or whether she was ever actually going to speak to Benjamin again, but she'd work it out … an early night would help … she was just so tired and …

Within seconds, she was gone, sleep rolling over her and wrapping her in its comforting numbness, her whirling mind finally at rest for a few blessed hours. And then a dream, in which she was back in London, in the newsroom, frantically trying to finish a script, and Jeanette was standing over her, screaming, and Cora started screaming back and Jeanette screamed louder and then ran, ran straight towards the window and plunged through it, and the ghastly sound of glass shattering and falling filled her ears and she screamed louder …

Cora woke, sweat streaming down her face. Trembling, she looked at the clock. Just after eleven. She'd only been asleep for a couple of hours. What a horrible dream. She sat up slowly, trying to get her breathing under control. It was just a dream. Nothing to worry about. Just a stress reaction to all the things that had happened recently. Her heartbeat slowed. She'd go down and make a cup of tea, maybe sit up for a while and watch some late night TV. She swung her legs off the bed. And then …

'Oh, shit!' She gasped in horror as she heard it again. The sound of glass, falling and smashing. Not a dream then. Here, in this house, somebody was breaking a window. There was somebody downstairs.

For a moment she sat motionless, horror-stricken. Then her mind started to race. What did one do, in this sort of situation? Call the police. That's what she needed to do. Call the police NOW. There was another noise from downstairs, a soft thud followed by more tinkling glass. Shit, shit, shit. Cora frantically fumbled for her phone on the bedside table. It wasn't there. She scanned the room, desperate now. Where had she left it? Nothing on the dressing table, nothing on the window sill. She stood for a second, breathing hard, trying to calm her brain enough for coherent thought. She'd been so tired, she must have left it downstairs. Yes, she had. She could see it now, in her mind's eye, lying on the arm of the sofa. So, no mobile. Was there a landline phone anywhere up here? Her parents' bedroom? Cora couldn't remember, didn't know. She looked around again, trying not to let panic take over completely. Definitely no handset in this room anyway. She'd have to go out, find a phone …

She grabbed her mother's dressing gown from the chair by the bed and pulled it on, just as there was another sound from downstairs, a gentle thump, as if somebody had bumped into something. Please don't come up here, please don't come up here, please …

Chanting the phrase in her head like a protective spell, Cora tiptoed to the dressing table and picked up a large and – she noted even in her state of abject terror – shockingly ugly yellow vase. She needed a weapon, and this would have to do. Still on tiptoe, she crept to the door and opened it slowly. It swung silently on well-oiled hinges. Thank you, Dad. Thank you so much, she thought.

She paused, listening. Silence. Where was he? Or she, or

whoever it was? Cora was suddenly filled with a white-hot anger. Was this her stalker, following her to Spain? Or just an opportunistic burglar? How dare they invade someone's home like this, how dare they break windows and creep about? Her fingers clenched around the vase, a steely determination taking hold of her. Why not just turn on a light, demand to know who was there, shout out that the police were on their way? They might just run. She looked around, saw the light switch that would illuminate the landing, stairs and hall in one quick movement, and reached out a hand.

Then a floorboard creaked in the hallway below, and the anger left her again as suddenly as it had arrived, fear flooding back, her fingers suddenly icy cold and her feet leaden. She froze, hand still outstretched towards the switch. No. No light. In the dark, she might be able to evade whoever it was, this stranger who couldn't know the layout of the house she knew so well. Maybe she could get out, run to a neighbour, get help. She took a deep breath and listened again. Nothing. OK, this was it.

One hand gripping the vase, and the other on the banister, she began moving stealthily down the stairs, one step at a time like a small child. She stopped every few seconds, peering into the darkness below, listening. Still nothing. Almost silently, she crept downwards, down and down, only a few steps to go now …

And then, suddenly, a dark shape loomed below her, and she heard a man's voice, shocked and loud in the stillness, and the untied belt of the dressing gown, dangling unnoticed, wrapped itself around her ankle and she was falling, crashing down onto the hard floor of the hallway, her skull smashing onto the tiles, the vase slipping from her hand and shattering, sharp yellow shards peppering the floor, and lights were flashing and stars bursting and pain searing and blood roaring in her head. And then, there was only darkness.

51

'Cora. Cora, please! Oh for God's sake, Cora, wake up, please wake up!'

The voice was loud and urgent, and startlingly familiar. Cora groaned. What was going on? She slowly became aware of a sharp pain in her forehead and a dull ache in her left ankle. And it was so hard, and cold, this bed she was lying on …

'I'm so sorry, Cora. I didn't mean to frighten you, please wake up!'

Who was that? She recognised the voice, but her brain wasn't working properly. Slowly, painfully, she opened her eyes, squinting in the glaring light, her vision blurred. Where was she? All she could remember was coming downstairs and then … she gasped in fright as the memories flooded back. There was someone in the house. Police. She needed to call the police. The phone. Where was the phone?

She hit out wildly with her right hand, using her other arm to prop herself up, then recoiled in shock as her flailing fingers made contact with skin.

'Ouch!'

Again, that familiar voice. So familiar …

Justin? It couldn't be. But it was, she was sure of it.

'Justin? Is that you?'

'Yes, it's me. I'm so sorry … but that's quite a right hook you have there …'

Cora sat up carefully and rubbed her eyes, her vision clearing. To her utter amazement, it was indeed Justin, crouching next to her in the hallway, rubbing his own eye.

'Justin, what the *hell*?' She couldn't quite take it in. Was *Justin* her stalker?

'I know, I know, I have a lot of explaining to do. But please, don't be scared. I never meant to hurt you. In fact, quite the opposite – I've been trying to protect you.'

Cora stared. 'Protect me from what, exactly? Was it you, stalking me? Am I dreaming? None of this makes any sense …'

'It's a long story. No, it wasn't me following you, but I know who it was. And he never meant to frighten you either. Look – can you stand up? We need to get you off this cold floor. You were only out for a few seconds, but we probably need to get you checked out by a doctor too. I was so scared when you tripped …'

Justin had slipped an arm around her and was gently easing her to her feet. She whimpered slightly as her weight shifted onto her left foot.

'Ow. Think I've sprained my ankle.'

'Lean on me.'

He half led, half carried her into the lounge and helped her onto the sofa, propping her injured foot up on a cushion. Then he pulled an armchair closer to the couch and sat down himself. Cora looked at him properly for the first time, her heart lurching a little. Despite everything, despite what he'd done to her, the callous way he'd simply left, it was so good to see him. He was a little thinner than he'd been when they were together, but the muscles were still there, his arms looking hard and defined through the thin fabric of his long-sleeved blue T-shirt. He ran his fingers through his dark crop and returned her gaze.

'You look good, Cora,' he said softly.

She smiled. 'I look like someone who's just woken up, had a horrible fright and then fallen down the stairs, but thank you.'

He grinned back, then reached out and gently touched her forehead. She winced.

'You'll have a bruise there tomorrow. I'm calling a doctor, OK? And once that's done, we'll talk. There's so much to tell you, so much I need you to understand. But I need you to know right now, that I've never hurt anyone, OK? And I will go to the police. I'll come back with you. Once I've told you everything. Is that alright, Cora?'

She nodded, slowly. She'd been so scared, but somehow she felt safe now. This was Justin, her Justin. Well, not hers any more, but she still trusted him, believed in him.

'Right, let me find a medic, and then – tea, maybe?'

'Tea would be great.'

It was nearly 1 a.m. by the time the local emergency doctor had been tracked down, arrived, declared her to be generally fit and well and issued a prescription of painkillers, 'taking it easy' for a couple of days, and a cold compress on her sprained ankle.

Justin had been a star. He'd lit the fire, arranged blankets and pillows around her on the sofa, fashioned an icepack from an old tea towel and something unrecognisable from the freezer, and made copious cups of tea. Now he settled down into the chair next to her, proffering a plate of buttered toast.

Cora took a piece, surprised at how hungry she felt at this strange hour. It was weirdly comforting to find herself being looked after by her ex after such a ghastly few days. But now she was suddenly desperate to hear what he had to say, to get some sort of explanation about his appearance on the CCTV footage, the odd tweets, the stalking. She munched her toast, waiting.

Justin carefully put his tea down on the floor and took a deep breath.

'Right. Here goes. Cora – this is going to sound mad, insane. And I know you won't believe me, or WANT to believe me, when I tell you what I'm about to tell you. But I'm pretty sure I'm right. I'd stake my life on it.'

Cora sat up a little straighter against her pillows, and swallowed her toast. She suddenly felt a little sick.

'Well – go on then. I'm listening. But first – you said you knew who was stalking me?'

Justin nodded, a little sheepishly. 'He wasn't stalking you, not exactly. He was … this sounds crazy, but he was a private detective. I hired him, Cora, because I was worried about you. I thought you might be in danger – I'll tell you why in a minute – and I wanted someone to be there, to keep an eye on you. I tweeted you a couple of times, trying to tell you to be careful, but I didn't want to terrify you, and I wasn't sure I was right, and ...'

His voice tailed off as he noticed Cora's face, which had taken on an astounded expression.

'But – I thought *you* were threatening me, when you sent those tweets. I thought that you thought I was going to tell the police about the CCTV, and that you were warning me off. I was really scared, Justin. I thought I had a stalker, for goodness' sake!'

Justin's head was in his hands. 'I'm so sorry. I thought I was doing the right thing. I'm an idiot.'

'Well, did he follow me all the way here? How did you know where I was? I don't understand ...'

'No, but he managed to follow you to Heathrow. He's been cursing you with all your tearing up and down the motorway! He watched you check in for a flight to Spain and then called me. I made an educated guess, thought it was likely you'd be coming here, and decided it would be a good place to come and talk to you, sort all this out. Amazingly, I remembered how to get here, and –'

'That car. That navy car! I *knew* I was being followed. He's rubbish at undercover work, Justin – I hope he didn't cost you too much. I spotted him loads of times. But anyway – back to you, you idiot – you couldn't have knocked on the door, like a normal person? What possessed you to break in in the middle of the night? I presume that was you, creeping around in the bushes earlier?'

'Yes, that was *so* stupid. I spotted you by the pool, and I didn't know what to do, whether to just walk up and say hello, or phone ... so I went for a walk, trying to decide, and ended up in a little restaurant. Then before I knew it, it was dark. It was just so late, and I didn't want to scare you, and also – well, also, I thought you might call the police or something if you saw me outside in the middle of the night, and then we'd never get to sort this all out. So I broke a window – just a tiny one, in the back door, I'll fix it tomorrow ... and thought I might nap on the sofa till you got up ...'

Cora sighed. Her brain was still racing, a thousand questions buzzing unanswered through her mind.

'But I still don't get it. Why did you think I was in danger? You weren't even in the country, were you, for the past few months? What on earth made you think I needed protection?'

There was a long pause. Finally Justin looked up, his face serious. He rubbed his nose, and Cora remembered the gesture from the CCTV footage, the gesture that had convinced her beyond doubt that her ex was the man police were searching for.

'Because, Cora, as you and only you know, I was outside TV Centre when Jeanette died. And I think – well, now I'm almost positive – that I know who killed her. I wasn't sure, not a hundred per cent, not at first, which is why I hired the private eye while I researched it all. I didn't want to just call you and tell you what I suspected, just in case I was wrong ... I didn't want to destroy your life until I was absolutely certain, Cora.'

Cora felt a chill run through her. 'Destroy – my life? What on earth are you talking about?'

She stared at him, almost willing him not to answer, and starting to hope that this might actually be a nightmare from which, any moment, she might wake.

'It's – it's because it's someone you know. Someone you're close to. And I was scared, Cora. Scared that you'd get hurt too.'

Cora's voice was barely a whisper. 'Someone I know? A friend of mine? A friend of mine pushed Jeanette out of that window?'

Justin nodded. 'I don't know how to tell you this, but yes, I think so. Oh and by the way – she wasn't pushed.'

'Wasn't pushed? What? It was suicide after all? You're not making sense, Justin!'

He shook his head. 'No, it was murder alright. But she wasn't pushed. She was pulled. Pulled out of the window. From the *outside*, Cora.'

52

Cora stared at her ex-boyfriend again.

'Pulled? From the outside? On the seventh floor of a tower block? How did that work then? Did Superman fly by and decide to be a baddie for a change?'

She laughed, feeling slightly hysterical. This night – or morning, as it was now – was taking on a rather surreal feel.

Justin took a deep breath. 'Look, let me tell you the story, how I saw it, from the beginning, OK?'

'I'm all ears. But this is feeling more and more like a weird dream, Justin.'

He smiled briefly, then his face was serious again. 'I bet. Right. Here we go. I felt bad, Cora. I felt terrible, in fact, that I'd ended things with you by telephone. It was a horrible, cowardly thing to do, and I should never have done it like that.'

Cora nodded vehemently, but didn't say anything.

'I think, if I'm honest, that I'd been, well, depressed for a few months before that – I mean properly depressed, not just a bit down. I wasn't sure where my life was going, what I wanted, and I just started to feel really … really low. Like a twat I didn't say anything to anyone, you know what us blokes are like. And we were hardly seeing each other anyway, were we, with work and everything, and things just got on top of me, I suppose. So I decided to go away, get out of the country for a little while, take a break from work and from everything, try to sort my head out. I just needed to be alone for a bit, so I even ditched my UK mobile – I knew I'd get a load of grief from everyone for dumping you like that, and I just couldn't take it. That's why I used Twitter to contact you, instead of phoning or texting. I just couldn't handle the angry phone calls I'd get from you … from

283

everyone, if they had my number. I even shut down my email account when I left, because so many people had my email address and I knew I'd be bombarded. I know that makes me sound like a pathetic coward, but it's the truth.'

He paused. Cora said nothing, suddenly feeling horribly guilty that she hadn't realised how depressed her boyfriend had been.

He carried on. 'I'd booked a flight to Spain for later that morning, the eighteenth of December, and I checked into a hotel in London the night before. But in the middle of the night, I suddenly decided I needed to see you before I went, just to say sorry, and to say goodbye. So I got up at stupid o'clock – I still have no idea how you do that every day, Cora – and called a taxi to take me over to TV Centre. I knew you'd be arriving at work in the early hours and I thought I could catch you before you went in. But the taxi took ages to arrive, and by the time I got there it was about 4 a.m. and I knew I'd missed you.'

'So you hung about, for *four hours*? You were on CCTV, Justin, lurking around till about eight o'clock! No wonder the police were suspicious!' Cora couldn't help it – she felt totally exasperated again.

He groaned. 'I know, I know, I haven't handled any of this very well, have I? Yes, I hung about. I nearly went inside a couple of times, to ask Reception if they could call up and tell you I was there, and then chickened out of that. And then I thought, I'll just hang about till the show's over, and catch you coming out. It was freezing, and there's nothing open round there at that hour, no cafés or anything, so I kept wandering off, doing laps of the building to keep warm. There was a security guard roving around a bit, and I avoided him in case he made me leave. It was sort of fun, in a perverse way, hiding in the shadows.'

He hesitated, coughed, and then carried on. Cora's eyes were fixed on his face.

'There were these cradle things on two sides of the building – you know, the kind window cleaners use? They were on the ground, presumably waiting to be used later on. And then, well it was still quite dark, but it was nearly eight o'clock, and I was doing another lap, and I heard this creaking sound, coming from above. I looked up, and one of the cradles was up there, instead of down on the ground where it had been earlier. I stopped and looked up for a bit, wondering why it was up there so early. And then I heard voices coming from up there, muffled voices. I couldn't hear what they were saying, but it sounded like a man and a woman, arguing. And then I was even more puzzled – what were two people doing on a window cleaning cradle, when it was barely light?'

Cora's heart was pounding. 'Are you saying the killer was in that cradle? Seriously? I suppose it explains why nobody saw anyone go in or out of her office. So – go on. You saw? You saw what happened?'

'Well – sort of. It all went quiet for a bit, and then I heard noises again, and it looked like something was being hauled out of the window above … it looked like a big sack or something at first. There was grunting, as if it was a struggle, something heavy, you know?'

He stopped again, breathing deeply.

'And then seconds later – oh God, Cora, the noise. I'll never forget it. Something whistled through the air just a few feet away from me, and then there was this thud, the most sickening, crunching thud. And I knew. I knew it was a person, a body. Right there, right in front of me.'

He moaned slightly. His face had turned white, his eyes suddenly brimming with tears.

'Are you OK? Justin?'

'Yes. Yes. I'm fine.' He rubbed his eyes fiercely.

'The cradle started to come down really quickly, and I was scared. I know that makes me sound like a total coward, but I was scared, Cora. If this person had just pulled someone out of a window and thrown them to the ground, what else were they capable of? So I just shrank back, into the shadows, flattened myself against the wall. The cradle hit the ground, and this man, a tall man, wearing a black balaclava or something like that, leaped out of it. He walked over to the body on the ground, and

285

pulled something off her face … there was a ripping sound, as if it was tape, I think. And then he just walked away.'

Cora could barely breathe. 'But you said – you said you knew who it was. How? How did you know? If his face was covered?'

'Because, as he left, he pulled it off. The mask thing. And I caught a glimpse – just a glimpse. But his face was so distinctive, Cora. I knew I'd never forget it.'

'So – who? Who was it?' Her voice was just a squeak now, hardly audible.

'It was Benjamin, Cora. Benjamin Boland.'

53

Cora leaped from the sofa, pain in her bad ankle forgotten, staggered to the kitchen and threw up, violently and for a long time, in the kitchen sink. When she'd finished, Justin gently wiped her mouth with a handful of tissues and led her back to the living room. She sat there shivering, hands shaking, brain numb. Benjamin? Her Benjamin? So not only was the wonderful man she'd thought she loved a dirty little two-timer, he was a murderer too? Really? *Really*? Well, this beat them all, didn't it? She knew how to pick them, didn't she? Yep, she sure knew how to pick them …

'I'm so sorry, Cora. That's all I seem to be saying to you today, but I really am so sorry, to be the one to tell you this. I just had to, I couldn't let it go on any longer – you do understand?'

Cora nodded, still trembling. 'How can you be sure, Justin? You saw him for – what, a couple of seconds? The man. The man who killed Jeanette. Are you positive, really, that it was – that it was Benjamin?'

Justin leaned forwards, taking her quivering fingers gently in his.

'That's just it. I wasn't, at first. I'm not a great TV watcher, as you know. But that glimpse, that glance I got – I only knew at first that the face looked sort of familiar. I couldn't place him, but I knew I knew him from somewhere. That's why I didn't say anything in those first messages I sent you. I just wanted you to know that I had nothing to do with the murder, but I didn't want to start throwing names around because I just couldn't remember where I'd seen that face before. And then I just stopped answering your messages, and I know that must

287

have been incredibly frustrating for you, but I was just trying and trying to remember who he was and I didn't want to talk to anyone until I'd done that. I desperately wanted to talk to you, tell you what I'd seen, but you can't accuse people of murder, can you, unless you're pretty sure? It wasn't until I was browsing the British newspapers online, and I saw that picture of you and him together – you remember, when you got photographed at some do?'

Cora nodded. That picture in the *Mirror*, the one she'd been teased so mercilessly about by the boys.

Justin was still talking. '... then, well, I still wasn't a hundred per cent sure, but he looked so like the person I'd seen. And I thought, what if it really is him, and Cora's dating a murderer! And I was so scared, scared for you. Which is why I sent that tweet.'

'The one – the one warning me to be careful? And not trust anyone? But Justin, that was so vague! I thought you were threatening me! Why didn't you just *tell* me what you'd seen, what you were thinking? You made me so scared, do you realise that? So scared, so many times! That night, when I saw the private detective outside my house, on his phone – I suppose he was texting you to tell you Benjamin was inside with me – and then you immediately sent me another warning tweet? I was terrified!'

Justin sighed heavily. 'Oh, Cora, I'm just so, so sorry. I don't know. I wasn't positive, and I thought that if I made such an enormous accusation, and I was wrong, that someone like him wouldn't hesitate to sue me to hell and back, and then you'd hate me even more than you did already, and ... so that's why I hired the detective, to follow you, make sure you were safe. I told him that if he saw anything, any hint at all that Boland might hurt you, to go to the police. I couldn't bear it, Cora, if anything had happened to you ...'

He sank his face into his hands. Cora stared at him for a moment, then reached out and stroked his head briefly.

'Fair enough, I suppose. But there are still so many questions, Justin. Why didn't you just go to the police there and then, when you saw Jeanette being pulled out of the window and …' – she couldn't bring herself to say 'Benjamin' – '… saw whoever it was getting away, on The Dead Dog Day?'

Justin sat up straight again. Cora noticed with a shock that his eyes were bright with unshed tears.

'Pardon? What day?'

'It's what we call it. The day Jeanette died. Because there was a dog, which died too … oh, never mind. Go on. Why didn't you go to the police?'

'Because I'm a moron. I wasn't thinking straight. I panicked – I stood there for a minute, two minutes, I'm not sure, trying to process what had just happened in front of my eyes. I could hear her moaning, and I know I should have gone to her, tried to see if I could save her, but I was in shock, I think. And then there were footsteps, and I saw the security guard coming round the corner, and – I don't know, I suppose I thought that as I was the one standing there, just feet from the body, that I might somehow be blamed. So I hid, behind a skip that was sitting there, until he'd gone running off to get help, and then I ran too. I ran away, Cora. Like a coward. It's something that will haunt me for ever, believe me.'

'And then, when you realised you'd been captured on CCTV? Why not come forward then, allow them to eliminate you from the enquiry?'

'I saw it online. Yes, it was me, but it could have been anyone, Cora. My face was never seen, just that coat you'd bought me, which I'd never worn before so I knew nobody else would recognise me from it. I gave it away to a charity shop in Madrid, though, just in case.'

He had the good grace to look shamefaced as Cora glared at him, then continued.

'I just thought, how can I come forward now? How can I explain running away from the scene of a murder? It would have looked so suspicious. So I just didn't come forward. Sorry, Cora.'

Cora rubbed her sore ankle, head still buzzing.

'OK, so if you're right – why? Why on earth would

Benjamin kill Jeanette? He barely knows her. In fact, I think he only met her once or twice, when she was trying to get him to work on the show. It makes no sense. What possible motive could he have for wanting her dead?'

A little bubble of hope suddenly rose inside her. Justin had this wrong, he must have. It couldn't have been Benjamin. Everyone has a doppelgänger, right? It must have been someone who just *looked* like Benjamin. Then the bubbles of hope burst as she realised Justin was shaking his head sadly and pulling a sheaf of papers out of his duffel bag that had been slung on the chair opposite.

He sat back down. 'I thought that too. It was one of the reasons I thought I might be wrong about him, at first. So, as I was at a bit of a loose end out here with not a lot to occupy my time, I did some digging. And – well, take a look. This is what I found.'

He handed the pile of papers to Cora.

'Read it, Cora. Because, in there, is the reason why I believe Benjamin Boland killed Jeanette.'

54

Twenty minutes later, Cora finally put the pile of papers aside, tears running down her cheeks. Was there really a motive in what she'd just read, a motive for murder? There *was* now, she knew, a tragic link between Benjamin and Jeanette, but if that link was a motive for murder, it was a motive of the most twisted and pointless kind.

Justin sat quietly opposite her, watching her intently. She returned his gaze with brimming eyes, and they sat there for a moment, motionless. Then Justin broke the silence.

'So. What do you think? It's only been in the past few days that I finally got all the documentation together, Cora. As far as I can see, it's pretty damning. But you're the journalist …'

Cora shrugged. She tried to speak, but her throat was so thick with tears she could only squeak unintelligibly. She coughed and tried again.

'He told me about it, you know. The plane crash. The one that killed his parents, when he was just a little boy. It ruined his childhood, he ended up in boarding schools and with foster families, it was so hard for him. It broke my heart when he told me, Justin. But – he never mentioned, never said … '

Her voice shook and she picked up the newspaper article again, the one that revealed the terrible link between Benjamin and Jeanette.

'FOUR KILLED IN BERKSHIRE AIR CRASH', screamed the headline. And then the detail, stark in black and white on the photocopied page that Justin had ordered from the archives of the *Leader* newspaper. It was so long ago that nothing had been available online – he'd certainly done his research, Cora thought, as she re-read the chilling words.

'Four people died today when a light aircraft crashed shortly after take-off at Green Lytham Airfield near Maidenhead. James Boland, 36, and his 35-year-old wife Miriam were passengers in the private aircraft which was en route to Scotland. The two crew, pilot Christian Kendrick and his co-pilot Guy Ferill, were also killed when the aeroplane burst into flames on impact. Mr and Mrs Boland leave a seven-year-old son, who was being cared for by a neighbour at their London home at the time of the accident. Mr Kendrick, who was 40, is survived by his wife Helen and their 14-year-old daughter. Mr Ferill, who was unmarried, is mourned by his parents and three sisters. Accident investigators are trying to establish the cause of the crash.'

Christian Kendrick. Jeanette's father? Jeanette's father, flying the plane that killed Benjamin's parents. Christian. Chris. Jeanette's last word. Was that what she was trying to say, that she'd been attacked because of Chris, her father? But would she call him Chris, and not Dad or something?

And then, another article, dated a few months later.

'ALCOHOL TO BLAME FOR FATAL PLANE CRASH?'

Cora scanned it again, the letters blurring in front of her eyes.

'A post-mortem examination revealed significant levels of blood alcohol in the bodies of both Mr Kendrick and Mr Ferill. Investigators believe the two men were drinking together at Ferill's home the night before the tragedy ...'

Cora wiped her eyes. 'So yes, it sounds as if Jeanette's father and his friend, the co-pilot, were at fault. But they all died, together, Benjamin's parents and Jeanette's dad. Two children, devastated. Surely that would bring them together, not lead one of them to murder the other years later?'

'I know, it doesn't really make sense. Revenge maybe, revenge on her family for what they did to his? The question is, why now? It's just that the combination of that, and – well, the fact that I'm so sure it was him I saw doing the deed – it doesn't leave that much room for doubt, does it?'

He leaned back in his seat and rubbed his nose again.

292

'I even got the private detective to break into Benjamin's flat a while ago, you know, to see if he could find any link between him and Jeanette, just in case it was by some miracle a different Benjamin Boland who looked a bit similar. He broke into yours first – well, not broke in, I sent him my key, hoping you hadn't changed the locks, and told him where the key drawer was. I figured you'd have a key to Benjamin's flat by then, so he borrowed it, you'd written 'Benj' on the keytag so it wasn't difficult …'

Justin noticed the furious look on Cora's face and stopped talking.

'I knew somebody had been in there. I *knew* it!' she hissed. 'Did he break in twice then, to put the keys back?'

He nodded guiltily and Cora glared at him. 'He did it all in one day. But it was worth it, Cora – there *was* something in Benjamin's place, a photo, of his parents, in a box in the wardrobe. The detective bloke took a shot of it on his phone and emailed it to me, and it was the same people as in the newspaper article, so I knew then. I just needed to wait to get all the archive newspaper stuff together, which took a while. I don't know what else to say, Cora. I'm just so sorry. So sorry about everything.'

Cora shrugged, suddenly too weary to think about it all any more. She looked at the old Victorian clock ticking away quietly on the sideboard. It was nearly 3 a.m.

'I need to sleep, Justin. We both need to sleep. And then tomorrow – well, later today really – I think we should go home. Go to the police, tell them everything. Then they can decide what to do. It's not up to you, or to us. OK?'

'OK. I'll help you upstairs. I'll get online now, book us some flights, and then sleep down here, on the sofa, alright?'

Cora nodded, struggling to get to her feet and wincing as the pain shot up her leg from her damaged ankle. Suddenly, all she could think about was Adam. Adam would sort this out. She felt a desperate urge to call him, but she ignored it. This needed to be done in person. Even with all the pain, shock and exhaustion the night had brought, she realised the thought of Adam was a comfort to her. He would fix this, he would find out the truth. And she drifted into an uneasy sleep, dreaming of green eyes watching over her.

55

Wednesday 11th April

Benjamin Boland was pacing. His head hurt, and he hadn't slept
more than a couple of hours since Cora had driven off leaving
him in the pouring rain on the Embankment, but he couldn't
rest. Pacing, pacing, up and down the long hallway of his
apartment, through the living area, feet tapping on the polished
wood, and then back again. Pacing, pacing.

Tomorrow, that was all he could think about. Tomorrow,
he'd sort this mess out, and then he could get on with his life.
His life, which despite all the trappings of success, had always
been such a mess really, ever since that awful day ...

He felt a surge of rage, his fists clenching so hard that his
nails dug painfully into his palms. The Kendricks had paid now,
they had lost two people they loved, just like he had. So there
was just one more person, somebody else who needed to be
dealt with now, before he could move on, move on to his
glittering future, be normal, be happy. It wasn't fair that he had
to do this, not to her. But he knew it would never be over unless
he did it, did what needed to be done to finish it.

He'd been planning to do it tomorrow. He slowed to a stop,
and slumped down onto the sofa, shutting his eyes. He
imagined her face, the expression on it, the look in those
beautiful eyes when she realised what was about to happen to
her. He didn't like to think about that, but it was the only way.
It had to be done. Suddenly, a surge of energy shot through him.
Why wait? He leapt to his feet. Tonight. He'd do it tonight. As
long as she was at home. If not, he'd go back tomorrow, and
every day until it was done. And then he'd be free, free from his

past, and ready to move on. As he moved swiftly through the apartment, gathering his new balaclava and gloves, and the spare key to her flat, Benjamin Boland was smiling.

56

DCI Adam Bradberry stared at the pale, exhausted looking pair on the other side of his desk. His head was reeling from the deluge of information they'd just imparted, and delighted though he'd been to see Cora suddenly appear at the police station reception desk, he couldn't quite suppress his irritation about the fact that she'd been withholding information from him for quite some time.

'I'm so sorry, Adam. I should have told you about knowing it was Justin on the CCTV,' she was saying now. 'But I just knew there'd be a valid explanation, and …'

'Alright, alright.' His tone was sharp, and she visibly winced. He instantly felt guilty, knowing that only part of his annoyance was due to the fact that she'd potentially hampered the investigation. He was, he acknowledged, feeling unaccountably jealous that she'd done so in order to protect her ex-boyfriend.

'Look, let's move on.' His voice was softer now, and he was rewarded with a ghost of a smile. Bloody hell, she was gorgeous, even with the bruise on her forehead, those dark circles under her eyes, and the pain that was contained within them. He had a sudden urge to wrap her in his arms, but busied himself with shuffling through the copious notes he'd spent the past hour scribbling down as Cora and Justin had told their remarkable story.

'Th … thank you. So much.'

He met her gaze, ignoring the boyfriend. Ex-boyfriend, he reminded himself. And presumably Benjamin Boland was an ex too, now, if all this was true. Quite a cheery thought. He looked down again for a moment, trying to drag his mind away from

Cora's love life and back to the matter in hand. He cleared his throat.

'I'll need full, proper statements from you both in due course, but that can wait. Cora, you look terrible. Go home. We'll take it from here. I'll keep you posted. And as for you, Mr Dendy – I'd advise you to go home too. And next time you witness a murder, maybe come forward, instead of fleeing the country?'

Justin was doing a good impression of somebody who was extremely interested in the faded and stained blue carpet of the interview room. He raised his eyes sheepishly to those of the policeman.

'I will. Sorry.'

Adam shook his head and waved a hand dismissively. They all stood up, Cora a little gingerly although her ankle was feeling much less painful this evening. She reached across the desk and touched Adam's hand.

'Call me, as soon as you can, please?'

He nodded. 'I will. Get some sleep.' He smiled, and she smiled back. Justin looked curiously from one to the other, but said nothing.

When they'd gone, Adam returned to the murder investigation room and started barking orders. First, they needed to get Benjamin Boland in for questioning. This story seemed completely surreal, but Dendy seemed pretty sure about what he'd seen. And as for this link between Boland and Kendrick … Adam thumped his forehead in frustration.

Of course, the TV star hadn't even been on the police's radar as a potential suspect, and so even though it had been known that Kendrick's father was a pilot and had died many years ago in an accident, that was simply a bit of interesting background with no possible connection to her murder. And even the long-dead father's name – Christian, so probably Chris for short – simply hadn't seemed relevant. One of the team *had* pointed it out, but the brief discussion which followed had ended in one detective joking that maybe Jeanette was calling the name out in her dying seconds because she could see her father waiting for her at the gates of heaven – or hell. And that had been it.

Adam sighed and rummaged through the case files on his desk until he found the full set of crime scene pictures. He flipped through them. There it was: that antique print on the wall of the murdered woman's office. A print of an old aircraft. He compared it with the photo on the old newspaper article Justin had handed over. The same plane. She must have loved her father very much, to have that on her wall so many years later.

A thought struck him, and he went through the files again, this time looking for a phone number. He reached for the phone on the desk and tapped the numbers in. Clancy Carter answered within a few rings.

'Hello?'

'Ms Carter. Sorry to bother you, DCI Adam Bradberry here. A slightly random question for you …'

Five minutes later, he put the receiver down, his hunch confirmed. It seemed that Jeanette Kendrick had not known that the people who died alongside her father that dreadful day had been Benjamin Boland's parents, certainly according to Clancy, who had been deeply shocked by the news. Yes, Jeanette had known that a young couple had also been killed, and their surname, and even that they'd had a child, but the connection to the handsome TV presenter had never been made. Benjamin had never talked about it in any of the many TV and magazine interviews he'd done since his rise to fame, Clancy had said – she'd read several times that his parents were both dead, but no further details had ever been given, and with Benjamin seemingly reluctant to discuss it, no interviewer had ever pursued the matter.

So, Adam pondered, maybe neither of the bereaved children had ever been given full details of the crash when they were young. And while it seemed Benjamin had, when he grew up, begun to look into his parents' death, maybe it had been too painful for Jeanette to do the same. Could Benjamin have been in the dark too, until the day he'd been called to Jeanette's office to discuss appearing on her show? Did he spot the picture on her wall, recognise the plane, and start his research then? Could that day have sealed Jeanette's fate?

Adam frowned. He wanted Boland here now, in front of him. He was angry, angry at himself for not considering that the murder could have taken place in a different way, for assuming that somebody inside had pushed her out, not that somebody *outside* had *pulled* her. But who would have thought like that? A better cop than him, maybe. He looked at the time on the scratched screen of his mobile phone. Just after 7 p.m. The cars were on their way to pick Boland up, and it wasn't far. As long as he was at home, maybe this case could be wrapped up by midnight. Adam tapped his keyboard and the dark computer monitor sprang into life. A little more research into that accident and all involved in it, that's what he'd do. Solid facts to throw at his best suspect so far. A little knot of excitement was forming in his stomach. He had a good feeling about this. A very good feeling indeed.

57

'He's not at home, boss. We've got a car outside his apartment building, in case he comes back later. And we've got patrols heading for some of his usual haunts. According to his agent he rang earlier to say he's not been feeling too well, wants to take the next couple of days off. In theory, he should be at home …'

Adam sighed, frustration building again. 'Alright. Let me know as soon as you find him.'

He put the phone down and turned back to his screen. Out of interest, and to fill the time while he waited, he'd started looking more closely at the fourth man who'd died, Guy Ferill. There were a few further articles in the newspapers in the months after the crash: first the accident investigation pieces, the ones Justin Dendy had discovered and handed over. But then several more – short articles about the funerals, and then a brief follow-up in a local London newspaper when a memorial service had been held for Christian Kendrick a year later. In the past two hours Adam had miraculously managed to acquire copies of all of them, calling in favours with journalists on the night desks of the relevant papers, promising exclusives when the case was resolved. Intrigued, and also because it was proving to be an otherwise quiet night and they were bored, the reporters had called up their own archives and emailed the pieces to him, hopeful of a scoop in return.

Now Adam sipped his fifth strong coffee of the evening and read each article carefully. Guy Ferill and Christian Kendrick had been close friends, by all accounts, as well as regular work partners. Their love of socialising was mentioned more than once, while Kendrick was twice referred to as a 'maverick' who'd been a little wild in his youth before settling down with the love of his life and having a daughter, 'the apple of his eye'. Jeanette, of course.

Adam put his mug down and absent-mindedly picked up a half-eaten pear that had been lying next to it. He took a mouthful and grimaced. It was nearly black. How long had that been there? He spat into the bin, threw the offending fruit in too and turned back to the screen. So – Guy Ferill. Here we go. Single, a few years younger than Kendrick, but from a big close family. There was a photo here, of the young man with his three sisters, and some children, his nieces and nephews. Adam's eyes flicked over the list of names under the photo.

'Guy Ferill, pictured from L-R with his sister Joyce Stratton and her son, James; sister Frances Cane, with her daughter Beth and son Peter; and youngest sister …

He froze, staring at the last few names on the caption. His eyes flicked from the words to the photo. One little girl stared out at him, eyes bright even on the black and white, photocopied page. His heart thudded. It was her, no doubt about that, even though so many years had passed. He'd know her anywhere. Dear God. What if Boland wasn't finished with his killing, his revenge? Could that mean …?

He pushed his chair back from his desk so violently that his coffee cup crashed to the floor, the dark liquid splashing onto the already filthy carpet. Oblivious, he ran from the room, shouting at a few bemused officers to follow him. He had to get to her, now. Before Benjamin Boland did.

58

'Thanks so much for driving me home. The offer still stands, you know. You're welcome to stay. Er, on the sofa, of course,' Cora added awkwardly.

Justin smiled. 'It's fine, honestly. It would be a bit weird, after all that's happened. I'm happy in a hotel, and I'll head to the parents' in the morning, hire a car. Don't worry about me.'

He paused, and then reached out and took both of her hands in his.

'I'm just so happy, Cora, that we're friends again. I'll never stop feeling bad about the way things ended, but if we can just put it behind us ...'

Cora squeezed his fingers and then gently pulled her hands away. 'Hush, it's fine. Water under the bridge and all that. Thank you for looking out for me, for caring enough to have me followed – and to follow me yourself! I *think* my ankle will recover, one day ...'

He groaned and covered his face, and she laughed.

'Teasing. Now go – I'm knackered and you must be too. Give my love to your mum and dad, OK? And keep in touch.'

'Goodnight, Cora.'

He headed off down the driveway, listing slightly with the weight of the holdall on his shoulder, and turned halfway to blow her a kiss. She raised a hand to catch it, and pressed it to her cheek, smiling, then shut the hall door and locked it. For a moment she stood there, almost too weary to climb the stairs, then took a deep breath and began the ascent, dragging her bag and tackling the steps one at a time like a toddler, wary of her still slightly delicate ankle.

It *had* been good of Justin to drive her car home from

London; his concern about her injury, her exhaustion and her mental fragility after discovering her boyfriend was probably a murderer was quite touching. They'd stopped at Reading services, suddenly ravenous after a day of travelling and the stress of the police station, and he'd even treated her to a burger and chips. And they'd talked, talked for a solid hour across the greasy table, happy to be in one another's company again despite everything that had happened. Justin had told her he'd felt the chemistry between her and Adam, teasing her into admitting that yes, there was an attraction there, an attraction that had somehow grown slowly even though he was a doting father.

Justin had looked at her then, a flash of hope in his eyes, but she had shaken her head.

'I haven't changed my mind, Justin. I still don't want my own. I'll never want my own. But maybe I could put up with one being around now and again, if the relationship was right.'

He'd nodded ruefully, and she'd reached for his hand, and they'd sat there for a moment, both finally accepting that this was the end. At least, she thought now, as she tackled the last few steps, she knew that things were good between them again. And now, what a relief to be home, what a relief to know her own bed was just a few metres away, and that her friends were close by.

'I'll ring Rosie and Nicole tomorrow, get them round,' Cora thought as, slightly out of breath, she finally made it to the landing outside her own front door. She fumbled in her handbag for her keys. 'They will quite simply *die* when they hear what's happened. And as for Sam and Wendy, and the boys ...'

She allowed herself a tiny smile as she slid the key into the lock and let herself into the hallway. Even though the whole thing was utterly horrific, and she was still reeling from the knowledge that Benjamin was involved, part of her still relished the prospect of the fabulous gossip she'd soon be passing on to her friends.

'I'm officially a disgrace,' she announced to the hall clock, which was glowing the time at her in purple neon. Nearly

10.30 p.m. She dumped her bags on the floor and flicked the light switch, kicking off her shoes with a happy sigh. It was *so* good to be home.

She headed straight down the hall towards the kitchen. A hot chocolate, a hot shower, and a hot water bottle were what were needed, she decided as she opened the fridge. Was there any milk that was still within date, though? She was cautiously sniffing the carton when she heard it.

THUD.

Cora almost dropped the milk. What the hell was that? It sounded as though it had come from the lounge. She stood still for a moment, but all was silent. She put the carton down on the worktop, heart pounding, then smiled shakily to herself. The events of the past few days were making her paranoid. It had probably just been somebody in the flat below.

'Pull yourself together, woman!' she berated herself out loud, at the same time half-wishing she'd insisted Justin had stayed the night. But heck, she'd better get used to evenings alone, seeing as she was single again. Might as well start now, she thought sadly.

She opened the saucepan cupboard, pulled out a milk pan and poured in enough for a generous drink, then put it on the hob and turned the power on. Then she wandered into the bedroom, retrieved her hot water bottle with its cuddly faux mink cover from its drawer and placed it next to the kettle. She was spooning chocolate powder into her biggest mug when she heard it again.

THUD. CREAK.

This time she did drop what she holding, the spoon clattering into the sink. There was no doubt now. That noise was coming from the lounge. There was somebody there. A burglar? Please, not again, not a repeat of what had happened in Spain. But there'd been no sign of a break in, had there? How could somebody be in the lounge? Didn't they hear her come in? Cora stood stock still, mind racing.

The police. She needed to call the police. With a horrible sense of déjà vu, she instantly realised she didn't have her phone with her. It was still in her bag in the hall.

'Oh, hell,' she groaned, casting her eyes around the tiny kitchen for a suitable self-defence weapon. The fire extinguisher next to the cooker, that would do. Grabbing it, she moved as silently as possible into the hall, realising halfway along it that she'd have to pass the open door of the lounge to get to her bag. And then what? How could she make a phone call? They'd hear her. This was impossible. What on earth was she going to do?

THUD.

Another noise, softer this time. She'd make it to the front door, run for it, get out onto the street and scream for help, she decided. Her heart was beating so fast that she was panting slightly. She was almost at the lounge door now, could see into the room, illuminated slightly by the glow from the streetlights below. Was there somebody in there? Where were they? She paused, torn between the urge to flee on down the hallway to freedom, and an unexpected desire to see who was in her home, and why. And how had they got in?

Suddenly, recklessly, she reached out and flipped the lounge light switch.

'Who's there? What are you doing in my flat?' Her voice, strong and resolute, rang out.

Out of the corner of her eye, Cora saw a startled movement in the far left hand corner. Gripping her extinguisher, she turned to face the intruder, then gasped.

'You! What are you doing here?'

59

Benjamin took a long deep breath and looked down at the slumped body on the floor. It had only taken a moment to overpower her and squeeze her throat, hard but not too hard ... enough to cut off her oxygen supply and render her unconscious, but not hard enough to kill her. Not yet.

He sat down suddenly on the sofa, his legs unexpectedly feeling weak. The first time had been so easy, but this time ... could he do it? Could he finish the job? She was so beautiful ...

'COME ON!' He thumped both fists on the coffee table, a flash of anger burning through his veins. She had to die, and she had to die *now*.

'DO IT. DO IT.'

He stood up again purposefully, marched over to where she was lying, and crouched down next to her. Her throat still bore the livid red marks of his hands, stark against her soft white skin. He stared at her, willing himself to feel the hate, the anger. Her eyelids fluttered and a soft moan escaped her lips. She was coming round. Now, Benjamin. Do it now. Do it now, and then it will all be over. Do it ...

He reached out and gently turned her fully onto her back. A minute, that's all it would take. A minute of pressure on her throat and it would be done. He breathed deeply again, summoning up the rage, the memories ...

He had always carried the anger with him. Ever since that day, when he was seven years old, and had come home from school to find his safe, happy little life torn apart. He could still remember the blue flashing light on the patrol car parked in the driveway, and inside on the sofa his Auntie Ellen, ashen-faced, a policewoman holding her hand. Auntie Ellen, of course, not his real aunt but a friend of Mummy's. And Mummy and Daddy dead, killed when the plane that was taking them to a party in Scotland crashed, and his world crashed with it.

He was considered too young to go to the funerals, too young to be told the details of what happened. But he was smart and cunning as a child, and he acquired the newspapers, read every detail, gazed with anguished eyes at the photos of the plane which had ruined his life. Revenge though had never entered his head, until that day in Jeanette's office, when he had seen the picture on her wall, the picture of the aircraft he knew so well, that caused a twist of pain in his guts every time he saw it. Suddenly it had all clicked. Kendrick. Jeanette Kendrick. Christian Kendrick's daughter.

The old anger had come surging back, and he'd decided, there and then, that the only way to heal the ever-present pain in his heart was to avenge his parents' deaths. He briefly considered killing Jeanette's mother, the wife of the man who'd stolen his childhood, but dismissed the idea. Jeanette would be so much easier. He'd noticed the big unsealed windows in her office, wondered if that was something he could use. He'd gone back too, not long before the day Cora called 'Dead Dog Day', on the pretence that he was reconsidering Jeanette's job offer, and placed a tiny listening device under her windowsill. He needed to listen to her, on the day, find out when she was alone. He'd swiftly removed the device again when he'd finally travelled up in the window cleaner's cradle, unsecured and so very convenient, and appeared at her window. He'd timed it perfectly, listening intently first via his earpiece from around the corner, hearing her office door rant about the stupid dog, hearing her slam back inside, the device so sensitive he could even hear the blinds snap shut, knowing she was there on her own and that now was the time.

He'd even bought his apartment in the building just along the road specifically so he could be close to TV Centre, watch and wait, consider his options, wanting to carry out the perfect crime. The idea had struck him suddenly one day as he lazily watched the building's window cleaners through his telescope, realising with interest that the cradles were always there overnight, tucked neatly away in the shadows along the side of the building, when the marathon monthly window cleaning task was being carried out. He'd wandered down there, casually checked them out, happy to see that they were the straightforward manual, hand-cranked wire rope style, no problem for him to operate after he'd once had to use one in a filming stunt. Then it was just some duct tape, a balaclava, and gloves. They'd probably shed a few black fibres, but he made sure he'd got rid of them immediately, stuffed deep into a bin outside a restaurant on the way home, never to be seen again. And he'd been so careful, walking away from the scene of the murder and not running, nothing to draw attention to himself.

His gamble had been that Jeanette might not come to the window when he suddenly appeared outside – that he'd have to climb in and throw her out instead, risk being caught inside her office. But in the end, she'd come so easily, so surprised to see him smiling there seven floors up, so curious, actually thinking at first that he'd changed his mind about joining the show and was making a dramatic, Benjamin-style gesture to impress her, stupid woman. As soon as she was within reach he'd grabbed her, leaning in through the opening and gripping her tightly by the arms, telling her the real reason he was there, and why she had to die.

'I didn't know … I had no idea … I'm so sorry. So terribly, terribly sorry. Please, if …' she'd stuttered, trying to apologise for her pathetic excuse for a father. He'd grown angry then, risked reaching into his pocket with one hand, still holding one upper arm in a vice-like grip, grabbing his pre-prepared strip of tape and slapping it across her mouth. He didn't want to hear any more, and he didn't want her to start screaming, to be stopped before he could finish what he'd come here to do, what he'd been planning for so long. And she'd been so weak, when it came to it, the great Jeanette. So easy to haul through the open window, so easy to drag out and over the window ledge, into the cradle. He'd had momentum by then, fury and anguish giving his gym-honed body even more strength, lifting her flailing body in one smooth movement over the side of the cradle, dropping her like a piece of litter. A vase or something had fallen inside, he'd heard it crashing to the ground, but that wasn't a major problem; it could easily have happened if she'd jumped, or if somebody had pushed her out from the inside, which was what the idiot police had instantly assumed. It had worked, worked beautifully. The perfect crime.

He hadn't been able to attend the funeral with Cora, too busy with filming commitments, but he had studied the TV news clips and newspaper coverage of the event with quiet satisfaction, noting the pain on the faces of Jeanette's mother and other relatives.

His revenge, though, had only been half finished. There was the other family, Guy Ferill's family. They too had lost just one person, while he had lost two – another score to settle. He'd got private investigators on the case, tracking down the man's relatives, and been shocked, astounded, to discover that one of Ferill's nieces also worked in television – not only that, but she also worked at TV Centre, alongside Jeanette. The perfect choice, so easy for him to access.

It had been a struggle, deciding what to do with her, especially as he'd foolishly decided to get to know her first, and then found himself, somewhat to his surprise, far from immune to her charms. His affection for her had crept up on him, frightening him, making him wonder if he could actually do this, go through with his plan.

Now, he looked at her, her eyelids still fluttering. Oh, shit. He closed his eyes, summoning up the image of his parents, his mother's soft voice, his father's gentle eyes, the wreckage of the plane, the pain of his childhood. The old fury bubbled up again, quietly at first, and then in a fierce torrent, and he opened his eyes and roared, just as she started to sit up, eyes wide with fear. He paused only for a second, looked at her, feeling nothing, his hands finally reaching for her throat, and starting to squeeze, and squeeze …

CRASH. There was an immense noise behind him, a sound

310

of splintering wood and smashing glass, but he was lost, fuelled by misery and anger and memories, squeezing, squeezing, listening to her gasping, oblivious to her hands clawing at him in terror, aware only that her life was ebbing away and that his could start again.

'STOP! STOP!'

The voice rang in his ears and then he was being dragged backwards, his hands being pulled from her throat, his body being flung to the ground, the room suddenly full of police officers and panic and noise.

And Alice. Alice was choking, men lifting her up, telling her to breathe, telling her it was all going to be alright, that she was safe now. Alice, still alive.

'I've failed,' thought Benjamin, as his face was ground into the carpet, his hands yanked violently behind his back. 'Mummy. I've failed you.' And then the tears began, and he cried as if he might never stop.

60

In Cheltenham, Cora put down her fire extinguisher and laughed with relief.

'How on earth did you get in? You scared me half to death!'

Oliver, the neighbours' cat, who'd sneaked in past her at the door as she'd arrived minutes earlier, stared at her with malevolent eyes and hissed. Cora hissed back.

'And be more careful in future. That's two ornaments you've knocked over there, you clumsy creature. Right, out!'

She pointed at the door and Oliver, having found nothing of interest in the lounge anyway, slunk out of it and headed down the hallway. Cora saw him out of the front door and locked it firmly behind him.

'What a day. Now – hot chocolate!'

And once more, she limped towards the kitchen.

60

61

'I just can't believe it, Cora. It's like something out of a book.
Or maybe even too far-fetched for a book. It's *insane*.'

Nicole, her hands cupping a virtually untouched mug of
black coffee, shook her head and looked at Rosie, who was
literally open-mouthed.

Cora grinned. 'Rosie, shut your mouth. And yes, I know, I
can hardly believe it myself. Nobody can. I sure can pick 'em,
eh?'

Rosie, mouth now closed, exchanged a sympathetic look
with Nicole.

'You've still got us. And what about the hunky policeman?
Any developments there?' Rosie poked Cora in the arm.

It was pouring with rain outside, the occasional crack of
thunder rumbling in the distance. In Cora's living room, the
three of them were snuggled together on the sofa, the table in
front of them laden as always with cakes. Rosie and Nicole had
both left work early, desperate to hear every detail, but neither
had expected the stupendous story they'd just heard.

Cora poked Rosie back. 'Stop it. It's too soon. But …'
She paused.

'Well, maybe. He's asked me out for a drink. We'll see.
He's got a child, remember. Not really my type.'

Nicole cackled. 'Not really your type! He's bloody
gorgeous.'

Cora smiled. Adam had been on every TV news programme
during the day, as the showbiz world was rocked by the news
that Benjamin Boland had been arrested on suspicion of the

315

murder of Jeanette Kendrick and the attempted murder of Alice Lomas. And yes, the policeman had looked rather gorgeous, she must admit. She put down her mug and picked up a Danish pastry.

'Anyway, he rang this afternoon, partly to suggest meeting up and partly to clear up a few things,' she said, then paused to take a bite.

She swallowed. 'Benjamin has told the police absolutely everything, apparently. Admitted murdering Jeanette, and that he fully intended to kill Alice too. He had a key to her place apparently, even though they hadn't been dating long, so he didn't even need to break in. It was just so lucky that Adam recognised that picture of Alice as a child in that newspaper, and acted on a hunch and rushed round to her flat. She was in a picture of Guy Ferill's family, and Adam says she was totally unmistakeable even as a small girl. He had her home address in the system of course – took all her details when she was questioned. Another minute or so and it would have been too late, he said. I've never much liked her, as you well know, but – bloody hell, I wouldn't have wished that on her.'

She closed her eyes for a moment, trying not to think about Benjamin's hands around Alice's throat, those hands that had been so gentle when they had been together, the hands that had done such wonderful things to her in bed. She shuddered and opened her eyes again.

'And she's pregnant, too. It would have been two lives he'd taken.'

Rosie was looking horrified, hands instinctively moving protectively to her own bump.

'Flipping heck, Cora. That poor girl.'

The three of them fell silent, each lost in her own thoughts. Cora sipped her tea slowly, remembering the phone conversation she'd had with Adam earlier that day. One of the biggest of the dozens of questions she'd fired tearfully at him was why Benjamin had felt the need to date and sleep with Alice before attempting to murder her. It was something she couldn't understand – why not just kill her, like he'd done with

316

Jeanette?

Adam, his voice full of kindness and sympathy, which had made Cora cry even more, had gently told her some of what Benjamin had explained to him, in what was apparently a full and open confession.

'He was having some doubts, Cora, about whether he was ready to settle down. And in his clearly rather sick mind, he thought he might be able to kill two birds with one stone – excuse the pun, sorry, that was ill-judged – and have a bit of fun with Alice before he finished her off. It made sense to him, apparently, although he also said he felt terribly guilty about sleeping with her, when it was you he really cared about. Every time it happened, he felt sick afterwards, he says.'

Adam filled her in on some of the details – how Benjamin had engineered a meeting with Alice in a club and asked her out, taking a gamble that as she and Cora weren't exactly friends, Alice would be happy enough to date him behind her colleague's back. How he'd put off the murder, using the newsreader to satisfy the sexual urges he still sometimes had, but then feeling disgusted at himself and terrified Cora would find out. How he wanted to pull off another perfect crime, biding his time. How he'd even tried to throw suspicion onto Alice herself.

'So sneaky. Unbelievably sneaky,' Cora said out loud.

Rosie and Nicole turned to look at her.

'Which bit?' asked Nicole.

'The recording.'

Nicole nodded, and took a large bite out of her chocolate muffin. Rosie shook her head slowly and reached for a second slice of Victoria sponge.

'He's a clever one, that Boland,' she mumbled through a mouthful of cake.

Cora plucked a sultana from her pastry and popped it into her mouth. Clever indeed, she thought, remembering the recording of Alice that Benjamin had made on his mobile phone, Alice talking about feeling guilty about something bad she'd done.

'According to Adam, who's spoken to her again at length, she's now admitted what she didn't say when he first questioned her – that what she was actually feeling terribly guilty about was dating Benjamin behind my back. Same as when we overheard her saying a similar thing in the café. And Benjamin knew that, of course. He just got lucky, realised he could use it to throw attention onto her. It certainly worked. I went straight to Adam with it, didn't I? Dammit, I kept Benjamin fully up to date with the police investigation, for goodness' sake. He knew exactly what was going on all the time.'

She groaned.

'Don't beat yourself up, Cora. None of this is your fault. And maybe Alice isn't as bad as you thought, eh? At least she felt guilty about what she was doing.'

'Yes, I know. I've been thinking about her a lot, actually. I'm going to go and see her, try to clear the air. I've had enough of this stupid feuding – there are so many more important things in life. If I can take anything positive from all of this, it's that life is short, too short for petty jealousy and bitchiness.'

Cora stood up and walked to the window. The sky was almost black, the rain battering the pavement below. A lone pedestrian scurried past, umbrella half inside out, coat flapping. She sighed and turned back to her friends.

'Oh, and the Chris thing? Pretty clear now that Jeanette was trying to tell the security guard she'd been attacked because of her father, Christian. He was never known as Chris though, according to her family – that's why the name didn't ring a bell for anyone. If it had, maybe the link to Benjamin would have been spotted sooner and …'

She felt tears welling in her eyes again.

'Oh, Cora. I'm so sorry.' Nicole's voice was gentle. 'Jeanette was very badly injured, remember. It's likely she was just trying to say something, anything, to get that message across. "Chris" was probably as much as she managed to say before she … '

Cora nodded.

'He's still claiming he loves me, you know. Benjamin. Adam said that he's saying it over and over again. "Tell Cora I love her. Tell her I would never have hurt her. It's just something I had to do, to move on with my life, I was almost ready to commit to her for ever." That sort of thing.'

'Oh Cora. He probably did, you know. He was just so screwed up, so obsessed with his twisted revenge ...'

Rosie's voice cracked slightly. She looked close to tears. Nicole leaned over and stroked her arm.

Cora turned to stare out of the window again. Yes, he probably did love her, she thought numbly. What a waste. What a terrible, tragic waste.

62

Sunday 15th April

Alice's eyes looked distended, the lids pink and puffy; her make-up-free face was blotchy and streaked with tears, her nails chipped and broken. Propped against pillows in her hospital bed, she clutched the pink pashmina that was wrapped around her shoulders, and shivered. But it was her neck that Cora's horrified eyes were drawn to over and over again, the livid bruising, the clear impressions of fingers etched onto delicate skin. She felt sick. Benjamin had done this. Those were Benjamin's finger marks, the visible, horrible proof that he had tried to kill this woman. She shivered too, and dragged her eyes back to Alice's.

They'd been chatting for over an hour, hesitantly at first, both wary after years of professional enmity. But eventually, the barriers between them began to crumble slowly in the face of their shared trauma. Now, in this little, private, London hospital room, which smelled of a mixture of disinfectant and Chanel N°5, Cora was actually holding Alice's trembling hand. She allowed herself a small wry smile. Wendy and Sam would think they were seeing things – who would ever have thought it!

'I was kept in the dark too, as a child,' Alice was saying. 'I was very young, and I knew my uncle had been killed in a plane crash, but no real details – not the fact they'd been drinking or anything. The family sort of fell apart after the accident. Everyone adored Uncle Guy so much, and without him all the fun seemed to go out of our lives - we'd all been so close before, but after he died everything changed. It was such a devastating time, it affected everybody, and although I never knew the specifics of what happened, I picked up on all the tension and unhappiness. It was horrible. I didn't have a very happy childhood, not after that. But we and the Kendricks always kept in touch, so I knew Jeanette, and that's why when I decided I wanted to work in TV, I came to her. It seems weird now that neither of us ever realised that Benjamin was the kid who lost his parents in the crash, but we really didn't – it was one of those taboo subjects in both of our families, and as we grew up I think we both just sort of wanted to put it behind us.'

Cora nodded. She could understand that. Alice shivered, even though the room was stiflingly warm.

'And Jeanette – well, she helped me. She was so good to me, Cora. I know I'm not the brightest girl in the world, but she took a chance, she gave me the opportunity ...'

A sob wracked her frail body again and she slipped her hand out of Cora's and fumbled on her bedside table for a tissue. She blew her nose noisily, then took a deep breath and continued.

'That's why I was so upset, when she died. I know everyone thought I was just being a stupid diva, but I was devastated. We were friends, you know? She was probably the only true friend I had, in all honesty. There are a couple of others, from school, who I keep in touch with – in fact, I was speaking to one of them on the phone, that time in the café when you overheard me, and again that time Benjamin recorded me. I assumed it was Agnes – you know, from *Sportsworld*? – who'd given that recording to the police, I feel bad about that now. That's another person I need to apologise to. I rang her up and screamed abuse at her down the phone, she must have thought I'd gone crazy!'

She managed a weak smile, and Cora smiled back. Alice sniffed and carried on talking, her voice hoarse.

'But I really don't have many friends, and I know it's all my own fault. I've been so horrible to everyone at work, and I've hated myself for it, but once I started with that sort of bitch persona it just got harder and harder to stop. All I really have is my looks, Cora, I know that – I'm not clever like you, or like Sam or Wendy or anyone else there, and I've just felt so scared and insecure ever since I started the job. It just seemed easier to keep everyone at arm's length, so nobody would know how out of my depth I was.'

She paused again and cleared her throat.

'So it ended up that in the last few years it was Jeanette I was closest to. We never let that be known, not at work, but we really were very close. And I know the way I was acting made the police suspicious of me, but I just couldn't control it. Every time I walked into that newsroom, walked past her office, it hit me again. And the funeral was just horrific. It's been terrible.'

She stopped and wiped her eyes. Cora sat quietly, letting her compose herself. Poor Alice, she thought.

Alice took a sip of water, slumped back on her pillows and stared at the ceiling.

'So – I wasn't myself, Cora. And I'm sorry, so sorry, for what I did to you. It was such an awful time, and Jeanette was gone, and then I was dumped by this guy I'd been seeing, and I was so desperate for someone to just hold me, and tell me everything would be alright. And you were nice to me, even though I didn't deserve it, and I still couldn't stop myself being a bitch. And then, after that day when I was being so nasty to you in the make-up room, and you ignored my question and walked out – do you remember …?'

Cora nodded.

'Well, it was just after that, that Benjamin came up to me, in that club. I knew he was your boyfriend, but I tried to justify it to myself, told myself you'd started being mean to me again so you deserved to be cheated on. I just went along with it. I deserve everything I got, Cora. I'm a horrible cow, and I deserve what happened to me.'

'No!' Cora said fiercely. She grabbed Alice's hand again.

'No, you don't deserve what happened to you. Neither of us do. It was not my fault, it was not your fault, OK? Never say that again. It was him. All him. You remember that.'

Alice's eyes filled with tears once more.

'Thank you,' she whispered.

They sat in silence for a while. The room was filled with

flowers, vases on every available surface, cards bearing messages of support and sympathy. At the end of the bed, the TV was showing an old episode of *Columbo*, the sound muted.

'He knows now, that I'm pregnant,' Alice said eventually.

Cora looked up. 'Benjamin does?'

'Mmmm. That police officer told him. He said Benjamin was glad, then. Glad that he didn't finish it. You know, kill me. He didn't really ever want kids, but he told the police he'd never hurt one.'

She paused and wiped her eyes again. 'He told me, over and over again you know, that he didn't love you. That he was going to finish with you, so we could be together. That's why I thought it was OK for me to be with him. But when I saw his face, that day on the Embankment, when you caught us together, I knew the truth straight away. I could see it in his eyes when he looked at you. He did love you in his twisted way, Cora. Everything he said to me was a lie. Just to get close to me, so he could use me for his final fling sex games and then … kill me.'

She lay back on her pillows and closed her eyes, looking suddenly exhausted.

Cora nodded, her heart hurting. It was so dreadfully sad, all of it. Benjamin, the little boy whose life had fallen apart, who'd grown up to be so wonderful in so many ways, but with the secret pain, the pain which had turned into a sickness which would eventually destroy him. And all of them who'd been dragged into it with him … Jeanette, Alice, and Cora herself. Jeanette was gone, and the two who were left would never forget this, never really get over it, Cora knew that.

She looked at Alice.

'The baby – it's OK?'

Alice opened her eyes and smiled for the first time that day. 'It's OK. And yes, I know its dad is a killer, and that's not going to be an easy conversation to have one day. But it's the only good thing to come out of this horrible mess, Cora. I'm having it. And then it'll be the two of us, and I won't need anyone else. I'll love it and protect it and care for it and everything will be alright.'

Cora swallowed a sudden lump in her throat.

'It doesn't have to be just the two of you, Alice. You have friends. We'll help. You won't have to do it all on your own.'

'Friends?' Alice's voice was barely a whisper this time.

Cora nodded. 'Friends,' she said.

63

Three weeks later

'I'm happy. I really do feel happy. And I feel lucky too – is that weird?'

'Well, you're always a bit weird Cora. But yes, you're lucky. Lucky to be alive for one thing, after the murderer boyfriend thing and all.'

Nicole rolled her eyes, then smiled and clinked champagne glasses with Cora. Rosie, who had finally given birth two weeks ago after what seemed to all of them like the longest pregnancy in history, grinned up at them from the sofa, where she was contentedly breast-feeding little Amy. Alistair, his arm wrapped around his wife's shoulders, looked up for a moment to smile at Cora too, then resumed his besotted gazing at his new daughter. Nicole's Will, sitting next to him, raised his eyes heavenwards, and they all laughed.

It was a beautiful day, the warm May sunshine streaming in through the open doors to the roof terrace. Inside, Cora's living room was all set up for a Sunday lunch party, table pushed back against the wall and groaning with food, white balloons tied to the backs of chairs, and plenty of champagne, white wine and beer cooling in the kitchen. She wasn't sure exactly why she'd felt the need to throw a party, but it suddenly seemed that after a horrible few months, lots of her friends now had something to celebrate. Rosie's gorgeous new baby, Alice's pregnancy, Adam's successful cracking of the murder case, and, for Cora herself, the news that she would be covering Alice's maternity leave. Six months, maybe longer, in the studio in London. And, amazingly, all with Alice's blessing. Their friendship had had a tentative start, but there was no doubt it was now a friendship.

There was a buzz at the door intercom and Cora whooped, put her glass down carefully on the mantelpiece and ran to answer it. It seemed everyone else had arrived at once, and within minutes the flat was full of chatter and laughter. Scott, Nathan and Rodney had come together, all with their partners, and all three wearing the silly T-shirts she'd picked up for them in an airport souvenir shop while she and Justin had been waiting for their flight home from Spain.

To her great delight, she'd found a white T-shirt with the slogan 'Idiot Seeking Village', now proudly sported by Rodney. Shaven-headed Scott's said 'Who Needs Hair With a Body Like This?' and intolerant Nathan had been thrilled with 'I See Dumb People'. She hugged them all happily. She'd miss them during her London stint, but Alice would be around for a few months yet so she and her crew would have the summer on the road together – the best time of year for morning TV reporters, with daylight from 4 a.m. and no need for thermals.

'Right – where's the food, Cora?' demanded Scott, after he'd stopped whirling her around in a huge, dancing bear hug.

She laughed, a little out of breath, and pointed across the room. Scott's eyes lit up.

'Marvellous! I could eat a hearse!'

'Horse, not hearse!' chorused Cora, Nathan and Rodney, to delighted laughter from everyone else in the room. Cora shook her head. Scott really was the original Mr Malaprop.

Leaving the boys to descend on the buffet like starving creatures, Nathan play-wrestling a recently arrived Justin away from the chicken legs, she went to join Sam and Wendy who'd caught the morning train from London and were currently arguing over who should get first cuddle of Rosie's baby.

'Oi! Cuddle me instead!' Cora demanded.

They both obliged.

'You look good. Better than I've seen you look in ages, to be honest,' Sam said, appraising her with a critical eye. 'Wonder why that it is, eh, Wend?'

She nudged Wendy, who almost spilled her drink.

328

'Sam! But yes, you do look rather gorgeous, Cora. And yes, I think we can guess why.'

Cora couldn't help blushing. 'Shut up,' she said, smiling.

She turned and caught a glimpse of herself in the big mirror over the fireplace. She did look good. Her skin was glowing, eyes bright, even her hair seemed shinier. Across the room, she caught Adam's eye. He was deep in conversation with Alice, but when he saw her looking at him he beamed. Alice glanced over her shoulder, grinned, and waved her glass of orange juice in the air to beckon Cora over.

'Thanks so much for inviting me,' she said. 'I'll stop hogging him now, there's a baby I need to go and bounce on my knee – get some practice in!'

'Yes, you'll need plenty, young Alice. Better get used to baby sick on your cashmere too.'

Alice groaned and headed across to where the girls were all still cooing over the angelic Amy. Cora watched as they all greeted Alice with warm smiles. Phew. She knew how they all felt about Alice, but they'd agreed to make an effort for Cora's sake, and she was relieved they were keeping their word. That was another thing she had to be thankful for. Her friends truly were wonderful.

'So – nice party,' Adam said, dragging her attention back to him.

'Delighted you could make it,' she said.

And even more delighted that you've asked me out, and that we're having dinner next week, she thought. They fell into easy conversation, wandering out onto the roof terrace where Harry was crouched in the sunshine, playing some sort of intense game involving toy cars and Lego, and chatting animatedly to Rosie's Ava and Alexander and Nicole's serious-faced little Elliot.

'Children, at one of my parties. I must be getting old,' Cora mused.

'They're not so bad. Honest.'

'I know. Well, some of them anyway. These four are pretty special, I think.'

They rested their glasses on the balcony ledge, a light breeze ruffling their hair and bringing the scent of roses across from the adjoining terrace where Oliver had appeared some time earlier and was now stretched out in the sunshine like a small, discarded fur coat. The cat reminded Cora of the night when Benjamin had finally been caught. She shuddered slightly and looked away. He was on remand now, awaiting sentencing. She'd been bombarded by requests from newspapers over the past few weeks, trying to sign her up for 'My Boyfriend was a Killer' exclusives once the court case was over, but she'd turned them all down. She wanted to move on now, not dwell on what had happened. She didn't know how things would work out with Adam – she still had no desire for full-time children in her life, but her attraction to him was so strong she'd been powerless to turn him down when he'd nervously asked her out. And she genuinely liked Harry. She drained her glass and smiled up at the policeman.

'Come on, let's go and eat, I'm starving.'

'Sure. Er – you didn't make the food though, did you? I'd quite like to be alive to see Boland permanently behind bars …'

'Cheek! How do you know I can't cook anyway?'

'I may have been chatting to your friends, possibly …'

Cora rolled her eyes. 'Some friends. They're right though. So, no, I didn't cook, it's catered, you're quite safe.'

They were still laughing as they reached the buffet table. Cora was just popping a goat's cheese canapé into her mouth when her mobile rang. She fished it out of her pocket. Work. Great.

'Hi, Alan,' she mumbled, mouth full of cheese.

'Cora. Sorry to interrupt your lunch – nothing urgent, I know you've booked today off, just a quick heads up for tomorrow's lives. Need you in Weston-super-Mare. Talking donkey on the beach. I'll email you the details later, OK?'

She swallowed, shaking her head. 'Talking donkey. Yep, fine. Talk to you in the morning.'

She ended the call. Adam was staring at her in amazement.

'A talking donkey? Your job is insane, Cora. Quite insane.'

'Oh, good, does that mean a trip to Weston? Ice-cream for breakfast then!' Nathan appeared at Adam's side, wiping his mouth with a napkin.

'Indeed.' Cora grinned and pulled her cameraman towards her for a hug. He picked her up and swung her around, her legs narrowly missing a small table laden with glasses.

'The A-Team, back on the road for a summer of fun!' he trilled, then plonked her down again. Adam watched them, grinning.

Cora took a deep breath and gazed around the room, at her friends and colleagues, all happy and healthy and here. Today was a good day. And tomorrow there'd be a talking donkey. She raised her glass, and laughed out loud.

THE END

Mark Lock
The Elmsley Count

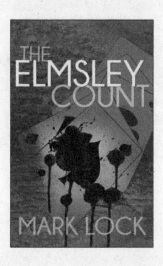

Somebody is targeting the former inmates and guards of a young offenders institution in South London, leaving messages at the crime scenes and taking body parts with them. It is down to Detective Inspector Hal Luchewski and his team to find the killer. The only problem is that this week happens to be the week in which Luchewski's past prepares to blow itself up in his face, and people's perceptions of him are likely to change forever.

Penny Kline
Nobody's Baby

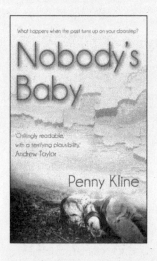

In the middle of the night Izzy Lomas finds an abandoned baby on her doorstep. It could have been left by any desperate person … except that the baby's name, pinned in a note to its carrycot, brings back a striking memory from her childhood. *If you had a baby what would you call it …*

If Izzy's suspicions are correct and she tells the police, it could end in tragedy. Allowing herself some time to investigate, she frantically tries to trace the baby's mother, but every twist and turn in her search seems to lead to a dead end. And the longer she stays silent, how many people is she putting in terrible danger?

Linda Regan
Guts for Garters

Life's not easy growing up on the Aviary Estate in South London. Alysha and her mates have survived being abused by people who should have cared for them, their lives ruined by crime and deprivation. Now they're taking control of the estate so children can grow up safe with real prospects in life.

When a rival gang starts encroaching on their territory, Alysha and the Alley Cats decide to teach them a lesson. The last thing they expect is to find one of their rivals murdered on their patch. DI Georgia Johnson wants answers. Johnson trusts Alysha – but will she still trust her when she realises her prized informant is leading a gang herself?

When another body is found – a teenage girl this time – Alysha decides to frame the evil leader of the rival gang … but he has a few nasty surprises of his own in store for the Alley Cats girls.

Anna Legat
Life Without Me

Georgie Ibsen is a successful, cynical, fortysomething hotshot lawyer. She runs her life, professional and personal, with precision and clear purpose. She's just made a breakthrough in a crucial case, her family is growing more independent … things couldn't be better.

Until it all comes to a screeching halt when she's involved in a hit-and-run and ends up in a coma.

Somehow, in her comatose state, Georgie is given unique glimpses into the lives of her nearest and dearest, their most intimate secrets: her boring husband's intense involvement with a colleague; her son's lovelorn yearning for his mother's nurse; her fifteen-year-old daughter's bad boy boyfriend, who *just might* be linked to the criminal mastermind involved in her last big case…

Jean G Goodhind
Something in the Blood

Honey Driver runs a hotel in Bath. She also collects antique underwear. As boss, she's in charge one day and washing dishes the next, resisting her mother's match-making attempts and managing multiple responsibilities - mundane, safe, and unexciting. Then one day things change. Honey lands the job of liaising with the police on behalf of Bath Hotels Association. No worries, she tells herself. Nothing will happen; then an American tourist goes missing and Honey is called in to help. Despite the on/off hostility of her police opposite number, D C I Steve Doherty, she sticks to the task. In the process Honey finds out that there's more to work than washing dishes, and more to murder than malice aforethought.

For more information about **Jackie Kabler**

and other **Accent Press** titles

please visit

www.accentpress.co.uk